INNOCENCE LOST

To Anna

Thank you so much for all your help at my Release party

Much
Love
Helen

HELEN JOHNSTON

Publishing
Covers & Formatting
http://paradoxbooktrailerproductions.blogspot.com.au

DEDICATION

As this is my first book, there are quite a few dedications. So as the advert on the TV says "Now for the science bit."

These books have got, blood, sweat, and tantrums in them, all mine! There are a few people that have been with me every step of the way and deserve a massive shout out.

The Tesco Tottie's, "Laughing." You all know who you are but esp. to Bev, who spent many a Saturday night reading and re-reading for me.

Penny, Debz and Jodie, who all helped one way or another and supported me. Love you three!

Lisa should get a long time service award for above and beyond friendship as she painfully deciphered my truly appalling hand writing at the very beginning.

And to my family, husband Darryl and son Aaron who have learnt how to eat burnt pizza, while I bash the keyboard. To my parents Brian and Chris for their unconditional love and support.

Lastly, to all the Role Players on Facebook that I've met over the last few years. There are so many raw and talented writers on there and I've made close friends with a few that I couldn't even have come this far without all my faceless friends on line. I LUBES YOU guys. But esp. to Cindy, Maritza, Em, Doreen, Rogue and Minxy…. You keep me sane!!

The amazing artwork was created and donated by the creative designer Mr. Phil Roberts.

DO NOT SPOIL WHAT YOU HAVE BY DESIRING WHAT YOU HAVE NOT; BUT REMEMBER THAT WHAT YOU HAVE WAS ONCE AMONG THE THINGS ONLY HOPED FOR.

EPICURUS

PROLOGUE

They'd been told to meet at a certain place at a specific time. Their horses seemed agitated but they pushed them faster and further into the darkness. The trees were so close together now, very little of the starry night sky breached their thick branches; a small light in the distance was their only guide

Incredibly bright, colourful caravans encircled a huge blazing camp fire, above which a crackling pig was roasting. It smelled so tempting, though neither Blake nor his men would be invited to take part in the celebratory feast later that night. They were here only for Blake to see the grandmother of the leader.

She, being the most infamous of all great fortune tellers.

Flanking them on either side, four riders, scouts, joined them as soon as they were heard approaching the camp. Not a word was spoken as they were escorted between the caravans and shown where to dismount and tether their horses.

The leader pointed to the caravan Blake was to enter.

Alone.

"Stay with the horses," Blake instructed his three men, with a curt nod. He climbed up the worn wooden steps, knocking gently on the open top half of the stable door.

"Come in," The voice that called him sounded like its owner

had difficulty breathing. He opened the bottom half of the door. At six foot four, he had to stoop to enter. At the end of the caravan, a tiny old lady smoked a pipe of sweet smelling tobacco. She grinned a toothless, gummy smile and pointed with an arthritic finger.

Once seated, she grabbed his hand and pulled his arm across the round, lace covered table with incredible speed and strength for someone who looked so frail.

"It is true! My vision foretold of our meeting. You are no mere mortal man. More of a Lord of your kind. So I will address you as such, my Lord," she went quiet, deep in thought, searching for the answers she knew he desired to hear.

He gazed around the interior of the small caravan. It was filled with knick-knacks, a lifetime's worth of collecting. Every available space was used. All the objects were lovingly taken care of and not a speck of dust was to be seen.

His attention snapped back to the woman when she spoke.

"You will meet your soulmate, your Queen. But it will be some fifty years from this date. You will travel to a hot and foreign land. Finding her will be easy. Holding onto her will prove to be your worst nightmare. Take heed my Lord, she is an innocent and must stay that way until the moons align. Do not attempt to dally with her. Be warned, your heart will break into a million stabbing pieces before she belongs to you fully. This journey is going to make you pray for death."

The gypsy suddenly sagged in her chair; she looked, if such a thing was possible, even older than her years.

"Now leave, please my Lord..." she gasped. "Your reading has drained me." The old woman closed her eyes and drifted off into an uneasy sleep. She missed the expression on his handsome face, and his startling green eyes watched her thoughtfully as he pondered her words.

CHAPTER ONE

Siobhan looked around her favourite bar, sipping a margarita. It was well into the six week holiday in the South of France with her friends, a 'job well done' present from their parents for great school exam results. Imogen's parents owned a ritzy villa here, up in the hills and had loaned it to them. For the past few nights, she'd felt as if someone was watching her and her friends. You know the feeling, the hairs on your arms or the back of your neck stand up with no reason and you shiver? Siobhan had noticed it again when they arrived tonight – but could see nothing out of the ordinary. She dismissed the thought and returned to the present, enjoying the company of her good friends, good wine and good music.

Suddenly, the crowds parted and Siobhan turned to see what was happening – only to be captured in a dazzling, intense, emerald green gaze. Her breath caught in her throat, and her hand stilled midway to her mouth as her glass was left hovering. She was practically drooling and Imogen, sitting next to her, elbowed her in the ribs.

But her attention was so not on whatever her friend was trying to tell her.

As the four girls stared at the men now walking - no scrub

that, stalking – in their direction, and quickly called dibs on the ones they wanted.

Seraphina fancied one of the twins, the one with the short crew cut. He was a massive mountain of a man and looked to be at least six feet six inches tall. Definitely mad, bad and dangerous to know.

"That is exactly how I like my men," she told her friends with a giggle, her eyes shining excitedly.

"I'll have the other twin, thank you very much. There is a God," Imogen whispered. He was just as large and ferocious looking, and his eyes were very nearly drilling a hole directly into hers. His hair was longer and highlighted naturally to a light blonde.

Charlotte, the quiet one of the group, smiled to herself.

I don't think I get a say in which one I want, Siobhan thought a little shakily, as it was perfectly clear who was intent on being hers.

Marching right up to her, he brazenly took hold of her hands, dipped his head and gently grazed the back of her knuckles with his lips. She shuddered at the touch.

From that first innocent contact, Blake had felt it – she was the one, this was his Queen. The old fortune teller had been right. Here he was, fifty years to the day, in a hot, foreign land, hand in hand with his soulmate. He quickly made the introductions.

"I'm Blake, it's a pleasure to meet you," he told Siobhan, never taking his eyes away from hers. His deep, masterful voice warmed parts of her she hadn't realised were chilled.

"Siobhan," she whispered breathlessly. Her eyes were wide, like a shy doe caught in the headlights. The other girls had got their dibs too.

"The twins, Nat and Alex, are easily distinguishable," he told them, as a smiling Alex sat down next to Imogen, and Seraphina let out a loud, happy squeal as Nat picked her up and sat her on his lap. "Alex has the blond highlights, and Nat has very little hair."

Their warm, liquid, brown eyes were mesmerising as they stared at the two girls.

Ethan, the fourth man, smiled at Charlotte and sat next to her as he introduced himself. Siobhan was surprised at how quickly Charlotte seemed to take to him. She was the most introverted of the group, with issues in her family life known only to the girls who had befriended her when she'd arrived at their private boarding school.

The evening flew past and Siobhan felt like she had been sucked into a void containing only her and Blake. He was impeccably dressed in a suit of the highest quality. All of the men were suave and sophisticated and she judged them to be in their late twenties, early thirties. It made her feel a little young and gauche.

But Blake was slowly and gently bringing her out of her shell, somehow knowing how inexperienced she was with the opposite sex. He didn't push too hard, didn't touch her inappropriately, but still was touching her enough to make her whimper as they danced the night away.

Siobhan was tall at five feet seven, but she felt dainty and very feminine as his arms wrapped her in a cocoon of sensuality. As they danced, her silk, backless halter dress gently caressed her hips, skimming her curves as she moved elegantly in his embrace. His hands continually ran up and down her naked back. It felt like the hottest thing she'd ever done – and it was only a dance, for Christ's sake. Her friends all seemed completely at ease with their chosen man, happily dancing or talking at their table.

It was the same for the next few fun-filled nights of craziness, as they got to know each other – and slowly, Siobhan let her barriers drop.

One evening, on a shopping trip, Blake presented her with an antique looking golden locket. She held it in her palm, and ran her thumb over the intricate pattern on the front. On closer inspection, she saw it was overlaid on top of some words that made no sense to her.

The whisper of a gold chain felt heated as he placed it gently around her neck.

"You must promise me, Si, never to remove it. Promise me. It will keep you from harm." His eyes seeming to darken as he gave her the order, his voice low and enchanting. She felt as if a sorcerer was weaving his spells around her. Her heart thundering in her chest, her throat felt dry and she swallowed hard, trying to find her voice.

"I promise, Blake," Siobhan whispered softly, because it seemed incredibly important to him. The gold chain was so fine and delicate she wondered just how long it would last, but she had immediately fallen in love with it, and vowed dramatically to herself, *it will have to be cut from my neck.*

The same night he bought himself a new watch and asked her to look after his old one, an elegant and stylish vintage Rolex.

It was timeless and beautiful.

It was a Saturday, four weeks into their holiday, and the girls had just finished their evening meal when four very large, white boxes were delivered to the villa – one for each of them. Each box was wrapped in a different colour bow - which matched the very elegant evening gowns inside. With great excitement the girls opened their boxes and held up their dresses for the others to see, before quickly disappearing to put them on. A little later, they were back downstairs, dressed, coiffed and made up when there was a knock at the door.

Blake looked devilishly attractive in his black tuxedo, as did his three friends – and girls let out an excited squeal as they ran to their respective man.

But Siobhan couldn't move. She studied Blake from across the villa's marbled floor, and knew she was falling in love with him. Standing before him, she felt a little afraid and bit her lip, as her body trembled slightly. She glanced in the old mirror above the fireplace and she saw a worried expression on her face. She felt winded, as she watched him walk towards her. He had the grace of a dancer and the powerful build of an athlete and the way he looked at her made her gasp. He raked her body with his eyes, from head to toe, like a predator waiting to pounce.

"What are you looking so pensive about, Si? You're the most beautiful woman I've ever seen," said Blake. She gave him a quick twirl. "That dress is perfect on you, as I knew it would be."

His eyes roamed appreciatively over her body.

"Thank you for the dress, Blake. You're right, it's perfect."

Putting her hands on his shoulders, she reached up and placed a gentle kiss on his lips while his hands slipped around her waist, pressing her body to his. The kiss that started off soft and gentle quickly turned into a passionate embrace. Forgetting all about the dress and trying to find out where they were going, she concentrated solely on the blistering kiss.

Her stomach was doing funny little somersaults again.

"You'll have to redo your lipstick now," he told her, grinning as he pulled away. "I have a funny feeling you'll be redoing it quite a lot tonight."

"I really don't mind," she said, a little breathlessly.

Placing his hand on the small of her back, Blake guided her to the black limousine where everyone was waiting for them.

"At last! We thought for a minute you two were going to stay there all night glued to each other," Seraphina told them with a fake tut and a saucy wink.

Siobhan rolled her eyes in mock agitation, and smiled shyly at

Blake.

The men made a very handsome group. They could have easily been models and seemed very much at ease in the expensive black leather interior of car.

All the girls except Charlotte were hastily redoing their lipstick.

"So, is anyone going to tell us where we're going tonight?" Seraphina asked, her eyes on Nat, who in turn was staring intently at her.

"You'll soon see." Blake said with a grin.

Nat tore his eyes away from Seraphina long enough to pour everyone a glass of champagne.

"Chin, chin!" They all said, clinking glasses.

Everyone settled back into the leather seats. Siobhan couldn't remember ever seeing her friends as contented as they appeared now. She noticed that the men's bow ties and cummerbunds matched the dress of the girl they were escorting.

Blake's was midnight blue, Nat wore emerald green, Alex lavender and Ethan's was black.

"Whose idea was it to go matching? It looks great," she asked.

"When we bought the dresses, it was the saleslady's idea. I wasn't sure about it myself, but now I'm seeing everyone dressed it does look rather special, doesn't it?" Blake murmured in her ear.

"I think you all chose just the right colour and dresses for each of us, well done." Siobhan said with a smile.

"It took a while for us to decide which ones to choose," Blake told her, as he lifted her hand to his lips and gently nibbled her knuckles.

Her heartbeat accelerated.

"Well, everyone looks very happy with the choices you made." Siobhan tried to clear her throat as her voice came out all breathy. How could a simple little touch have affected her so much? Before she could ponder the question any further, the car came to a halt and the driver opened the door.

They were at the harbour.

Taking hold of her hand, Blake walked toward vast lines of yachts moored at the water's edge, eventually coming to a halt in front of a stunning yacht. Two men hurried down to welcome him and his party on board, after a brief conversation with them Blake walked the group down the side of the yacht and gently manoeuvred Siobhan until she stood with her back to him. He put his arms around her waist and drew her close and she let her head fall back and rest on his shoulder, loving the fact he was still taller than her, even in her heels.

"Look at what I've called her, Si," he said, and pointed to the name, written on the side in deep crimson.

"This is yours?" She asked, her eyes wide with shock.

"Yes, it was delivered earlier today. I thought we'd all enjoy a night-time cruise. Now, look at her name," he answered softly.

The Lady Si.

Seraphina let out a squeal of excitement, as she pointed to the name in fancy lettering and hopped from one foot to the other in glee.

"Look, Siobhan, he named it after you!" she said.

"Oh my God Blake," Siobhan looked at it in wonder. "That's the most amazing thing anyone has ever done for me," she said, her voice full of excitement.

The evening and night was spent on the cruiser – fifty five feet of the highest spec luxury. The furnishings were sumptuous, with thick, plush carpets, lavish gold fixtures and inviting cream leather sofas.

The night was one of Siobhan's most pleasurable experiences, the kind that stays with you forever.

They all happily posed for photographs, and a deck hand

snapped them all laughing and joking, pulling faces and striking silly poses. There was Champagne and cocktails for the girls and bourbon for the men. Siobhan spent much of the night wrapped around Blake like a blanket, while she laughed so much her cheeks hurt.

Standing up he gently tugged her up to join him. The air had become a little cooler as they sat outside on the upper deck. They went hand in hand back down the stairs to the inside cabin and settled on the butter soft leather couches. Siobhan leaned her head on his shoulder and promptly fell asleep.

Waking later, Siobhan found her head was in Blake's lap and her long legs were stretched out in front of her. They were completely alone and she blushed. He leant down to kiss her with such passion that she was left breathless and wanting more. But she didn't have the first clue how to tell him to hurry up and seduce her.

His hands travelled inside her dress, cupping her breasts. He felt her nipples spring up under his skilled touch, and continued to kiss her, his tongue encouraging hers to tangle with it.

Her whimpers of need filled his hungry mouth. Siobhan had never been kissed like this, touched like this. It was scorching her, burning her from the inside out. Her back arched , silently begging him to seduce her completely while his fingers slowly inched towards her panties, then slipped inside. Her body bucked involuntarily as Blake's fingers gently brushed against her and she gasped as his fingers softly skimmed against a spot, a bundle of nerves that made her want to cry out. She was absolutely soaked down there. Her face flamed with heat as there was no way to hide her arousal from him.

Hearing a growl from him, she stilled her attempt to try to hide how wet and ready she was for his touch.

Her will left her, her body was his to command.

His fingers continued to stroke her, slipping between her wet folds. Using first one, then two fingers, he slowly entered her slick core and she moaned, her body rippling at the exquisite sensation. She was completely washed away by what she was experiencing for the first time. Blake couldn't help but to grin as he gazed into her eyes, open wide in wonder, glazed with passion and lust. She stared into his which were half-closed and dark, mirroring her own feelings as he made her body move in a way that was completely foreign to her.

His eyes were filled with a primeval savagery as he fuelled her delighted body, awakening it, moving it to a final destination that she had never, ever felt.

Suddenly it felt like she was about to explode, she shuddered and pulsed on the end of his fingers while he took her body higher and higher. Shutting her eyes tightly, she screamed as she came. He laid claim to her lips, capturing her scream in his mouth.

As her body slowly calmed, she blushed with the afterglow of her orgasm. She looked directly into his eyes as he slowly lifted his fingers to his mouth, his eyes flaring as he sucked each finger until they were clean of her glistening enjoyment.

After smoothing her clothes, he pulled her onto his lap, wrapping his arms around her.

"You Si, were made for my touch, my kiss. Your body is made for pleasure," he whispered. His lips touched hers, a gentle brush, not wanting to scare her. "What your body felt was completely natural," his lips nipped her ear as her head nestled in the crook of his neck, her hot breath tickling his skin. "And this is only the start of our story."

They stayed there until the others walked back inside. Siobhan felt so loved, so cherished by Blake that any embarrassment she might have felt was tenderly kissed away.

She was in love and couldn't fight her feelings for him. They were far too strong.

Many nights of pleasure followed, but they never had full sex. Siobhan came so many times, she lost count, his hands wove a spell upon her body that was addictive.

Her dreams on that holiday were highly erotic, almost pornographic, involving her and Blake doing things she had no clue people did to one another. She soon lost all of her inhibitions and was begging him to touch her and set her alight.

One night, the girls saw another side to their men. They were in a bar, and Siobhan had been to freshen up and was on her way back to Blake when a horrible, short, sweaty, drunk man made a grab for her and tried to drag her onto the dance floor. She looked around frantically and caught Blake's frozen snarl as the man brought up his hand as if to strike her.

His eyes seemed to have glazed over and looked almost black, while his mouth was open in a ferocious snapping of teeth. He shouted an order to Nat, who jumped up and was by her side in an instant, his speed amazing Siobhan. She watched in fascination as Nat pulled the disgusting man away from her and Alex and Ethan helped him to eject the troublemaker from the bar. . As she turned to run into Blake's waiting arms, Siobhan spotted Nat's elaborate, thick black tribal tattoo. It started at his right wrist and went up his arm, over his shoulder and down his back. She watched how it moved and flexed under his shirt as he helped to carry the man off into the dark night.

As Blake soothed her, her friends gathered around. She felt tears welling up.

"Please take me home Blake," she whispered, her face buried in his neck.

They all started to move before she had even finished the sentence. That night he stayed with her at the villa, the first time he'd stayed all night. He held her and soothed her until she finally fell asleep.

While she slept, he studied the bruises on her tender wrists. He was beside himself for letting her out of his sight for even a second, and was furious with the drunken man who had dared to try to hurt her. He was loath to leave Siobhan, but all the men left before daylight – with Blake vowing to the other men that they would be more vigilant around the girls from now on.

The girls were horrified by the bruises on Siobhan's wrists.

"That fucker! I'd like to get my hands on him!" Seraphina shouted as they were eating breakfast the following morning.

CHAPTER TWO

The holiday carried on, with the weeks speeding by far too fast. Blake and Siobhan used the time to get to know one another – but still did not complete the seduction.

The girls found out that Nat, Alex and Ethan worked for Blake, doing what they didn't ask but they were all exceptionally wealthy. The holiday was nearly over and Siobhan was buzzing with the need to have him fuck her. She blushed as she thought of the uncharacteristic curse words. It was unbearable – she would shake as soon as he entered a room. He only had to look at her with his mesmerising hooded, feral green eyes and she'd be a shuddering wreck.

His chiselled face, with its aristocratic straight nose, and beautiful full lips could wreak havoc on her body. His well built and muscled body could have her tongue tied just by moving underneath his clothes. Her hands would run all over and underneath his silk shirts, feeling the hard ridges of his stomach and the smooth planes of his chest. He was simply beautiful and she knew that she would never, ever, feel like this about another man.

She belonged to him, and he to her. It was that simple.

With only a couple of days left, they were awakened by a loud banging on the doors of the villa. A member of staff answered it and the girls thought nothing more of it – until Imogen found the handwritten invitation on the dining room table.

In perfect calligraphy, it read:

Mr. Blake Warren, Mr. Nathaniel Benedict, Mr. Alexander Benedict, Mr. Ethan St Williams.
Would like to invite:
Miss. Siobhan Taylor-Smith, Miss. Seraphina Stanford, Miss. Imogen Hutchinson, Miss. Charlotte Johnston-Tyne.
To the midnight, summer Masquerade ball... We will pick you all up at 6pm, so please be ready for a fun-filled, fantastic night of hedonistic pleasure...

"Hedonistic pleasure" – just thinking about the phrase brought Siobhan out in chills. Was tonight the night when she'd finally lose her virginity? She hoped so.

Looking at each other, the girls screamed and jumped up and down with excitement.

"Oh my God, oh my God!" Imogen said. "What's the time, Si?"

"One o'clock," she answered, flipping the invitation to read that the men had arranged for them to be dressed, and have their hair styled and make up done – so they weren't to worry about a thing. With that, the girls scattered, each going to their own rooms to have a quick shower and prepare for when the women arrived to help them dress. They met downstairs after their showers, wrapped in huge fluffy white towels, and only had to wait a few minutes before they heard cars being parked, followed by footsteps approaching the villa.

Imogen opened the door and four women walked in, each with

four assistants whose arms were full of equipment for the evening's events. Four dress rails were wheeled in, each with a different name on it, and covered so the girls couldn't see what they contained.

Imogen chatted in French with the stylists and then turned to her friends.

"Okay, everyone. We're to go to our rooms with our particular team, and get ready in private." This caused a few raised eyebrows as they were used to getting ready together, but soon each girl led the way to their room.

A few hours later, Siobhan cautiously made her way downstairs, careful not to stand on the hem of the skirt. At least her soft leather, black ballet pumps, with satin ribbons wound up her delicate ankles were flat and not some killer heels that could have tripped her up. She couldn't wait for Blake to arrive, and hurried up to get downstairs. At the bottom step, she gasped. Her friends were all waiting for her.

"Oh my God, Si honey, look at you! You look utterly delectable. Blake will be unable to keep his hands off you." Seraphina said, admiring her gorgeous gown.

The heavy boned corset, in a rich purple and gold brocade, accentuated her breasts. It was tight and made breathing difficult, and Siobhan knew by the end of the night she'd be glad to take it off, no matter how good it made her look. But hopefully, Blake would be the one who removed it. Her waist looked tiny, accentuated by the skirt which was a frothy concoction of midnight black tulle netting that reached the floor.

Her makeup was dramatic, her eyes made up in rich purples and gold's to match the corset – although her simple mask hid most of it. It was black with matching purples in a lace overlay. She performed a very ladylike and demure curtsey to her friends, then they excitedly inspected each other's costumes.

Each gown was unique and complemented their personalities perfectly.

Seraphina's was in jade green, to match her eyes. Its tight corset had her impressive breasts bound tightly, but they were still very nearly overflowing. Her gown had a bustle, and the waterfall of taffeta silk skirt made a crisp sound as she twirled before them. Her mask was catlike, and highlighted her eyes.

Imogen's blood red gown showed off more of her gorgeous skin than it hid. Her killer heels and feathered mask added inches to her height. *Alex will bust something when he sees her in this,* thought Siobhan. She grinned as she marvelled at her friend's confidence in wearing such a gown and wondered wistfully if she'd ever have such confidence in herself.

Charlotte was also grinning, and the friends gaped at her transformation. In school, she was their Goth girl, complete with black nails and makeup. All through school they'd tried to encourage her to have her hair cut, but she was adamant that she needed it to hide behind. Now the fall of long, unruly, black hair was gone and in its place was a smooth, sleek bob with platinum blonde streaks.

Her pale blue, almost silver, eyes stood out like shining stars and her black sequinned dress shimmered as she walked. It was slit up to her thigh, showing off long slender legs covered in silk stockings. The little matching jacket fitted her like a second skin and her lips were a vibrant slash of red.

She looks simply stunning, Siobhan thought, hugging her friend. At the strange sound of horses sedately clip clopping up the drive, the girls picked up their bags and hurried to the door – just in time to see four horse-drawn carriages come to a halt in the large circular cobbled driveway.

The doors opened and the men stepped down and stood waiting for their respective partners to join them.

Each wore an old fashioned cape over his suit. Masks covered their faces and each was holding a long-stemmed red rose. Siobhan ran eagerly to Blake, but came to a stop just before him. She smiled as he bowed low to her, then curtsied to him and fell into his open arms.

The journey to the chateau was eventful. Within the privacy of their carriage, he gently unlaced the restrictive corset and lifted her breasts free. He knelt on the floor in front of her and gently opened her thighs, while he talked to her in a soothing voice, in the foreign language that she didn't recognise, but found as sexy as hell. Blake used his fingers to bring her to an almighty climax, which left her breathless and shaking with desire. His eyes blazed with a near-fanatical ownership that took her breath away. She grabbed his thick hair and pulled him to her as she sought his lips, kissing them passionately. Her hands lightly traced a trail down his face until he nipped her fingertips with his teeth.

"I love you Si, more than you could ever know," he breathed into her ear, "This is the sole reason we came to this country, to meet you, go to this ball and fall in love." His eyes were full of love and she stared in wonder at him.

Sitting back, he explained a little about the chateau.

It was owned by a French couple, Monique and Solomon, whom he'd known for a very long time. It was their life's ambition to bring it back to its former glory.

He continued to kiss and caress her while the carriage gently swayed as the horses continued their journey up the long, tree-lined drive, then he quickly dressed her and she caught her first sighting of the chateau. It was an impressive sight – an incredible old building with imposing stone gargoyles, their wings open wide, as though protecting its inhabitants from attack.

At first, she thought they were bats, but who in their right mind would have huge stone carved bats by their front door? They joined their friends in the spacious entrance hall, where they attracted a lot of admiring glances from the other guests, both male and female.

Entering the very grand ballroom, which Blake whispered to her, was known as the Great Hall, Siobhan soaked up all the little details. It was decorated with unusual flags, attached to the high wooden beams of the ceiling. She stared at the multi-coloured costumes of the women present. They were as proud as any of the peacocks strutting in the grounds outside.

Their table was sumptuously laid with large silver wine goblets and silverware. Their seats were scaled down versions of his and hers thrones and were extremely heavy. The scene was lit by a huge, ornately carved, black marble candelabra placed on the heavy white damask tablecloth.

They danced the night away, and Siobhan even danced with other young bucks who dared to ask her. Even before Blake pointed out their hosts, Siobhan could feel ice cold eyes following her every move. She couldn't explain why they intimidated her – they had never met before. There was something a little off, especially with Monique.

Her smile was just a tad too wide, her eyes a little too bright and her perfectly styled hair was just too perfect. Siobhan couldn't put her finger on what was unsettling her.

She snapped her attention back to Blake as, with a brush of his lips against hers, he handed her off to another dancer.

This man's mask had a long, caricature-like nose, white with two black tears weeping from the right eye. Beneath his cape he was wearing black trousers with a long sleeved white silk shirt with a high pointed collar and a white lacy jabot around his neck and ruffles at the cuff. His waistcoat was heavily embroidered, with a black tailcoat made of doeskin finishing off the outfit.

He looked like a regency gentleman straight out of one of her school history books.Without a word, he led her to the middle of the dance floor, and his hands reached out for hers. Her heart thumped in time with the music which was now a fast-paced Latin beat. She had taken dance lessons at school and was proficient in most of the ballroom and Latin dances. So when her new dance partner started to lead her into a salsa routine she relaxed, and followed the steps without too much trouble. She started to enjoy herself. He was a very skilful dancer and by the end of the dance she was laughing, and felt a little disappointed when it was over. They had not exchanged a word as they danced. Once again her partner bowed to her, but unlike Blake's simple bow, it was done with a theatrical flourish.

He was making her feel a little uneasy and she curtseyed quickly, then turned to walk away, but he grabbed her hand. Siobhan panicked slightly as she remembered the awful man from the bar. Maybe this man wanted another dance, but all she wanted was to be returned to Blake. She was about to tell the man to let go when he started to walk to where Blake was sitting.

Relief flooded through her and she followed him.

Blake stood up and watched as she was led back to him. The man placed her hand in Blake's and again bowed low to them both before leaving. Just before midnight, their hosts called for silence.

"Good evening to you all and welcome to our little party," Solomon said in a quiet but dignified voice. *He's got the same presence as Blake*, thought Siobhan. He didn't need to raise his voice to gain everyone's attention. She looked around and saw all eyes were on the two figures spotlighted on the stage.

She could tell they were a very powerful couple.

"We've been having these little get togethers for over fifty years." Siobhan gasped. *Fifty years? He must be talking about that his parents? He doesn't look a day older than thirty and Monique only looks a few years older than me*, she thought.

"Each year your costumes and gowns amaze Monique and I," she couldn't place his accent, not French or Italian, she must remember to ask Blake later where he was from. "So, for my toast of the evening I raise my glass to my guests, you," he raised his silver goblet to the audience, who clapped, raising their goblets in return.

"Good evening everyone, and welcome once again. Like Solomon your costumes inspire us to continue these parties. My toast for the night is also to you. To our many friends, who travel miles to be with us, I salute you." Monique said, and raised her goblet.

Again, everyone followed, taking a sip. She also had a quiet voice, throaty with a dry, smoky tone, which radiated a cold power from within.

"Now the midnight hour is very nearly upon us, so I would like everyone to please stand up and raise their glass and toast to a wonderful night. For the night is still young and plenty of fun is to be had by those wishing it!" She raised her voice, as if to emphasise the point.

Removing their masks, Blake pulled Siobhan into his arms, softly kissing his way down her face until he planted a wet, warm kiss on her mouth, moving down her neck to place gentle kisses on her neck. It sent shivers all over her and she whimpered in his arms, forgetting for now the sinister feelings she was receiving from Monique.

It's all in my head, she told herself. She lowered herself down onto his lap to return his passionate kisses, leaving herself literally gasping for air, her cheeks flushed with pleasure. He'd told her they were guests here for the night, his eyes letting her know exactly what they'd be getting up to later.

She felt nervous, but so excited and aroused that she couldn't wait until the ball was over.

The girls decided to freshen up, and were ushered into a room that was out-of-this-world beautiful, all black marble with a gold thread running through it, and gold fixtures, including a mammoth gilt framed mirror. They elbowed each other out of the way, giggling like schoolgirls as they repaired their makeup.

Suddenly the door opened and in walked Monique, surrounded by a large group of women. Siobhan's stomach dropped. The two groups eyed each other.

Monique was beyond pale, skinny, with long black shiny hair. She stared haughtily at Siobhan, and looked down her nose at her, until her eyes rested on her locket. Her open hostility prompted Siobhan's friends to protectively gather around and shield her.

"I hope you are enjoying yourselves," Monique said as she glided over to wash her hands, walking right through the middle of the girls. She looked at Siobhan. Her eyes were now glazed over, and her earlier moment of hostility had vanished.

"I do like having Blake's little... what are you? A girlfriend? Or just a holiday fuck?" She asked, not seeming to hear the sudden intake of breath from Siobhan's friends.

Not wanting to be uncivil to a supposed friend of Blake's, Siobhan bit her tongue and tried to smile. She didn't want to show how hurt she was by this women's hostility. Monique gave the girls one last sneering glance, and her eyes lingered on Siobhan as she told her, "I'm sure I will see you very soon, Mon petit." With that, she snapped her fingers and walked out with her posse.

The four girls stood stock still and stared at each other in dead silence.

"Okay," Imogen said, shaking her head in bewilderment.

"What the fuck was that all about?" Seraphina snapped, and made to follow Monique. Charlotte caught her arm and tugged her back into the bathroom.

"What? Get off, she needs to know no one talks to my Si like that and gets away with it!" Her eyes flashed dangerously and she glared at Charlotte as she pulled her arm away.

Charlotte walked back to Siobhan and put her arm around her shoulder.

"What do you want to do?" she asked.

Taking a deep breath, Siobhan looked at her friends, all willing to do whatever she asked.

"Let's ignore her. She's just a little strange, that's all. Let it go. I want this night to be magical and I'm not letting her or anyone else ruin it for me or Blake." She watched as Seraphina huffed and stalked away.

Imogen and Charlotte just shrugged and followed her out of the bathroom. The four men sensed a change in the girls when they arrived back at their table. Blake saw Siobhan slowly pick at her food, then sip her drink as she watched the dancers on the floor, – looking anywhere other than into his now-hooded eyes.

Gently pulling her onto his lap, he slowly lifted her chin, and waited patiently for her to look at him.

She knew he'd somehow guessed what had taken place in the bathroom and silently pleaded with him to not make a scene. His eyes flashed cold hard steel and she noticed how they briefly moved in Nat's direction as though issuing a silent order. She quickly covered his face with kisses, and delighted in sending his pulse skyrocketing, and then muttered loving phrases to him until his defences melted and he murmured them back to her.

In the early hours of the morning, Imogen crouched down by the side of her chair.

"Si," she whispered. "It's time to go up to our suites – are you sure you want this?" Siobhan blushed and closed her eyes briefly, then nodded.

"Yes, yes I do," she smiled shyly at her friend and then Blake.

Everyone stood to make their way out of the Great Hall

together, only to be stopped at the doors by a murderous looking Monique. She pointed at Siobhan's locket and very nearly reached over and ripped it off her neck. Only when a furious-looking Solomon suddenly appeared, did the other men walk behind Blake to make the couple back down– all in a language the girls didn't understand. Blake snarled something so obviously nasty that Monique paled even more before stomping off with Solomon following in her wake.

Blake stared after them for a split second before he marched out, dragging Siobhan along behind him. Whatever had happened had pushed him over the edge. He stopped dead and let everyone else pass, and then pulled her to him. He was so tender that it left her speechless. Pushing her right up against a hard, cold, stone wall, she felt his body and whimpered with desire. He gently tipped her face up for his lips to devour.

Time stood still.

She realised that this was somehow goodbye and she wept, and his lips chased the tears down her cheek, kissing them away. His lips continued to devour her with a ferocity that left her breathless. With great difficulty he pulled himself away and she gasped at his haggard look.

He cuddled her to him, nearly squashing her in his embrace.

"Remember this if nothing else, Si, I love you," he whispered and before she could utter a word, he led her away from the chateau and placed her in a waiting car with her friends.

She was devastated, and could only watch as he turned and walked back inside the chateau without so much as a backwards glance.

The four girls were suddenly alone.

The car journey back to their villa was hell, with Imogen pitifully crying, Seraphina so angry that her spectacular green eyes looked like ice chips, and Charlotte silently looking out of the window.

No one could work out what the fuck had just happened.

Arriving back at the villa, Siobhan hastened out of the car, tiredly shaking her head at her friends as she fled to the peace of her own room. For the first time in her life, she didn't want to discuss what had happened. Quickly removing the makeup and costume, she took a red hot shower. She didn't want to think; didn't want to imagine what she should have been doing with Blake right now.

She went to bed naked and sank into oblivion, with tears rolling down her cheeks.

The next day was filled with packing and getting ready to travel back home.

Their dream holiday had ended as an absolute nightmare.

CHAPTER THREE

TEN YEARS LATER.
Present day

Gasping, Siobhan woke with a jolt and realised she was still on the train, with tears rolling down her face. She glanced around, horrified that someone might have seen her as she stupidly cried at that dream, again. She sighed. It was the same each time she dreamt the bloody thing. She ran a hand self-consciously through her hair, shook her head, and tried desperately to not think of the past. To clear her mind of the upsetting memories, she gathered her belongings together. The designer luggage that Imogen sent her last Christmas was safely assembled and hauled into the waiting taxi.

She was moving to a new village, because life had suddenly become far too claustrophobic in London. She'd broken off her engagement to Harry, to the approval of her three friends. They had seen unmatched the pair was, but kept their counsel, hoping she'd figure it out, in time. Siobhan had sold her flat, and bought a large and airy house in the countryside. A recent interview had successfully landed her a new job, so here she was, at nearly twenty nine, starting a new life.

She'd been on regular visits to her house as the interior designer waved her magic wand over it, enjoying the time to explore the countryside and introduce herself to her new work colleagues. It was a much smaller veterinary practice than she was used to, but the four people who worked there were friendly and welcoming.

Her father had bought her a new sporty little car, in her favourite colour, purple, and the villagers soon became used to her zipping around, singing loudly with her music blaring. Her mother had sent in her interior designer ahead of the move date, so everything was ready to go. The taxi dropped her off, and she smiled when she opened the door and saw that everything was ready for her to move straight in. *Bless my mother*, she thought. She made herself a cup of coffee, and then flopped down onto her leather sofa. She started to flick through the channels on her huge plasma TV and was just about to nod off when her phone rang.

"Hey, girlfriend!" Imogen's voice called out. "Are you all settled in?"

"Yes, Mother's been very efficient." Siobhan laughed, making herself comfortable and looking forward to a good old fashioned chinwag with one of her best friends. "How's life across the pond?"

Imogen now lived in a Las Vegas penthouse. One of the new metal and glass structures springing up there, it was one of the most spectacular apartments she'd ever seen, and among the most expensive. Not that money would ever be an issue to one of the world's most famous supermodels.

Imogen had been at university studying law, to become a lawyer and follow in her mother's footsteps, when she'd been spotted by a top model agency. After her initial *should I, shouldn't I?* She had tentatively dipped her toe into the modelling world and discovered she was a natural. She soon became the darling of the world media, her face instantly recognisable across the globe, and she was now in the enviable position of being able to pick and choose who she worked for.

She had become a British institution and the people loved her.

At dead on six foot tall, Imogen had enviable long, shapely legs. Her eyes were often called pools of liquid chocolate, and were framed by long eyelashes. She didn't believe in the waif look, and always portrayed a healthy attitude towards her body and eating.

"Oh, life here is just fabulous, darling," Imogen laughed. "But I'm not ringing up about me. I want to hear everything that's new with you."

"Well, you've already seen the photos of my new house." Siobhan said.

"And I love it, it's very cool."

"I've only been here a couple of hours, so ring back in a few days and I'll let you know what's going on." Siobhan laughed. "Oh, and thank you very much for the flowers, wine, and chocolates. They're lovely. I'll have to ring Sera and Charlotte to thank them in a mo."

"Have you heard from Charlotte?"

"No, why? She's all right, isn't she?" she asked.

"Yes, yes, she's fine. Don't worry. But I do know she has some great news she wants to share with you. I don't know what it is exactly, as she left a message on my machine. So make sure you ring her after me," Imogen said. "And also, I'm over your way with work in a couple of weeks, and that just happens to be a bank holiday weekend. Will you be free? Will it be all right for us all to stay? We really need a girly weekend."

"Let me get my diary," Siobhan was already walking to her bag where her diary was kept. "Yes, I'm free. I so can't wait to see you guys. I'll ring round and double check with the girls, but I can't imagine there'll be a problem. Book your ticket and I'll see you in a couple of weeks. Take care honey, big hugs, love you!"

After hanging up, Siobhan dialled Seraphina's number – but without any luck. Her messenger service told her she was at her swimming academy which she owned with her partner Dale.

At school, apart from boys, Seraphina's passion had been swimming. She was exceptionally good at it. Representing first the school and then the country, the teachers claimed it helped calm her somewhat explosive personality and focus her fiery temper.

Seraphina had been the rebel of the group, the one who always had something to say. Continually in trouble with the teachers, her tall, athletic body, with her glowing red hair earned her the nickname Miss Fire Cracker. Her breasts were high and full, even after all the training she did. She was even more incredibly beautiful now, her pale luminous skin covered in freckles. Her sparkling jade green eyes were always the first to betray just how angry she was.

She was incredibly loyal to her friends and would fight hell and high water to protect them. Siobhan left a message telling her friend the dates and not to bother ringing her back, but to just turn up when she could.

Now it was Charlotte's turn. Luckily, this friend was available to talk.

"Si?" Charlotte asked in her soft voice.

"Yes, honey, it's me. You okay?" She always asked her dear friend this at the start of any phone conversation. They all secretly worried about Charlotte.

She'd come to their school later in the year than the other three and was the last one to join their group. She'd been a scrawny little thing, not trusting anyone, and kept to herself. But at night she'd wake the whole dorm up with nightmares.

Her life had been troubled before she came to the school. As well as the nightmares, she used to self-harm. The girls found this out one night when the whole sad tale that had been Charlotte's life had came flooding out. The girls had helped her to conquer all of her fears and she'd made a full and wonderful recovery.

Charlotte now was a hugely successful business woman, owning a company that set up support groups all over the country in schools, aimed at combating adolescent self-harm. Some of the stories she told them had been truly gruesome. With her passion, understanding, and dedication, she'd quickly made a name for herself and was very rarely at home.

"I'm fine, Si, how are you? Are you recovered from your move?" Charlotte asked quietly.

"Yes I did, thank you. Now, I know you're our superwoman, but are you free in a couple of weeks to come down to me for a girly piss up?" Siobhan said. She heard Charlotte chuckle, and that in turn made her smile, remembering a time when Charlotte had very little to laugh about.

"I've already cleared my schedule. While I presume you were on the phone to Sera, I was calling Imogen."

"Bloody hell! You know, we should set up a conference call thingy, so we can just arrange a time and all chat away instead of calling each other and trying to find the ones that we miss." Siobhan sighed, but then smiled, realising all of her girly friends would be under one roof very shortly.

"Actually, I was ringing Imogen, as I've a bit of exciting news to share. I was going to wait until we were all together, but I can't." Charlotte took a deep breath, never one to be rushed.

Siobhan knew it was hopeless to try and hurry her along.

"I've been invited onto a very popular TV talk show in America. I fly out tomorrow and I wanted Imogen to come with me. At least that way I'll have one friendly face in the audience."

"Char, that's wonderful. I'm so proud of you. You deserve all the recognition that you get for how hard you work."

"I'm absolutely petrified Si," Charlotte whispered.

"Don't be. You'll have Imogen with you, and Sera and I will be there in spirit." Siobhan hoped this wouldn't be too much of a strain for her fragile friend. They were continually worried that past bad habits would resurface, but so far, Charlotte had been fine.

"I know, and I love you all. I've got to go honey. I'm sorry, but I have to be up so bloody early and I want to get all my notes and things ready. I'll see you in two weeks. Big hug! Love you!"

Siobhan had been desperate for a pet while she was living in London, but it was just impractical and downright cruel.

She was determined to have a couple of cats now she had the room for them to run around freely – and luckily a young farmer's wife advertised the day after she'd moved in, wanting someone to give a loving new home to brother and sister kittens. When she drove over to the farm, it had been love at first sight.

The black and white boy kitten she called Able, and the smaller brown striped tabby she called Dora, because to her they were *adorable*.

No, they were priceless and she loved them immediately.

She wasn't due to start work for a week and had a few extra days of freedom to enjoy herself. Driving to the nearest town, she started planning her weekend of fun with her friends. Sitting outside a coffee shop, sipping her caramel latte, she noticed a very large building that looked like it had only recently been renovated. A group of attractive men and women were obviously trying to entice people into joining whatever it was. With her curiosity piqued, she took a slow walk over to see what all the fuss was about.

The building was massive, and looked like three large Victorian houses knocked into one. Painted a crisp, bright white, the only sign on it was a small plaque above the impressive double door entrance, which said, "Club 1" in blood red paint. The tiny sign was understated, classy.

So it's obviously not another new gym opening, she thought with a chuckle.

A good looking man approached her. All blond hair and come-to-bed brown eyes, she imagined under his well-cut suit was a body to die for. He was incredibly tall and very masculine. Breathing in, she closed her eyes. He smelled exactly the same way as Blake had all those years ago.

That smell was pure sex. Shaking her head, she had to concentrate as he introduced himself.

"Hi, my name is Trey," the man told her, reaching out to shake her hand warmly. It sent electric currents up her arm.

"Uh, hi, I'm Siobhan," she told him a little unsteadily, shaking herself again to gain some control before she made an utter prat of herself. Trey smiled as he talked to her about what the Club could offer her. It sounded so exciting and such an original concept she signed up for the opening night, which was on the weekend of her friends' visit.

It was excruciatingly expensive.

There were four floors including a basement that boasted a famous burger joint franchise, plus a casino, a dance floor, a first class restaurant and a Tequila and Vodka lounge that had leather bean bags and chairs hanging from the ceiling.

She couldn't wait to could take her friends there.

Trey explained that it was intended to be a member's only club and that she could sign her friends in for free on that weekend. After taking her credit card details, he gave her special red foiled embossed tickets for opening night, explaining if the tickets were lost, they wouldn't be getting in.

He also gave her the club's glossy promotional brochure.

Whoever ran it operated a first class venue. Just before Siobhan left, he remarked:

"That's a very special locket, and it looks fabulous on you."

He didn't wait for a reply. Smiling at her, he bid her goodbye with a cheeky wink.

The two weeks passed in a work and kitten haze, and she enjoyed them both. Soon it was the day of her friends' visit. She'd sent them all their own keys so if they arrived before she finished work they could let themselves in.

Pulling up outside the house, she noticed gleefully that they were all there and let out an excited squeal when her front door opened and her friends engulfed her in a group hug, all talking at the same time, with Able and Dora weaving in amongst them excitedly.

Soon they were all chatting, catching up with gossip and reminiscing. They had already sorted out where they were sleeping and they'd had a good old rummage through the house. As the night wore on, they all relaxed with a few bottles of wine. Getting out her camera, they posed for a few photos on the sofa.

There were pictures of the girls all over the house.

Her favourite pictures, the ones they took on that fateful holiday where she had met Blake, hung in her study. They'd been professionally framed and mounted on the wall behind her computer, so as she was working she could ogle him to her heart's content.

They didn't get to bed until the early hours, but the next day, her phone rang way too early. It was Trey, from the Club, phoning to explain that she'd won a day in a spa, including a free hair style and manicure. She and her guests would be picked up and taken there in the Club's car and returned home afterwards. Then later, when they were ready to go to Club 1, they'd be picked up and dropped off home at the end of the night.

Her friends greeted the news with excitement once they had surfaced from their sleep.

The time spent at the spa was relaxing, once the staff had got over the fact that the famous Imogen had walked through their doors. All the girls loved it when their friend was recognised and Imogen was happy to pose for photographs once they'd washed and blow dried her hair. She only let the world's top stylists cut her fabulous locks.

Seraphina had her gorgeous red hair snaked into sexy ringlet waves that ended just below her shoulders.

Siobhan decided it was time to cut her golden locks. The cut took about six inches off and the hairdresser gave it some lovely choppy lengths. A wispy fringe brought her stunning blue eyes into focus.

Charlotte's hair needed very little as she'd only just had it styled for the television show.

Later that night, once they were ready in their finery, looking devastatingly sexy, they met up in the living room to show off their outfits. Siobhan was particularly pleased with her black maxi dress. It dipped low, showing off her cleavage. Her new haircut made her look younger than twenty-eight. With her eyes made up by Imogen, she was breathtakingly stunning.

The Club's car arrived promptly at eight thirty, and the girls piled in happily. Champagne on ice awaited them, and they giggled their way to the club with the music blaring, thoroughly enjoying themselves, happy to be in one another's company once again. It wasn't a long ride, and as they neared the place, Siobhan pointed out the huge spotlights in the night sky. As they pulled up outside the club, the girls grimaced at the huge queue.

"I sincerely hope we do not have to join that!" Imogen said, but Trey was waiting for them. He spoke into his headset, and smiled charmingly at her and her party as entertainers milled around, entertaining the crowd waiting in the queue.

Some men did magic tricks, while other performers juggled chain saws. Half naked women on stilts caused Seraphina to nudge Siobhan in the ribs and snicker.

"Welcome, Siobhan, may I say that you and your party are looking quite decadent tonight," Trey said, lifting her hand slowly and kissing her knuckles. She couldn't take her eyes off him and felt the girls looking on in interest.

They all knew she was still in love with Blake but didn't bring it up very often. Just wearing his locket and watch was enough evidence that her heart still hadn't recovered.

But she knew they all kept their fingers crossed that one day soon she would find a man who could unlock her heart from the deep freeze she seemed to have buried it in.

CHAPTER FOUR

"Thank you, Trey," she finally managed to mumble, blushing furiously, while gazing into his brown eyes and biting on her bottom lip, a habit left over from school.

She only did it when she was unhappy or under stress or just plain confused. She fancied Trey – it would have been difficult not to – but she wasn't ready to take a step in that direction.

She sighed and followed him up the five steps and into the impressive foyer. Trey led them into the heart of the club and let them soak up the spectacular ambiance. The ground floor was where you could eat; the tables surrounding the dance floor were cosy and intimate. There were private rooms you could hire, in fact anything your hearts desired could be had, for a price. He showed them to their table and waited for them to be seated. Another man walked over, Trey introduced him as their personal waiter. Anything they wanted, they only had to look his way and he would find it for them.

Looking around, Siobhan was reminded of the masquerade ball all those years ago. Security here was just as tight, with staff walking around, talking into their headsets, assuring their clientele were safe and protected. Cursing, Siobhan gave herself a mental slap and brought her attention back to her friends, laughing as Seraphina whispered.

"Do you think the waiters are for hire too?"

Seraphina giggled – then stopped dead as their waiter winked at her.

The girls burst out laughing and Seraphina winked back, thoroughly enjoying flirting with the man. They had a round of their favourite cocktails, Margaritas, followed by more Champagne. By the time lights dimmed, the girls were ready to hit the dance floor.

They spent most of the night dancing, laughing and having a great time. They watched as Imogen danced with Seraphina, which caused quite a stir, but no one bothered her.

Charlotte was talking to a man at the next table and seemed to be relaxed and enjoying herself. Siobhan grabbed her bag and signalled to her friends that she wanted to go to the ladies room. They all nodded, but made no move to join her.

She didn't mind, they were having too much fun. A grand staircase led up to the next floor. It was wide and sweeping, and reminded her of the one *Gone with the Wind*, where Rhett Butler swept Scarlett into his arms.

If only she could find a man to come along and whisk her off her feet too.

Slowly walking up the stairs, she thought how nice it was to be somewhere where you weren't jostled. Usually a place was so jam packed that you had to fight your way through.

At the top of the stairs, a wide balcony wrapped around the whole floor, so you could watch everyone below enjoying themselves. Siobhan stood there for a few minutes watching her friends, loving the fact they seemed to be having a great time. Turning away, she walked off to find the ladies room and bumped straight into another woman.

"I'm so sorry," Siobhan stepped back, and then smiled at the woman she'd collided with.

"Hello, Siobhan, I didn't know you'd be here. Are you enjoying yourself?" It was Valerie, the owner of the vets where she worked.

"Yes I am. I think it'd be difficult not to here. The owners seemed to have thought of everything. It's quite breathtaking, isn't it?"

"Yes, they have. Well, you enjoy yourself, and I'll see you at work on Tuesday," Valerie told her, and with a smile and a quick goodbye Siobhan left her and wandered off.

She came across a huge security guard, standing outside a large door, his arms folded across his chest. He didn't acknowledge her so she walked past him, pushing open the heavy door.

The room she entered was very dark, but stranger still was just how quiet it was when the door gently closed behind her – as though she wasn't in a club any more but maybe an old museum.

As her eyes became accustomed to the dark, she took stock of her surroundings.

It was an immense square room with worn stone flooring. There was a small, fully stocked bar on the right and all along the left side were booths for people to sit in. In the centre of the room was an extremely long, highly polished table, surrounded by leather chairs. It looked like a boardroom ready for a meeting.

The room was lit by what seemed hundreds of fat white candles dripping wax down their black wrought iron holders, dotted here and there, and it took a while for her eyes to become used to the darkness.

She turned, ready to leave the room, as she'd evidently got the wrong set of doors, when a voice called out to her.

"Hello, Si. Come in, you're in the right place."

It was a softly spoken, very masculine voice; a man's voice she instantly recognized. A man she didn't think she'd ever see again.

"Blake!" She whispered, hardly daring to turn around, her brain in turmoil.

On the one hand she felt she should run and not look back. But on the other hand, oh, how she wanted to stay and see him again. She craved seeing him. She'd been dreaming about this moment for nearly ten years.

She knew her hands were shaking; in fact, her whole body was trembling.

Breathe, she told herself, standing motionless.

In that split second she was back in the South of France, meeting him for the first time. *Just breathe,* she reminded herself. She slowly turned around, holding her breath, her eyes firmly on the floor. *Come on, get a grip,* she ordered. *You're not an immature eighteen year old anymore, for Christ's sake!* She let out a deep, long breath, and slowly raised her eyes. Nervously biting her lip, she almost stumbled back as he appeared before her.

Her breath left her in a quick whoosh.

Blake, her Blake.

Her heart was beating nineteen to the dozen in her chest, as she thought, *After all this time I still love him.* She closed her eyes for a brief second and let out a long sigh.

But now *Anger* was overtaking the love she still felt for him.

How could he have left her in France those many years ago?

Broken hearted, completely innocent, not knowing what the hell she'd done for him to treat her in such a cruel manner.

With a monumental effort, trying to pull her spiralling, out-of-control feelings together she bit back on how she really wanted to greet him, with a smack in the face.

How. Dare. He.

He left me. He told me he loved me, but he still bloody left me.

"Hello Blake, long time no see. How are you?" She asked. Even to her ears her voice sounded a little pissed off and she hoped he noticed.

Her legs moved towards him of their own volition, her heart still hammered with anger, but pure lust shot through her as she slowly walked towards him.

It had been too damn long.

Had he really been this handsome, sexy, and downright gorgeous? She silently wondered. Her memories hadn't done him any justice. Goose bumps erupted all over her. She detested anyone other than her closest friends calling her Si, but had allowed Blake to call her that.

Hell, she wouldn't even let her ex fiancée Harry call her Si when they'd been together.

And now is so not the time to be thinking of the wedding that never was, she sternly told herself. But when Blake called her Si, her insides seemed to go into meltdown, even after all these years. *Get a bloody grip on yourself!* She shouted to herself, mentally slapping her face.

Blake walked towards her, all six feet four inches of pure animal magnetism. *He is simply the best looking man I've ever seen.* His skin was a little paler than she remembered, but she reasoned that he was now in England and not in the sunny South of France. His skin was almost translucent, reminding her of Monique, the nasty woman who'd owned the chateau where they had all gone on that fateful night. She grimaced as her feelings of abandonment rose up swiftly.

But those green eyes of his, which would draw you to him, hadn't changed. She loved his thick, dark brown hair and was glad to see that he still wore it a little long. The easy way he wore beautifully cut suits, without looking effeminate. Not that anyone could ever question his sexuality. It went deeper than looks, this man knew her, really knew her.

It was as though their souls had been entwined for all eternity.

He opened his arms and before she could stop herself, she walked into them. She just couldn't seem to control her body. It was on auto pilot. She rested her head on the hard planes of his chest and let out another sigh.

She was home at last.

His arms came around her in an embrace, a hug, a cuddle; whatever it was, it felt right. They stood there for what seemed an age, oblivious to their surroundings. Her hands gripped his shoulders – not wanting to ever let him go again, even though she knew he didn't belong to her.

He never did.

"Come and sit down, Si," Blake smiled at her, took hold of her hand, and led the way to a booth.

"Hold on a moment." She shook her head as if to clear away the cobwebs, and removed her hand from his as she slowly backed away. "Wait, I really need a drink, a large one."

"Please, help yourself." Pointing to the bar he continued walking to the booth and sat down, watching her. He knew that right now what she needed was space, and a little time to catch her breath.

She wanted a very strong drink – and quick. Grabbing a large bottle of Jack Daniels and a couple of glasses, she headed back to him. Her heart was still playing hammer jack drill in her chest, but she felt slightly more in control. Even so, she knew it might be prudent to put some distance between them, so she sat on the other side of the booth and poured them both a very large drink.

"Chin, chin!" Siobhan said, plastering a smile on her face. Tipping the glass back, she swallowed the dark liquid quickly, and nearly choked in the process. It burned her throat as it went down.

She poured another one, took a small sip and tried to muster her dignity. He knew the smile was fake as it hadn't reached her eyes. She raised her glass to him and he smiled at the familiar toast.

"Chin chin," he drawled, tapping her glass with his. Taking a small sip of his drink, he placed it back onto the table and studied her with a probing gaze.

Drumming her fingernails on the table, she asked.

"Why did you abandon me? Where did you go? You just disappeared. No word, nothing, not even a letter. That was truly cold." It came out in a rush and she was appalled that she'd said it all out loud.

Her eyes quickly found his, and then hastily looked at her nails, at the floor, anywhere but him. *I didn't just say that, did I?* She thought, furious that she would seem utterly pathetic.

"Look, let's forget it, okay?" she said, quickly trying to recover a tiny bit of self-respect. "It's been a really, really long time, and frankly I don't want to hear your excuses, or lies. I'm out of here." The JD pounded through her veins; she was furious at him, at herself, at the whole damn world. She made to get up from the booth, but he reached across the table and gripped her wrist. Her skin felt hot and clammy compared to his cool touch. Absently, she noticed he still had on the Rolex she'd helped him choose all those years ago.

She wondered if he expected her to return the Rolex he'd given her. It meant enough to her that she still wore it, but if he wanted it back, then fuck it.

How dare he grab her. Who did he think he was? After all these years, he had no right.

He was nothing to her.

She glared at him, her anger spiking. Then just as quickly it drained away. She knew she was lying to herself. She was furious with him, but he would never, could never, mean nothing to her.

"Sit down," Blake said, his voice commanding. But his eyes were soft and gentle as he pondered how damn close he was to her walking out on him, not that he didn't deserve it.

"Please sit down, Si. I've waited too long to say this to lose you again. Please." It was said quietly, pleadingly, but then, she'd never heard him raise his voice. Sitting back down, she stared at him mutinously, folded her arms across her chest, and waited for him to speak.

Inside, she was still shaking with pent up hurt and anger. He was delusional if he thought she was going to make it easy for him. But she desperately wanted, no craved, to hear what he had to say.

Her emotions threatened to overwhelm her. Just to look at him again after all this time was a gift. Would she now, after all these years, find out some answers that she desperately needed to hear?

She'd been so sure he'd loved her, that he felt the same way she did.

Leaning forward he took her hand in his. His hand felt cool – or was hers hot and clammy because she was suddenly extremely nervous? Her eyes dropped to the table. What if, after all this time, the answers she sought were not the answers he gave her?

"I loved you," Siobhan whispered softly, so quiet it was barely audible. "I even loved you for a long time after you disappeared. I gave you my heart!" Her voice broke and a lone tear slid down her cheek. She grabbed her hand back and brushed it angrily away. She felt like a hurt teenager all over again, and after Blake, she'd vowed never to allow anyone the power to hurt her. *Can I not control my mouth tonight?* She asked herself angrily. *He obviously didn't love me.*

"Don't think I never loved you, Si!" Blake said, uncannily guessing her thoughts. He was watching her as though he could see all the conflicting emotions that threatened to overspill from her at any moment. "I have loved you... you Si, more than I loved anyone in my whole long life. Please look into my eyes and see that I'm not lying to you." He squeezed her hand gently.

Trembling she looked up, squaring her shoulders.

"I was just eighteen when I loved you. You were my whole world, for such a short time. You told me..." She screwed her eyes shut tight, and shook her head before she continued.

"You led me to believe everything you said. But you have to know I'm not that sweet innocent little girl any more. And believe me, I was innocent, full of naiveté, when you found me. I'm an adult now, and have been around the block a time or two. You can't expect to walk back into my life and tell me that you loved me and expect me to fall at your bloody feet." She stared at him, her blue eyes flashing contemptuously at him as she dared him to argue with her.

All the while willing herself not to break down.

"You know what? This was a mistake. I have to go and find my friends. They'll be wondering what the hell happened to me. I can't wait to see their faces when I tell them where I've been and who I've been with."

Grabbing her bag, she stalked away from him. She almost made it as far as the door and was surprised to find he was now barring her way.

Don't look at him, she screamed, *just don't,* but her eyes slowly and painfully dragged themselves up the body she knew so well. She'd used this body as her fantasy for the past ten years. And it hurt, it hurt so bloody much. She wanted him like a drug, he was her drug. *No,* she screamed at herself, *he left you broken, he abandoned you! Do not forget.*

"I need you to understand why I had to walk away from you ten years ago." His voice broke and he ran a hand through his hair. Taking a deep breath, he looked at her.

Now he had her full attention. Never had he sounded unsure of himself. Looking at him, she saw he looked worried.

"My God! What is it? Were you dying of some sort of mysterious disease or something? Were you already married? Are you gay?" At this she let out a small hollow laugh, her eyes wide, pleading with him to deny what she'd said, then she struggled to get herself under control.

"You could've told me then. Whatever it was you, could've told me. You owed me that much, at least." Siobhan said, looking into his eyes, shaking her head sadly. Her emotions were running far too high for her to cope with him standing so close to her. *I need to touch him so badly, it hurts*, she thought sadly, but took a step away.

"I had to separate myself from you because of the people I had to deal with. If they'd known you meant more to me than life itself, they would have come after you, just to get to me. And I could never have allowed that to happen. You meant too much to me. You always have and you always will." He whispered quietly to her, his body still blocking her exit.

He could see the taut lines of her body. He knew again how damn close he was to losing her, for good this time. Taking hold of her shoulders, he gently turned her, until she was leaning against the door for support. Her breathing was shallow, she was so near to breaking point. He placed his hands either side of her face. She knew full well what was about to happen and hated herself for wanting it, wanting him, so badly. She held her breath as her heart jumped erratically, but he didn't lean in to kiss her as she thought. He lowered his eyes to look at her lips. They were parted, ready and waiting for him to make his move. He traced her lower lip with his thumb, feeling her suck in air. She was transfixed to the spot. She closed her eyes. Nearly groaning at the contact, she trembled with longing. *Please*, her mind screamed.

When he lowered his head as though to kiss her, she lifted her chin to meet his lips eagerly.

He moved as though in slow motion.

All was quiet, and time stood still.

At last, their lips finally met.

He gently nibbled on hers before running his tongue along her bottom lip, following the path his thumb had just taken. And she was transported back in time to when she was just eighteen. Just eighteen and had never been kissed.

He'd been the one who showed her what her lips were made for.

He'd been the first man who had made her legs wobble from a simple kiss. She'd been searching for a man who could kiss her with the same amount of passion and intensity ever since. Even after all this time his lips felt so familiar, and their bodies atomically moulded together, touching in all the right places.

Somewhere in the back of her mind she knew she should move away, to demand the answers that she was bloody well entitled to. But she couldn't stop the kiss, not now, not after all this time, not even if the building collapsed around them.

He knew how to kiss her like no one else.

It was as though her lips were made to fit only his. He slowly ran his hand up her spine, stopped on the back of her neck and pulled her even closer. Her hands came to rest on his powerful shoulders, clinging to them.

Suddenly, he tore his lips away. Dazed, she whimpered in protest, needing him to continue.

No one could light her up the way he could.

CHAPTER FIVE

"We need to go somewhere private, to continue our... talks," he murmured softly against her lips. "Let me take you home, Si? To my house. It'll be private and quiet."

"But my friends...?" She protested. "How will they know I've left them? They're staying with me."

"It'll be taken care of. I'll have someone let them know you're safe and they'll be driven home whenever they want."

"Let me ring them, let me at least try to explain..." She fished around in her bag, her hands a little shaky, to find her phone, but she didn't have any reception. Besides, she didn't think they'd hear their phones over the loud music the club was pumping out.

She knew that if she went home with him, it would be an open invitation to continue where they'd left off. She didn't know if she had the willpower to stop him, especially after all these years of dreaming about what it'd be like to make love with him, would she even want him to stop? If his kisses could affect her so, and also remembering what talented fingers he had, what else could he do to her?

And most importantly, once in his house, would she ever have enough courage to leave again?

She was sure her friends wouldn't mind if she left them for the night, and anyway she'd be home in the morning, wouldn't she? But she was determined to have this one night with him. Perhaps that would be enough and she could finally move on with her life. Perhaps she'd even walk away from him this time, see how he liked it?

But she knew it was a foregone conclusion.

"Okay, I'll come with you," she whispered, feeling slightly nervous, her whole body trembled a little with the thought of what was to come. Blake took out his phone and tapped in a number, it was answered immediately. *Funny,* she thought, *he seems to get signal without any trouble.*

"Bring the car around to the back. I'm going home now." As he talked into the phone, she barely heard the reply, but knew the car would be moving into position to meet them. Taking hold of her hand, he led her towards the far end of the room.

Her heels clip clopped on the stone flooring.

"...No, out the back. I don't need the hordes downstairs gawping. Take care of everything tonight, okay? No, I don't want to be interrupted. I think we'll be safe for tonight. No, Nat..." He sounded quite aggravated now.

"Keep everyone away. We'll pick up tomorrow night. The car's here, so keep in contact with Alex and Ethan, and if anyone asks for me, I'm up here in the club but not contactable. Thanks. Good night."

By the time he finished his conversation, they'd reached the back of the room. He pressed a button near the roof that she hadn't even noticed, as her eyes flatly refused to be torn away from his face. The wall slid open and behind it was a door. Blake tapped a code into a box at the side of the door, and she watched as it swung open to reveal a metal fire escape.

As they climbed down, the door silently closed behind them.

"So, Nat, Alex and Ethan are all still with you? I can't believe the gang's still together," she murmured, chuckling to herself.

It was information that made her feel uncomfortable. She'd have to tell her friends all the men were here.

"Oh my God." Siobhan gasped. "Imogen," The sudden realisation that Imogen loved Alex just as much as she loved Blake made her stop abruptly. Blake took her hands into his and gently tugged her down the steps and into the waiting black limo.

The driver silently closed the door, slowly pulling away. Sitting in the back of the limo in a daze she thought of all the explaining that was going to happen.

What a bloody nightmare. This isn't turning into the fun night I'd been expecting. First of all, Blake appears after nearly ten years of silence. Then, I discover the man who'd caused Imogen's heartache is also here.

And it was quite likely Imogen was going to meet him again, and soon. He was probably talking to her right now. She could just see her friend's faces, if all three men turned up to explain where she'd disappeared.

Seraphina's likely to scratch Nat's eyes out and I wouldn't put it past Imogen to slap Alex, she thought bemusedly. She let out a little sigh and slowly shook her head, then looked up at Blake, who could clearly see the sadness in her expressive blue eyes.

"I can tell you've lots of questions to ask me," he said. "If it involves other people, namely our friends, can we please leave them until tomorrow? I want to concentrate on us tonight. Is that acceptable?" He looked relaxed with his top shirt buttons undone, his suit jacket lying casually on his lap and his arm draped along the leather seat.

Pouring himself a brandy from the crystal decanter, he loosened his tie.

"Would you like one?" He raised an eyebrow questioningly at

her. "Or perhaps you'd prefer me to open a bottle of Champagne?"

"No, thank you. I've had quite a lot to drink today and I drank the JD a bit too fast. If you remember, I've a really low tolerance to alcohol." Siobhan made a point of looking out the window, as she tried to push all thoughts of that night out of her mind. She didn't want to think of his strong arms around her, as he guided her up the steps to the villa after a night of drinking too much because her legs were a little bit on the wobbly side.

She could still hear his chuckle as he'd helped her to her room.

Hoping to throw him off the scent of what she'd been thinking because he seemed to have an uncanny knack of knowing her thoughts, she studied the landscape and realised the car was gliding past dark fields and not city lights any more. Looking at her watch, she was surprised to see that half an hour had passed.

Time really does fly when you're having fun, she thought.

"I know small children are supposed to ask this, but, are we nearly there yet?" Her eyes drank in his features. *He is truly stunning,* she thought.

"Just pulling up," he pointed out of the window. She pressed a button for it to go down, she wanted the fresh air to settle her equilibrium, which was out of whack, with him so close.

It was a cold crisp night, and she looked up to see thousands of twinkling tiny stars in the clear sky. It was just the kind of night she enjoyed. She could pinpoint the main constellations and sought out the moon – for some reason, she'd always found comfort in looking at it. She pressed her hands over her stomach and felt it tighten in apprehension of what was to come. *Perhaps I should've had that drink after all? She* thought. *Just to steady my nerves.*

He slid over and gently turned her to face him.

He saw her eyes flare slightly in panic and wanted nothing more than to calm her. To reassure her, that he wouldn't hurt her or allow anyone else to hurt her ever again. The car came to a gentle stop and she leant back, her head on the headrest.

Closing her eyes briefly, she took a steadying deep breath as she heard the doors being quietly opened.

Blake stepped out and silently held out his hand to her, as if he knew what inner turmoil she was feeling and after a few seconds she took hold of it.

Her hand looked small and fragile as he curled his cool fingers around it.

Holding her hand securely in his, she followed him as they walked up a few steps towards an impressive door, which opened immediately. She tried looking around, wanting to see where he'd lived all these years. But it was pitch black and she couldn't see much, although she could make out was a large and exceptionally old building.

"Good evening sir. I was informed that you were on your way home," a man much shorter than Blake, round, with a merry looking face, and a shock of unruly, curly black hair, opened the door to them. He looked to be in his fifties and faced Blake as he addressed him, smiling politely at her as they entered.

"Hello Robert, how are you this evening?"

"Very well thank you, sir. Your rooms are ready as you requested. If that is all sir?" Robert asked politely.

"Thank you Robert, only one thing. Nathaniel has been asked to make sure that I'm not disturbed tonight. Only in the most catastrophic event will he allow that to happen. Please make sure those wishes are upheld within the house. If anyone needs me please redirect them to Nathaniel, is that clear?"

"Of course sir, good night sir, miss." Bowing his head, leaving them alone he walked away.

Looking around the spacious entrance hall, with black and white marble squares on the floor she saw it led off to five ancient, dark wooden doors surrounded by smooth, light, coloured stone arches.

The staircase, on the right, was so grand, so overpowering, it was almost impossible not to stare at. It was breathtaking and obviously only the most talented craftsman had been used to build it. It had tiny little lights buried into each step and it went up nearly three stories. It was the most beautiful staircase she'd ever seen. She went over to the first step, looking up at the stunning stained glass window that reached up nearly to the roof.

The colours that were reflected against the creamy walls were exquisite.

She hoped she didn't have to walk up three flights or she feared she'd be too damn knackered to do anything when she reached the top!

Hearing water running, she looked around. At the far end was a modern steel structure, a massive indoor water feature.

"That's pretty impressive," she said, nodding her head towards it,.

"Yes, isn't it?" said Blake, trying to keep his face straight, Ethan had designed it so they'd had little choice but to have the ugly monstrosity. But he watched her, enjoying the sight of her looking around his home. "Come on," he gestured to her to follow him up the stairs.

This is it then, no going back now, she thought; *time to put on your big girl panties.* She followed him, her heart beating loudly and erratically, the house was so silent surely he could hear it? She tried to control her breathing but found it impossible to slow down her heartbeat. She walked on her toes, tiptoed up the grand wooden stairs, and tried not to make a sound. She let her hand trail over the worn, wooden banister, which felt warm to her touch and paused midway to gaze at the stained glass window. It reminded her of the windows of a church and she wanted to find out if it told a story.

He waited patiently for her – luckily, he'd stopped at the first floor – and held out his hand to her. She thought he seemed so sure of himself, calm, quiet, and controlled. He held her hand, watching it tremble as he gripped it.

Pull yourself together girl. It's not the first time you've ever had sex! So get over it! She thought, *but it will be the first time with Blake.* She took in her surroundings. It was very spacious, decorated in cream, calming colours, with high ceilings. The house was very beautiful, with ornate plastering and lots of natural wood.

Very gothic like she thought, *not that I'm an expert historian.*

With her hand tightly gripped in his, he led her down a wide corridor towards the largest set of doors she'd ever seen, huge things, with ornate carvings in the dark wood, again extremely old looking. Reaching into his back pocket he pulled out a large, old fashioned key. Compared to the high-tech door in the club, this door was from a completely different age. Siobhan put out her hand to trace the pattern carved onto the wooden doors. It felt warm, just as the banister had, she wondered how many hands had done the same, and then shook her head – not wanting to think about other women here with Blake. The key made a deep clunking sound as the mechanism opened.

Blake gave both doors a gentle push and stood back against one of them.

"After you," he gently guided her into the room.

She gasped and covered her mouth in surprise. It was a bedroom, an incredibly masculine, large square room, which was softened only by the romantic soft glow of white candles. The floor was pale stone squares. She didn't know what to look at first.

The bed, no, she wouldn't think of that, not just yet anyway. Instead, she walked to the far end of the bedroom, towards the most enormous and elaborate fireplace, she'd ever seen. If it wasn't lit, she would have been able to fit in it standing up. She couldn't reach the sides, even opening her arms wide. The fire surround was glistening white marble, with two ornately carved columns and a squared off mantle. Above that was a gilt framed mirror, which reminded her of the large mirror in the bathroom at the French chateau, all those years ago.

On either side of the columns were white marble vases, at least three feet tall, full of her favourite white stargazer lilies. Their delicate petals were open, the pale pink interiors utterly feminine. Picking up a stem, she closed her eyes and inhaled deeply. The perfume was delicate, fresh, and pretty. Placing the flower back, Siobhan turned to look at the rest of the room, everything about it, indeed the whole house, seemed oversized.

The only other piece of furniture in there was the bed.

If she was shocked by the stunning fireplace, she felt her stomach plummet when she took in the sheer scale of the bed. It was magnificent. She was sure she'd seen a picture, once, maybe in school, of a bed just like this, a king's bed, all stately and so very, very masculine.

This bed was so very Blake.

It was made of rich dark wood and covered with the same ornate carvings as the door and staircase. The curtains tied to each of the posts were heavy, deep red, with burnt gold thread embroidered through them. It was high with an incredibly thick feather mattress, the cover matching the hangings. There were a pile of cushions of all different shapes and sizes, all covered in the same colour scheme of dark reds, creams, and gold. She couldn't believe she was really here. In Blake's bedroom, after all these years of fantasising. She felt overwhelmed.

Closing her eyes, she heard him approach. He stood behind her, and she found she couldn't move, it was as if her feet were nailed to the floor. Her blood pounded in her ears and her body trembled slightly. He placed his hands on her shoulders, gently squeezing them, and lifted her hair until it trailed over her right shoulder. Which freed the left side for him to kiss his way down from her ear to her collar bone. They were light teasing kisses, with his fingers gently stroking the same path down her neck.

"I adore you, Si," he whispered against her heated skin.

Her head fell to the right, allowing him greater access to her sensitive soft neck, and she whimpered at his touch. Her neck – especially the left side – was one of her favourite erogenous zones. She wondered if he could feel the beat of her heart, as her vein was positively dancing. She slowly turned around, with the help of his gentle hands, but found it damn near impossible to look into his eyes.

All these years of wanting him, of needing him – and here he was stood before her. The enormity of the situation wasn't lost on her. She didn't know whether to bolt out of the door or to stay and see where this night led her. All she knew was only his touch could awake her body from the years of hibernation it'd been in.

His hands cradled her face, lifting it slowly, gently, wanting to gaze into her eyes.

"I promise I'm not going to hurt you Si," his eyes were full of passion, with such a tender smile on his lips that it melted her heart.

He brought his head down and pressed his lips against hers. This kiss was completely different from the kiss in the club. It was fuelled by passion, forceful, and demanding a response from her mouth, which she gave back in full. She reached up, entwined her hands behind his neck and arched her body into his, a whimper escaping her throat to which he responded with a low guttural growl that spiked her arousal nearly through the roof.

Lowering one of his hands, he stroked the side of her breast.

The dress was not much of a barrier; and even though he was nowhere near her sensitive nipples they hardened immediately to erect little pebbles. Feeling this, he made a sound of a man purely running on sexual desire, as she moved restlessly against him.

His hand continued to work down her supple body, ending up around her waist as he pulled her to him.

CHAPTER SIX

In a heartbeat she felt how much he wanted her, how much he desired her. His hard arousal pressed into her stomach and she could almost feel it throb through the material of his trousers.

He feels so large she thought, *so thick, I want him.*

Breathing hard, wanting more, needing more, she wanted to demand he give her everything he had to give. She knew this time he wouldn't stop, as he'd done many times before, all those years ago. Reaching up, stroking his handsome face, she felt the slight stubble on his chin, a square jaw line and full lips which were continuing to devour her own.

Feeling her heart pounding in her chest she thought, with excitement, *it'll be working overtime tonight.*

Continuing to explore, her hands ran through his thick dark hair. He growled at her again, teasing her tongue with his own. Their tongues danced in each other's mouths as the air around them positively sizzled with passion and raw desire. *I've got to feel some skin,* she thought dizzily, and then lost the ability to think rational thoughts.

He was ahead of her as he wrapped his arms around her and picked her up, as though she was as light as a feather. Cradling her body against his he walked to the bed, all the while keeping his eyes fixed on hers, murmuring such sweet loving terms of endearment it almost brought tears to her eyes. He made it in a few strides and gently lowered her back onto her feet, pressing her backwards until her back rested against one of the posts at the foot of the bed and not on the bed as she had thought. She reached out her hand, wanting him closer, but he took it and turned it over, bringing his mouth down, kissing her palm. Placing feather light kisses up her wrist where the skin was thin and tender, flicking his tongue over her pulse, feeling it flutter.

No one had kissed her wrist before, but it felt electrifying now as he caressed it.

But he was moving too slow, damn it!

Reaching out, she undid his tie, threw it to the floor, and then worked her fingers down the neat row of buttons on his shirt. Her breath was coming out in small soft pants and she hadn't realised he'd come to an abrupt stop, watching her every move hungrily through vivid green eyes which had darkened with the swell of his desire.

Finally the shirt was undone, but instead of removing it she ran her hands up underneath it, sighing with pleasure at the first touch of his satiny smooth skin. His body was so well defined she felt each individual hard ridge of stomach muscle as she traced them with her fingers. His muscles rippled, there were no words to describe the feel of her fingers finally on his body.

Using her fingertips, she began to explore, first circling his flat nipples – and to her satisfaction they hardened, peaked, just as hers had. When she had finished teasing his nipples her fingertips danced over his firm chest and onto his powerful shoulder blades, where she forced the shirt off his arms.

Letting out a triumphant sigh, leaning forward she kissed his shoulder, her hands still roaming all over his upper body.

His skin felt a little chilled to her touch; *it must be because I am on fire* she thought. She couldn't get enough of him and he stood perfectly still for her, as though he knew she needed this time to explore his body intimately. The glow of the fire cast wonderful shadows. Not that she was paying any attention to anything other than how his body felt to her touch.

His eyes drank her in as she walked around him, her fingers on his body making his thoughts a mass of riotous sexual ideas.

He was broad shouldered and powerful. *Not even Michelangelo's marble statue of David compares to his physique,* she thought. Not an inch of fat, his skin completely unblemished. Leaning in, she brushed his shoulders with her cheek. He smelt so mouthwateringly good, so manly, she wanted to touch, lick, and bite her way to finding out what turned him on. *What would it take to turn this huge man into a jabbering mess of need?* She wondered, but knew instinctively it would be she who would be reduced into begging tonight.

"Siobhan," he growled, his voice low, husky, and sexy as hell. Turning around, he took hold of her, dragged her to him. His hands were in her hair, tugging it, sending little pleasure shocks down her body. She was tall, but he was taller and it felt good to be made to feel tiny and vulnerable.

But never afraid, knowing in her heart of hearts he would never hurt her; she was, and forever would be, safe in his arms.

His mouth dropped onto hers, taking ownership, his tongue penetrating her mouth thrusting in, making her moan. Feeling weak-kneed, she realised hazily he was holding her up, otherwise she be on the ground in an undignified heap. Her body pressed tight against his, breasts flattened against his chest and his erection hard against her.

Seeking her entrance, he slowly ground his hips against hers, making her pant with need.

Oh God, she thought, she'd never felt this aroused in her life; she desperately wanted him to take her now. To put that heavy, thick cock where it was meant to be and make her scream with desire until she was spent.

Lifting her up, he placed her gently on the bed. Kneeling up she moved into the middle, slowly starting to undo the long zip down the side of her dress. Glancing at him from under her eyelashes, she beckoned to him.

He needed no further encouragement; kicking off his shoes he quickly joined her.

He didn't have far to go to reach her, gently pushing her down into the mattress. Looking up at him, she stretched her arms out to him in a gesture that was as old as time itself. *Wow,* she thought, *those muscles are something else,* suddenly, she needed to touch him, really feel him, in places only he would know how to fill.

Lying down beside her, resting on his elbow he lent over her, gently stroking her face.

"You're so beautiful Si. I want you so much," before she'd time to reply he kissed her, a soft, heart stopping, kiss that melted her heart and made her insides go gooey.

"I love you Si, and you alone," he murmured onto her lips.

Teasing her mouth open, he gently brushed his tongue against hers, while her hands ran over his stomach, feeling his muscles clench, his skin so smooth to touch.

Looking directly into his eyes, she saw they were filled with love and sexual hunger for her.

His hand continued stroking down her body and finished the job of undoing her dress zip. The thin straps gently pulled off her shoulders and he tugged the dress down her body until just her bottom half was left covered. Running an appraising hand over her flat stomach, he felt it quiver before carrying on up her body and came in contact with her bra, a lacy, frothy concoction. It was pretty, but it still needed to come off.

Quickly dealing with the clasp; gently, teasingly, he slowly pulled the straps down over her shoulders. He rained kisses down onto them, but he was still moving way too slow and she made a move to remove it herself, faster.

He chuckled, pushing her hands away.

"We've waited nearly ten years for this. I'm going to take my time to enjoy you," he removed it and flung it off the bed, sitting back, admiring her now naked breasts.

"Beautiful." Siobhan felt a slight blush spread over her body. She wasn't used to being so scrutinised, but she enjoyed it because it was Blake. Suddenly his hands were everywhere, leaving a trail of burning kisses in their wake. He was stroking, kneading, keeping up a pressure on her breasts, they'd never felt so sensitive.

Arching her neck off the bed, she closed her eyes tightly. She knew before long she would be seeing stars bursting when her release took her higher than ever before.

She ached for him to take a nipple into his mouth and groaned with near despair as he moved up her body instead. Pressing soft kisses up her throat on his way to reach her mouth, finding her soft, already kiss-ravaged lips he began to kiss her with raw passion. He stroked his fingers down her body until he circled a nipple. Taking it between his thumb and finger, he gently pinched it.

She gasped for air as he repeated the erotic pinch over and over. It felt as though electric shocks were connecting her nipple to places he seemed in no hurry to explore. He made his way with torturous slowness back down her neck, licking, kissing, and occasionally nipping at her tender flesh.

She had never felt such bliss, *this is pure ravishment,* she thought hazily. But, any attempt made by her to touch lower down his anatomy, to touch him more intimately, made him move just, oh-so out of reach. And she needed to touch him, she craved to touch him desperately.

"Stay with me Si, you'll get there," his whisper tickled her breast, and then he kissed his way between the sensitive valleys of her breasts.

"Oh my God. Please." She begged him, and even to her it sounded like a whine. His mouth closed tightly on a nipple while his hand mimicked its action on the other one.

Her back arched off the bed in an attempt to encourage him to take more of her breast into his mouth.

"Do you have any idea how good you taste, Si?" His tongue flicked at her nipple, flattening it against the roof of his mouth.

He wanted her to talk? She found it impossible to answer, concentrating solely on his exciting touch; he was bringing her body to life, demanding she felt every erotic sensation possible.

It took her a while to realise that he'd stopped touching her and she let out a whimper for him to resume, but he ignored her and scooted down to her feet, quickly removing her shoes and chucking them onto the floor to join her bra, his shirt, and tie. Picking up a foot he gently kneaded, and massaged it. Bringing it up to his mouth, he placed a gentle kiss on the arch.

Next to come off was the rest of her dress.

Lifting her hips, she allowed him to slowly pull it down over her bum and down her long legs, leaving her in her white lacy thong. Reaching up, he gently tugged at her belly piercing, leaving her thong on. Her eyes were wide, and he saw the pure lust and passion shining out of them.

She felt hot, achy and everywhere he touched was suddenly super sensitive. But she wanted the rest of his clothes off, now. Kneeling up she took hold of his belt buckle, began to take it off – and then decided to have some fun while she was doing it.

He noticed the mischievous glint in her eyes, but hid the

knowledge from her. He would let her think she was in charge, at least for the time being.

Undoing his trouser button, she slowly undid the zip, closing the gap between their bodies so her breasts brushed up against his downy soft chest hairs. The friction made her nipples harden even more and a soft moan escaped her mouth. Her hands left his zip and ran slowly up his body, to his shoulders and down his arms, where her hands entwined with his.

They were body to body, both kneeling up, staring into each other's eyes.

It was a highly erotic pose and she wanted to stay in this position for the rest of her life. But, as soon as that thought appeared she knew it wasn't enough. Tearing her eyes away from his, she continued her quest to remove his clothes. To even up the balance, not that she was self conscious of her body in front of him. In fact, this was the first time she wasn't self conscious of being naked with a man, it felt completely right, natural, a coming home.

Taking her hands out of his, she trailed them up his back, letting her nails gently rasp his smooth skin, feeling his powerful muscles ripple under her touch. Moving to his chest, she leaned forward and kissed and caressed him. She wanted him to feel the same burning passion for her as she felt for him. Lower and lower her hands and mouth moved, flicking her tongue over his hard little nipples and delighted in hearing him gasp, swirling her tongue in his belly button while her hands ventured lower still.

She followed the thin line of hair down to where to zip was undone. She really wanted those trousers off now to allow her better access to what they concealed from her.

But, in a sudden burst of fluid movement, he stood up on the bed.

Oh my God, he's so tall, she thought, looking up and watching in wonder as he let his trousers pool at his feet then kicking them off the bed. She rapidly breathed in as her stomach knotted, underneath he wore, black, figure hugging underwear that showed off his lower body to perfection, leaving her under no illusion whatsoever, how much he desired her.

Reaching out both hands she ran them up his powerful legs and kept going until she reached his butt. It was delectable. Her hands crept underneath his underwear and kneaded his muscled cheeks. She was so nearly at her objective, but he reached out and gripped her hands, coming back down onto the bed, pushing her back down onto the soft mattress.

His face was so close to hers and she saw he was having difficulty remaining calm and in charge. She was loving the idea that he found her as sexy and exciting as she found him. He stretched his body out on top of her, supporting his weight on his elbows. His hand was on her breast, moulding it, squeezing the nipple before he moved back and forth between the two.

Desire raced through her veins, adrenalin, pumping through her heart. If he were to withdraw from her now she would die, she ached for him to finish what he'd started nearly ten years ago.

"Blake, please!" She begged him. "Please hurry, I need... I need," her voice a husky, emotional whisper.

He drowned out whatever she was about to ask him by kissing her savagely. Her hands on his head pressing him to her, digging her fingers into his scalp so he couldn't escape.

The kiss left her drained and weak, but she knew she wanted more, oh-so much more.

Shifting his body, he laid on his side, facing her, while she was still on her back. He traced a finger down her body, slowly, as if to draw out this strange form of torture he was inflicting on her. She began to squirm, tried to do everything in her power to get him to release her as it felt like a volcano was threatening to erupt.

"Argh… please Blake…"

Both his hands travelled down her body, making her squirm excitedly. She sighed happily when his hand finally made it to her thong, her hips dancing to entice him to remove it.

Her eyes squeezed tightly shut.

"Please."

In one powerful motion her panties were ripped from her body, her eyes flew open in shock and watched as they flew through the air to land on the floor at the foot of the bed. Luckily they didn't land on one of the many candles that lit the room.

At last she was naked before him, staring up at him as he looked at her appreciatively. His eyes were scorching hot, blazing a trail of goose bumps where she felt him stare. Now it wasn't enough to be naked, she desperately needed him to be naked as well.

She needed a lot of things now.

He stood up and she watched in fascination as his hands moved to the elastic of his underwear, she held her breath. Her eyes didn't waver as he lowered them slowly.

Her lust for him was shining out like a beacon.

Once they were around his ankles, he revealed his long, thick, and extremely hard cock.

She felt her mouth gape open.

"Oh," she murmured, in utter wonder of his perfect physique.

She wanted him in her, she knew he would fill her completely, stretch her. Her body began to ready itself for him, her juices pooling in the area which, at any moment would be filled by him.

Swallowing hard and sitting up slightly, she ran a hand lightly up and down the long length of him, loving the feel of him in her hand.

His skin was silky soft but at the same time he was as hard as steel and she heard his sharp intake of breath. Her thumb gently wiped off a drop of fluid that had appeared at the small slit, she licked it off her finger while staring into his eyes and licking her lips at the earthy, slightly salty tang of his taste.

He exhaled slowly, watching her tease him, grinding his teeth together to gain some small semblance of control over his body.

Lowering himself down to the bed once more, he gently pushed her down onto the mattress. His hands were not moving slowly now, he seemed impatient to touch her. He lay on his side, running his hand down, teasing her body to a fever pitch.

Stroking her until he suddenly came to a stop.

She opened her eyes, looked directly into his with a silent plea to continue. Licking her lips while her hands reached up to gently trace his lips. She cried out when he sucked her finger, swirling his tongue around the tip, nipping at the pad with sharp teeth.

"Now, Blake."

He needed no further encouragement, his fingers dipping into her silky wet folds and she lost all rational thought. Her hand fell out of his mouth, her eyes closing and she concentrated on the powerful feelings he was evoking with every stroke. His fingers slowly teasing her as he slipped into her entrance, feeling how hot and ready she was for him.

Finding her most sensitive bud, he strummed his fingers against it. Never missing a beat, playing her as though her body were a fine instrument. Her belly trembled and her head was thrown back in pure unadulterated lust. Panting, her body swelled, her back arched right off the bed as he bent his head to her ear and whispered softly.

"I want to watch you come, Si, come for me, let me watch you explode."

His crafty fingers rolled her bud between them and her world shattered into a thousand fragments. Screaming out his name in release, it felt as though her body was suspended off the bed as her body arched and her muscles locked.

Her hands gripped his shoulders, as though to tether herself, her nails digging into his skin, nearly drawing blood.

Kissing her with fever, on and on her orgasm lasted, spiraling up as far as the stars and his fingers kept her going until at last she was spent, wringing out every last drop of pleasure she had.

Collapsing onto the bed, her hands fell away from his shoulders, her body felt totally relaxed, sublime in a way she'd never felt.

He didn't miss a beat, moving his body over hers he thrust himself into her as the last tremors of her orgasm were still pulsating through her. Propping himself up onto his hands he continued to watch as she throbbed and pulsated around his cock.

Knowing that he'd never known anyone as beautiful as his Si. And make no mistake, she was his.

CHAPTER SEVEN

Wrapping her long, slender legs around his hips, her heels dug into his ass, while her arms went around his neck. His fingers slipped between their bodies, stroking her bud as his hips moved in long, hard thrusts into her.

She was panting, short, gasps, and her hips thrusted up to meet his with every powerful stroke.

Every forceful thrust was felt deep inside her, the tip of his shaft almost nudging her womb. He was simply the largest and thickest man she'd ever known. Not, that she'd known many, she'd only had two other lovers, but she knew he was larger than average and she knew she'd be a little sore and tender come morning, and looked forward to it.

Lowering his head, he bit one of her nipples.

"Blake! Blake," She moaned, her nails raking his skin, down his back, very nearly drawing blood.

"Tell me what you want, Si," he whispered, staring down into her face, watching it contort with pleasure.

"You, I want you, now."

She only just finished answering him as a wave of pleasure broke over her. Her back arched, her hands splayed out by her side, gripping the cover tightly. Every muscle locked as the orgasm raced through her.

As she shuddered around him, he felt every little touch around his cock, her rippling core soon sent him spiralling out of control and he found his own release.

"Siobhan!"

Roaring out he collapsed on top of her, listening to her heart galloping along, their sweat licked bodies cooling rapidly. He pushed himself up, brushed a few tendrils of her hair off her flushed face.

"You look so very beautiful, Si," he kissed her with a tenderness that was at odds with his size, feeling a little tearful laying in his arms, after dreaming of this, this moment, for the past ten years.

"I love you Blake, I've always loved you," she choked back her tears as she stared into his eyes.

"I love you, Si, I've loved you forever," he murmured against her lips, as he kissed her, covering her face in soft kisses. He started at her forehead and worked down to her closed eyes, her nose, flushed cheeks, and finally her lips.

Her heart gradually calmed down to a steadier beat, she felt languid, so relaxed she was afraid she was going to fall asleep. She wanted to wrap her arms around him and never move ever again.

But he obviously had different ideas, after slipping free from the tight grip her body had around his cock, he bounded out of the bed.

"Don't move, that's an order," he grinned. Leaning down, he pressed his lips quickly against hers. "I'll be right back."

She enjoyed the view of his naked body as he walked over to the fire place, and opened a door leading into another room. She heard him press buttons and then the sound of, water. Struggling up onto her elbows, wondering what he was up to. He walked out of the room, unfazed at being completely naked. She ran her eyes appreciatively over his fabulously hard body, licking her lips wanting and craving more.

All his muscles were defined to perfection. She was now only beginning to realise one night was never going to quench her thirst for this man, indeed one lifetime wouldn't be enough for her. He walked over to the bed, already looking completely re-energised for a man who'd just got up to what they'd just got up to.

"Come on," holding out his hand, he grinned at her, his eyes twinkling with hidden mischief.

"What are you up to Blake?"

"Come on, you'll see, you'll like it – I promise." She rolled in a most unladylike manner over to his side of the bed, but instead of taking her hand, he scooped her into his arms.

She couldn't help herself, bending her head down to his chest, she licked her way up until she got to his ear and helped herself to a suck of his fleshy lobe.

"Are you cold Blake? I've not noticed before, but you feel slightly chilled."

Her hands stroked his chest, but he only chuckled and kept walking through the door. Looking around, she saw they were in an enormous wet room. *Is everything here oversized?* She wondered.

Looking up she smiled, the roof was made of glass and she could see the stars. It was quite breathtaking.

"Blake, it's beautiful, I love it."

He pressed a button by the door and hundreds of tiny bulbs flickered on in the dark slate floor. It now looked as though you were walking on stars as well.

Up to this point she hadn't paid much attention to the actual shower. It was in the centre of the room and had a huge square shower head, about one meter square. It was so large she guessed both of them would easily fit underneath at the same time. As Blake put her down, she walked towards it and stood under the flow, it felt like soft falling rain. Looking up, the water softly splashed her face, like warm rain water. *It's unbelievable* she thought.

Joining her underneath the falling water, he knelt down behind her.

"Stand still, Si," he ordered, while proceeding to lather her up.

Starting with her legs, he worked his way up her body. Paying particular attention to her sexy, soft and feminine rounded ass, kneading it, making sure he worked his way into all her nooks and crannies, enough to make her squirm.

Looking over her shoulder, she wriggled her butt at him cheekily.

He chuckled at her as he carried on, the shower gel he used was heavily scented. *It must have a base of aromatherapy oils in it,* she thought, taking a deep appreciative sniff, it smelled heavenly.

When he was finished with her ass, he slowly worked his way up her back, standing up as he finally arrived at her shoulders. Gently massaging her, all her cares, her worries, were being washed away and down the plug hole. She'd never had any man pay this much attention to her body before.

And now at long last she understood why the lucky few made such a fuss about sex. Because, if she was honest, the two men she had slept with before didn't have a clue. She'd wondered what all the fuss was about. But, now she finally got it, and she knew she'd never be the same again after this amazing, eye opener of a night.

Slowly turning her to face him, his eyes raked up and down her body, from her eyes to her collar bone, down to her high and full breasts, which she felt swell under his ardent gaze. He took his time to inspect her before he knelt back down and started the process over again, this time on her front. Washing her from her ankles, he lathered her up, with the smell of the delicious fragrance filling up the room once more.

Starting to tremble as he worked his way up her legs, she wanted his fingers to once again inflame her. But he was working at his own speed and wouldn't be rushed. She couldn't believe she wanted him again, not after what she'd just experienced and how satisfied he'd only a few moments ago made her feel, but want him she did.

Standing up, he wrapped his left arm around her neck and pulled her to him. Closing his mouth over hers he kissed her while plunging his tongue into her mouth. Working his right hand down her body, he smoothed it over her soft skin, all the while kissing her with such passion it left her breathless. His hand was painstakingly working its way down to where she needed his attention the most.

"God Si, I could kiss you forever, and ever. But there's somewhere else I have to kiss you, I have to taste you."

With that he knelt in front of her, his hands gently pushing her legs apart to give him better access to her most private parts.

She gasped in shocked realisation of what he was about to do.

"Blake... No,"

But, he didn't answer her, instead, opening her lower lips he gently licked her from her entrance up to her full lips. Hearing him groan, she looked down her body to watch, his face was full of determination and longing, looking as though he wanted to take his time and fully taste her. Her fingers entangled tightly in his hair, whether to hold him there or to quickly yank his head away she hadn't yet decided.

Her whole body started to tremble and her nipples hardening to little pebbled peaks. He licked his way through her wet folds until he found her sensitive flesh, her little bundle of nerves, using his tongue he sucked it right into his mouth. Her head fell back onto her shoulders. She was moaning without even realizing. His talented tongue worked and at the same time his fingers slid their way into her, slowly penetrating her.

Fucking her, in and out, in and out. It was a double whammy and she couldn't help herself, her hips starting to move on their own accord, rolling in time with his tongue.

Her breathing was shallow, and she knew she'd never felt anything like what she was now experiencing.

The volcano was peaking inside of her.

"Blake, oh my God Blake," she managed to gasp out huskily.

Her toes curled, and her hips rolled to an invisible beat his tongue was playing on her. He was indeed wreaking havoc on her body. One of his well oiled fingers worked their way into the tight puckered hole that was her virgin ass hole.

Her eyes snapped open, looking down her bewildered look met with his and he grinned up at her, winking.

It was incredibly erotic, looking into his eyes while his tongue was... there! It only took a couple more well aimed flicks with his tongue against her bud, to push her over the edge. Screaming out his name she came, seeing stars burst behind her closed eyes. Her whole body shook with the ferocity of her release.

She slumped down, her knees finally giving way.

Catching her before she reached the floor he picked her up effortlessly, kissing her neck, nibbling at any skin he could reach. Once again he murmured to her, but what he was saying she couldn't make out, his lips were muffled against her skin.

With her legs straddling his waist, he found the nearest wall and with strength and precision she would have thought impossible, he held her to him and up in the air. Her back wasn't against the wall, his strength and hands protected her as he thrusted himself into her while his mouth found hers, kissing her on and on. His tongue mimicking the speed at which he was penetrating her.

Slowly fucking her mouth and core.

She thought she might die from all the passion, her arms were around his neck but her hands were not satisfied with not touching him. They fluttered against his skin. All the while he kept up the steady beat of thrust with his hips, grinding into her, then changing to a circular motion.

Clinging on for dear life, throwing her head back in ecstasy, she exposed her throat. Taking immediate advantage of that he kissed and nibbled it. He could feel she was close to coming again and stepped up his pace.

"Si, I want you to come again, come on, come now my darling," he whispered against her throat just as her world fragmented again. She was so in tune with his command that it acted as a trigger to her body and she came again, bucking wildly against him. Her voice was hoarse as she screamed out his name.

With a final, forceful surge he came too, and she watched hazily as his neck muscles strained with the force of his orgasm.

It showed his strength that he didn't drop them both to the floor, but after a while she felt him slipping out of her. Gently lowering her legs to the floor – they were a little on the shaky side – she took a few precious seconds to catch her breath before she leant back against the wall, pulling him into an embrace. She couldn't even think about moving as she was far too sated.

They stood in silence as there was no need for words. After a few minutes he placed gentle butterfly kisses all over her face.

"Blake, I had no idea, I never knew sex could be anything like that. Is it always like that for you?" His hand soothed her by stroking her body, not enflaming, but relaxing her.

"No, never before. Only with you," he looked at her tenderly and understood just how special this was, for both of them, before leaning down to very gently nip her kiss ravaged lips. He pulled her back towards the shower and they washed each other, taking time to get to know each other's bodies. Then he grabbed two huge, white fluffy towels which were more like fluffy blankets. Patting her dry, he wrapped her in one, holding her to him briefly before wrapping the other around his hips.

Putting his hand in hers he led the way back to the bed. Siobhan suddenly felt very tired, in fact she couldn't remember ever being this utterly shattered. Dropping the towel and getting into bed, she smiled dreamily as he pulled up the covers, tucking her in and making sure she was warm. Dropping his towel he joined her, pulling her to him until their bodies were tight against each other and she settled in the crook of his arm. Looking up to him as he placed a gentle loving kiss to the tip of her nose, she let out a contented sigh and closed her eyes.

Siobhan woke up sometime just before dawn on Sunday, but before opening her eyes she took a moment to go over last night's incredible events. Not in her wildest dreams did she ever think that she'd end up in Blake's bed, well maybe in her dreams, but never in real life. She wiggled her toes in excitement, a very self satisfied smile playing on her lips.

This was altogether a new concept for her, she was satisfied, sexually. Blushing fiercely, remembering how wonderful he'd made her feel, so loved, cherished, beautiful and sexy. *Oh my God* she thought, *some of the things he did to me*, well, it made her blush even more violently thinking about where he'd put his tongue.

She let out a silent giggle.

She wanted to run to her friends and shout at the top of her lungs: "I get it, I get what all the fuss is about sex now." She stretched her leg muscles, her whole body felt wonderful, a little tender in certain areas but even that felt good. She turned on her side to look at Blake, only to find he was already watching her.

"Good morning Si, you're looking very pleased with yourself.

I can't imagine why." He winked at her while his hand stroked from her shoulder down her arm. The light touches made her body tremble. She smiled at him, wondering if he could see the brief flashes of what he'd done to her the night before galloping through her mind. Closing her eyes, she tried, unsuccessfully, to banish the exceedingly sinful thoughts.

"Morning Blake," she said "Those are words I didn't think I'd ever get the chance to say to you."

Reaching up, she stroked his face, greedily drinking him in, she was amazed afresh at how little he'd changed.

Here we are almost ten years later and it seems that he hasn't aged in the slightest. She stared hard at his face, *nope,* she thought, *not a day older, how strange.*

CHAPTER EIGHT

But before she had a chance to ask him any questions, he said.

"I know baby, you've no idea how wonderful it is to have you here. Good morning. You and I need to talk, after our shower we'll go downstairs, you can have some breakfast while we talk," a look of concentration, mixed with weariness flashed across his face.

She cast her eyes down, nodding.

She wasn't in the mood for serious talks, but knew they'd have to have them, they both needed to confront the past if they were to have any kind of future together. She was putting off calling home to talk to her friends, who were bound to be furious with her for deserting them last night.

As if reading her mind, Blake said: "Here's my phone, call home and let them know you've not been murdered or something worse, I remember how vivid Seraphina's imagination was," he chuckled as she took the phone.

Before making the call, she touched his face, feeling the light stubble that had grown overnight, and drawing him to her. She kissed him, just to remind herself that he was real and not some figment of her wishful thinking or deepest desires and fantasies.

He lowered his lips to hers, gently cupping her chin, his thumb lightly caressing her skin. She sighed, giving herself up to the kiss, losing herself in the moment. Her tongue probed into his mouth and raising her hand she ran it through his thick hair. But before the kiss could deepen as she wanted it to, he pulled away to gently kiss her chin, her cheek, her closed eyelids, and her forehead.

Feeling him smile as she closed her eyes, enjoying the feel of his lips on her skin, she marvelled at the fact that this was actually happening. She was still in wonder that she was here, in his house, in his bedroom and in his arms at all. Opening her eyes she took a deep breath, needing to steady her thoughts and breathing before she spoke to her friends. It took a few minutes with him looking on with a sexy smile on his lips, which didn't help her to calm down.

Pressing the number to her landline, she smiled as it was picked up almost immediately.

"Si?" Imogen asked.

"Yes Imogen, it's me. You're not to mad at me for ditching you last night?" She worriedly asked and tried to keep her voice steady.

"Mad? Of course we're not bloody mad, duh. All Sera wants to know, as she's hanging on my arm, so she can hear exactly what you're saying, was it as good as you've dreamed it would be?" She laughed and Siobhan heard Seraphina call out to her,

"Did you have many?"

Blushing bright red, Siobhan shook her head and laughed, hoping Blake didn't hear what her slut of a friend, who she loved dearly, was shouting out. But, looking at the smug smile he now had on his face, it was doubtful she was that lucky.

"Tell Sera, yes lots," she whispered, almost hissing at her friend. "And thanks, for being so understanding. I'll be home in time for tea. Or do you need me to come home now?" She didn't want her friends to feel that she had completely dumped them.

"Don't you dare come home until you're ready to, we're all

fine here. Dora and Able slept the night curled up in Charlotte's bed. I'm so bloody pleased for you, that you've found him after all these years, it must be fate. But enough chatting for now, don't worry about us, if you can't make it home today, I'm sure we can find something to entertain us. So you have fun and stop thinking about us. Char and Sera say bye and if they don't see you, thanks for having them and we'll all get together soon? Big hugs, bye, bye Si. Say hi to Blake from us."

"Say bye to both of them for me but I will make it home to see you all before you go. Big hugs, bye, bye." She hung up, handing him his phone then snuggling back under the covers, not ready to move just yet.

Reaching up she pulled him down to join her, and snuggled into him as he wrapped his arms around her, holding her close.

"Do we ever have to move?" she whispered, placing kisses down his throat.

Noticing he still felt slightly cool to her touch, and thought it strange as she was toasty warm. Her tongue darted out to steal a few cheeky tastes of his skin – he tasted so good.

She slowly made her way downwards, wanting to tease him. Her lips brushed over one of his nipples and she bit it, not too hard but hard enough to get a response from him. He effortlessly pulled her back up the bed. She smiled up at him in a shy pretence, fluttering her eyelashes.

"Yes we do madam, let's shower and then you and I'll talk," he pulled back the covers and picking her up as if she were weightless he carried her into the shower.

She pouted up at him, swinging her legs.

"But I want to play," she said, licking her way up his neck.

"We can play to your heart's desire, but not until you've listened to what I have to say to you. Deal?"

He looked serious again.

"Okay," she huffed a little, and he chuckled.

"Didn't you play enough last night?" He set her down in the middle of the wet room and gently slapped her very cute behind.

"No, I did not! Why, did you?"

She stood before him, completely naked, hands on her hips and glaring at him. He laughed and turned on the shower and quickly joined her underneath the water, pulling her to him.

"I could never get enough of you, Si,"

Grabbing the soap, she lathered it up in her hands, reaching down to wash the part of him she wanted to feel again. It was soft only for the briefest of moments, soon rising and thickening to her touch, again she was amazed about his size.

"Si..." he moaned in her ear.

He let her hands explore to her heart's content.

They stroked, pulled and probed into places that made him breathe heavily. Then, when he didn't think he could take much more, she dropped to her knees, and took him into her mouth. All the while her hands played with his balls, gently tugging and weighing them both. Stroking her finger along his perineum, she sucked, licked, and thoroughly enjoyed herself listening to him lose control.

She'd never done this to anyone before, but had known it was a sexual act she'd enjoy doing, once she had the chance. Now she was doing it, for the first time, and to Blake, she more than enjoyed it. She had no idea he'd taste this good, he was as hard as steel and covered in the softest silk. He was breathing hard, calling out her name, in his low, incredible sexy voice.

He was close to coming she could feel his muscles contracting, but he didn't let her get him off, instead, he pulled her up until she stared into his darkened, lust filled eyes.

Pouting, she told him.

"I wanted to taste you Blake," He kissed her, tasting a little of himself, and growling as he lay down on the slate tiles, pulling her down on top of him. Without a word he took the soap and shifted her up his body until she had a knee either side of his head.

In this position she felt a bit vulnerable, being completely open to his very hungry gaze. He proceeded to use the soap and lathered it up so his hands slipped their way into her private folds easily.

It was his turn to play and tease her as she'd done to him.

Reaching up, he soaped her breasts, kneading them, pulling at her nipples until she was squirming on top of him. Craning his neck, he leaned upwards and had her sensitive bud in his mouth before she knew what he was doing. He drew it into his mouth and sucked on it gently.

With one hand tweaking her nipple, the other one slipped a few fingers into her, and found a place deep within her that had her crying out.

"What? Oh my God what is that, Blake," she watched him, desire darkening her eyes, her thigh muscles straining to keep her upright.

She felt her orgasm rising. She needed to feel him in her now and she quickly slid down his body, until she'd impaled herself on his cock. Both moaned as she encased every delectable inch of him. Siobhan sat up and stayed still, wondering if her own eyes looked as feverish as his.

Moving slowly, up and down, she rode him, using her internal muscles to squeeze him tightly. He filled her so completely, and never before had she felt a man who could stretch her as he did, it was intoxicating. His hands held onto her ass and she loved the slight bite of pain as his fingers dug in.

He watched the storm brewing in her expressive eyes and knew it wouldn't take long before she would be falling apart on him again.

Gripping his shoulders, she continued to rise and fall, with ever increasing speed. Slipping a finger between their two straining bodies, he found her bud, and stroked it. He made her writhe, arch and buck, silently begging for more, he watched her through half closed eyes thinking she was so exquisite as she took her pleasure. Pulling her forward, he nibbled on her nipple, gently biting into the tender flesh, while all the while keeping the pressure on her bud.

She was so close; she could feel her release approaching, like a speeding freight train.

"Blake, I'm going to come, now," she hissed. Riding him for all she was worth, her head flung backwards.

Meeting her thrusts hungrily he called out her name – and in one final, almighty thrust, he met her in paradise. Their cries of passion filling the room. Then she fell on him, breathing heavily, kissing him hard while they both panted. Tangling his hand in her hair he pressed her to him possessively.

Not wanting to move, but she knew it was time to talk.

Slowly, rolling off him, both groaning at the loss, she lay on the slate floor beside him, waiting for her heart to return to a normal rate. His arm was draped over her, and her leg was casually thrown across his body, as the water from the shower washed away their sweat.

"This is just a thought Blake, but what am I going to wear today? As I remember a certain person ripping my panties off last night," she tilted her head and smiled cheekily at him. "I don't mind walking around in front of you naked, but I don't think Robert would be all that impressed."

He chuckled.

"Oh I don't know, I think he'd be very impressed, but don't worry, I'm sure you'll look incredibly sexy in one of my shirts and I've unopened underwear that you can have. No one will disturb us, so don't worry about anyone seeing you dressed like that. Not that you've anything to worry about, you're so sexy," he leaned down, softly nipping her ear lobe.

Soon it was time for them to leave the shower and he towelled her dry, until her skin glowed. He seemed to take great delight in caring for her. The slate floor was heated and she felt she was cocooned in a womb. Following him back into the bedroom she took a moment to admire his back view, his body had her licking her lips for another taste and she knew the bond they shared would never be broken.

"I won't be a minute." He walked out of the bedroom and she heard another set of doors opening. Wrapping the white towel around under her arms securely, she followed to see where he went. Once outside the bedroom, she could hear him, but couldn't see him.

"Blake?" She called out to him and he quickly reappeared, pushing open an invisible door in the wall. When she looked closer she could see the very thin crack that opened up into a secret room behind the bedroom.

"Come on in, Si,"

The secret room was in fact, a fully fitted dressing room, with open door-less closets. The cupboards wrapped around the walls and in the centre was a large, comfy looking, cream couch. A mirror the size of the wall was at the far end and it was extremely well lit.

Every item of clothing was on show and it had to be the tidiest closet she'd ever seen. She made a mental note to not let him see how untidy she was. Walking along a line of suit jackets, she trailed her hands over the superior fabric. The trousers and shirts were hung up in their own sections, all colour blocked. It was amazing. All his shoes were lined up beneath the trousers, there were also racks for ties and belts. Being nosy and opening a drawer, she found every kind of underwear possible.

His casual clothes were on the opposite side of the room, again, all hung up in groups and then colour coordinated. There were jeans of every colour, T-shirts, casual trousers, shorts and swimming trunks. For a man, he had a huge amount of clothes. Again, trainers, sandals and boots were standing to order beneath his jeans.

She shook her head, looking at him.

"And I thought I liked to go shopping," she laughed, he in turn rolled his eyes at her.

CHAPTER NINE

"Come here wench and let me dress you."

She skipped over to where he was standing, smiling at him. He had something behind his back, holding up his hand he dangled her bra from his fingers. Tugging the towel, he let it fall to the floor and stood back, looking at her naked body.

She blushed as a look of awe and wonder spread across his face. Pulling the straps up her arms, he had great fun placing her breasts into the underwire cups.

Making sure he played with her nipples until they were standing to attention before he was quite happy, he quickly fixed the clasp behind her back and she stood still trying not to giggle as he played with her.

He hunted for the right colour shirt to give her, holding many different shades in front of her. In the end he decided on a plain white silk one. He took his time doing up the many tiny buttons. Letting his fingers brush against her nipples, he seemed to be in no hurry to get it buttoned up. She began to breathe heavily and he chuckled, knowing exactly what he was doing. Next came a pair of his trunks, opening a brand new packet of white designer ones for her to wear.

Kneeling in front of her he lifted one leg, then the other, before slowly pulling the underwear up her long legs, smoothing her skin as he went. His hands stopped between her legs to have a quick play, and she quickly became aroused again.

"Don't start something you're not prepared to finish," she growled to him, while secretly hoping he would continue and make her come. But he smiled at her, pulling his fingers away. The underwear was a little large on her, but at least they covered the bits necessary to be seen in polite company.

Once she was dressed, he quickly dressed himself in a casual pair of black trousers and a black linen short sleeved shirt. When he was happy with what they had on, he took her hand and walked them out of the dressing room. He led her back down the impressive staircase and through one of the arched doorways that led off of the main entrance hall. The room was a sitting room with very high ceilings, and the incredible old beams in the ceiling were impeccably preserved. The windows to the left were huge and mullioned. On the right, was a fireplace not dissimilar to the one in the bedroom, over large, and again with a gilded mirror that took up most of the wall above it.

The walls were painted in a neutral cream to match the modern leather couches. There were three, all four seaters and they didn't make the room feel overfilled, considering their size. The flooring was the original dark wood parquet, a little uneven in places due to years of people walking over it. *It must be an old house, maybe a gothic manor house?* Siobhan thought, *but it definitely has a contemporary twist.*

She liked what she'd seen so far.

Hanging on the walls were colourful portrait paintings all different sizes, of people whose eyes seemed to follow her. They didn't look that friendly, so she quickly looked away and walked faster to catch up to where Blake was waiting for her.

They didn't stop in the room, just passed through, but she soaked up all the little details so she could tell her friends all about his house later.

Walking through another stone archway at the rear of the room, they arrived in an enormous glass annex. It was extremely warm due to the sunlight filtering in through the many windows. The floor was covered in black and white tiles and it was furnished with white wicker chairs and settees, covered in a blue and white floral patterned material.

The room had many small trees dotted about in oversized colourful glazed pots. Any walls which weren't windows were painted white. The whole room had a Mediterranean feel, and with the sun shining, she felt like she was on holiday somewhere extremely beautiful.

It was light and spacious and the view from the windows overlooked the rear grounds. They looked to be meticulously cared for and landscaped, with not a blade of grass out of place.

"You have a beautiful home Blake," she told him, looking out at the garden, it was so large that she couldn't see where it ended. "Do you live here all alone?" Still looking out one of the many windows, but turned to face him when he answered.

"Not at all, I have Nat, Alex and Ethan. They all live here and then we have a large number of staff. Of course, they don't live in the main house, they have houses of their own on the land. You'll get introduced to them sooner or later." He was watching her with thoughtful eyes as she moved around the room, finally sitting down in one of the many seats.

Walking over he joined her, and sat down, taking hold of her hands. She shivered, feeling as if someone had just walked over her grave. Raising an eyebrow, she was about to question him, but watched as it was his turn to take a steadying breath.

What the hell's going on? she wondered silently.

"Siobhan, I've got something to tell you, and I really don't have a clue about how you are going to react," Blake glanced at her and then carried on before she could interrupt him. "I've wanted to tell you from the first day we saw you sitting in the restaurant in the South of France. I knew that I wanted you by my side, but it's, well it's complicated." Letting out a sigh, he turned his head away.

She watched him with a growing feeling of dread.

"What is it? What can be so terrible that you won't even look me in the eyes?" She asked him, putting her hand on his face, and turning him to look at her.

"I want you to believe me when I tell you that I love you. You are my woman and no one else will ever do. Okay, here goes, I'm a vampire and I'm actually nearly four hundred years old."

It all came out in a rush, trying to speed up what he was telling her, as if, somehow, if he talked faster then it would make it more believable for her.

She gaped at him, her mouth open, and her blue eyes staring at him.

"Pardon?" she whispered, sure that she'd misheard.

"Si baby, I'm a vampire, so are Nat, Alex and Ethan. That's why we couldn't stay with you in France, that's why I had to abandon you. I've far too many enemies who want to take me out of the picture. If they found out about you, how I feel about you, they'd come after you and hurt you, or worse," his eyes implored her to believe him.

Snatching her hand from his, she jumped up off the seat and walked a little unsteadily to the window. She couldn't believe what she had just heard. She shook her head and turned to him, her face, a deathly pale.

"A vampire, eh? Well that's a new one!" Shouting at him, her hands clenched by her side, her fists in tight angry balls. "How fucking dare you lie, after everything we've just done together? Oh my god, I pined away after you left me in France. It took me forever to get over the near catatonic state you left me in. It took ages to get my life back from the chaos and destruction that you left behind! I wished I was dead so many times – and all the time, here you were, actually fucking dead!"

Fat angry tears poured down her face as she shouted at him. Her whole body was shaking with rage, her hands still locked and held tightly by her side.

"You are a first class cunt!" she screamed at him before storming out. She ran back across the sitting room and had made it halfway up the stairs before coming to a halt. For there he was – already stood on the landing that led off to his bedroom.

"How did you get there?" Bewildered, her hand holding the banister so hard her knuckles turned white. Her face was drawn in panic as icy cold dread started to trickle down her spine.

Can he be telling me the truth? She wondered.

"You have to believe me, my darling Si, I'm telling you the truth. I was born in the late sixteen hundreds, this property, the land, and the club's land, have been in my family all this time. I was born a vampire, I'm not dead, I'm one of the Elders, I'm one of the oldest vampires still around. This life was not a choice I made," he said in his calm voice, standing perfectly still, watching her reactions. She stared at him, horrified, tears still pouring down her face.

"Liar..."

She turned and bolted down the stairs, flinging open the front door and running outside into the sunshine.

"Well, we both know you can't follow me out here. If you're truly a vampire." She sneered the word vampire at him. "Everyone knows you can't walk in sunlight." she shouted, all the while walking backwards, away from him.

Still only wearing his shirt and trunks, she was thinking fast. Her bag with all her stuff including her phone was still up in his bedroom.

She didn't have a clue where she was or how far away from town. *How the hell am I getting home? I'm stuck here,* she cringed at the thought. *No I'm not, I'll walk all the bloody way home if I have to, barefoot or not,* she shouted to herself.

"You've been watching too many B-rated movies and bad television stories. They're no more the truth..."

She held up her hand.

"And, what you're telling me is the bloody truth? I don't think so." She asked him, still shouting. "What, stakes through the heart won't kill you? Garlic won't repel you? I guess next, you'll be telling me you don't drink blood?"

She was still backing away, gasping in air, but to her surprise he followed her. Yes, he stayed in the shadows, but he was out in daylight.

"No, and I've still got a reflection in a mirror. But yes, I do have to drink blood. We don't go around savaging people any more. Well most of us don't. Of course, you do get the odd rogue one as you do within any large group. We're much more civilised than we've been portrayed. We're integrated within the human race, and have been for many centuries. As a rule we don't go round biting people. We try to carry on with our lives as normally as possible,"

He was almost pleading with her to believe him; he had known she'd take the news badly.

"But I watched Buffy; I know wooden stakes can kill you. And what about crosses, do they burn you? Hang on a second, I'm talking as though I believe what you're saying and I bloody don't. If you wanted just a one night stand, I'm a big girl now, you could have just sent me home. You know, a quick fuck for old time's sake? But to come out with all this bullshit is unbelievable. You've sullied what we shared and I hate you for it."

Turning she bolted as fast as she could down the gravelled drive way, trying to ignore the pain in her feet as the sharp stones tore into the skin.

Staying in the sunlight, even though she really didn't believe him.

She didn't get very far before she noticed him, he stood in front of her with his arms folded and was beginning to look angry.

His sexy green eyes were turning a darker shade.

"What will it take for you to believe me Si? Tell me," he demanded, watching her every move. "So I'm a little different from you, if I had some incurable disease I bet you'd be full of compassion. Not the hatred and disgust you're feeling right now. And that is all it is, an incurable disease." He was not quite shouting at her but he was getting close to it.

"So I'm a little older than you thought, but with age I hope comes wisdom. I can show you a world you never even thought possible." His voice returned to normal as he gained a little control. Walking over to her, he pulled her to him, trying to soothe her, but knowing it was going to take more than a cuddle to settle her now. She rested her head against his forehead, but kept her hands by her side.

"I don't know what to think Blake, but I do know I need to go home," she looked at him forlornly, her large blue eyes full of tears and it broke his heart, he was the one that had caused her pain. "This has been too much to take in, in one go. First you appear, and then we make love. Oh my God, I've never felt anything like how it was with you last night. Not even close. Then you drop the bombshell, *"hey babe, don't worry, I am a bloody vampire!"* I want to go home Blake, please just take me home." She begged him, sounding lost, hurt, and bewildered.

"Of course I'll take you home – but I want you to promise me that you'll think about what I told you to begin with, and that's I've always loved you and I always will." Taking hold of one of her hands he led the way back to the house. His fingers stroked hers and he brought her hand up so he could brush his lips against her knuckles. He took out his phone when they reached the house, and instructed whoever answered that he would need a car at the front door in about half an hour, while still holding her hand as though never wanting to release her.

Entering the house, going back up the stairs, this time she was oblivious to her beautiful surroundings. She was dazed at everything that had happened, too much to think about, her brain in turmoil, she followed Blake in silence.

How the hell am I going to explain this to my friends? She thought sadly.

"Oh my God, Char joked about you all being vampires in France," she started to laugh, but it sounded a little hysterical.

"It's okay, Si, come here," he gently pulled her to him and stroked her hair. "Everything will work out, you'll see," he whispered. "Nat has already explained it all to your friends, they know as much as you do. I told Nat to ask the girls to grant me this one favour and not tell you when you rang them this morning. I wanted to tell you in my own way using my own words. They're all fine, Seraphina found it all rather exciting. That is, after she threw her glass at Nat. Imogen, I understand, took it a little hard, I think she slapped Alex a few times. But she's okay now. Charlotte didn't bat an eyelid and said she's known all along and was waiting for everyone else to find out. She is an old soul, that one." He told her, watching how she reacted to the news.

CHAPTER TEN

Cocking her head, she looked up at him.

"Do you have ridges on your face when you vamp up?"

"Vamp up...?" He chuckled.

"You know what I mean, in the films the vampires have a normal face and one when they turn into a blood sucking beast?" she said, looking away from his probing stare.

"As I said before you've been watching far too many bad movies. But yes, my face does take on subtle changes. Do you want to see?" He began to wonder if in fact it had, perhaps been too much for her to take in.

Did she want to see him? Did she really believe him? As they were standing on the stairs still, not quite at the landing which led off to his bedroom, she backed away from him, but there wasn't a lot of room and her back hit the wall.

"Go on then," she said, far more bravely than she felt. Inside she was quaking; her legs were actually starting to shake. And before she had time to whisper that, "no, actually she wasn't ready to see him looking any different thank you very much," his face changed. She felt her stomach plummet, her eyes widened with shock and the tiny hairs on the back of her neck stood up, she covered her mouth with her hands, gasping her horror at what she was seeing.

"I'm dreaming aren't I? This can't be real," she managed to croak out, "Oh my God... Blake?"

He walked towards her looking like a feral predator straight out of her nightmares. Her legs gave out and she slipped down the wall, ending up on her bum with her legs sprawled out in front of her.

But she couldn't take her eyes off him.

His eyes had turned black, like bottomless pits of hell. They looked dangerous, they were hooded by slight ridges under the skin that joined his eyebrows together.

There were also slight, indentions on his nose and his forehead was more pronounced, a subtle change, but a change all the same.

He does look a bit like they do on the TV programmes, she thought, *but he's far more gorgeous than any actor, and incredibly frightening at the same time.* He held out his hand, and silently waited for her to take it. She looked at his hand before she took it, unsure if she should or not, and noted his fingernails had grown much longer and looked razor sharp. After a hesitation, she took it, and he helped her to her feet, her legs felt a little shaky but she was staring at his face. She was mesmerised by what she saw. Raising her hand, she gently traced all that was different about it

"Do you have fangs? Let me see them," she moved so her face was close to his, inspecting him.

Opening his mouth wide, he stood still so she could get a good view.

And, there they were, the two glistening teeth, so much longer, and deadlier than hers. She wanted to touch the razor sharp, deadly teeth, but he pulled her hand away.

"No, don't touch them, Si, you'll get cut and neither of us is ready for that particular consequence," he said gently, shaking his head until he was once again the Blake she thought she knew and loved.

Closing her eyes, counting to ten, she tried to control her emotions, tried desperately not to cry again. But tears began to fall. Pushing herself away from him, she walked to his bedroom, her shoulders drooped in defeat.

When he unlocked the doors and they opened, she hurriedly walked around collecting her clothes and her bag. She stared at the bed and tried to block out the happy memories she had.

She'd been so bloody happy just a couple of hours ago.

Look at the mess I'm in yet again, she thought, walking back to where he was waiting for her.

His eyes hadn't left her, he'd tracked her as she'd quickly gathered her belongings together, watched as she fell apart right in front of him, and there was nothing he could do. He'd never, in all his years, felt so helpless.

"The car is waiting for us, Si, come on, I'll take you home. You've had a rough time, my darling and I'm sorry – that's down to me. I love you so much, that I've broken so many of our rules just by telling you. Please, let me love you," he sounded so sincere and she looked into his eyes as he pulled her to him, gently kissing her tears away.

"Please don't cry, it's killing me," he lovingly wiped away more tears. Siobhan felt drained, her emotions in a tangle.

I want... I don't know what I bloody want, she thought angrily.

"I need to get home Blake, I'm sorry if I've not reacted how you wanted. I just need to get away from you, and that's something I never thought I'd say to you or want. Let me go and..." she lost the thought, and gently shrugged her shoulders, feeling as if she'd gone into shock, not knowing what she wanted.

"Okay, don't worry, we'll sort it all out. For the time being let's just get you home."

Putting his arms around her, he gathered her against him, needing to hold her, and then they walked out of the house to where the car was waiting.

He was about to get into the car when she shook her head.

"I want to go home alone Blake. Can you leave me alone now?" She begged him, shrugging off his arm, without looking at him, she got into the car. The driver looked to Blake for his orders.

He was loath to send her away from him this pale and upset, but what else could he do?

"Please take Miss Siobhan home."

The driver gave him a curt nod, quickly getting into the car and driving away.

Turning, she looked out of the car's rear window, staring into his eyes as she was driven down his driveway, until he'd disappeared from her sight. She didn't wave or smile to him then, putting her head in her hands, she cried all the way home.

It's a good job it's a hot day, she thought, as she calmed down a little, looking at what she was wearing. She still had on Blake's shirt and shorts. She'd grabbed her dress but had forgotten her shoes, so she was still barefoot. Her feet were starting to throb after her earlier dash down his driveway.

I need a long soak in my tub, she thought sadly, feeling bruised and battered.

In no time at all the car was pulling up at her house.

Her door was opened immediately and her friends rushed out. Siobhan couldn't get the car door open quick enough. She jumped out and ran over to them, already in tears. They bustled her into her house, paying no attention as the car drove away. Siobhan sat down on her sofa and breathed a sigh of relief.

"I like your new clothes, Si." Seraphina took in what she was wearing and winked.

Shaking her head, Siobhan looked at her friends with a small, sad little smile.

"Well, I think we all owe Char our apologies, seeing as she guessed what they were, when we were in France," she told them, sniffing.

"We already have, don't worry. We've eaten humble pie, haven't we Char?" The three girls nodded.

"Don't worry about it." Charlotte laughed and shook her head.

"But how the bloody hell did you know?" Siobhan said.

"Just from little bits I picked up from Ethan. He didn't tell me. Rather it was the things he didn't say. I don't know, I just sort of guessed,"

Siobhan looked at Imogen,

"How are you? Are you okay? I heard you hit Alex a few times, I wish I'd thought to do something like that to Blake. I just might yet, if I ever see him again that is,"

"I'm okay, I'm still trying to get my head around everything. But I'm glad to have seen Alex again after all this time. I don't know what will happen now," her eyes told everyone she was more upset than she was letting on.

"And, what about you Miss Fire Cracker? Did you really throw a glass at Nat?" Siobhan laughed at her friend.

"Yep! I was the first one to see them in the club. They were walking towards us, the three of them. I just couldn't believe my bloody eyes. I marched over to them and just chucked my glass at Nat. I'd meant to throw my drink over him. But my hand slipped and he got the glass in his face as well. It didn't cut him any and he flicked his hand and brushed it away as if it was inconsequential. Then, he had the bloody audacity to laugh," she was scowling as she remembered. "The security started to pay interest in what was going on. But Ethan gestured for them to stay away. They walked over to our table, Imogen had just returned from the dance floor and Alex smiled at her. She walked to him and I thought it was going to be a wonderful reunion, but get this, as Alex made a move to kiss her, her hand came up faster than greased lightning and she bitch slapped him good and proper. It was fantastic!" Her eyes glittered in excitement. She took a deep breath before continuing.

"They grabbed us and dragged us into a private room. Ethan and Char here," nodding towards their friend, "just ignored us and sat down. They were chatting as if they'd never been apart. But the four of us were shouting. We'd separated into our pairs and were giving the men hell. I hadn't realised just how much repressed anger," she stuck her tongue out at Charlotte as she used her, what she considered psycho babble speak, and continued. "I'd bottled up all those years ago, but, my-oh-my, I went a little crazy at Nat and I could hear Imogen ranting at Alex. When we had released all of our negative feelings as Char would say, we sat down – and that's when they told us what they are." She took a gulp wine, as Charlotte had opened a bottle of wine and poured everyone a large glass.

"Thanks Char," they murmured, all taking an appreciative sip.

"We, of course didn't believe them. We called them all the names under the sun," giggling at the memory. "Just picture it, Imogen and I, two tiny girls blasting these great hunks of men. It was seriously funny. But then, they changed right there in front of us. You've never seen the two of us move so fucking fast. We ran for the door, but of course, they beat us to it, they were stood in front of the thing with their arms folded across their chests. And all the while, Ethan and Char were sitting there chatting, even when he changed and was all fangy like!"

Charlotte laughed. "I happen to think that it made him look kind of sexy," she replied haughtily.

Imogen looked up and asked Siobhan.

"Nat asked us not to tell you about them as Blake wanted to tell you himself, was that the right thing to do? I've been worried about this, and have been wondering whether we should have told you when you rang us?" Siobhan closed her eyes, took a deep breath and thought for a few seconds.

"No, I think I had to hear this straight from the horse's mouth, so to speak. I don't think I'd have believed you, if you'd told me. I would have thought you were just having a laugh," she reassured her friend, taking a long and satisfying gulp of her wine, sitting back on the couch she carried on. "So, my first love's a vampire, I don't know what to do now," she wailed, looking at her friends for help.

"Did you at least have great sex?" Seraphina enquired, in her typically blunt manner.

After a few minutes she sniffed and told them.

"Yes, it was the best sex ever. Of course, thinking about it, he would be a fantastic lover. He's had nearly four hundred years to bloody perfect his technique. Just think of how may lovers he's had. God, I must have seemed pathetic to him," Seraphina gathered her into her arms to hold her while she cried.

"If you don't mind, I need a little time to myself, to think about what I'm going to do next, if anything."

It seemed to her they'd been talking for hours.

"We've already run you a bath, Blake called while you were in the car. He told us you were feeling a little bruised, and to give you some space if you needed it. He also wanted us to remind you, that he loves you. So go up for your soak, we aren't going anywhere. We can talk if you want later, or you can go straight to bed, it's up to you."

Nodding to her friends, she walked to her bathroom, thinking about Blake and the fact that he'd called her friends to warn them that she wasn't in the best of moods. Well, that was an understatement. Looking at her watch, she was surprised to see it was late in the evening.

Entering the bathroom, she smiled.

Her friends had lit all the candles she kept dotted around, and placed lovely scented flowers in vases on the floor. Stripping off Blake's clothes and stepping into the bath, it felt fantastic, the water was warm and gently lapped her body.

What to do now? She wondered. It was just too unimaginable. Never did she think vampires were real, not in her wildest dreams, she'd thought they were the imagination of some writer.

She couldn't think clearly, feeling dead tired. There was a bottle of wine opened with a glass ready for her to drink. Pouring herself a long drink, she drained it in nearly one gulp.

God what a fucking mess, she thought sadly.

After about an hour in the warm water, when her skin was turning wrinkly, feeling drowsy she decided it was time to get out. Drying herself, she knew she didn't want to face her friends, she walked out of her bathroom and straight to her bedroom. On top of her mirrored bedside little table, was a small intricately carved wooden box and from it she removed a sleeping pill. She didn't like taking them, but decided this was an emergency and swallowed it with a glass of water and got into bed.

Dora and Able joined her in the bed, nudging her hand and licking her face as if to say.

"It's okay, we still love you."

She stroked them, kissed them, and fell asleep while hugging them to her.

CHAPTER ELEVEN

The next morning, Siobhan awoke to the wonderful aroma of coffee.

Seraphina's got my complicated coffee maker working, she thought. Getting out of bed she slipped on her silk wrap and headed downstairs.

She was right; Seraphina was in the kitchen making coffee for everyone.

"Hey honey, thought this might wake you up," her friend called out.

"That smells really good Sera," said Siobhan. She sniffed the air appreciatively and took the large mug of frothy latte from her.

"Let's go and sit in the sun."

Picking up a kitten each, they carried their drinks into the conservatory, where the kittens made themselves comfy in their laps. Siobhan took a sip of her coffee, sighed and put her mug on the low table before turning to her friend.

"Sera, I'm in such a mess. I can't get my head around the fact that Blake's a bloody vampire. He drinks blood for fuck's sake, and he's seriously old," she said, her eyes focusing on the horses running around in the fields that backed onto her house.

"I know, it's an awful lot to take in," said Seraphina "If I hadn't seen Nat and the others with my own eyes then I wouldn't believe it. But I did see them, and I do believe. To quote Shakespeare: *There are more things in heaven and earth, than are dreamt of in your philosophy.* I think the old man got something completely right. But don't ever let me hear that you've told our old English teacher Mrs. Godly that I actually learnt something in her boring class."

"I know you're right. But I was thinking last night – if vampires are real, does that mean werewolves and all the other things in horror films are real too?" said Siobhan.

"You'll have to ask Blake that one," Seraphina shrugged. "Now talking of Blake, when are you going to see him again? He's already rung here this morning. He loves you Si, so very much. I can understand why they left so suddenly in France now, it wasn't the ideal way, but he did it for everyone's safety. And, it nearly killed him, Nat said. But he had to do it, if he hadn't we might not be here today. So please, go and see him, at least to learn more about him. He's a really important man in their world, like a King or something, and I think he wants you to be his Queen."

Siobhan gaped as she listened to Seraphina.

"So, come on spill, what was the sex like?" Seraphina giggled. She curled her long legs under her, and watched her friend blush a dark red. Siobhan closed her eyes and images of what they'd done together danced behind her lids.

"That good eh?" Seraphina said with a saucy smile.

"Sera, I've never felt like that with another man in my life," Siobhan touched her still-hot cheeks. "Of course, I now understand why he's so bloody good. He's had a long, long time to perfect his moves. He certainly knew his way around a woman's body. It was as though my body already knew his. And he knew exactly what I needed. It was incredible. Was it like that with you and Nat? And if so, how the hell does your Dale compare?" She stroked her kitten, loving the sound of her contented purring.

"He does just fine. Of course, I had to teach him a few things to bring him up to speed, but it's great now. But what I wouldn't give to be able to have just one night with Nat again," Seraphina sighed long and dramatically, her eyes glazing over with a wistful expression. "Go and see him, he's been the love of your life for so long. Talk to him, find out all the facts. You owe that to yourself at least."

A smiling Imogen walked in with a cup of coffee.

"I bet I can guess what, or who, you're talking about?" She sat beside Seraphina and stroked Able.

"Personally, I think you need to talk to him, maybe do some physical damage? You never know, it might make you feel better. It helped me a tiny bit." Siobhan laughed. How could she do any kind of physical damage to Blake – a man who was as large as a house? So not going to happen.

"I think you're both right, this has been going on far too long for me to just walk away from. Do you fancy a drive to see his house? I really want you with me this time."

Both the girls nodded their heads and she felt relieved.

"You should've heard the names I called him, I even used the C word and you know how I hate that. But it felt good." Siobhan shook her head as she remembered how angry she'd been with him.

"Do you want me to call him and let him know we're coming to see them?" Seraphina said.

"Yes, you'd better, I don't want to walk in and see them doing something I'm not ready to see," Siobhan said, sadly.

"Go and get dressed and I'll ring him, we can spend the day with the men. You do realise I'll have to fight myself not to jump on Nat as soon as I see him?" Winking at them, Seraphina walked over to the phone.

"Well, I might jump Alex, he's still so damn sexy. I could do with a bit of no-strings-attached sex to iron out a few kinks before I fly back to the States." Imogen was smiling as she got up and walked out of the room.

"Oh great. As Charlotte now finds Ethan all sexy when he's got his vamp going on, it looks like I'll be the only one not to get fucked. That's just not bloody on." Seraphina muttered to herself, dialling Blake's number.

Siobhan sat for a little while, enjoying the kittens and the warm sun. She could hear Seraphina's muffled voice, talking to Blake. Finishing the call, she came back and sat down beside her.

"He said that we are all very welcome at his house any time, and he can't wait to see you. And for me to tell you that he loves you very much. So come on, get your ass in gear. Apparently, he's getting his chef to cook a Sunday roast, so please hurry up as I'm bloody hungry," Seraphina said, stroking Dora.

"I'll go and wake up Charlotte and get her moving." Siobhan's thoughts were in chaos as she walked up the stairs. In a few hours she'd have to face Blake once more. Only a few days ago, she would have sprinted there to spend time with him – now she was dragging her heels.

A few hours later they were dressed, ready to go and they piled into Siobhan's car.

"Do you remember the way, Si?" Charlotte asked.

"Now you come to mention it, not really, we were driven there last night and I didn't pay any attention to where we were going, or anything."

She groaned, wanting to slap her forehead for not remembering.

"It's okay, I've got directions." Seraphina called out from the back. She passed them to Imogen in the front.

"You're looking very nice Si." Charlotte said softly, trying to calm her nerves.

"Thanks Char, you all look fab too," said Siobhan, with a confidence in her voice that she didn't feel. She was feeling a little sick. She wasn't ready for round two with him. But her body ached for his touch, she wanted to feel his lips, his tongue, every delicious part of him really. She worried he'd be mad at her for her reaction to his secret.

She had to get a grip and deal with the fact that he is a vampire, if she wanted him in her life.

The girls kept up a constant line of chatter all the way there, trying to keep her mind off where they were headed. They only got lost a couple of times, but as they turned into the long drive, Siobhan pulled over and came to a stop.

They sat there in silence for a few minutes.

"Are you all right, Si?" Imogen turned to face her. Reaching over, she gave her hand a gentle reassuring squeeze. "It's okay, you know, you're not alone in this. We're all here for you. Why don't we just drive up to the house? Hear what they've got to say. If at any time you want to leave, well, we'll be right behind you."Siobhan closed her eyes and took a couple of long, deep, breaths. She looked in the rear view mirror, where the other two nodded at her encouragingly, and after a couple of minutes she started the car.

"I did a runner from him yesterday down this drive, barefooted. At least I have my car with me today, for a quick getaway." They drove down the tree-framed driveway and came to a stop right by the front door. For several minutes they all waited in the car for her to get out.

"Okay. Okay, let's do this," she smiled at them, but the smile was brittle and false. Siobhan unfastened her seat belt and got out of the car, just as the front door began to open. Her stomach dropped in fear, she hoped that it wasn't Blake, she wasn't ready yet.

But Robert stood there.

"Hello again Miss Siobhan. If you'd all follow me please?" he greeted them, his arm sweeping back inside, indicating they were to enter. They all stood by the car, drinking in the details of the old house. Taking another deep breath, Siobhan walked up the steps, knowing her friends were close behind her. As they entered the house, the muffled conversation came to an abrupt stop as they took in their surroundings.

Charlotte walked over to the stairs.

"This is amazing, just look at this," she said, as she ran a hand appreciatively over the wood, just as Siobhan had done when she'd first seen it.

"You ain't seen nothing yet," she told her friend with a wink.

Robert waited patiently by a door that she hadn't yet been through. When they'd all admired the entrance hall they followed him through the second stone arched doorway.

"I love these old doors, are they part of the original house?" Charlotte asked him, her eyes eagerly drinking in all the little details.

"Yes they are, Miss Charlotte," he said as he led them through the mansion.

Charlotte nudged Imogen.

"How the hell does he know my name?"

"I have no idea," Imogen whispered.

Siobhan walked at the back of the group, subconsciously trying to prolong the time when she would, once again, be face to face with a group of vampires.

"Oh. My. Bloody. God!" Charlotte said in awe, as they walked into a two storey library.

She came to a stop and sighed.

"Okay, I'm officially moving in here," she gazed around the room in rapture. Seraphina took her hands, tugging her, so she had no choice but to follow Robert.

"I don't want to, I'm quite happy to stay here. This is the most impressive private library I've ever seen," Charlotte moaned as she was dragged past hundreds of books. Some were so old they were locked away behind temperature controlled glass cabinets.

"I promise you can come back later, but first we need to be polite and say hello." Charlotte was looking back hungrily at the books and didn't take any notice of Seraphina.

There was another stone archway at the end of the large library and Robert, waited for them.

"Miss Siobhan, ladies, you'll be dining in the formal dining room today for lunch. They are waiting for you. If you could continue straight down the corridor and go through the door at the far end."

"Thank you Robert," Siobhan smiled at him, trying to look natural, but she knew it was unconvincing. Robert smiled back and bowed to them all as they passed. Then he turned and walked back the way they'd come.

"Come on, let's get this over with."

With a grim look of determination on her face, Siobhan marched down the dark wooden panelled corridor. The floor was uneven stone and this part of the house seemed to be much older than what she'd seen so far. Her hand hovered on the door handle for a fraction of a second, suddenly unsure of her welcome. Imogen placed a hand gently on her shoulder to remind her she wasn't here alone.

The door creaked as she opened it, and they walked in.

The room was quite dark but there was a huge welcoming fire crackling in the oversized fireplace at the far end of the room. The walls were a deep shade of red and there was a great deal of black wrought iron work. The candle sticks, placed on most of the surfaces were alight with long, fat, white candles, matching the chandelier hanging overhead. A heavy dark wooden table with ornately carved cabriole table legs dominated the room, and looked as if it would seat fifty easily.

The chairs lining both sides were covered in rich red velvet that matched the walls. The table was laid for the eight, with silver or pewter platters and ancient looking silver wine goblets. The flooring was again large stone flags, worn with age and a dull grey colour. The fire was burning what smelt like apple tree logs, which filled the air with a warm scented perfume. Suddenly, Blake was standing in front of them.

"Hello and welcome to our home," he smiled at them.

Siobhan stared at the floor. Her head was pounding, her hands felt clammy and she was finding it hard to breathe. She wanted to run away again, she didn't want to be here. She began to back away, one small step at a time.

"Si," Blake whispered and he walked towards her, holding out his hands for her to take.

All eyes were on her. She berated herself and told herself to stop being a coward. Dragging her eyes off the floor, she looked him in the eyes – and at that moment everyone else melted into the background.

CHAPTER TWELVE

"Blake..." she whispered, her body trembling.

"Come here, Si. Let me hold you. I know you're feeling a little bewildered and hurt at the moment and I'm sorry for that," he talked in a low deep voice, anything to calm her nerves.

After a few moments of indecision she stepped forward and into his arms. But he could see she was still wary of him.

"What can I say to ease your mind?" He wrapped his arms around her, flattening their bodies together. She tentatively put her arms around his neck and let him hold her, feeling his hands stroking her back, soothing her taut nerves.

They stood there holding each other for a long time. He could feel her heart beating erratically in her chest and wanted nothing more but for her to feel safe and at ease around him.

Gently tipping her chin upward, he covered her lips with gentle kisses. She closed her eyes and kissed him back, but felt wretched at herself for giving in so easily, when all she wanted to do was to shout and scream at him, or at least throw something. The others had already sat down at the table when they came up for air.

Looking up, staring into his startling green eyes, she smiled a timid smile.

"Don't think just because I let you kiss me that everything's all right between us," she whispered, as he guided her to the head of the table and pulled her chair out for her to sit.

"I understand, Si," he sat with her to his right, never taking his eyes off her.

"Do vampires eat normal food then?" Seraphina said loudly, and then looked around innocently as everyone choked out a laugh. Even Siobhan's mouth twitched a little and the ice was broken.

Nat shook his head at her, laughing.

Siobhan watched Alex, who was staring at Imogen with longing, *he looks just as in love with her as he did in France,* she thought.

"To answer your question Seraphina, no we don't. We can eat, it won't cause us any danger, but we no longer have any taste buds for what I suppose is normal human food. Now," said Blake, as he looked around the table, "this meeting is a time where I hope you'll all get to ask as many questions as you can think of. And we will answer them all, as honestly as we can. Now let's eat, I hope you all like the traditional Sunday roast?" People entered with platters piled high with delicious smelling food.

Once they'd all been served, they tucked in.

Siobhan's favourite was the roast potatoes, and they were finished to perfection. Not, that she was eating much, thought Blake, as he worriedly watched her pushing her food around the plate.

The wine flowed freely and soon the girls relaxed. The conversation was loud, with everyone talking over the top of each other as good friends do. They recalled good memories of France.

Charlotte was huddled with Ethan, telling him about her business, and Siobhan thought how relaxed she looked in his company.

Well, you never know, perhaps after all this time she's at long last ready for love, she mused.

But he's a vampire, her mind screamed at her, *and so is he.* She focused on Blake. *Never mind how damn sexy he is, and oh my God he so is!* She fought for breath while she studied his features. *I want that man,* she thought, as she tried to cover her sudden fit of giggles with her hand.

Blake moved his chair closer.

"How are you Si? Tell me, is this so different to going out for a meal with a human man?" he said in a low voice, refilling her goblet .

"If you're trying to convince me that you're just a bunch of normal men entertaining some ladies, I'm not that gullible. Or maybe I am, because I believed every word, every damn word you said to me in France all those years ago!" she snapped at him, her eyes flashing with anger.

He didn't get the chance to answer, as Charlotte scraped back her heavy chair and stood.

"Don't tell us, you're going back to the library?" Seraphina teased with a shake of her head.

"Yes, Ethan said he's got something of interest to show me," Charlotte said, a huge smile spreading across her face.

"I bet he has, honey," Seraphina winked.

Charlotte poked out her tongue at her and linked arms with Ethan, their heads close together as they walked out of the room with a quick wave. Siobhan thought she looked calm and confident and was pleased for her, but also a little worried. She turned to Blake – she really didn't want Charlotte turned into a vampire or anything else to happen to her. If any of her friends were hurt because they were here, because she didn't want to face Blake alone, she wouldn't be able to live with herself.

But he was way ahead of her thoughts.

"Don't worry, Si; didn't they spend all their time together in France? She'll be completely safe. You have my word on that," he said softly.

"If I wanted to become a vampire like you, would you have to bite me? Drain me of my blood and make me drink yours? Isn't that how it works? Is that why you're all a bit pale looking and slightly cooler than us? And why didn't we notice this in France? I'm pretty sure you all had tans." She turned to see how he reacted, goading him. The heady wine felt as though it was racing through her veins.

"Will I become one of the undead and have to live forever drinking other people's blood?" She was beginning to enjoy herself. It was fun, picking on the vampire.

"Hey, I got another one; do you have any other kind of talents? Other than being a most excellent lover? Like..." Tapping the side of her cheek, as if pondering what his talent would be. "Do you fly? Or turn into a bat? Or any other animals? What else do you do?"

Her voice had risen and she was almost shouting, unaware that everyone had stopped talking and was listening to her tirade.

"You did say we could ask you anything, right? Well, how many lovers have you had? How many people have you turned into a vampire? Have you killed people just for the fun of it? Answer me, damn you!"

She screamed and threw the contents of her goblet in his face, then watched in horrified fascination as it slowly dripped down his white shirt, like blood from a deep wound.

There was a stunned silence and an audible gasp as everyone waited for Blake's reaction, but he just sat in his chair and looked at her. She was appalled at her behavior, and felt her anger drain away as she looked at his eyes. A sliver of fear snaked its way down her spine and she bit her lip, wondering what was about to happen.

"Um, Si honey? We're going for a walk in the grounds, if that's okay with you?" Imogen said.

"Yeah, sure, whatever," she waved her hand in a vague dismissal. Imogen knelt by her side, took hold of her hand and gave it a squeeze. Siobhan looked at her friend with sad blue eyes, the colour had dulled as if she was in great pain and they were fast filling with tears.

"I don't think I can do this Imogen," she sniffed, as a tear ran down her cheek. Blake was by her side in an instant, picking her up out of the chair. She gasped at the suddenness of his actions, but wrapped her legs around his waist and fastened her arms tightly around his neck as he strode out of the room.

Nestling her face in Blake's neck, she breathed in his unique male scent. Knots of apprehension formed in her stomach as he strode through his house and up the stairs to his bedroom.

After kicking the door shut and locking them in, he walked over to his bed and dumped her unceremoniously in a heap in the middle, then turned and walked away. Leaning against the far wall, he glared at her, his hands clenching and unclenching into fists, looking like he was ready to strike something.

His eyes had a dark, dangerous glint to them.

She began to think she might have overstepped the mark, but she had far too much anger pumping the adrenaline around her body to heed the warning.

She stared at him, unshed tears, hurt, mistrust and anger in her eyes.

"Siobhan!"

Suddenly it all became too much for her.

The news that he was back in her life, had watched her live her life and that he was a vampire, a vampire for fuck's sake. She could see he was having trouble controlling his darker instincts. He shook his head a couple of times, and she watched as the transformation began from human to vampire. She shrank back on the bed in fear, as though it would protect her. But he wouldn't hurt her, would he? Terrified, she watched him, deliberating whether she could ever trust him.

She looked hastily around the room, *I'm sure he locked the door when he stalked through it. So I'm locked in with a blood sucking monster from the old horror films,* she thought, her anxiety spiking.

Her heart pounded and her nails bit into her palm as she balled her fists tightly, trying to fight the waves of panic. *Breathe, just breathe,* she silently willed her body to obey. *Yes, but he's a vampire!* her mind screamed at her.

Well thanks for that little reminder, she told herself wryly. He was still leaning against the far wall, as if trying to make himself look smaller and less terrifying to her, but he'd never taken his eyes off her.

He'd watched with horror as her face mirrored her conflicting emotions. She was ready to bolt, and he could feel her panic and terror from way across the room.

Am I just about to lose her? After finding out about me, will she try to run away and hide away from me? he thought worriedly. He wanted to grab her and never let her go, to hold her and calm all her worries.

And to simply love her...

Sorrow and defeat began to etch itself onto his face and she watched it as it reached his emerald green eyes.

He knows what I am thinking, he knows exactly how I'm feeling, she thought.

Suddenly, she wanted nothing more than to comfort and reassure him. Taking a deep breath, she pulled her courage together, got off the bed and slowly and hesitantly walked over to him. Only when she was standing right in front of him did she feel his power, it was emanating off of him in waves, the air around him sizzled.

Raising her hands slowly and nervously, she brought his head down, needing to feel his lips on hers. She let her emotions go and in that split second she realised how much she loved this man.

It suddenly made no difference that he was a few hundred years older than her or that he wasn't human; she loved him like no other. He was the other half of her soul, he somehow completed her.

"Si, my darling, tell me you love me. Tell me we can find a way to be together," his breath was labored, still fighting his inner demon. "You must know how much I love you, and you alone. I've wandered for centuries looking for you and now I've found you, I won't live if you walk away now. Please... I lost you once and I'm begging you with all my heart. Please tell me you belong to me."

He'd stopped kissing her and his hands gently framed her face, his eyes pleading with her.

Pulling away from him, she turned and walked a couple of paces towards the bed.

With her back to him, she didn't see the raw, shattered feelings that flitted across his face as he thought she was rejecting him. He couldn't fathom how he kept his knees from buckling.

Still facing away from him, she slowly lifted her tee shirt over her head and dropped it to the floor. Then, unzipping her jeans, she shimmied them down her long legs.

She stood in her black lacy balcony bra, which pushed her breasts up high, and her black matching thong.

Looking over her shoulder, she smiled a shy smile at him. And she nearly made it to the bed.

But he beat her to it and stood watching her approach him.

He looked as if he was casually leaning against the heavy bed post, but inside he was coiled, ready to pounce. Her eyes never left his as she gazed at him from under her eyelashes. He saw her feelings for him, she couldn't hide how she truly felt any longer.

I love you, her mind screamed to his.

He was still in the red wine stained shirt and leaning forward, she brushed his lips gently with her fingers before using them to undo his shirt buttons. The wine was still wet, and bending her head forward, she licked it off his chest.

Growling, Blake lifted her effortlessly with one arm. She wrapped her legs around his waist and within seconds he'd removed her bra, allowing her breasts to rub freely against his wet chest, hardening her nipples instantly.

Tilting her head forward, she bit his neck, not hard enough to break the skin, and she delighted in feeling his body tremble as she licked her way slowly till she reached his ear.

With only one hand holding her up, it allowed the other to explore her body. Resting her back against one of the bed posts, he lifted his free hand to mould a breast, running his thumb over her nipple. Their eyes locked and she could see the desire building and darkening in his.

She couldn't believe he could hold her up with one arm.

It must be one of his vampire traits, she thought, as a raw tide of pleasure threatened to tear her apart.

CHAPTER THIRTEEN

As he held her up in the air, her hands were free to do as they pleased. She slipped them under his shirt, kneaded the muscles in his back and thought *I want it off.* Quickly removing the offending shirt she kissed his bare shoulders, enjoying how the muscles flexed beneath her light touches, but she craved more.

"Blake, let me down, I want to touch you," she breathed in his ear.

Immediately complying, he slid her down his body, both of them groaning as her body rubbed over his hard erection. She quickly undid his trousers and pushed them down his legs impatiently, his underwear with it.

He was naked in all his glorious perfection before her.

Licking her lips, she slowly took in every detail of his incredibly sexy body, and knew she'd never stop wanting him.

Still as a statue, he watched her as her eyes travelled over him, but she knew he was ready to pounce at any second. Which he did, moving with lightning speed he had her bent over the bed, her bottom sticking up saucily, before she even realised where she was or what he was doing.

Standing behind her, he roughly ripped off her thong.

His weight imprisoned her on the bed. He'd trapped her, not that she wanted to be anywhere but underneath him. He slowly kissed his way down her back, each vertebra treated to a gentle kiss, while his hands were underneath her, stroking her nipples.

Building the fire until it was raging inside of her.

Turning her head so her cheek was pressed against the soft bedding, facing the end of the bed, he prowled up her body needing to kiss her hard. His tongue thrusted into her mouth mimicking what his cock would soon be doing. She tried to reach back and touch him, but frustratingly he was just out of range. Sighing, she decided to relax and let him continue whatever he had planned for them.

She would bide her time, knowing she'd get her chance to touch him later.

Shifting his weight, he stood between her legs, and massaged her ass with firm hands. Then he left her briefly, before she felt something warm and thick trickle onto her skin. She gasped. It felt like an oil of some sort and he caressed it into her until she was almost purring. He worked first one, then a second well-oiled finger into her extra tight ass hole, while slipping the other hand under her, finding her sensitive bud, gently rubbing it between two slippery fingers. Her breathing- came in short gasps, and she closed her eyes to concentrate, thrilled by the delicious new feelings created by his clever finger tips.

Tucking an arm under her stomach, he gently lifted her so she was not rested so much on the bed. Kneeling down behind her, he ran his hands up her thighs, pressing outwards, making her open her legs wider for him.

His fingers opened her body up so he was looking at her most intimate of places.

"Blake..." Siobhan moaned, the anticipation was excruciating and she trembled as he continued to study her body.

Slowly leaning forward, he found her bud with his teeth and she hissed as he gently grazed then sucked it between his soft lips. Bucking back against him, she nearly went into orbit as he slid a couple of fingers deep inside her.

Suddenly Blake backed away, breaking off all contact. She'd been so close to coming, whimpering, she turned her head to see what he was doing. The sight that greeted her nearly made her legs buckle.

Blake poured some of the oil onto his hands and wrapped them both around his cock, stroking himself from base to tip, slowly. It was so erotic, looking into his eyes as he pleasured himself, all the while staring into hers.

Letting out a long sigh, her eyes bored into his, shining with unsatisfied lust. Leaning over her again, he slipped his hands under her body letting his fingers graze her nipples.

Making her arch and undulate under his touch. Then his hands travelled downwards, finding her bud, stroking her until he felt the tremors of her approaching orgasm.

"Fuck me now Blake!" She begged him. "Now... please!" He leant over her until his chest was pressing her into the mattress, then removed his hands from her pleasure point and put them either side of her head.

He whispered to her.

"I want to worship your body Si."

Flicking his tongue into her ear, he sent chills through her body.

"I want to penetrate you everywhere," he murmured – and comprehension dawned as a well oiled finger slowly teased her tight puckered ass.

Not entering, but teasing, the little light touches felt so damn good and she was lost in a sea of feeling. He shifted them both until they were lying on their sides with her back pressed tightly against his chest, then lifted her top leg, back and over his so she was open to him.

"Blake, I've never..."

She gasped, feeling embarrassed about what he was doing to her, how he was making she feel.

His finger gently pushed past the tight ring of muscle, opening her, then slowly slipping further inside her tight virgin sheath.

It shouldn't feel this good, should it? she silently wondered.

Her mouth opened as her neck arched back so he could run a fang up and down her. She was panting as his other hand slipped down her body, caressing her bud.

"Am I hurting you Si?" Blake gasped, slowly inserting another finger to join the first and watched as her back arched. He knew she'd never been penetrated in this way before and wanted to make it as enjoyable for her as he knew he could. He just had to bite down on his own needs and desires and concentrate on her, only her needs were important now.

He slightly scissored his fingers inside of her extra tight channel, and she gasped and started to gently rock her hips slightly in time to his gentle thrusts.

"Blake..." She moaned as his hand moved in a rhythmic motion, demanding her body dance to the silent tune. His fingers were still stroking her bud, teasing her, as she made little mewling noises. He slowly removed his fingers and re-oiled his now throbbing cock, desperate to be inside of her, but he hammered down all his wants and slowly started to penetrate her ass.

Concentrating on her every move and sound, not wanting to hurt her as the tight ring of muscle held him on the outside for only the briefest of resistances, then he was slowly sliding all the way into her.

As a torturous moan left her lips, he couldn't keep the growl of primal ownership silent. This was his Siobhan, his Queen. His to worship and to belong to for eternity. Once fully in he stilled, allowing her to become adjusted to the new sensations that were swamping her. He didn't want to frighten or to overwhelm her.

He would wait until she felt safe and in control to carry on before he would move. His fingers still gently stroked her bud, his mouth never leaving her neck, and his tongue flicked at her fluttering pulse.

Tremors started to build deep within her and she moaned loudly.

"Oh my God Blake!" she cried out, writhing beside of him as their bodies locked together. "I've never... I've never, Jesus Christ!" she shouted as he began to slowly move his cock in and out of her.

Her hand gripped onto his arm, her nails digging into the skin, nearly breaking it and drawing blood.

"I know baby, I know," he murmured to her, as he felt her orgasm approaching fast.

She growled in such a seductive way, he nearly forgot this was her first time. He growled back as his hips tried to break free from the chokehold of discipline he had placed his body under. Biting the inside of his mouth, he very nearly drew blood while trying to regain some control, but her body, oh her body was made to fit his exactly.

And this was such exquisite torture he was feeling now.

"Blake!" She restlessly called out to him, she could feel she was just about to come and she wanted more. More thrusting. More penetrating Harder! She could feel he was holding back, trying not to frighten her and she loved him for it, but...

"Blake, I need you," she managed to gasp. "Please, harder, take me! Show me, please."

"This?" He whispered into her ear, picking up the pace, suddenly going from short shallow thrusts, to hard then harder, pushing into her, his breathing coming out in short deep breaths. He was determined not to let go until she had, but it was the hardest thing he'd ever done, she was so tight, like a fist surrounding him.

And then, feeling his fingers pinching her bud over and over, suddenly she became rigid, arched her back into him, and screamed out his name as she came with such a force she thought her back would surely snap.

It was such an intense darker orgasm and it carried on for ages. She was pulsating and her muscles were clenching him as he came to an explosive end, shouting her name and collapsing by the side of her. Their bodies were covered in a light sweat, but she was too shattered to move.

She lay still while her breathing gradually returned to normal, her heart crashing against her ribs. She felt him shrink and gently pull himself out of her, and she couldn't contain the whimper as he turned her over and wrapped his arms around her, letting her rest her forehead on his chest.

Gently bringing her face to his, he kissed her so softly that she felt a tear run down her cheek.

"Blake, I've never felt anything like that in my life," she whispered as he continued to kiss and nibble her mouth. "I do love you, I trust you more than I've trusted any man. My body is yours to do with whatever you want; I belong to you and you alone," she told him as tears continued to fall.

"Darling Si, I love you and I want you to feel everything your body is capable of. And my body is yours to do with whatever you want. I belong to you, and you alone. You know our love is for all eternity," he said, wiping away her tears.

They lay together for a while, staring into each other's eyes, sharing little touches to one another's bodies. She still felt overawed at what she felt for him, but knew she'd never again be able to leave his side.

Cradling her naked body to his, he picked her up and walked to the wet room.

"I wonder if Seraphina has given up and jumped Nat's body?" she dreamily said as he set her down once again in his shower.

"I wouldn't be surprised. Those two have a connection even Nat can't deny – and he is the most damaged of us all," he said softly, as though talking to himself more than to her.

Siobhan wondered what he meant and just hoped Seraphina would be okay.

"And as for Alex and Imogen, well they're in love and fighting it as well. And Ethan and Charlotte seem to get along fine but I don't know about romance there, Ethan is a bit of a free spirit and I can't imagine him wanting to tie himself to one woman for all eternity," he said as the warm water ran down their bodies once more.

After they had showered, kissed, touched and played for quite long enough, they dried each other and got dressed, all the while sharing small sly glances and smiling secret smiles. Siobhan considered how much her life had changed in the past forty eight hours.

"Come here Si, you're looking all pensive again on me, what are you thinking about?" he walked over to her, wrapped his arms around her and held her cocooned in his love for a few minutes.

"Blake, one day you're going to have to tell me what's happened in your life. The stories you must be able to tell."

She searched his eyes for any clues of what he kept hidden from her, but they stared back at her, full of love.

"I promise I'll tell you anything you want to know, I give you my word."

Taking her hand in his, he brought it up to his mouth and kissed her knuckles before he led the way back downstairs to the dining room where they'd left their friends. In the library, they saw Charlotte bent over a book, listening intently to whatever Ethan was telling her. His arm was around her waist and Charlotte's hand was running up and down his arm. Looking up at Blake, she smiled and nodded to them. They tried to walk past quietly as possible, but Ethan heard them and the two girls smiled at each other while Blake and Ethan nodded once to each other.

Neither couple said anything as they carried on their way back to the dining room.

"I am so pleased for Charlotte. You know, if any of us deserves a little fun, she does. She had an awful family life, especially before she came to our school," said Siobhan once they were out of Charlotte's hearing.

"Ethan told us everything after France. You know, I could have her father killed if it would help her?" Blake said, his face completely blank of all emotion. Once again she was reminded that underneath the human facade was a ferocious killer.

"I know you're deadly serious and it doesn't faze me. But I don't think we should. It was a lovely idea though," she giggled softly as her eyes strayed up to look into his.

Blake laughed, a deep rich rumble that vibrated through her hand on his chest. Leaning down, he placed a kiss on her forehead, and once again she noticed the difference in their skin temperature. As they reached the dining room, he said.

"There's no one in there." They entered the candlelit room, and she saw that he was right, the room was empty.

"Where do you think they are Blake?"

"I don't know, but let's give them some space. I think they all have a lot to talk about. I could give you a grand tour of the house if you'd like? Or we could find somewhere cosy and sit and talk some more?" Blake raised his eye brows suggestively and grinned roguishly.

"Talking...? I hadn't realised we'd done much of that this afternoon?" she teased, and took his hand as he led the way back to the sunny glass conservatory where they had sat on Sunday morning. They sat down on the white wicker seats and she leant against him as he wrapped his arm around her waist. Kicking off her shoes and tucking her legs underneath her, she tipped her face up as he dipped his head down to kiss her. It was a kiss that had them both breathing hard before they broke apart.

CHAPTER FOURTEEN

"I don't want you to ever get bored of kissing me," she whispered against his lips as they lingered.

"You have my word; there's no possibility of that happening. You've the most kissable mouth on this planet. Didn't I tell you all those years ago, that you were made for kissing?"

She nodded, remembering. Breaking apart, she gazed out into the garden.

"You have a wonderful house Blake. Has it always been in your family?" She turned back to face him. There was so much she didn't know about him.

"Yes, all those paintings you see dotted around the place are my ancestors; they're ugly bunch aren't they?" he laughed, enjoying watching her try not to snigger, then continued the history lesson. "It's an old building; I really can't remember just how old it is. It's been burnt down, bombed and added onto a few times over the years. I think there are a few original features left, but you'd have to ask Robert, as he's the one who keeps all the records to do with the house. And he just loves anyone who's interested in the old place – but be warned, once you get him started talking about it, you'll be hard pushed to ever get him to shut up." They both laughed.

"The dungeons are still intact, if you'd like a tour?" he said, and laughed at her shocked expression.

"I think I'll give that one a miss, not really my cup of tea," she was blushing and he found it utterly adorable.

"Oh I don't know. I can just see you in full dominatrix outfit, all kitted out in leather and PVC. Standing in thigh high shiny PVC stiletto boots..."

She saw his face take on a dreamy expression and arched an eyebrow, pinching his arm.

"Hey, come back to me Blake. You were miles away."

"Ouch!" he said, rubbing his arm, and grinning. "Okay, maybe not yet, but you never know."

"Blake, how did you know I was at *Club 1* on Saturday night?" she said. He took a moment to answer, and then sighed.

"Si darling, *Club 1* belongs to me. The land it sits on is the same as the land and the house here. It's always belonged to my family. It has been many businesses including a bakers, a pub and a fashion shop. You name it. We have to keep changing it so people think it has different owners buying it all throughout the years," he said, but she felt that he wasn't telling her the whole story.

"Yes, I understand that, but how did you know I'd be there Saturday night with my friends?" He took hold of her hand and brought it up to his lips as he gently nibbled at her knuckles.

Such a small gesture, but it still raised goose bumps on her arms. Again he took a moment to answer.

"I've always known where you were and what you were up to. Throughout the years, I've had you watched for your own safety. Please don't look at me like that, I had to make sure you were safe. After what happened in France, your safety was my responsibility." He watched her expression change to one of shocked outrage. She looked at him, horrified, her eyes huge as she stared at him. Her mouth was opening and shutting as if she couldn't get out the words to reply to him.

She took a deep breath, untangled her hands and stood up, needing some space between them both.

"Let me get this straight. While I was pining away for you, you were having me followed and watched? Did you know I was at one point going to get married?" she said, as she paced back and forth in the sunny room.

"Of course I knew Si; he was one of my men. But when he was assassinated we knew they'd found out about you and that you'd have to come here and at long last be with me." He walked over to her and pulled her into his arms. But she looked up, horrified, as she pummeled her way out of his embrace.

"Hold on. So you've known every single intimate detail of my life. You've had me watched. You ordered one of your henchmen to play make-believe boyfriend, no, fiancé to me. To make love to me! Did you know all the intimate details too, or would you like me to show you just how well he must have followed your orders! Did he give you bi-weekly details of what he'd done to me that week? And now you're telling me that he's dead?" She backed away from him, her hands clenched by her sides.

Her face was ashen and her whole body trembled.

"My new job here, I suspect you set that up as well. It was all a game to you, wasn't it? You don't love me, you never have!" she shouted hysterically, feeling sick.

With her hand over her mouth she ran out of the glass doors, not stopping until she was at the nearest tree. Bending over, she vomited. Her body shook with anger at all she'd just learnt and she was crying so hard that she didn't hear him approach.

Wiping her mouth, she turned to look at the man she thought she knew and loved. But the truth sucker-punched her, she didn't know him; he was someone she'd thought she'd trusted above all others.

The only man she'd ever given her heart to.

But now she looked at him as though he was a stranger – and she didn't know what to do.

"Do you realise I was dreading telling you this even more than I was dreading telling you that I'm a vampire? I kept putting it off, I'd hoped you wouldn't put two and two together because I knew just how bloody hurt you'd be." He whispered, going to put his arms around her and pull her to him.

But she backed away, tears spilling silently down her face, her eyes wildly looking around for an escape route.

"You could've just found me after France; you could've found me and told me all about yourself. If you had, then the last ten years of my life wouldn't have been a fucking lie!" She screamed the last bit at him, her face contorted in utter rage, while her body was shook like a sapling tree in a storm.

She ran away from him, but tripped over, falling flat on her face.

She just lay there on the carpet of grass, sobbing into the ground.

I can't believe it, my whole life after France is a fucking lie. He's controlled my life while watching me from the shadows, she screamed silently.

Blake was with her in an instant, throwing himself down by her side, pulling her to him. But she fought him off, kicking, biting and scratching him, while her clenched hands thumped him as hard as she could.

All the while she screamed obscenities at him; needing desperately to hurt him.

But Blake kept repeating her name, whispering it over and over. Shielding himself the best he could but letting her work her anger out on him. She needed to go through this to hopefully come back to him.

Siobhan didn't know she could be so violent, deep down knowing she couldn't really hurt him, what with him being a vampire and all. But she was going to have a bloody good try. On and on she fought him, but her body was beginning to tire. Her muscles hurt and she ached and she slowly came to a stop, her hands loosely held up against his chest. She was sniffing and gasping for air as her tears slowly abated. She rested her head wearily against his chest. Her breathing was heavy, and her emotions in a tumble – she was totally confused about her feelings for him. She knew she loved him, but how could she also hate him at the same time?

She stayed with her head rested against his chest for a while, her eyes closed, as she tried to get a grip on her emotions. Slowly, moving her head she opened her eyes, expecting him to be looking back at her in anger.

But all she saw was love and compassion in his eyes; without thinking she reached up and kissed him slowly.

Letting her set the pace, he gently stroked his hands over her body.

Her heart was still beating wildly and she was breathing hard, but she was beginning to feel other sensations building up inside her.

"Si, darling, come back to me..." he murmured against her lips. She gasped as she took in all the scratches on his face, the buttons that were missing on his shirt and the nasty looking gouge marks on his arm.

All this inflicted by her in their struggle. Mortified, she felt tears well up again.

"Oh Blake, look what I've done to you!"

But he silenced her with very gentle kisses.

"Don't worry about them. They'll disappear in a few hours, I heal very fast," he said, chasing a few tears with his lips. "And anyway I deserved them, you had every right to react the way that you did. But don't ever think I don't love you. Because I do and if you think it was easy to have people watch you and report back to me and to know exactly where you were and never to be able to touch you, and to just watch you live your life from the shadows was easy, then you are mistaken. It was the hardest thing that I've ever had to do."

He looked so drawn, so unhappy, that she pulled him to her, kissing him hard. Her tongue probed into his mouth and her lips sucked gently at his tongue and she enjoyed his growl of appreciation at her actions. She was only beginning to comprehend just what he'd gone through.

Just think what it must have been like for Blake she thought, *he could see me but he couldn't touch or talk to me.*

"It was hell knowing every little detail of your life, but not having any part of it. It very nearly drove me insane and I wanted to die," he said, while gently nipping her lips as she'd stopped kissing him. Smiling, she nibbled his lips in return.

After a few minutes she pulled her mouth away from his.

"What? Again, do you mean? You wanted to die again?" She was smiling tentatively at him but her eyes were still awash with tears.

"I have never died Si. I was born to this life," he laughed at her "huh?" expression.

"I will explain everything later; we've a lot to talk about and to sort out."

To him, she'd never looked more beautiful, her eyes were huge and full of her true feelings. He knew the worst had passed and they could work everything out, in time. They continued to lie on the soft grass, in the shade.

She was thinking about what he had told her. She wondered if they would be able to merge their two very different worlds together and meet somewhere in the middle.

"Hey you two, there are plenty of beds for you to lie in, you shouldn't have to lie on the grass you know," Seraphina called out in loudly.

Siobhan laughed and sat up as her friend and Nat approached.

"Hey you," she called out, as Blake stood with unnervingly grace and held out his hand to help her up. Blinking a couple of times, she pulled herself together. As she brushed off the grass from her jeans, she tried somewhat unsuccessfully to tidy Blake's ruined shirt. Seraphina did a double take at the mess he was in.

The scratches had already started to heal, but they were still very angry looking. Seraphina raised her eyebrows questioningly at Siobhan, but she just smiled and shook her head.

"It's a long story, tell you later.

"Come on let's go and get a drink, more of that wine sounds like a good idea," Siobhan said, watching as the other two turned to walk to the house. As they did, Blake tugged her towards him and held her against his chest. He wrapped his arms around her and held her against his rock hard body.

She relaxed, snuggled up against him and placed a gentle kiss on his neck. She was becoming used to the slight coolness of his skin.

They stood there for a few minutes, then made their way to join their friends.

"So, what have the two of you been doing all this time? Or shouldn't I ask?" she teased Seraphina.

"Not what you've been doing, obviously." Seraphina laughed, sticking her tongue out playfully as Nat passed round the goblets filled with the wonderful wine that they'd drank earlier. "Nat's been showing me around the house, it's truly spectacular. The history that's in these bricks is amazing. If only they could talk, what wonderful stories they'd tell."

"Did Nat show you the dungeons?" Siobhan asked her friend slyly, wondering how she would react.

"Yes, they were. Um... Interesting to say the least." Seraphina quickly changed the topic of conversation. Through the window, Siobhan watched Imogen and Alex strolling towards them. Looking as they had in France, just as in love.

"Hello you two," she greeted them as they came into the conservatory, taking a seat. Both smiled, and she watched Alex as he folded his larger frame around Imogen's, continuing to touch her.

Yep, she thought, *nothing much has changed there,* she smiled to herself.

"Is anyone else hungry, as I am starving?" she asked the group. She'd barely touched her meal when she'd arrived.

"We could go to *Club 1* and eat there," Blake said, he brought her hand up to his lips, and placed a tender kiss on her palm.

"I hardly think we're appropriately dressed for your Club, Blake, plus have you seen your cuts and bruises? I think we'd cause a bit of a commotion," Siobhan said softly, now deeply regretting her earlier actions.

CHAPTER FIFTEEN

"Well, you could go home and get ready and we could pick you up. Or you could go and collect whatever you need and come back here to get ready? There's plenty of room for you all, and Si..." Leaning in so his breath tickled her ear. "Baby, do not give these marks a second thought. They'll have disappeared by the time we leave this house, I promise you."He ran his tongue up along her ear and enjoyed making her shiver. Siobhan managed to pull herself together and looked at Seraphina and Imogen who both nodded their heads in agreement.

"Okay then, we'd better go and grab Charlotte." Siobhan's legs were a little shaky and she waited until she felt Blake's fingers lace through hers before they walked to the library to find Charlotte and Ethan.

They were still engrossed in some old book, oblivious to everyone.

"Char? We've decided to go to Blake's club to eat, you want to come?" Siobhan asked.

Charlotte looked at Ethan and they smiled at each other.

"Would you mind if we didn't join you? There's a lot here I want to have a look at." She dropped her eyes and blushed a little, and they all knew it wasn't just books she was going to be studying that afternoon and night.

Nodding her head, Siobhan smiled at her.

As they trooped by, Seraphina whispered loudly to Charlotte.

"You go girl, have fun!" She winked, making Charlotte laugh, and shake her head. As they left the library, Siobhan turned around and studied Charlotte silently, biting her lip. Blake caught the glance and whispered to her.

"She'll be perfectly safe Si."

"I hope so." She lifted her head and closed her eyes, waiting for him to kiss her. He made her sigh with pleasure as his lips grazed across hers.

The girls left the men at the front door of the mansion, waving to them as Siobhan drove away. They weren't even out of the driveway when Seraphina asked.

"So, Si, how did Blake get all those scratches and bruises? I didn't think you could harm a vampire, are any of the myths about them true?"

Siobhan took a deep breath and filled her friends in on what he'd told her and how she'd reacted to it.

"Does that mean we've all been watched? That we've all been guarded? That they knew where we were and what we've been up to all these damn years?" Seraphina looked at her in disbelief.

"I think so, yes, he didn't get to talk much after he admitted what'd happened. I went a little mad, and freaked out. I have never bit or scratched anyone in my life. I've never had a fight, but he got the full force of an anger I didn't know I was capable of. But give him credit, he didn't try to stop me or retaliate – and I went crazy woman on him for a long time. He just tried to fend me off and kept repeating my name over and over. And you can hurt vampires, but their pain threshold is way off the chart, you can't kill them as they would be far too strong to let you get that close, and they heal incredibly fast. That's about all I found out. Oh and another thing, you remember Harry?" They nodded, puzzled.

"Well, he was one of Blake's men, and he's now dead." The girls' jaws dropped in shock. They all sat in silence for a short while thinking about what they'd learned.

She had loved Harry. Okay, it hadn't been the all-consuming, passion burning, love she felt for Blake, but she had been comfortable with him. She knew her friends didn't think it was a match made in heaven, but they'd had their moments of passion. Actually, knowing now what she did about sex, they'd been lacking there too. She shifted uncomfortably in her seat and sighed, looking at Imogen who'd remained silent as she had explained everything to them.

"Are you all right Imogen? You look a little shell-shocked. I know it's an awful lot to take in."

"That's an understatement! Yeah, I'm fine; I'm finding it hard to believe that Alex might've been watching me and not contacting me," she said in a small voice, as she curled herself up on the front seat and looked out of the window.

"You still love him, don't you honey?" Seraphina said, leaning forward and rubbing Imogen's shoulder.

"Yes and I thought he was still in love with me, but he couldn't have been, could he?" she said sadly.

"Yes he is, I saw how he was looking at you when we sat down to eat lunch. He's just as much in love with you as he was in France," Siobhan told her, and smiled as Imogen's mouth turned up at the corners slightly.

Well that's a start she thought.

"So Sera, what about you and Nat? Are you still in love with him?" she glanced in the rear view mirror to see her.

"To be brutally honest, I really don't think I was ever in love with Nat. Yes, I loved his body, his lovemaking, the things that man could do to my body... but I wasn't in love with him per se. I think he's great; I could talk to him about anything, and forever. But not love him. I'm glad to have met up with him again. God, I think I just might have got old and respectable. Fucking hell, I didn't expect that to ever happen." Seraphina laughed loudly and her laughter was infectious, soon they were all laughing along with her.

Parking the car outside Siobhan's house, they ran inside and quickly gathered all the girly stuff they'd need to be able to get ready for the night at Blake's house. She led them into her study and took out the provocative and extremely sexy lingerie she'd bought on one of their many shopping trips to France, which she'd never worn.

Unwrapping the tissue paper she lovingly inspected it all, trying to decide which set to finally wear for Blake after all this time.

"So, which do you think he'd prefer? I like the peep hole one with the ribboned crotchless panties." Laughing and blushing, she held them up for inspection.

"Definitely!" Seraphina agreed.

"I still can't believe you never wore any of this for Harry," Imogen said.

Siobhan shook her head ruefully.

"Are you both ready? We need to get going." They both nodded and the group headed downstairs. Siobhan checked that Dora and Able had enough food and water, as well as giving them each a long cuddle and smothering them with kisses. She hated to leave them for so long, but knew she would be back tomorrow to love them some more.

Back in the car, Siobhan turned up the music and they sang all the way back to Blake's. As they drove through the village she waved to a few people she knew. Then they were zipping past open fields where cattle grazed contentedly.

This time when she pulled into Blake's driveway she didn't hesitate, but drove straight up to the front door. And this time it was opened by him and he was smiling at them as they quickly got out of the car and collected their belongings for the evening.

"Are you moving in here by any chance? Not that you wouldn't be made most welcome."

Seraphina stuck her tongue out at him, making him laugh.

"We need all this to make ourselves beautiful!" she told him, dragging her overnight case behind her.

"You're all too beautiful already." he replied, holding the door open so they could enter.

"Good reply." Siobhan whispered, passing him to enter. He grinned at her and took her dress bag and case.

Alex was waiting for Imogen and he stepped forward to take her bags with one hand, the other slipping around her waist and pulling her to him for a lingering kiss. When they came up for some air they walked off so Imogen could get ready – or whatever else was in their minds to fill the time.

"Now Seraphina, it's up to you. Nat said he'd be quite happy for you to use his rooms to get yourself ready, or if you'd prefer you could use one of the guest suites?" Blake enquired tactfully.

"I think it'd better be one of the guest suites, otherwise who knows what would happen?" Seraphina said with a giggle.

Robert walked forward to take her bags from and lead the way to her suite.

"And Si, of course you're with me..." He smiled at her and they began to climb the stairs to his rooms. In the dressing room he hung up her dress, a beautiful, long, pale blue silk concoction, with a wide, darker blue ribbon which ran underneath her bust, tying and left trailing down her back; with matching shoes and clutch bag. She was saving the special lingerie for when they got home, as she was planning on seducing him.

"Blake I need a shower before I get dressed and do my makeup," she said, sorting out lots of little bottles and makeup onto a clear work surface that he'd made available for her to use. Once done, they walked into the bedroom and he sorted out the shower while she sat on the bed looking around the room and thinking about all that had taken place over the past couple of days.

"Si, come on, it's ready for you."

She heard him calling to her from the wet room, and her heart gave a little jump, still unable to believe she was with him after all this time. Crossing the room, she entered the shower.

"Have you forgotten something Si?"

He looked at her with a grin on his very sexy mouth. Looking down at herself and laughing, she stared at him as she slowly pulled her T-shirt over her head.

He was over to her in a heartbeat and it was he who unzipped her jeans, pulling them down with her panties. It was also Blake who unhooked her bra, freeing her breasts and gently massaging them. He was already naked and his body glistened from the water, she couldn't help but to stare unashamedly as she licked her lips, leant forward and sucked one of his nipples into her mouth, delighted when he hissed his pleasure at her. She stood up and smiled at him, feeling all powerful and female, wanting him to feel as aroused as she did when he took her hand and led her to one side of the room. On the wall was a different shower head, connected to the wall by a bendy hose.

"Stand against the wall Si, with your legs apart." He commanded, greedily kissing her mouth. His hands roamed all over her body and she thought about how quickly he could enflame her, turning her on by a mere look or the slightest of touches. She did as she was asked, wondering what he had in store for her.

Blake left her standing with her back against the wall and

walked over to where the towels were hanging. She had a chance to check out his incredible body, his back was broad shouldered, tapering in to his waist. She watched how his muscles flexed and her mouth watered, wanting to run her tongue up the curve of his spine, to tease him until he moaned for her.

With his back still towards her he said:

"Close your eyes Si."She did as she was told, then heard him walk slowly back to where she was standing.

He leaned into her so his mouth was next to her ear.

"I am going to blindfold you Si. Do you trust me?"

His voice dropped to a deep, sexy growl as she nodded her head.

He slowly slipped the black satin blindfold over her head until it completely covered her eyes, then he moved so he could gently nibble her mouth before plunging his tongue in and kissing her with a fever.

Her body started to tremble, and she whimpered against the onslaught of the kiss.

Being in darkness added an extra thrill for her, and her nipples were rock hard as she rubbed herself against his chest, enjoying the sensation of having his fine chest hairs tickling her sensitive peaks.

Taking hold of the shower head, he made sure the spray was warm enough for her before bringing it down and spraying her tender breasts, while his mouth enjoyed and pleasured her nipple.

The feelings he was inducing on her body felt wonderful, and her mind was just sinking to a place where nothing existed but him and her, when suddenly she let out a squeal.

He'd turned the water temperature to freezing cold, making her breasts tighten, and her nipples throb. Using his mouth, he quickly warmed her up, continuing to alternate between the cold water and his warm mouth for a few minutes.

Her breasts had never felt so sensitive, and she thought she might come just by him ravishing them. Her breathing changed to short gasps, her hands held onto his shoulders, her nails digging into them as she tried to ground herself while the feelings threatened to swamp her.

He knew she was close to coming so he moved down her body. She presumed he was knelt before her as the water, now warm, was directed at her most sensitive of places between her legs. Her thighs trembled in anticipation of what he might now do next.

Gently opening her lower lips he sat staring, thinking how glorious she looked, how aroused and ready for him she was.

He couldn't hold back any longer. Moving slightly forward, he sucked her bud straight into his mouth. She shuddered and let out a low moan as he introduced the water alongside with his lips and tongue.

With one hand holding the shower head against her, he slowly and gently slipped two fingers into her, sliding them in and out, fucking her in a slow, lazy rhythm.

She began to pant, her hips moving in time with his mouth and fingers.

He quickly replaced his mouth with the water spray, a powerful jet of water hitting her bud over and over

"Blake...!"

Her body was coiled ready; ready to break apart; she was desperate now for release.

"I'm watching you Si; I'm watching you standing there blindfolded before me. With your nipples just begging to be squeezed and the water making you quaver ever so wantonly. Come for me Si." His low sexy voice demanded her.

Her mind was filled with images of him kneeling down in front of her, watching her, with his green eyes darkening with arousal, as she moaned and writhed before him.

Blake's fingers were still moving in and out of her, the spray of the water hitting her sensitive bundle of nerves with precision every time.

Throwing back her head, she strained against the water, her body locking, she let out a wail as she came apart. His fingers milking her on and on, making sure every last drop of her orgasm was felt and she was spent.

CHAPTER SIXTEEN

She collapsed, panting, into his arms.

Whipping off the blindfold he smothered her in kisses and rolled them both onto the floor, where he pushed himself into her while she was still having the last of the tremors.

He loved the feel of her tight muscles pulsating around his cock.

Sitting up, bringing her up with him as he did, he sat cross-legged and she wrapped her legs around him, her arms going around his neck as she went on an exploration of his face and neck with her lips and tongue.

They gently rocked back and forth. She loosened her grip around his neck and placed her hands on the floor behind her, arching her back, so she could push him deeper into her.

His hands roamed all over her, stroking her face and neck, gently pinching her nipples, watching her expressive face as she lost herself to the sensations he was making her feel. Slipping a finger between their fused bodies, he ran it around her bud. Soon he had her begging for him to release her again, while his cock pumped powerful and deeply within her.

"Look at me Si, I want to look into your eyes as you come

again," he said.

She lifted her head and opened her eyes, and he saw how she pleaded silently with him to let her come. Her eyes kept fluttering shut but each time he pounded into her she stared deeply into his.

"Please... please!" she begged him. "I can't take much more..." she whimpered.

Still staring at her, he pinched her bud, hard, and she shrieked at him.

Her body bucked while she screamed out his name, coming powerfully, all the while staring into his eyes. While she was still coming he changed positions, and he was now on top, thrusting into her with all his might. Winding her legs around him, with her heels digging into his ass, it only took a few more deep pushes and he called out her name, collapsing on top of her.

As they lay panting on the wet, warm tiles, she took her time catching her breath, running her hands up his arms.

"You were right, these scratches are very nearly healed." He looked down to watch her hands as they travelled up his arm. Such an innocent touch, but he thought it was one of the most powerful sensations that he had ever felt.

"We vampires heal very quickly." he explained. "Now we really need to hurry as we have to get ready to go out and I want to show you off tonight as my woman." He helped her up to her feet, kissing her all the while.

After they were dressed and happy with how they both looked, they joined the group waiting downstairs.

"Before we leave, I want to go and say goodbye to Charlotte and Ethan," Siobhan said.

"I don't think you'll find them in the library any more. I looked for them earlier and couldn't see them anywhere," Imogen said.

"Oh, well, Blake can I leave them a note?" Siobhan said.

"Of course," he said. "Follow me." He found a note pad and an old fashioned feather quill and ink.

"I can't write using that, I don't know how to use it," she smiled at him.

"Never mind, I'll write it."

So she told him what she wanted to say and he wrote it down, in very neat, perfectly formed, old fashioned script.

Once the note was written they rejoined their friends, Nat was outside making sure the car was ready. Blake helped her in and Nat opened a bottle of Champagne, which they all toasted each other with the usual "chin-chin". Siobhan leant against Blake, enjoying his touch as his arm went around her neck and his fingers teased the sensitive skin behind her ear.

The journey was full of happy chatter, with the music blaring.

In no time at all, the car was pulling over in front of the club. Even though it was a Monday evening, there was still a queue to get in. The doormen jumped to attention as they saw Nat getting out of the car. He walked over to them, checking up on the night's events.

The rest of the party walked up the steps, she noticed that every member of staff greeted Blake – and he in return greeted them each by name.

When Blake reached the entrance doors, Trey appeared.

"Good evening Mr. Warren, your private room is all ready for your party. If you'd like to follow me?" he asked, but Blake slapped him playfully on the back.

"It's okay Trey, I know the way thanks. Is anyone here I should know about?" He asked his employee.

"Not as yet, but Tony and Simon have just rang up to ask if they could have an audience with you at some point?" Blake looked at Trey thoughtfully.

"I'll get back to you on that." Trey inclined his head

respectfully at Blake.

"Good evening Miss Siobhan." Trey said as she walked past him to follow Blake into the club. He showed no surprise at seeing her with his boss.

"Hello Trey. Have you been home or have you just slept here for the night?" She asked him.

"No, I've been home briefly, but as it's the club's first weekend open, I wanted to be here so nothing could go wrong. Have a good evening." Trey said with a nod of his head. She smiled at him, then carried on to reach Blake who he was waiting for her. He put out his hand for her to take as they entered the club.

It was as full as it had been on Saturday night. And everyone seemed happy to see him, it took a while to make it to the stairs as Blake wanted to introduce her to everyone.

She was generating a lot of interest, especially from the women, wondering who she was and how she'd managed to snare Blake, who looked devastatingly sexy.

But that's nothing new, she thought as her eyes drifted over his body. She knew firsthand what his fine clothes hid.

"I thought we could eat first and then maybe end up in the vodka and the tequila lounge? Is that all right with everyone?"

Nodding their agreement, everyone followed Blake and Siobhan up the stairs into the room where she had first met him on Saturday night.

Was it only the night before last? she wondered. So many things had changed in such a short space of time.

The room was a little better lit than on Saturday night.

"Now, do you want to split up and sit in the booths or would you prefer to sit all together at the table?" Blake asked them.

The booths got a unanimous vote.

"I'll be bar lady." Seraphina laughed as she walked over to the bar and got behind it. "I've always wanted to do this. Now love, what'll it be?" She called out in an exaggerated accent, to which they all laughed at.

They let her pour them a drink, laughing as a fair bit ended up on the floor rather than in the glasses.

"Remind me never to give you a job as a bar person," Blake told her, grinning.

"No, it's a lot harder than it looks." Seraphina said, walking away from the bar and following Nat to sit in their booth. "If anyone wants any more drinks, you can get it yourselves."

Smiling, Siobhan slid into the booth where Blake was waiting for her, and this time she didn't sit on the other side but as close to him as she could. She rested her elbow on the table and put her head on her hand, tilting her head to look at him.

Bloody hell, she thought incredulously, *I'm in love with a vampire!*

Bending his head down, he kissed her. Leaning back with his hand gently cupping her chin, holding her against him, his kiss enflamed her senses.

"What do you want to eat Si?" He whispered in her ear, his tongue following the curves.

She giggled as the light flicks of his tongue didn't miss a beat, tickling her as it led a deadly path down her neck.

"You of course."

She smiled against his lips, feeling a rumble of laughter in his chest.

"Later my darling Si, you may eat me to your heart's content. Now be a good girl and choose what you'd like to eat."

She hadn't even noticed the menus on the table, never mind the waiter patiently waiting to take her order. Taking a deep breath she tried to concentrate on what was written on them.

"All right, I'll have the brie and salad ciabatta, please."

Nodding his head the waiter moved away.

"So, you can eat, I mean it won't kill you? But you just can't taste anything?" She asked him, he nodded before answering her.

"My brother Anthony wasn't born a vampire as I was, and I'll remember his favourite food was mashed potato. He used to describe everything he ate for me. Sadly, I lost contact with him, I found out he'd entered the priesthood, but I haven't seen him since he and I were quite young. Perhaps he's still alive and has been turned, I don't know if that would have been a good thing. Don't get me wrong, he's my brother and I loved him, but I do remember that he had a vicious streak to him. Even so, I do miss him," he explained.

"You have a brother? I didn't know you had a brother. Bloody hell, there's so much I don't know about you," she said.

"You will do in time, I promise you. You already know the most important thing about me," he said.

"What, that you're a vampire?"

"No, not that, that I love you and you're the most important thing, no, the only thing in my life." He picked her up effortlessly, pushing the heavy table away from them at the same time. Hitching her dress up, she sat back down on his lap with a leg on either side of him.

Very unladylike.

She felt his arousal pressing through his suit trousers into her as she arched her back enjoying the sensations of it. She ran her hands over his face, thinking about how different, yet the same somehow, he looked when he had on his vampire face.

But whatever face he wore, she knew she would love no other.

Pressing her lips to his she realised that she could stay kissing him forever, but her salad had just arrived at the table. But instead of letting go of her, he fed her, bite after little bite, all the while she sat astride him.

She found it arousing to be hand fed by him while she was sat on his lap, especially as his erection was sending delicious little thrills racing about her body.

"Do you fancy a dessert?" he asked her, after she'd finished her meal.

"Is there any chocolate mousse? I have a thing for chocolate," she said.

"Of course." He nodded to their waiter as her plate was taken away.

"Oh and some good coffee?" She added. "I still can't believe we're sitting here together, after all these years. I'd nearly given up hope of ever seeing you again." Siobhan told him, putting her mouth on his and gently nipping his lips.

I really can't get enough of this man, no vampire, oh what the bloody hell ever! She thought to herself as her mousse arrived. .

"There's a lot of ways to eat and enjoy this, but this will have to do for now..." he said.

Her eyes widened as he dipped his finger into the smooth, rich mousse, her mouth opened as he slipped the finger in. She sucked the sugary delight off his finger, while her eyes locked with, his clouding with desire. They repeated this several times, until she dipped her finger in for him to suck, she felt his teeth gently scrape on her soft finger pads and whimpered as his tongue flicked across her finger before it popped out of his mouth. She wiped a chocolate finger across her lips, and then leant forward for him to lick them clean. He took his time, running his tongue first along the top lip, gently sucking it into his mouth, and then repeating it with the bottom one. She was beginning to squirm in his lap causing both of them to gasp, especially when he gripped her bottom hard, pushing her down against his hard cock.

"I can think of more fun places to put this mousse for you to lick off, Blake..." she whispered against his mouth.

"We'll take some home with us," he promised, a wicked, sexy

gleam in his eyes.

"Siobhan." Imogen called out. "Alex and I are going to the vodka and tequila lounge, you coming?"

She laughed softly into his mouth.

"I damn well could be..." This was whispered for Blake's ears only and she felt his hips lurch involuntarily, pressing hard up against her. She spoke louder for Imogen to hear.

"Yes, we're coming with you. What about you Sera, are you going to join us?"

"Yes, we're with you all." Seraphina answered her. Blake picked Siobhan off his lap and placed her on her feet. Her dress fell into place automatically, but he had to rearrange his trousers to try and deflate his monstrous erection.

She tried to hide her giggles behind her hand, *nothing would hide that,* she thought, and warmth filled her body as she thought of what she'd be doing later.

He shook his head, giving up and just moved in behind her, close, so no one would see. He growled as she bent down to pick up her bag and cheekily rubbed her ass against him.

"Si, baby, you are not helping. And you will pay for that when I get you home." He ran his hands down her back and enjoyed her quick intake of breath.

She couldn't walk anywhere for a few seconds, she was so close to coming she felt wobbly. The earlier teasing with the chocolate mousse had already heated her up, now she was ready to explode.

Sensing how close she was, he grabbed her to him, kissing her with such passion it left her completely breathless.

"Come..." was all he whispered and her body convulsed. He held her up against his hard straining body as she came, shaking, and moaning softly. Opening her eyes in wonder, she quickly looked around, hoping no one knew what had just happened.

"No one saw anything," he whispered, as she looked relieved.

"That's never happened before to me, you didn't even touch me."

She was stunned. He smiled at her tenderly, and brushed a few stray hairs back in place as he took her hand and led them to where their friends were stood talking.

The men were chatting together as the girls stood by one of the booths. Siobhan was still flabbergasted by what she and Blake had just shared. He looked over to her and winked when suddenly there was an almighty crash.

The whole building shook like an earthquake, instantly followed by screaming and shouting from downstairs.

It sounded like all hell had broken loose.

Yanking open the door, Nat was about to go and investigate when the doorman from outside the door came running in.

"Mr. Benedict!" he shouted to Nat, "There's unfriendlies downstairs, they've taken out a lot of our men. Part of the front of the building has been blown away. There are casualities on both sides." He took a breath, waiting for his orders on what to do.

Moving with preternatural speed, Blake raced over to where Siobhan and the girls were clinging onto the tables for support, their eyes wide with terror.

"Blake, what's going on? Is it an earthquake?" she shouted, clinging to him.

"No, nothing like that. Si, I want you to lead the girls down to the car waiting for you all to take you back to mine. You'll be safe there. Okay? The number password for the electronic door is your date of birth. I'll see you at home, after this has all been sorted. Now go! I have things to take care of here, I love you!"

Grabbing her, he kissed her briefly but thoroughly, then turned and ran back to Nat and Alex.

As they hurried off, Blake turned and the girls gasped – he had on his full vampire face, and it was cold with fury.

"Come on!"

Siobhan shouted, and they as they punched the button on the ceiling a second secret door reappeared. Turning, to Imogen and Seraphina, she saw they looked shellshocked and pale.

CHAPTER SEVENTEEN

She keyed in her date of birth and watched the door slide open. Down the steel fire escape the girls ran, the heels of their shoes echoing down the stairs.

"Trey!" Siobhan called out, spotting by the waiting car. "What's going on?"

"I'll explain in the car, Blake was very specific about getting you three to safety." Trey said, opening the car door for them to get in. They were not alone in the car – two men already sat there, watching them climb in. They looked old, with weather worn lined faces, and reminded Siobhan of a couple of bounty hunters from an old western movie. Their clothes were worn and very dirty and they looked completely out of place sat in the immaculate car.

The driver set off so fast that the tyres made an awful screeching noise and the girls were thrown around in the back seat. The men silently stared at them, silent. One smiled a gap toothed smile and Siobhan was repulsed. She couldn't believe that Blake would want her with these two men. The smiling man pulled out a gun – and the girls screamed and clung together.

"Trey!" Siobhan shouted. "What the hell is going on?"

The man with the gun pointed it at Imogen, pulling the trigger.

Seraphina pulled Imogen out of the way, but she was hit in the arm and let out a wail as she crumpled back into the seat. He fired again – and this time Imogen was hit. She fell hard against Siobhan who screamed in terror.

She begged him to stop, and prayed that her friends would survive. But the man with the gun just smiled at her, a smile that never reached his cold jet black eyes.

"Oh calm the fuck down bitch, they're only tranquiliser darts. Your friends will wake up in a few hours time, unhurt!" said Trey, looking at her in disgust. Something about his voice that made her look at him. Through her tears she could see that his face which had seemed charming, so happy, was now looking hard, angry and very arrogant.

Even his mannerisms had changed; he wasn't the same man who'd chatted to her when she had joined *Club 1*.

"Why?" She whispered, while trying to decide if he was telling the truth about the tranquiliser darts. She couldn't see any bullet holes.

She sobbed uncontrollably, wiping away her tears, not caring if her makeup was being smeared across her face

"Why Trey?" she shouted, staring at him, wondering what evil had possessed him to try something like this.

"Why? Because I'm being paid an exorbitant amount of money to deliver you." He sneered.

She gulped a deep horrified breath.

"Delivered? Where the bloody hell are you taking me Trey? If you're after money, I bet Blake would pay you a hell of a lot more than you're getting! Please ring him and find out!" She screamed begging him to show some mercy, but as Trey just glared at her, she looked around the car for a way to escape.

She would jump out of it while it was still moving if she had to.

Suddenly, the other men lifted Seraphina and Imogen , opened the car door and tossed them out, as if they were garbage. She watched in horror as her two friends bounced on the hard ground, hitting it at unnatural angles.

"No!"

She screamed and threw herself at the two men, trying to jump out of the open door. She didn't care how fast the car was travelling, she just wanted to reach her friends and make sure that they were unhurt. The man who'd shot her friends turned and slapped her with such force she fell back into the seat. Her eyes were huge and the welt marks were already appearing on her cheek as she sat there in shocked silence, staring at Trey.

"Might I make a suggestion? I don't want you hurt. Don't get me wrong, I really don't give a fuck about you. You're just a means to an end to me. But I think if you get delivered and your body is all covered in bruises it might lessen my payout. And if you do that, I will let my two friends here kill you very, very slowly and painfully – and believe me they know a few ways of doing that. So don't do anything so fucking stupid again, you dumb whore!"

As he ranted at her, she stared at the floor – not wanting to antagonise her captives. But she was shaking like a leaf in a gale and was so scared about what was going to happen to her.

She prayed that her friends were not seriously hurt or worse. Suddenly, she remembered her mobile phone in her bag.

I need to call Blake somehow and leave it on so he can track me, then he'll be able to figure out what's happening to me and come and find me, wherever I'm being taken, she thought, *but how to do it without being caught?*

"I need the bathroom." She told Trey, hoping he might stop the car long enough for her to ring Blake.

"So go, we aren't stopping you." Trey leered at her and she

shuddered, she would be no match for the three of them if they tried to rape her.

Oh fuck! She bit her lip, trying unsuccessfully to stop her body from shaking so much. She watched as Trey nodded to one of the men, and then froze as he raised his arm and she saw the gun. She felt the sting of the dart as it pierced her skin.

"Please don't hur..." She couldn't finish what she was saying as the tranquiliser immediately took hold. Her eyes closed and she slumped back into the seat.

Sometime later she came to, she shook her head, which felt like it was full of cotton wool, all fuzzy from the tranquiliser dart. She felt woozy, like she had a major hangover, and realised that she was hung up, naked, her arms stretched above her head and her feet a couple of inches off the ground.

Her eyes were having trouble focusing and her arms ached badly but she had no way of knowing how long she'd been hanging there. Her watch was gone – in fact, the only thing she had on was Blake's locket.

Blake will find me, she kept repeating to herself over and over again.

She tried to concentrate but her brain didn't seem to want to work. The room was dark, damp and looked very old. She was hanging in the centre of it and found that she could swing herself around by the cord holding her up. She was alone – and wanted to keep it that way. There were no windows, and there was a smell of something rotten, but she didn't want to know what was causing the stench. The walls weren't modern bricks, they were all different shapes and sizes and for some reason didn't look English. She began to wonder if she was still in England.

She must have passed out again, and when she awoke she sensed she wasn't alone. She could hear murmuring. There were several people there. She kept her eyes shut and hoped that one of them would give away something useful, like where the hell she was or who Trey was working for.

She strained her ears, but she couldn't make anything out, then she realised they were speaking in French...

An icy trickle of fear ran down her spine as it she suddenly dawned on her. She knew where she was.

"Allez!"

A female voice was raised amid the murmurs. Siobhan heard shuffling of feet as people hurriedly left and realised she was now alone with the voice's owner. As she opened her eyes, she wished with all her heart she was wrong.

But it was not to be...

"Monique!" she whispered.

"Siobhan, so nice of you to hang around to see me!" she laughed cruelly as her eyes roamed over Siobhan's naked body. "You have got a little fuller than I remember you." She roughly ran her hands over Siobhan's breasts.

Siobhan kicked out wildly, but all that did was make Monique chuckle.

"Has Blake not taught you enough yet to appreciate a woman's touch? Oh, little one, you've so much to learn – and I'm going to enjoy teaching you." Monique mocked in her throaty deep voice. She sounded like she smoked about forty very strong cigarettes a day.

But her English was excellent.

"Why are you doing this?" Siobhan glared at her captor.

"Is it not obvious?" asked Monique, eyeing her like a slab of meat, prodding, pinching and pulling her hair. Her eyes were black and cold, staring critically at her prisoner.

"I see that you still wear my locket." she said and fondled the pendant where it lay nestled between Siobhan's breasts.

"Your locket?" Siobhan's body shuddered at the touch of the

woman's cold bony hands.

"Yes, little one, my locket." Monique's eyes flashing dangerously, as she ran a finger almost lovingly over the locket. "I shall tell you a short story, that goes back a few hundred years. Don't ask me how many exactly, even I can't remember now, but what's a few hundred years between friends?" She picked up an old wooden chair from the far corner of the room and dragging it over, so it scraped on the stone floor tiles. The noise set Siobhan's teeth on edge. Monique placed it down in front of Siobhan, her face in line with her midriff, and sat there studying her body. Before continuing her story, she reached forward and gently ran a fingernail up her thigh.

The scratch went deep and blood oozed down Siobhan's leg.

Monique growled; a sound that came from deep in her throat, and leant forward to run her tongue lazily up the wound, licking it clean. Biting her lip, Siobhan tried to hold back the the sobs that threatened to break free at any moment. But inside her head she was screaming – stupidly, she'd only just realised that Monique was a vampire just like Blake.

Holy shit, she thought, *I'm in serious trouble here.* The cut hurt so much she thought she might pass out.

"Good girl, I like no noise when I drink. In time it will not hurt as much and you may even get some pleasure from me drinking from you." Monique licked her lips, obviously taking pleasure as Siobhan gagged at the thought.

"Now where was I? Oh yes. I was a young innocent just about to marry my sweetheart, when a stranger came to our small village. He was the most handsome man I'd ever seen, and he seemed to want me and only me. Can you guess who that could be? Of course you can, you're not stupid. Blake, he was the one who behaved abominably to me. He charmed me and promised me the entire world; I think the saying today is that he groomed me. In those days he was my vile seducer! He lured me away from my fiancée, my family and friends. He showed me a new and exciting world, until I was so in love with him that I would have died if he had left me. And of course die is what I did do – he turned me; made me what he is. Then suddenly he left me, he grew bored of me, he wanted someone new. And do you know? He has kept doing the same thing to different women all throughout the years. The locket you're wearing was given to me by my then fiancée, it has a powerful spell cast on it, but Blake had it removed – so the spell only now works for him and anyone he chooses to put it on."

Siobhan felt horrified at the story she was hearing.

"But you see, never before has Blake placed my locket around the neck of one of his tarts, his sluts – and believe me, there have been legions of them. He has paraded them in front of me to see, but Blake has finally met someone he actually seems to love and cherish. He's decided you're fit to be his Queen after all these years of searching. You are the one who has been given my locket!" Monique screamed.

Siobhan looked on, petrified, as Monique got more and more angry. Monique's face began to change, her eyes darkened, and Siobhan saw the tips of her fangs as she hissed. Monique shook her head and took a couple of deep breaths as if to clear her thoughts.

"But that will not happen if I keep you here with me, as my new pet, as my new plaything. Perhaps I'll come to understand what it is that Blake sees in you – you, who are just a pitiful human. Now rest, little one, I'll come back for you soon. You never know, Trey has been asking to come and have a play with you. He has a nasty little trick that he's dying to share with Blake's little tart. I don't think you are ready for Trey just yet, but it could be fun watching and maybe joining in." She stood up and slapped Siobhan hard across her face, the force of the blow sending her swinging.

Monique had vanished by the time Siobhan was still again. Once again alone, she allowed herself the luxury of crying, hard loud sobs, as hot tears poured down her face. She felt dirty and sticky and her scratched thigh was throbbing. She had to try and keep her spirits up until she was rescued.

Her arms felt as if they were about to drop off and her face was sore from where she'd been hit by Monique and the thug in the car.

Oh my bloody hell, the thug in the car, the man who shot me, was the same man that dragged me onto the dance floor all those years ago in the South of France. It was the same bloody man! He must work for Monique and so must Trey, she thought as she drifted off into unconsciousness.

CHAPTER EIGHTEEN

"Argh...!" Siobhan screamed as she was rudely awoken by a man throwing a bucket of freezing cold water over her. She gasped as the water dripped down. It was icy cold and to her embarrassment it made her nipples go rock solid.

The man grunted at the effect the cold water had on her body.

He looked to check that no one was watching, then he leant forward and pinched her nipples hard with both hands.

She let out a wail of torment.

"Please don't!" she begged. He was panting and she looked to see what he was doing. And immediately wished she hadn't.

The man was staring at her and pleasuring himself – a truly repulsive sight. Using his right hand he was pumping harder and harder, going up and down, up and down, with long even strokes.

She thought she was going to throw up as his rough, work calloused left hand roamed over her body. When he pinched a nipple and she begged him to stop, that seemed to get him really excited. He turned her and slapped her ass very hard, making her jerk in response, but she bit her tongue and didn't make a sound.

He was nearly finished, she could tell. His face was flushed bright red with the exertion. His breathing was getting faster and faster to match the hand on his cock and she closed her eyes, not wanting to see any more. She couldn't do anything to stop him, just wished he'd hurry up and come so he'd leave her alone.

He came in a wail, spurting all over her breasts and she felt the warm gloopy substance slowly drip down her body. She opened her eyes, and before she could even think of the consequence she kicked him as hard as she could in the balls.

"Fuck off!" she screamed. She couldn't even brush the disgusting stuff off.

He yelled in pain and raised his hand to hit her, just as the door opened.

He immediately backed down and with a scared look towards the door he scuttled away, then was gone. Another man was looming over her.

At least he has a bucket of water with him, she thought, bracing herself for the coldness as he threw it all over her, but this time she was grateful as it washed her clean.

But there was something about this new man that made her skin crawl.

He was exceptionally tall, and thin to the point of starvation, with long matted black hair, and naked, apart from a filthy dirty loin cloth. His toe nails were unusually long for a man, making him look more like a feral creature.

The whole of his body was covered in what looked like whip scars. She shuddered as she studied him. He walked around her, taking his time, running a bony hand over her as though examining an animal. Grabbing her backside he gently smoothed a hand down where the other man had left a hand print. Her eyes still smarted where it had stung her.

The gentleness of his touch caught her off guard.

"Please, please can you help me escape from here?" she begged.

He didn't reply, just continued the examination of her body; his large hands probing into places she didn't want him to touch. Kicking out she tried to fight him off with her legs, but she was no match for him. He was still standing behind her and she felt his hips rubbing against her ass when the door opened again.

"Allez!" A female voice shouted. "Away, honestly you cannot find good servants these days." Monique stared angrily, almost wildly, at him, and he flew out of the door, cringing as he passed his mistress.

"Now are you going to be a good little one and not fight if I let you down? Because if you fight, you can just stay up there." Monique said, tapping an elegant shoe on the stone floor, as if bored by the whole situation.

"Please let me down."

Reaching up, Monique slashed the ropes with a large knife. Siobhan fell to the floor in a heap, her shoulders throbbing with the relief. She sat and massaged her arms.

"Get up; we start your training today. It's a good day, just wait and see what fun and games I have in store for you." Monique cackled like a witch in a bad movie as she led Siobhan, still naked, out of her cell and up into the main part of the house. She blinked rapidly as her eyes became accustomed to the bright lights, and wondered just how long she'd been tied up for. She stumbled on still-wobbly legs and Monique yanked hard on her hair.

"I'm going to put this on you so whenever I want you to be taken somewhere, you can be led." It looked like a large dog collar, made of black thick leather, with a metal loop at the front and a long heavy metal chain attached. Siobhan's eyes opened wide in horror, and she backed away, not wanting to wear it.

But Monique looked at her with cruel eyes, and gestured with her head that the choice was simple, put it on, or return to the cell and continue being tied up. Siobhan took a deep shuddering breath and bent her head in defeat as Monique to put the thing on her. It felt alien, stiff and cold around her neck, and the chain was heavy as Monique gave it a tug.

She walked away and Siobhan had no choice but to follow. The hard unforgiving foreign object around her neck felt like a brand and strangely made her feel more naked. It told anyone she came in contact with that she was now a slave. They climbed stone stairs in silence and passed many people on the way, but when they saw their mistress they stopped talking and looked away. Monique stopped at a door, quickly unlocked it and tugged her metal lead to enter.

Siobhan looked around at the strangest room she had ever seen.

The stone floor felt cold under her feet and the furniture was odd. Everything had metal hoops attached, like the one on her collar but bigger. Her jaw dropped as she scanned the room. There was a leather covered table with holes cut away, a large metal cage and a bed was covered with shiny PVC sheets. The large wooden headboard had metal hoops, as did the foot posts.

Taking up one whole wall was an array of different whips, handcuffs and objects that she didn't even want to think about. On the opposite wall was a large wooden cross, again with metal rings attached all over the place and black leather padded cushions along the centre.

She felt terrified and tried to block out what her eyes were showing her, but Monique had other ideas.

"Siobhan, heel!" she ordered and Siobhan obeyed, walking to Monique's side. Her head dropped to her chest and a tear escaped down her cheek.

"Now, now little one, do not cry. You wait and see, where there is pain there is also pleasure and everyone has to learn to enjoy both." She lifted up Siobhan's face and stared into her eyes.

"Now I'm going to leave you alone. The door will be locked – and look up – we will be watching your every move." Monique laughed and pointed to a video camera in the ceiling. She removed the metal chain, letting it drag along behind her on the stone floor – a noise that reminded Siobhan of fingernails being scraped down a blackboard – then stalked out of the room.

Alone at last, Siobhan sank to the floor, her legs finally giving way. She wrapped her arms around her knees and let herself cry. The situation she found herself in was utterly unbelievable. It couldn't be real. *That's it,* she thought, *this really isn't happening and in a second I'll wake up.* But after a few minutes she shook her head, *okay, so it's really happening.* She hugged her knees to her, trying to control the growing feeling of horror.

She idly wondered what Blake was doing. Hopefully he was looking for her, and her friends, she prayed they were safe and unhurt.

After a while she took another look at her surroundings, *what the hell are they going to do to me in here?*

It looked like a torture chamber.

Was there a bathroom? She spotted a door and slowly got to her feet to investigate. *Yes,* she thought gratefully, *it's a bathroom.* A nice normal bathroom that housed a huge walk-in shower and a very large sunken bath. The walls and floor were covered in black marble and a huge crystal chandelier hung from the middle of the ceiling.

It was similar to the bathroom that she and her friends had visited at that fateful party all those years ago. *I need a shower, I feel so dirty and sticky,* she thought, and quickly fiddled with the knobs. As soon as she figured it out she stood under the hot water, trying to scrub herself clean.

When she'd finished she felt a little better. Wrapping a large black towel around her, she went to check out the huge wardrobe in the corner of the room. It contained some very odd looking clothes, all in rubber and leather. And the shoes! They were all PVC, with spiked heels. Feeling a little shell shocked, she took a deep breath and tried to find the least offensive piece of clothing. She pulled out all sorts of outfits, including strange moulded rubber contraptions that she had no idea how to put on. Everything seemed to be covered in buckles, spikes and straps. Eventually, she pulled out a pair of shiny black PVC stretchy trousers, with cutaway sides and laces crisscrossed all the way up. She hurriedly pulled them on, doing all kind of strange moves as she tugged and wiggled into them. They fitted her like a second skin and made her legs look long and lean. The zip went from the front all the way to her back.

Now for a top, she thought, running a hand down her thighs, they really didn't feel too bad, *and hopefully some shoes.* She pulled out and held up a dozen or so tops before putting them back into the wardrobe, then she found a black rubber boob tube. This was even more of a struggle to put on than the trousers and it was so tight, she didn't think she'd be able to breathe, but it was incredibly stretchy.

The black rubber outlined her full high breasts and showed them off to perfection, holding them up and moulding to their shape with her nipples invitingly sticking out through it. It was very short and stopped just below her breasts. Her narrow rib cage and small waist was on show with her diamond belly piercing glittering against the black. Although she didn't realise it, she had the perfect body for the outfit.

Eventually she chose some black patent stilettos with a silver spike for a heel – the most normal shoes she could find. She didn't think she could walk in any of the others. She then pulled out two long thin tubes of rubber, wondering what they were for. They looked too small for leg warmers, but she worked out they were for her arms and quickly pulled them up; subconsciously trying to cover as much of her flesh as possible.

They had crisscross laces up the sides to match the trousers and went past her elbows, coming to a point on her fingers. A small loop held them in place, so she put a finger through it. Looking in the mirror, she didn't recognise herself. The clothes she was now wearing were a complete contrast to her usual attire. Digging around a bit more, she found a thick rubber band and put her hair up in a high pony tail. She also found a black face mask and decided to put it on, thinking it was good have something to hide behind.

She wondered if Blake would like to see her dressed like this. With a sad smile, she remembered how dreamy he'd looked when he was talking about her in dominatrix clothes. *Is this what he was thinking about me wearing?* She wondered. She didn't know. Hell, kinky to her was not doing it in the bed.

I wish my friends were with me; she felt frightened and alone walking back to the bed, stroking the strange covers. Feeling tired, she decided to have a rest and she laid down, first of all tossing and turning in the strange bed, then falling into a deep sleep.

She was having a very erotic dream. In it, someone was stroking her body through the PVC and it felt so good, she didn't want to wake up. In her dream her trouser zip was being undone and warm gentle fingers began to fondle her until her natural reaction was to move her hips in time with the fingers. Her breasts were also being fondled, through the rubber, making her arch her back towards the unknown touch.

She sighed in bliss, feeling two sets of hands on her body. Two people were playing with her, and she realised she never wanted it to stop.

Her boob tube was gently pulled down and her nipples sprang free, they were hard and tight already and begged to be sucked.

Which they were, sucked and nibbled, as the fingers playing with her bud started to speed up.

Siobhan slowly opened her eyes. She wasn't dreaming, there really were two people in bed with her.

She struggled to get away, not willing to admit it to herself that she was actually enjoying what they were doing to her.

I was dreaming! she screamed silently, trying hard to find excuses to why she would find something like this pleasurable instead of damn degrading.

"Please stop!"

She shouted at the pair and struggled some more, then realised she couldn't move as her arms and legs were shackled to the bed with leather cuffs. She was trapped. Her new bed mates ignored her, carrying on using her body as their plaything. The pretty girl was sucking on her nipples, then frowned, and got off the bed. She quickly returned with a strange looking device, opened the padded little pincers on the end, and attached them to Siobhan's already aching nipples.

She let out an involuntary moan. The padded pincers were biting into her extra sensitive nipples while stretching them outwards. It hurt for such a short time, then turning into a dull ache.

The girl played a game, licking and sucking her nipples then returning the pincers every few minutes, making her buck uncontrollably when the delicious sensations sent electric shocks all the way down to where the man was teasing at her bud.

Shamefully, and not understanding how the hell she could be gaining any kind of pleasure from this, she felt her orgasm start to build. She was shocked that she could feel like this with two strangers, doing things to her body that she didn't want them to do.

Letting out a low moan, she began to pant.

The man bent and bit her now very sensitive bud, she jerked in response, crying out for him to stop. But he just laughed and put a mini pincer on her now swollen bud. It was just like the ones the girl was using on her nipples.

CHAPTER NINETEEN

It squeezed her bud and she squealed and bucked, trying to move her body away from the sensations she was being forced to feel. While she was bucking she felt something slide inside of her, the man was fucking her with a large dildo, sliding it in and out. He picked up speed, and then slowed his pace, alternating the speed and even though she didn't want to, her hips began to dance along with it.

All the while, the girl worked on her nipples, licking them gently then replacing the pincers. Her bud was still held in place by the other pincers as she was stroked and teased by the man.

She knew she was going to come, but didn't want to give in and admit how much she was enjoying all these new feelings that they were inflicting on her.

But she couldn't hold off any longer and with a scream that rent the air apart she let go and came, her whole body lifting off the bed with a spasm, her muscles locking as her body pulsated with the force of the release.

Coming back down to earth and while her body was still humming with pleasure, she heard someone clapping.

"Well done little one, who knew you'd be so easy to train?"

Monique sneered. "I wonder what Blake would say if he could see what you just did? Oh wait a minute, he will!"

She waved a silver disk at a horrified Siobhan.

"I'm going to be sending dear old Blake a copy of all your new fun and games!"

The man and girl left the room without uttering a word or looking at her again.

"Get some sleep little one, I'll send some food later. I need you to keep your strength up as we have lots more in store for you."

With that, Monique swept from the room.

Closing her eyes, Siobhan wept. She knew there was no way out. She was stuck here with her captors. She sobbed as she thought of Blake witnessing all the humiliating and shameful things Monique would force her to do.

If only he could find her. Was he even looking for her? She could be anywhere in the world, would he think of his old flame Monique? Surely he'd figure it out and come and rescue her – and hopefully it would be sooner rather than later...

Sometime later, she awoke. Her body achy and sore from the earlier rough handling. While she slept, someone had been in the room, released her from the shackles and left wine, bread and cheese for her. She couldn't remember the last time she'd eaten and tucked in ravenously. The wine left her feeling a little woozy, so she crawled back into bed and dropped off to sleep again. This time she woke up feeling awful after a dreamless sleep. Her limbs felt heavy and her head was pounding. She stared at the wine goblet and wondered if she'd been drugged. She couldn't get out of bed and lay there looking at the ceiling, her mind blank.

Her eyes wouldn't focus, so she wasn't sure that she really saw movement by the wardrobe. Dismissing the thought, she closed her eyes and fell into a drug induced sleep.

She woke to a sensation of being lifted off the bed – but couldn't do a damn thing about it. She was carried out of her room, along a passageway and into another room, filled with warm steam. Her clothes were gently removed until once again she was naked apart from her collar.

She felt warm water caress her as she was lowered into a rose petal filled bath. Many hands gently washed her, soothing her taut nerves. She tried to concentrate on her new surroundings. There were many filled baths and it looked like the room was used as a communal bathing area. It was very noisy as lots of people were in there too, chatting and washing or just relaxing.

Someone had removed her mask and she felt vulnerable again. She liked the mask, it hid the real her – and she desperately wanted to hide.

The steam and the hands soon began to work their magic and she relaxed. The hands belonged to young girls, *they must only be around eighteen or nineteen,* she thought hazily.

They smiled and continued their ministrations. Ripples of pleasure blossomed as one of the girls firmly massaged her breasts, her soft hands full of creamy soap bubbles. She didn't want to admit how wonderful to be caressed by a stranger in a room full of strangers. Another girl had moved down her body and was intent on washing her most private of areas. Her fingers gently parted her folds and soaped her while someone else's fingers entered her and began sliding in and out.

Lazily opening her eyes, Siobhan looked to see if anyone was paying any attention to what the girls were doing to her. But no one appeared interested. *It must be the drugs*, she thought hazily.

She would never allow this to happen to her if she wasn't drugged. The thoughts evaporated as intense feelings of pleasure began to reach a crescendo.

Resting her head back against the rim of the bath and closing her eyes, she let the ripples of her orgasm ride through her. It left her gasping, wanting more.

But the girls melted away, leaving her alone in the warm water. Looking up, she spotted a camera pointing right at her bath and realised she was being filmed, again. Shame washed over her as she thought of Blake watching another game that Monique had no doubt set up. She longed to get out of the bath, but hesitated as she was naked and self conscious – and there didn't seem to be any towels. She watched as a man got up out of his bath and walked through a door at the far end of the room.

That's where the towels must be, she thought as she climbed out of the bath. Her head was a little clearer, but she was still a little wobbly on her feet. Walking slowly and a little unsteadily to the door where the man had disappeared, she realised her mistake. This certainly wasn't a towel room. It was bare, with whitewashed walls, no windows or furniture except for a harness style swing, suspended from the ceiling by thick metal chains.

The man she had seen earlier was still naked and he walked purposefully towards her, took hold of her wrist, and led her towards the swing. She went with him without a fight, putting the heavy limbed feeling down to the drugged wine, *that must be the why,* she thought, her mind already racing ahead. The swing had many black leather straps and chains, and the man turned her around, and helped her to sit in it. Once in, he tilted her until her back felt the coolness of the leather and then spread her legs wide open and fastened them in place. Next, her hands were tied up high above her head, which tilted her breasts provocatively. Siobhan felt utterly exposed – all her body parts were now on show and she was tied up to be used and enjoyed.

The man hadn't uttered a word to her and she held her breath, dreading whatever was about to happen. He turned and picked up something from the floor, then walked around to her head. Then he placed a soft silk blindfold over her eyes, plunging her into a world of darkness.

With the blindfold in place, her other senses suddenly felt heightened. She heard the faintest rustle, and the slightest of touches felt more probing than if she were watching it. *I was never blindfolded in my life and suddenly I'm blindfolded twice in a matter of days.* It was all so new to her and she was ashamed as to how much she was enjoying it.

She should feel disgusted and she should be trying everything she could to escape. *It's the bloody drugs!* she shouted silently once again.

Hearing the door open, she trembled to think what was about to happen. Her skin was still damp from the bath and she felt goose bumps over her naked body. Footsteps made their way to where she was hanging; she could hear breathing, but still no one spoke. Without warning she felt the swing/harness being raised. She gasped as fingers ran slowly up and down her spine, someone was beneath her. At the same time, a man's hand covered in warm oil began to massage her, slathering her body until she was slick and slippery. Whoever it was touching her made sure their oil slicked fingers went everywhere. She tried to wriggle away from her assailants but was bound to the harness/swing far too well.

The door opened again and she heard more footsteps, then a buzzing noise filled her senses and she felt a small cold metal vibrator held against her bud. It sent her pulse racing and her body started to act on its own accord, undulating to the pulses. She heard a whooshing sound, micro seconds before feeling the sting of leather as it made contact with the soft skin of her ass. Crying out in shock, she tried to arch away from the bite of pain, her knuckles turning white as she clung to the chains holding her up, but it was repeated over and over again.

Her ass cheeks began to feel red hot and sensitive, smarting from the kiss from the leather. She begged the person to stop, strained against it, almost whimpering, when at last she heard the whip being dropped to the floor before they licked her skin, little soft licks where the leather had kissed her, instantly soothing the burning sensation. Siobhan sagged back into the harness/swing as the person beneath continued to caress her, then almost screamed as an object was slowly inserted up her ass. She bucked wildly, but to no avail. Whoever held it was slowly and determinedly pushing it into her and it was dripping with a lubricant. Clenching her internal muscles, she fought the unwanted intrusion. The anal sex she'd enjoyed with Blake had been her first time– and her extra tight puckered hole was untrained for this kind of invasion.

Once it was lodged in her, she felt a flared end sticking out of her ass and against her soft hot ass cheeks. It felt alien but made her feel incredibly filled. Meanwhile, the buzzing vibrator was still being held against her now throbbing bud. Being blindfolded made it all the more intense, making her feel every touch, every lick and bite a hundred times more forcefully than if she was watching what they were doing to her. She felt a man grip her ankles, pull her forward and slowly ease his cock into her. But once he was balls deep in her a sudden urgency took hold of him, and he pounded into her body, moving in and out of her by using the harness.

He swung her away and drove into her with relentless force. Siobhan was helpless, and couldn't do anything but allow it all to happen to her.

He was an incredibly endowed man and his cock stretched her to her fullest. The vibrator was still buzzing against her bud, and at the same time whoever was beneath her began to move the object up her ass in and out. It all became too much for her. Her senses on overdrive, she screamed, bucking, coming, her back bowing off the leather. She threw her head back, her body bucking and straining against her restraints.

On and on her orgasm lasted, while the man was still pounded into her, feeling her internal muscles milking his cock. Crying out gutturally, he came with a long grunt, and after a few moments of catching his breath he removed his now limp cock from the tight hold she had on him.

The buzzing stopped and the object up her ass was withdrawn at the same time.

She was spent, bruised and a little sore from the sexual excess. Her body flopped back into the harness as her heart raced and she gasped for breath, like a fish out of water. She heard the room empty and began to panic. Would she be left hanging here to be a plaything for anyone who happened to walk into the room?

Suddenly her senses sharpened. She could hear breathing! She was not alone – someone was watching her.

"Who's there?" she called out.

"Well done little one, you are progressing much faster than even I would have thought possible. Who knew you had these dark desires hidden away?" Monique said with a malicious laugh. "I would never have guessed you would enjoy sharing your body with so many at the same time. Your films are being made up even as we speak, and I think Blake will find his little Miss Innocent is not so innocent anymore." Her manic cackle filled the room as she walked out, leaving Siobhan alone again.

"Shit, fuck, oh my God!" she screamed.

After Blake watches me he won't even bother to come and find me, she thought sadly, wishing she was at home with her cats. She must have dozed off, only to wake as she was untied and dropped to the floor.

Once her hands and legs were free, she removed her silk blindfold. Standing on slightly shaky legs, she reached back to soothe her bottom, which felt tender and bruised. The chain was reattached to her collar, and the man who'd released her pulled it for her to follow him. Head down, she walked behind him. She was led back through the bathing room, which was still filled with people in various stages of sex.

Her eyes widened as she took in the sights and sounds.

Bloody hell, she thought, *I'm in a completely different world.*

She looked around wildly for an exit, but the man yanked at the chain, giving her no choice but to follow him back to her room. He removed the chain and roughly pushed her inside, before slamming the door shut. There was the sound of a heavy lock being bolted, and she turned to find more food and wine waiting for her. Siobhan studied the wine in trepidation before taking a huge gulp. She was thirsty and ravenous and took huge bites of the food. She ate like someone who hadn't seen food for months, grabbing and stuffing it into her mouth, past caring what she looked like.

When she'd eaten and drank her fill, she walked over to the wardrobe to choose another outfit. She was dead tired again, but didn't know whether it was due to the wine being drugged or the fact that her body ached from being pulled around and so thoroughly fucked.

CHAPTER TWENTY

Flinging the clothes she'd chosen onto the bed she shuffled to the bathroom needing to get herself cleaned up.

Once the shower was switched on and at the right temperature she stood under the needle like spay of hot water and leant her head against the white tiles trying to work out what day it was or how long she'd been held here. There were no clocks on the walls, so she no idea of the time or date. Days and nights here seemed to roll into one. She showered quickly and decided she couldn't be bothered to get dressed as no doubt whatever she wore would be removed again very shortly. She climbed into bed, her eyes closing before her head even touched the pillow.

Her dreams were of Blake, of him rescuing her and telling her that he loved her no matter what she'd been forced to do. His strong arms lifted her, sheltering her from the pain of what she was experiencing.

Waking, she felt a little happier.

At least she was alone and the wine didn't seem to have been drugged this time, because her head was clear. *Actually, the whole place seems quiet*, she thought. She walked to the door and tried the handle, but it was still locked.

As if it'd be left open, she berated herself. Shaking her head, she turned back towards the bed, but was startled by the sound of the lock being opened. Who would it be this time? And what would they want her to do? Her hands clenched at her sides and she trembled in apprehension.

"Good evening little one." Monique entered, giving her an evil smile as her cold black eyes roamed over her naked body. "You've slept the day away, now you have to work. Oh and by the way, I thought you'd like to know that Blake received your film debut in the early hours of this morning. He's had plenty of time to watch it by now. Do you think he would have had a wank while watching his precious Miss Siobhan being fucked by all those strangers? But not only being fucked, but actually enjoying it all as well."

She threw her head back and laughed.

Siobhan was filled with rage, and without thinking about what the hell she was doing or the consequences of her actions, she stalked over to Monique and slapped her hard.

The sound echoed around the room making her almost smile in satisfaction at the handprint left on the pale woman's face.

Monique roared in anger. Her face transformed in an instant, and her fangs were fully on show as she hissed, her face contorting in rage. A terrified Siobhan backed away, but Monique's hand grabbed her by the throat and threw her onto her bed. Siobhan screamed and landed in a heap,.

"So, little one!" Monique hissed, pinning her down on the bed with a hand wrapped around her throat. "You think you're ready to inflict pain, do you?" She ran her fingers up and down Siobhan's arm. "We shall see!" She screamed, and then flipped her over, laying her face down on the bed.

Grabbing some silk ties, Monique tied her arms behind her back, then roughly grabbed Siobhan's hair, lifted her face off the bed and gagged her with a rubber ball attached to a strap, securing it behind her head. It made Siobhan gag and she tried not to panic as she was rolled roughly onto her back again.

She looked helplessly into Monique's eyes.

"I will enjoy this, I'm feeling a little peckish." Siobhan tried to fight, but it was a losing battle. Monique was a vampire and infinitely stronger. Monique pinned her to the bed with one hand as the other turned her head to one side. The collar was slipped up her neck so Monique had a clear view of the vein she wanted.

Her eyes were black and terrifying as her tongue flicked out, licking Siobhan's neck a few times. Then she opened her jaw wide and her razor sharp fangs slipped through Siobhan's skin like a knife through butter. Her screams were muffled by the gag as she tried in vain to move her neck away, but Monique's grip was like a vice. She heard the faint sucking noises of Monique drinking, until, thankfully, she lost consciousness and then felt no more...

When Siobhan awoke, her neck was dressed with a large plaster and her collar was back in place. She was shackled to the bed on her back, with thick leather cuffs.

She was in a star position, her arms and legs stretched apart. *Open wide, for whatever is going to happen next,* she thought sadly.

Her neck throbbed where Monique had bitten her. She knew it was inevitable, but she dreaded being bitten again. She desperately wanted to see Blake, needing him to come and find her and get her out of this hellhole.

If he's watched those films, surely he'd have recognised this place? He'll be coming soon, she told herself, trying desperately to keep her spirits up.

She must have dozed off again, because when she opened her eyes she realised she was being watched by a familiar face.

"Trey!" she said, eyes flaring with hatred. She struggled

against her restraints, wanted to hit him, to hurt him in some way.

He looked at her coldly, clinically and laughed. At a click of his fingers, a man and woman entered the room. They walked over and stood passively beside him, awaiting their orders.

"Dress her. I want her ready and in my room in ten minutes," he ordered, while appraising her body. "You and I, my darling, are going to have a little fun together." he said in a voice devoid of emotion. His eyes once again swept coldly over her and his lip curled in satisfaction as he watched her recoil from his glare.

The couple worked fast, undoing all the restraints and dragging her over to the closet. The man held her while the woman searched for suitable clothes. She chose a very skimpy schoolgirl's uniform, which made Siobhan laugh.

"You've got to be kidding me? Trey gets off on schoolgirls. How bloody predictable is that?"

As she was dressed she chuckled to herself. Perhaps this was a dream and she would wake up laughing, telling Blake all about it.

But it felt far too real.

The lady dressed her in crotchless panties, then a plain white bra with a front clasp. A white shirt covered her top half, tied up in a knot under her breasts so her slender waist and belly piercing was visible, then a blue pleated school skirt was added – so short, her ass cheeks were clearly visible.

Next she was handed white knee high socks to pull on and low pumps were placed on her feet. Her hair was put up into high pigtails tied with ribbons.

Looking in the mirror she thought, *I look like I am going to a very naughty fancy dress party.* She giggled to herself until she remembered who she was dressed like this for. The man stepped towards her and ripped off her neck dressing. He stared at the two tiny puncture marks, the bruising surrounding them almost gone. Siobhan dropped her head and wondered for the hundredth time if she'd ever get out of this alive.

But Seraphina would laugh if she could see her dressed up in this.

I bet she's done the naughty schoolgirl lots of times. But I bet even she hasn't done some of the things I've been made to do while I've been here, she thought sadly, praying silently that she'd see her friends soon.

After attaching the metal chain to her collar, the man led her out of the room with the woman following meekly behind.

Don't people talk around here? she asked herself, *as so far no one's talked to me apart from Monique and Trey, very strange.*

The man suddenly stopped, turned, and quickly injected her before she knew what he was doing. Siobhan yelped in pain as the needle was pushed into her neck.

The drug started to work straight away.

She felt like she was floating along instead of walking. Taking a deep breath, she felt all her worries and fears about being here and what they were forcing her to do disappear. She smiled at the man and woman through unfocused eyes.

Bloody hell, a tidal wave of desire washed over her. She felt incredibly horny, like she'd never felt before. She ran her hands over her breasts and felt her nipples harden. The woman walked up close behind her and began stroking her nipples, making Siobhan moan loudly.

But the man had other ideas. He roughly pushed the woman off and tugged at Siobhan's neck, using the chain to pull her along.

She didn't care where she was going, as long as it ended in the possession of her body and gave her the ending she craved. She took no heed as they moved along a succession of corridors, and only raised her eyes when they came to a stop outside another door. The man knocked loudly. It was opened by a beautiful, completely naked woman, who silently beckoned Siobhan to follow her. The man handed her chain over in silence, then he and his companion turned and left, leaving Siobhan alone with her new caretaker. She was breathtakingly beautiful, with waist-length jet black hair which curled and draped over her pale ivory skin – so fair, it seemed to glow. An intricate black tattoo wound sexily around her right leg, appearing to flex as she walked. Starting at her ankle, it wound its way up her leg and back, ending in the centre of her neck. Her eyes were pure white; *she must have contacts in*, thought Siobhan.

She spotted Trey, who lounged on a bed, like an over indulged Sultan and watched her approach. His eyes were heavy with lust, and his black silk shirt was undone, showing off an amazing, hard, pale body. The drugs were making her act without thinking; she stood at the foot of the bed and waited for Trey to tell her what he wanted her to do.

There was an almost overpowering aroma of incense, the walls were papered with a black, silk embossed paper patterned with gold swirls, and the only illumination was from a few fat black candles. The massive four poster bed was the only piece of furniture in the room, and it was covered with black satin sheets, plump pillows and black silk drapes.

Trey continued staring silently at her, his eyes raking over her body. The woman walked up behind her and gently lifted her skirt, letting her long blood red nails gently scrape along Siobhan's thighs.

"Who's been a naughty little girl?" she breathed in Siobhan's ear, in an accent she couldn't place.

She pushed her forward from the waist and bent her over the bed, placing her hands onto the wooden foot end. All the while Trey watched them, his impressively thick erection reaching past his belly button already oozing with pre-cum.

The woman pulled down Siobhan's panties so her bottom was

sticking up in the air with her skirt around her waist. She leant forward and pinched her nipples, making Siobhan moan low and restlessly move her hips. Her eyes now glazed with desire, staring into Trey's, which were black and filled with the erotic promises of what was to come. Her mouth gaped and she panted as he took his cock into both hands and worked himself, staring into her eyes.

"We're going to have to punish you, are you ready?" the woman asked her. Siobhan bit her lip and nodded, she really wanted to be punished.

Moving off the bed with predatory moves, Trey stalked around the bed and swapped places with the woman. Taking hold of her ass, he bent down and kissed each cheek before spreading them apart and licking around her tight puckered ass hole.

She whimpered as she was licked, even through the drug induced fog, she could feel every lick, every probe of his inquisitive wet tongue. He then moved away at preternatural speed to again stand and watch. The woman returned, and stared up into Siobhan's eyes. She was so close to Siobhan's spread legs that the coolness of her breath tickled her secret folds. She stroked her hands up the inside of Siobhan's legs, making her tremble with sheer abandonment. The woman's tongue flicked snakelike on the insides of her thighs and Siobhan silently wished she would move upward and find her bud. Looking up at the ceiling, she saw a camera filming her. It was in the mirror hanging over the bed, the little red light flashing, indicating it was on and filming her every move. Trey looked on as she watched the woman under her skirt. He held it up, bunching the material in his hands so they could all see.

The bed was at the perfect height for the woman to reach her sensitive bundle of nerves. While she sucked on Siobhan's bud, Trey released the skirt and began to tweak her nipples and slowly undress her.

"After you've come, you naughty little girl, we're both going to fuck you, at the same time," he whispered.

By now she was gently rocking her hips back and forth in time with the pressure of the woman's clever tongue. Trey finally stripped her and his hands caressed her breasts, hard. Feeling his hard cock pressing into the small of her back, Siobhan reached round to feel it, letting out a sigh when her hands made contact and she started to stroke him.

She felt her orgasm beginning to build, and began to pant, little moans of enjoyment escaped her mouth as she moved her hips, demanding the lady lick and suck faster. Bending to her neck Trey bit into her just as her orgasm burst. She screamed, bucked and swayed, very nearly passing out again.

Trey didn't drink for long and when the ripples of her orgasm abated, she turned to look at him, but felt too drugged to be repulsed by the blood dripping from his teeth and lips.

The woman quickly knelt up and kissed Trey, while noisily licking away Siobhan's blood. Moving as one, they picked her up, placed her in the middle of the bed then lay down on either side of her. The woman kissed her passionately while Trey's hands and mouth found her breasts, sucking on her hard little nipples, nibbling them, demanding they become even harder.

She'd never kissed another female before.

It felt forbidden and so very erotic that she carried on – not that she had a choice with the drugs fuelling her desire. Trey quickly pulled them apart, lifted her up and in one forceful thrust slid his cock deep within her.

Arching her back, she moaned as he filled her deeply, and began to ride him, bracing her hands on his shoulders.

The woman left the bed, and then returned with a strap on dildo around her waist. She stood and watched by the side of the bed as Trey and Siobhan fucked, then slipped her fingers between their bodies and rubbed Siobhan's bud. Siobhan jerked at the touch then moaned as delicious waves of pleasure overrode her horror.

Normally she'd have died rather than endured what they were both doing to her but now, here, drugged she let go of normal and enjoyed extraordinary.

Taking the initiative, she leant over and pulled the woman toward her, kissing her, as Trey still pushed his cock into her with long forceful thrusts.

CHAPTER TWENTY ONE

The woman lubricated the dildo as Siobhan watched. She slowly stroked it before quickly jumping onto the bed and pushing Siobhan down until she lay flat against Trey's chest. She aligned the dildo with Siobhan's ass, and she trembled as she was slowly entered from behind.

Trey stopped moving and she sobbed, crying out as the woman pushed into her tight ass. Once the woman was in she also stopped moving, allowing Siobhan to savour the feeling of being filled in such a way for the first time. As she lay on top of Trey, the sensations started to gather deep within, dark tendrils of pleasure whipping her into a near frenzy. Need clawed at her. Trey lifted a breast and sucked her hard sensitive nipple while his other hand stroked down her body and rolled her bud between his fingers.

"Trey?" she said, the quiver in her voice betraying how her body was craving release. She was overwhelmed at the pleasure of being taken by two lovers at once, and Trey saw with satisfaction that she was enjoying what was being done to her.

"Stay still and let us fuck you."

With his fingers rubbing and pinching both a nipple and her bud, he knew it would only take a few hard thrusts and she'd be flying.

Slowly he started to move again, the extra tightness of her core now making it doubly pleasurable for him. His cock rubbed along the dildo, making him almost hiss with pleasure.

She obeyed, enjoying the very intense feelings that were building. Faster and faster he pounded into her and with the woman fucking her ass, her orgasm came quick. She threw back her head and screamed her pleasure, her glazed eyes taking in the three of them in the mirror above. The woman ran her tongue up Siobhan's neck and caught a few drops of blood as Siobhan shuddered with the last tremors of her release, then slowly withdrew from her ass. Trey shouted and came with a force that nearly unseated Siobhan from his cock. Her body was sweat slicked and heaving as she slumped down onto Trey's chest.

Impatiently he pushed her still quivering body off him, got up off the bed, and stalked around to where she was now sprawled.

"Suck me Siobhan, now!" his voice was dark and hypnotic. She looked into his eyes as his surprisingly still hard cock slid inside her open mouth. She moved until she lay on her side, cupping her head so she was comfortable. Using her other hand she played with his balls, gently pulling and rolling them in her palm.

The woman stood at the foot of the bed, now with a different dildo strapped around her waist. It was ridged and far thicker than the one she'd used on Siobhan and she spread thick lubricant over it while watching them, her eyes glazing over with lust. Once finished she ran her hands over her own breasts, her eyes feasting on Siobhan's greedy mouth sucking Trey, making him buck his hips while he fucked her mouth. With a wave of his hand he beckoned her over.

Silently she stood behind him and waited as he bent from the waist, giving her all the access she needed. Placing her hands onto his powerful shoulders, she pushed the dildo deep into his ass.

Grunting, he thrusted his cock deep into Siobhan's mouth.

The lady snarled loudly, pushing the dildo in deep then pulling out without losing her balance. It didn't take long until he roared out his release, flooding Siobhan's throat. She gagged, but he stayed in her mouth while she lapped his cock clean.

She fell back, closing her eyes as his cock slipped from her mouth.

She wasn't alone on the bed for long.

Removing the dildo, letting it thud to the floor, the woman joined her, curling her body around Siobhan.

She began slowly.

Gently touching her breasts she enflamed her desires, then turned Siobhan around until they faced one another. Siobhan mirrored what the woman was doing to her, gently cupping her breasts, letting her fingers stroke her nipples and feeling encouraged with the moans she got in return. The drugs had taken all her inhibitions.

Watching the erotic scene unfolding, Trey took his already hard cock into his hand and caressed himself. But it wasn't what he wanted; he wanted to feel a female body, a snug, warm sheath to make him cry out again.

Getting up onto the bed and moving behind her, he lazily ran his hand up and down Siobhan's spine. Reaching down, he slid her ass cheeks apart again, slipping a finger inside her.

Moaning at the intrusion, she arched back into his touch.

Being between the pair of them again, she started to whimper when his cock started to slowly inch into her from behind. Giving her one last sinfully sexy kiss on her lips the woman turned on the bed so she could lick Siobhan's bud. She opened her legs wider, allowing her all the access she needed, while she did the same to her female partner. Siobhan felt the dull ache of another orgasm build as her bud was sucked deeply and a wet tongue dragged across it.

"Oh my god!" she screamed as another orgasm raced over her body and she bucked back against Trey, which only made his cock slam into her more. Meanwhile, the woman had never stopped suckling on her bud.

Suddenly she felt a white hot burning needle pierce her and she cried out, bucking harder, trying to pull away – only to find herself in a choke hold.

"Don't move," Trey breathed into her ear, holding her steady as the woman quickly pulled out the needle, fastening a tiny hoop through the hood of her bud. She then licked her and gently pulled the loop with her tongue, which made Siobhan's body splinter – and she immediately came again.

With her internal muscles gripping his cock in tight, Trey couldn't hold off and came as well, slumping against her shoulder. Leaning forward, he bit into her neck and drank a little of blood.

"Look." said the woman. Siobhan glanced at the mirror on the ceiling and watched Trey licking her neck. Then her eyes travelled down her body to where her sensitive bud was throbbing.

The woman pulled her lips apart and she saw that she indeed been pierced.

The tiny hoop was protruding between her lips and it made her feel like she needed to orgasm by just looking at it. Arching her back into Trey, the woman gently pulled the ring and her world was blown apart again.

After that, things got a little hazy.

She was fucked in every hole possible and she in turn fucked Trey and the lady and came so many times she lost count, before slipping into unconsciousness.

When she came to, she felt Trey wrapped around her holding her tight up against his cool, hard body. The woman was nowhere to be seen, they were alone together in the silent bedroom. She suddenly felt repulsed at the things she was remembering, *oh my God!* she cried silently, *what did I do?* She had brief flashes of what she'd taken part in and more shockingly, had enjoyed. Feeling dirty she looked around for a bathroom and began to cry, half climbing, half stumbling out of the bed.

"Where are you going Siobhan?" Trey called, his eyes tracking her pacing around the room.

"I need a bathroom, I need a bath." she said, her back turned to him, not wanting to look into his cruel eyes.

"We'll take a bath soon, I've booked it so we can have a bit of privacy. Just the two of us, that is unless you want my friend to join us again?" He laughed as she shook her head vigorously. "No? But you so enjoyed her touch and I know I enjoyed watching the two of you together. You made a delightfully decadent picture writhing on my bed with her head between your legs."

He was taking delight in tormenting her.

"You may well have fucked me, and your friend may well have done things to me. But it was only my body you affected. Not my soul! That still belongs to Blake, as it always will!" she screamed, her face ashen with disgust. In one fluid movement he had hold of her throat, lifting her up the wall. She gasped for breath, her hands trying to pry his hands away, but he was far too strong.

"I could break your scrawny little neck with one hand, you little bitch! But I won't, I enjoy bending you to my will, making you do things I know you don't want to do. But think on this, if you really didn't want to do those things, you certainly wouldn't have had as many orgasms."

Laughing, he threw her back onto his bed.

"And as for your soul being Blake's property, I hardly think he'll want you back when he sees what we all got up to. Do you think he'd want to fuck you when you show enjoyment in being fucked by strangers doing degrading things to you?" His words struck home and she bent her head, knowing she'd never be able to look Blake in the eyes again. Then she lifted her chin up defiantly.

"But it was the drugs that made me do those things, not me!" she shouted.

"They weren't drugs as such; they were just a mild tranquilliser mixed with a little herbal aphrodisiac to help you relax. I knew you hadn't taken part in anything like that before and wanted to relax you. You wouldn't be much fun if you were shit scared of us, would you? See, I'm not that much of a monster; I didn't want to frighten you. But we needed to see how much you could be taught." Trey said walking towards the bed slowly.

"Trey, I want to go home, please wont you let me go? Please talk to Monique and see if she'll let me go!" she begged. "You've had your fun; everyone's had their fun..." A tear slowly rolled down her cheek.

"Fun? We haven't even begun to have fun yet," he said, laughing at her stricken face. "Monique's been planning this from the moment she first met you all those years ago. After Blake spirited you away from the masked ball, he returned with his security and nearly wiped out Monique's whole Order. She and a handful, including myself, managed to escape that night. It was a bloodbath, I've done many things in my lifetime but to murder on such a great scale was more than Monique could allow to happen without retribution. Hence why you are here now. You and I have already met; do you remember a stranger you danced with at the ball all those years ago? If I remember correctly we danced a salsa and you enjoyed it." Trey added.

She remembered that dance, and he was right – she had enjoyed it. Her eyes widened in recognition.

"Now, let's go and have that bath." He held out a hand for her to take, and when she hesitated, he snapped.

"Do I have to lead you there by your chain?"

"No, no, I'm coming."Siobhan said, quickly scrabbling off the bed, but she couldn't bring herself to take his hand and instead walked by the side of him, her face to the floor.

"Trey, if I keep getting bitten, won't I turn into a vampire?" she asked as they walked along the hallway.

Laughing softly he explained.

"No, Siobhan, you won't turn into a vampire. No one here can turn you, your locket makes it impossible for any of us to turn you. Blake's the only one who can do that. This is why he made sure you promised to never remove it. There's a spell on it which is bloody powerful and no one here will try and mess with it. So you're safe, but that does not mean we can't drink from you."

The bathing room door was locked, but he produced a key and they entered.

It was empty and very quiet, and only one huge bath was filled with warm, scented water. She didn't wait to be told, but got straight in, completely submerging her body under the water.

It was very soothing on her bruised muscles and she held her breath for as long as possible and then sat up and brushed her wet hair from her face. Trey was sitting against the edge of the bath watching her and Siobhan blinked at him.

"What?" she said.

"Nothing, I'm just thinking how beautiful you are." Trey said, watching as she blushed. "And that you can blush after everything we've just shared is very appealing. Now come over here and let me wash you." She did as she was told, and sat between his legs with her back pressed up against his chest. Lathering up his hands he gently rubbed them all over her body. The hot water and steam were making her feel drowsy and she let her head loll against his shoulder, her eyes fluttering shut as Trey continued to gently wash her.

Her breasts were bobbing above the water, her nipples sexily peeking through the bubbles – and they seemed to need a lot of washing.

Smiling she shook her head.

"What are you laughing at?" Trey asked her, cocking his head.

"What is it with breasts that excites the opposite sex so much, whether its vamps or human men? I just don't get it." She turned in the water so that she could watch him. He looked at her and laughed.

"I think all males are fascinated by them aren't they, and some females?" he said.

Before she could answer he leaned forward, took a nipple into his mouth and sucked it until it became a hard nub. Moving to the other nipple, he repeated the sensation, drawing it into his mouth and making it hard. Her body reacted to his very talented tongue. After a few minutes she reached forward, tweaking one of his nipples, making him yelp.

His eyes darkened with desire.

"I only wanted to share a warm bath with you, but I see you want more fun and games?" He swiftly moved them until her back was pressing against the side of the bath. She rested her arms and head on the rim, with her long legs in front of her, floating before him.

Bloody hell, she thought, *I must still have whatever those drugs were that man injected me with last night, they must still be in my system, I do not act like this! No matter what I've been given I should still fight them,* she thought hazily. But she couldn't seem to help herself.

Slowly, she opened her legs in front of him.

He growled, walked between them, and she wrapped them around his waist, continuing to stare into his eyes. Gripping his cock in his hand he slowly entered her, it gently nudged her new little gold hoop, making her gasp.

She felt the pull of it on every push in and on every pull out, it heightened her pleasure tenfold. Her body felt like one giant erogenous zone and every time she begged him to allow her to come he withdrew and waited for her to settle down before repeating it all over again.

She was nearly driven out of her mind with pleasure.

Sinking down into the water, pulling her on top of him as he went, he stopped moving, holding her against him so he could feel the erratic beat of her heart. Trey started to move slowly as he sat up and she wound her long legs around his waist.

They were slowly rocking against each other, their whole bodies locked together.

"Now..." she begged.

"Yes, Siobhan, now!"

They came together as he pulled her forward, locking his lips on hers so he could feel her cry reverberate against his lips.

After she stopped shuddering and she had felt his cock slowly slip out of her she floated away on her back, ducking underneath the water again, coming up on the other side of the bath.

"We haven't got much time left together as I'm leaving here and going back to England tonight. Will you miss me?" he said.

But she could see he didn't mean it so she laughed and told him the truth.

"No!"

CHAPTER TWENTY TWO

"Good, don't get attached to anyone here Siobhan, people are here to only further their own lives. They don't care who they've got to take down to get what they desire," he said solemnly.

With that he got out of the bath, gesturing for her to follow him, quickly patting them both dry. Then he reattached the metal chain and led her back to her room.

"Remember me, whenever someone plays with your little gold hoop."

Laughing, smacking her on her behind, he undid the chain and allowed her to walk through the doors. She heard him lock up and walk away.

Once again, there was food and wine for her to eat and drink. She tucked in while replaying the events of her time with Trey and whoever that woman was. *God,* she groaned, *I can just see Blake's expression when he watches my exploits.* She shuddered at that thought, *with every touch, every lick on my body from someone else, I'm bloody betraying him.* She sniffed, tears threatening to fall again.

Think of something else, she thought quickly, so she thought about the sex she'd had with the woman in Trey's room.

She'd never in her wildest dreams thought about making love with another woman before. She knew it had happened at her school, but she had never been interested.

Seraphina might have experimented briefly but she had soon turned back to men. Siobhan looked down at her new piercing – she couldn't believe anyone would want to get pierced down there! But it did have its uses, and she couldn't wait to show Blake it, if he would even talk to her after this.

She was so tired she nearly fell asleep right there eating the food, so she slowly pushed herself up from the table and slipped between the sheets, falling asleep immediately. Again, she dreamed about Blake rescuing her from this nightmare, telling her he would still love her, no matter what she was made to do. In this dream he charged in on a magnificent white steed and fought off everyone. They had ridden off into the sunset to live happily ever after.

Waking up she felt her hot tears running down her cheek, and brushed them away angrily. He wouldn't love her once he'd watched her take part in everything she'd done since being here. She hoped he'd viewed them alone. She would die of shame if any of the others had seen them. Feeling her face blush a fierce red, she thought about what she'd done since being captured.

She knew she wasn't the most experienced when it came to sex and what she'd done with Blake recently she thought had been very daring, kinky. Now she realised just how tame her past sex life had been.

Did Blake enjoy all the things she'd done here? Would he like to see her with other women? Would he enjoy it if she had on one of those things the woman had worn so she could fuck his ass? What about if she dressed up for him in all the gear that was in the wardrobe? She recalled the dreamy look on Blake's face when he'd been joking about her dressing up as a dominatrix for him.

She didn't really know what a dominatrix did, but being here, she could certainly guess.

Well, with all the clothes in the closet I'm bound to find something to fit the bill. She opened the doors and started to rifle through the clothes, bringing out each piece and trying to think if Blake would like to see her in it. She wanted to be as daring as she could, and decided that she may as well learn as much as she could while she was here; as there seemed to be lots for her to learn and plenty of willing teachers.

I f Blake ever finds me again, I can wow him with all my new knowledge. She remembered that he'd mentioned thigh high boots, so she picked a shiny black PVC pair with silver spiky heels. Next was a rubber skin suit, with a long zip from her neck right around to the small of her back. It also had two zips where her breasts were, so when they were opened her breasts poked through the holes.

It wasn't the easiest of things to put on, but after a lot of huffing and puffing she managed it.

The sleeves made her arms look long and slim. Pulling on the boots and zipping them up, she looked at herself in the mirror. Running her hands over her body, she had to admit to like what she saw – and knew instinctively that he'd love her in this outfit.

But something was still missing, thinking back... *Something about a whip, that's what he'd said,* she thought, and walked over to the wall that until now, she'd tried to ignore.

There was a large selection of whips hanging up, and she chose one that looked like a riding crop, except the handle was covered in purple crystals. It looked much too pretty for its intended use.

She gave it an experimental smack against her leg, where it made a throaty thwack. She giggled to herself, wishing Seraphina could see her in this get up, it was so completely different to anything she'd worn before.

She wanted a mask though, as she still didn't feel confident enough to pull this off without one. Rooting through the closet, she found a black rubber mask and quickly put it on, then put her hair up in a high ponytail before studying the finished result.

She looked incredibly sexy and again wished that Blake was here with her. Her skin looked pale against all the black and she wished she had a bit of makeup. She explored the room, and inspected all the different objects.

It was all so alien – there was a wrought iron metal cage big enough for someone to sit in, a bright red leather table with holes cut away where she presumed certain body parts could be placed and fondled, and dentist's chair, which was something she didn't even want to think about as she had a fear of the dentist's. The largest piece of equipment, apart from the bed, was a huge wooden X, which was fixed to the wall, with padded leather cuffs to buckle around ankles and wrists. It could be hoisted into the air and suspended either upside down or the right way up. Siobhan ran her hands over the leather and wood and wondered what Blake would do to her if she was tied up on it.

He did say his house had a dungeon, and if so, who does he use it with? she asked herself. *Will I ever get the chance to ask him?* Shaking herself, she thought sadly, *like hell have I any right to question him about his sex life.*

On the wall to her right, where all the whips and other odd things were hung, were an array of nipple and clit clips. There was also a huge selection of dildos and vibrators of all different shapes, colours and sizes. Some making her eyes water just looking at them and some just plain freaky, while the rest looked positively dangerous to your health. She also recognised a long thin piece of plastic with little balls all the way up.

That looks like what was put up my ass when I was tied into that swing, she thought. She remembered the sensations that the toy evoked. There were lots of things she didn't have a clue about. The door opened and Monique walked in looking as pale and as haughty as ever. She looked distastefully at what Siobhan was wearing.

"As I said before, little one, I hardly think you're ready to cause other people pain. Not yet anyhow. Maybe with a few more weeks of training we may have you up to some sort of acceptable standard."

A few more weeks! Siobhan screamed silently, her eyes still firmly on the floor. *I'll never make it, I'll never survive away from Blake that long!*

"But, what you have on will suffice for now. You're looking a little pasty, so you can go outside for the day, hopefully that will bring a little colour back into your face. I forget humans need the sunlight, to look, well, to look human. You'll not be alone. You'll be on your lead at all times. If you try to escape you will be hunted until you are found then you will be killed. Do you understand, little one?" Monique asked, attaching her metal lead.

"I understand." She whispered.

Outside! She thought, she hadn't realised how much she was missing it.

Another woman stalked into the room and Monique said:

"This is Xandrella. She'll be your guardian while you are outside. If you prove you can be trusted I'll let Xandrella come and get you every day. We might bring some colour back into that pretty little face of yours."

With that she turned, marching out of the room, leaving the women eyeing each other.

"You should see what I wear for my night job." She mumbled to Xandrella with a small smile, hoping to break the ice.

But Xandrella didn't smile back.

Instead she continued to stare at her with distaste. Then she opened her mouth, showing extraordinary teeth, all filed to sharp points. Siobhan couldn't help but gasp as the old fairy tale of Red Riding Hood came to her mind.

"Oh what sharp teeth you have," and the answer was. "All the better for eating you with," she thought with a shudder. All Xandrella was wearing was a number of black leather straps, held in place by a lot of metal buckles, and not a lot else. *Does anyone wear normal clothes here?* Siobhan wondered.

Xandrella had very short bright blue hair that was styled in hard little spikes all over her head.

Her face was scrubbed clean, no makeup at all, with high, proud, and well defined cheek bones. Her lips were full, with a little gold stud in the corner above the lip on the right hand side. In her eyes were contacts, or so Siobhan thought, which made them look like cat eyes and gave her the look of a lean, hungry predator.

She didn't look as if she laughed often.

Her left ear was completely pierced from the lobe right the way around with little studs. She was very lean and muscular, with many scars. In her right hand she carried a long quite thick stick, made of old pale looking wood and she had such a well defined six pack that Siobhan wanted to touch it to see if it felt as hard as it looked. You wouldn't want to tangle with this woman.

"I am trained in the arts of Kendo, Taekwondo, kick boxing and cage fighting." Xandrella said without making any eye contact as she led Siobhan from the room.

Oh boy! She thought, letting out a long sigh.

No wonder Monique had Xandrella to watch her, there was no possibility of her trying to escape – she looked like she could take on the twins, and win. Xandrella marched along at a fast pace, forcing Siobhan to trot behind her.

Soon they were outside and she squinted and shaded her eyes

from the unaccustomed sunlight.

Standing still and taking in a deep breath of fresh air, she relished the sunlight on her face, until Xandrella growled, giving a sharp tug on the lead.

She had no choice but to follow her until they came to a stop under a large willow tree. Xandrella freed her from the metal lead, and moved to sit in the shade.

But Siobhan wanted to feel the sun on her skin so, finding a soft bank of grass, she lay down. It was wonderful to feel the sun on her body and she closed her eyes, thinking, *I thought I was meant to be on my lead at all times? But, Xandrella must know that I wouldn't dare to try and make a run for it, what would be the point? I know just how fast they can move.*

She felt overdressed, so unzipped the boots and removed the rubber suit, which was nearly as hard as putting the damn thing on, and then lay back down once she was naked. The sun felt glorious on her body and she stretched her muscles like a cat preening itself on a window ledge. She closed her eyes, enjoying the moment.

She felt peaceful, which wasn't an emotion she'd felt since arriving here.

It was such a different world, a world she hadn't even known about until Blake had told her, and look at what she had been through since finding out. *Just how long have I been here?* she wondered, running her hands over her warm, naked body. She didn't feel ashamed at being naked in front of Xandrella, who was watching her through her half closed, cat like eyes.

She sat under the tree in complete shade, smoking a strange coloured cigarette and blowing smoke circles. She didn't seem at all interested in Siobhan, who continued lying on the grass looking up at the incredible blue sky.

She heard footsteps approaching and turned her head to look at the newcomer. He was a short man, similar to the man who'd shot her. Her skin crawled as he walked over to her and stood with a leg either side of her body, trapping her.

"Hello my little flower, look at you just lying around all warm and naked. Were you waiting for me to come over and fuck you?" he said, his eyes gleamed as he rubbed his already straining cock through his dirty trousers. He was very ugly and very sweaty. Then he was flying through the air as Xandrella's stick hit him between his legs and sent him airborne.

He landed perfectly, crouched on his feet, his face distorted with rage.

He made to return and Siobhan shrank back, only for, Xandrella to put a hand roughly on the top of her head, locking her in place.

CHAPTER TWENTY THREE

"Sit very still!" she barked. She moved to stand in front of Siobhan, holding her stick thing loosely in her right hand and placing her body in between Siobhan and the man. As soon as he saw Xandrella, the man came to an abrupt stop, and seemed to cower.

"Rella! I didn't know you hired yourself out to guard humans," he said, his skin paling in fear.

"I didn't know the bitch was under your protection. I've heard the rumours that Monique had a human whore that any one, male or female could do with whatever they so desired! I know how you like your females Rella; of course you could have first go" Siobhan's heart froze at his words, the news that she was just a whore to be used by anyone had her retching.

"Fuck off Raoul!" Xandrella said in a low voice, she didn't need to shout – and Raoul didn't need telling twice, he scampered away as fast as his short fat little legs would carry him. Xandrella stepped over Siobhan and resumed her position under the tree, smoking her strange cigarettes. Siobhan turned to look at her new protector.

"Why was that vampire so scared of you?"

"That's fuck all to do with you really. But I will indulge you. I come from a long line of female warriors. My whole Order is female, and we are turned and trained at a very young age. I have trained and fought all my life, I'm over five hundred years old and I've been in many battles, so of course I'm well known. I'm called in when someone or something needs protection. We're paid very highly to do our job and I happen to be the best of my Order – so don't worry about any more Raoul's annoying you. Once the word gets out that you are under my protection, that incident will hopefully be the last."

Siobhan mulled over what she had just learnt.

"But you'll not protect me from Monique and everything that she wants me to do, will you?" she shouted in temper.

"Of course not you stupid human, she is my employer," Xandrella shouted back, blowing a smoke ring and not even bothering to look up.

Siobhan turned haughtily on her heel and strode back to where she'd been lying earlier. She had hoped to rediscover the peace she felt before Raoul had rudely interrupted. But instead, she felt restless. She stared at Xandrella and remembered Raoul had said about: that she only liked women *I wonder if she fancies me?*

Stop it! she giggled to herself. *Before coming here I wouldn't dream of wondering if another lady fancied me, but since I've been here I know now that sex doesn't need to be so predictable.*

There are many ways to enjoy it, and if it's a little different, so what? She was desperate to see Blake. *Would he enjoy everything I've learnt? Perhaps he'll be disgusted with me and reject me? Well there's no point in worrying about it.* She bravely tried to tell herself, *I'll have to cross that bridge when or if we ever meet again.* Sighing, she wondered how long it would be before she could touch him again.

"Get dressed Siobhan." Xandrella called out to her.

A lady of few words, she thought, quickly doing as she was told. Xandrella attached the chain and led her back to her room in the dark chateau. Before opening the door, she told Siobhan: "I will see you tomorrow." She stalked away, not giving Siobhan a chance to say goodbye. Sighing, she walked into her room and closed the door. But she wasn't alone, a man was waiting for her.

"My, my, you are just as beautiful in the flesh as you are on film." He drawled, his Southern accent thick, as he got off the bed and stood in front of her.

Lifting his hands, he ran them appraisingly over her body. Siobhan took a few hasty steps away from him, only to back herself against the door. He stood with his hard body pressed against hers, and unzipped her breast zips, allowing them to pop free. His head came down and his mouth nipped at the tender flesh, making her cry out.

He took a moment, looking her in the eyes. He appeared youthful, not that it meant anything around – here he could be eighteen or a few hundred years old.

"I know how you like it Siobhan, I've had the privilege of watching the films that you've made since being here. For someone so young and so innocent you have picked up your new way of life incredibly quick." All this was spoken softly as his eyes travelled over her body. She felt sexual heat and power coming off him in waves and quailed before him.

"Now, what have I done to make you look like I am about to turn you? You know I can't, you know why, so why look like I just hurt you? Or do you want to feel pain?" His eyes bored into hers and he saw she looked very wary. "My name is Jarryd and I am from New Orleans, but I am staying here for a while and I came across your films, completely by accident, I assure you. You are one sexy lady. I decided I wanted a piece of you, so here I am."

His lazy Southern drawl, which she had always found alluring, would have been inviting and sexy at any other time.

But not now, not here.

Glancing up, she saw his gleaming white fangs. He was incredibly good looking, and had a stunning tan. He was dressed with an elegance that befitted an old southern gentleman – an immaculate suit of cream linen, with a white, open necked shirt. His hair was a rich chocolate brown , with natural blond highlights, cut short but with a long, floppy fringe. It was a casual image that must have taken hours to create. She could imagine him owning a huge plantation with a few hundred slaves, producing cotton.

"Where are my manners? They do seem to have left me. I was more interested in your beauty, I do hope you can forgive me?" Jarryd drawled, then grinned as he picked up her hand and kissed her knuckles where she felt the graze of his fangs. "I do seem to be getting a little ahead of myself, so let's start again." Fastening up the zips, he led her to the bathroom where he had run a deep bath, the jets were on and it was bubbling away. She smiled.

"Baby doll, let's get better acquainted over a few glasses of bubbly and a good long soak."

As they stripped, Siobhan watched Jarryd out of the corner of her eye. He had a lovely all over tan and she wondered if all vampires had great bodies. Could she ever go back to normal men? She doubted it. *Did vampires have groupies?* She nervously laughed to herself, thinking, *well if they didn't, they do now.*

She was nearly undressed and Jarryd was already in the bath watching her.

"I just might get you to wear just the boots when we are ready to get out of the bath." he commented as she removed her footwear and lowered herself into the warm water.

The water felt delicious around her body as it bubbled away, and she leant her head back and closed her eyes. Jarryd moved silently through the water until he was standing in front of her, taking a long sip of Champagne, he brought her head up so he could kiss her, letting the drink dribble out of his mouth and into hers. He held her close to him.

"Now listen closely, Si." he whispered softly into her ear, his voice serious.

Her head jerked as he said her name. She stared helplessly into his eyes – which were now as black as midnight and not the piercing blue of earlier.

"Blake sent me here, he knows you're here and is doing everything possible to get you out. Stay still!" He hissed to her as she tried to jerk away. "I have to act like this with you, remember we are always being filmed. He has a plan, but it'll take a while yet. He tells you to stay safe and to do anything you have to do to achieve that. And by anything he means *anything* baby doll." She started to cry, and he pulled her to him so she could rest her head on his shoulder. His powerful arms wrapped around her as she wept.

"I thought he'd forgotten me, or when he saw the films, he then decided that he didn't love me or want me anymore," her voice broke as she sobbed against his shoulder.

"Oh baby doll, he loves you so much, he'll do anything to get you out of here. But you must remain here until he comes and frees you, you must not do anything yourself. He will be pleased for me to tell him that you are unharmed. He was beside himself until he saw the films. No, don't look like that, you were hardly in a position to argue with anyone were you? But seriously, he was as mad as I have ever seen him – and I have known him an awfully long time. When he finally releases you, it's going to be a battle to end it all!" Jarryd said with a smile.

"And do not forget you now have Xandrella on your side."

She took an unsteady gulp.

"What do you mean? I thought she was working for Monique?" she said, puzzled.

"Monique thinks she is working for her, but Xandrella's a spy working for Blake, she has always worked for Blake. It is her job to keep you safe, well as safe as she can. That is why Xandrella was so rude and nasty to you today, she couldn't let anyone suspect that she isn't on Monique's side. I know she was pretty terrifying, but it was a necessary step. She will become friendlier as time goes on, but not in front of anyone else. What else was I meant to tell you?"

Jarryd ran his hands up and down her spine, trying to calm her as he spoke.

"Oh yes, all your human friends are safe and unharmed, but of course worried about you. Imogen had to return to the States so they told your parents you went with her for some more training for your new job. Your parents are fine, and everyone, including your parents are being guarded. They don't know anything of course, but Blake wanted to make sure they remain safe and he's now not willing to take any chances with anyone."

She slowly began to relax and felt a little more relieved that Blake still wanted her and everyone was fine. *But he's seen the bloody films,* she shuddered at the thought, blushing a fierce red.

Shaking her head and wiping away her tears, she looked at Jarryd.

"Are you in any danger by being here?"

"Only if we don't enjoy ourselves, baby doll," he said in his deep southern drawl. She nodded, pulling her emotions together and wrapping her arms around his neck tightly. She whispered in his ear, always mindful of the cameras.

"Thank you for telling me all this, for bringing me news on everyone. I desperately needed to know that he was at least thinking about me and that my friends were all safe. It'll make being here a little more tolerable. I miss them all so bloody much," she cried softly against his shoulder. He kissed the top of her head, holding her for a few seconds, letting her pull herself together, before telling her.

"Turn around Siobhan, there's something I want you to feel."

Turning from him, he moved her so she was pressed against the side of the whirlpool.

He then stood directly behind her, grinning as she squeaked.

"Ouch!" She felt her arm being injected. "Why did you do that?" Her body started to feel incredibly hot and achy.

"I will explain later, I promise you," he murmured in her ear.

"Do you feel it?" Suddenly she felt completely aroused and she was aware of nothing but Jarryd behind her, naked.

"Yes!"

The "it" he was talking about was one of the jets of water. It sprayed her bud at just the right speed, making her arch her back into him. His cock was already hard as she felt it rub against her, the drugs making her feel exactly like they did when she'd been with Trey and the woman. Dipping his hand under the water he reached around her to spread her lower lips apart so the jet could be felt even more intently. She was pinned against the side and he bent his head down, running his tongue along her neck. She tensed, thinking he was about to bite her.

But he just teased her, murmuring.

"Think of me as an extension of Blake, close your eyes and imagine that it's his mouth on your neck, his hands touching you, he will bring you to orgasm then carry you to bed and make love to you all night long."

She shivered against the sensuous flick of his tongue on her neck, her eyes closing.

"Do things you would only want him to do to you."

His words inflamed her and sent her flying, and she was soon having an orgasm, bucking against Jarryd's strong hold.

Once she'd calmed a little, she turned her head.

"Kiss me Jarryd," she demanded.

He moved in to ravish her mouth. She turned to face him, wrapping her arms around him to draw him closer and gave herself over to the delicious feelings the drugs were enhancing. She wrapped her long legs around him and enjoyed the way he kissed her.

It felt like he hadn't kissed anyone for a very long time and he left her gasping and wanting more.

CHAPTER TWENTY FOUR

With her eyes closed, she really could have been kissing Blake. She ran her tongue over his lips and flicked his fangs as she gently kissed him; such a gentle, sweet kiss to render her breathless.

Jarryd ran his tongue over her teeth, his arms around her waist as he ran his hands up and down her spine – not to comfort this time but to enflame.

Lifting her up out of the water and sitting her down on the side he pushed her down so she laid flat on her back on the floor tiles with her legs dangling in the water. He pulled her to him until her bum was right on the edge of the tub.

Kneeling, he put her legs over his shoulders.

"I've been looking forward to getting my teeth around this little gold hoop," he whispered against her body, ducking his face low.

He bit it, giving it a little pull.

Her back arched and her hands pushed against the hard floor as she ground herself into his willing mouth. He knew exactly what she needed, he began with small little licks which were more like hot little kisses to her bud. His hands roamed all over her body exploring, getting to know by the sighs she made if she liked something he was doing.

He was in no rush even though she implored him to speed up.

"Have patience, Si!" he chuckled, taking hold of her hands and placing them on her breasts. "Pinch your nipples and enjoy yourself, while I enjoy myself here."

Feeling the drugs override any embarrassment, she pulled tentatively at her nipples – and then bucked at the electric shocks they sent down her body.

Jarryd's fingers were buried deep inside of her, while his tongue was pushing her towards another orgasm. She began to pant and writhed on the tip of his tongue.

"Please, please, I need to come now," she begged.

"As you ask so sweetly, I will help you come," he whispered against her heated flesh, seconds before plunging two fingers deep inside of her while his other hand and tongue did delicious things to her bud and brought about an almighty orgasm. She cried out and came with such a powerful force, she felt her body rise and then crumble beneath his expert touch. Lying on the tiles with her eyes shut, her mind was locked away in her own private world.

Jumping out of the water and scooping her up into his arms, Jarryd carried her to the bed. She was still in the throes of her orgasm, and felt warm, soft and wet to his touch. Placing her gently on the bed and walking over to the wall he picked out some things to enhance their pleasure. Turning, he looked into her eyes, they were watching him, showing him the drugs in her system were keeping her very aroused.

He quickly reached the bed and slipped a blindfold over her eyes, bending his body over hers until his mouth was sucking a hard little nipple into his mouth. Only when he was satisfied they were both as hard and as peaked as they could be did he attach the nipple clamps to each, making her cry out and whimper.

Her body trembled with the erotic pinch, the clamps were

padded but they still had enough force to make her cry out with the pleasure and pain.

Quickly and efficiently, he cuffed her hands to the bed, stretching her arms above her head, holding her secure for his pleasure.

Stroking his fingers through her lower lips, his eyes feasted on her as he felt she was still incredibly wet. Rising her hips she followed him, mewling slightly as he pulled away from her – but when she heard a buzzing sound she opened her mouth to start begging.

But a second later she felt him spreading her legs wide and in one forceful thrust he pushed himself into her. He was impressively endowed, filling her, spreading her internal muscles and only when he was in her did he pause so she could feel what was making that buzzing sound. She let out a low moan as whatever he'd attached to his cock brushed erotically against her bud. It was made of soft rubber, she could feel that much, with what felt like little rubber spikes all over it and it was vibrating against her most sensitive place while his hands gently tugged at the nipple clamps.

His mouth closed over hers, swallowing her cries, devouring her with long, hard kisses.

Feeling her body was close to another orgasm, he picked up the pace. His hips pushed himself deeper and deeper into her and she lifted her hips up so she could receive him.

"Now Jarryd, please God now..." She called out to him, becoming almost frantic for release.

Pulling off the nipple clamps, he bit down on a nipple, very nearly drawing blood. It was enough to make her scream out as the first wave broke over her. Her legs and internal muscles clamping him to her as she held onto him until she was spent, not caring if he had come or not, but it only took one final hard push for him to reach his own release.

Quickly he quickly reached up, freeing her hands and rolling them over so she was now sprawled on top of him.

"Come here."

Growling deeply he pulled her down to kiss her, running his hands through her hair. He was satisfied she was panting heavily and seemed quite content to lie on him and relax. She was trying to catch her breath. Wondering what on earth Blake would be feeling about someone he'd sent into the lion's den to try and guard her, and she'd ended up sleeping with him.

What a mess, I think I must be turning into a nymphomaniac, she thought sadly.

"I hope you are not too tired, as the night is young, and so are we – well you are. There are lots of fun things for us to try." Jarryd said as he lay on his back looking down at her still sprawled over his chest.

"Are you hungry?" he enquired, just as there was a knock on the door.

It was opened by a couple of young servants, carrying large platters of delicious smelling food. She walked a little sluggishly to where they'd placed the platters and sat down, looking at him gratefully.

"Tuck in, Blake thought you could do with some proper food, so enjoy. You'll understand if I do not join you? But I like to watch a human eat, it brings back fond memories. So please, do carry on," he softly told her once the girls had left the room.

On the table was an array of her favourite shellfish.

"How the hell did you organise this?" She helped herself to an oyster.

"Blake told me you loved of shellfish, so I ordered it from Monique's kitchen and had them bring it up. Monique thought it terribly quaint that I wanted to woo you with food; she laughed and said as I have paid for you I could do anything with my time with you. But she thought it was a waste when there was far more interesting things that we could be doing." He watched her eat a mussel, then dip a large piece of lobster into a sauce and suck it clean before swallowing it whole. She closed her eyes and licked her lips and fingers clean, savouring the flavor.

"This is so good, it's a shame you can't taste anything," she said between bites.

Opening a bottle of Champagne, she greedily drank it straight from the bottle. It dripped from the corners of her mouth and dribbled down her breasts and she giggled as she watched it progress down her body. It was too much for Jarryd, who let out a hiss and scooped her from the chair. Standing her on the bed, he grabbed a second bottle of Champagne, shook it and let it spray all over her body.

She squealed as he knelt before her, licking the Champagne off. She wriggled in pleasure, holding his head and rocking her hips so he could reach everywhere it had touched.

"Do you want anyone to join us or are you happy to continue with just a private party?" he said.

"What did you have in mind?" said Siobhan, nervously biting her lip.

"Baby doll, would you like another man to join us or perhaps a lady? It's your choice, I want to go back to Blake and tell him you had fun and that it was your choice what we did." Jarryd smiled, and then went back to running his tongue along the inside of her thighs.

"Jarryd, I've already tried the two ladies, one man combo, I think I'd like to try another man with you, if that's okay?" She blushed scarlet, not believing what she was saying, but she saw him grin, and he winked up at her.

"Consider it done." He jumped off the bed, opened the door

and walked out into the corridor. When he returned, she gaped. With him was a hug black Maui. He was at least six feet five and heavily tattooed with traditional Maui tattoos on his back, arms and face. Siobhan thought he was gorgeous, with amazing piercing brown eyes which looked at her as if he couldn't wait to eat her alive.

His long jet black hair came down in waves to his waist.

I can't wait to feel that against my body, she thought, still blushing. He wore only a black leather loin cloth which did nothing to hide the fact that he was hugely hung, and definitely aroused. Jarryd stood and watched as she inspected the new arrival. She obviously felt an instant attraction to him.

"Well, baby doll, what do you want our guest here to do? He is at your disposal, think about what you would like to do with two men at your beck and call." Jarryd grinned at her.

Siobhan studied the two men.

They contrasted perfectly against one another, both were tall and had amazing well defined muscles. One was deliciously dark and tattooed, with a sheer bulk that could snap her in half if he so wished and one was tanned and muscular but had a gentleness about him.

Or maybe, she thought, looking Jarryd over; *that's what makes him so deadly, his outward persona belies a deadly force he holds in check by sheer willpower.*

"I want to be dressed, dress me in what I had on before the bath," she ordered.

They picked up her clothes from the bathroom floor and returned to where she stood waiting for them. Jarryd poured her a glass of bubbly for her to drink while they were dressing her.

Kneeling in front of her, Jarryd lifted up a foot and she rested her hand on the other man's very large muscled shoulder. He kissed and sucked each toe before running his tongue between them, while his hand kneaded her arch. It sent different sensations rushing all over her body before he slipped on the leg of her rubber suit, pushing it up to her knee. He then nodded to their new playmate to do the same.

This time she placed her hand on Jarryd's shoulder for balance, watching while the other man picked up her foot in his large dark hands, bending his head down so he could place her toes into his open mouth, his tongue flicking snake-like at her foot, his long hair falling forward.

Not being able to resist, wanting to feel it was as soft as it looked, she reached out a hand and slowly ran her fingers through it.

I was right, so soft, she thought, wrapping her hand around in his hair. She looked down her body. Her foot looked so dainty in this man's huge hands and the sensations she was feeling were beginning to make her tremble. She gripped Jarryd's shoulder a little tighter as he slipped the suit over her foot up to her knee just as Jarryd had done a few seconds before. She took a large gulp of Champagne and closed her eyes, imagining she was no longer being held captive but back in Blake's bedroom and it was he who was dressing her, for his pleasure. She could feel the men working as one, kneeling behind her, kissing and nibbling the sensitive skin at the back of her knees.

Tugging at the rubber suit, they pulled it up her thighs until it was resting just below her ass. They were still behind her, and she could only imagine what her bottom looked like with the black rubber framing it. She felt feverish as they enjoyed a taste of her, licking and nipping, making her giggle and preen. Pushing a finger gently between her cheeks, Jarryd slowly caressed her puckered tight hole. With his finger covered in some sort of oil, it slipped into her with very little force. She gasped as it burrowed deep in her, her hips bucking, she clenched his finger, while the other man continued nibbling and licking her ass cheeks. Jarryd didn't stay there for long, just long enough to tease her before gently removing his finger and both men moved around to face her.

Kneeling back down, Jarryd slipped a finger into her folds, sliding his way along the length of her, from her asshole to her little gold hoop, giving it a quick sharp pull as he watched her bite her lip.

Her head fell back as intense pleasure flooded her senses. As Jarryd worked his magic, the other man looked on approvingly, his dark eyes filled with lust.

Jarryd continued slipping his finger around her bud, teasing her, then the other man's hand joined in. He slipped a couple of his fingers inside her, matching the speed of Jarryd. It felt intoxicating and she was soon on the brink of coming, rolling her hips, moving in time to their fingers fucking and pleasuring her.

Her breath came out in wild shudders, she was on the edge but Jarryd laughed and both men took their hands away from her straining body. Whimpering, she very nearly demanded they continue, but they'd moved up her body, pulling the suit a little higher.

The black rubber suit was now sat on her rib cage, her breasts beautifully framed by the black. They each took a nipple into their mouths. Their hands gently brushed the underside, circling around, while their tongues laved at her swollen nibs. Rolling the sensitive nipples in their mouths almost synchronised in their movements. Lifting and pushing her breasts together, they enjoyed darting their tongues over her nipples.

CHAPTER TWENTY FIVE

Siobhan gave a pleasure-soaked moan; it was heaven to be stood there letting them pleasure her. She felt worshipped and knew they'd do anything she asked. She felt Jarryd's hand pulling up the zip ever so slowly until her breasts were covered and thought about telling him to undo it and start again, but didn't. There were other things to do, maybe even more thrilling and wicked, before it was removed again.

Her arms were the last to be covered and they were also treated to light caresses, kisses and nibbles, before she was finally dressed. Jarryd was smiling at her, but his eyes flashed erotically as he took in her body incased in the black PVC.

"I want my boots on, Jarryd."

Wondering if that was really her voice, *does it sound as husky to them?* she wondered. He nodded and picked up her boots while the other man effortlessly lifted her into the air. Her head fell back, resting on his chest, as Jarryd held open the boots. She was slowly lowered into them and Jarryd pulled up the zips, all the while looking into her eyes which were filled with unspoken promises of all the wicked things that were to come.

"Now Siobhan," Jarryd whispered, moving in tightly to her

body, his body touching hers, his lips brushing against hers in the lightest of kisses. She sighed as the kiss ended far too suddenly, her body aching for a touch, feeling small and feminine being sandwiched between the two huge men.

"Tell me, what would you like to do? What are your most secret desires?" he asked, continuing to kiss her gently. She was finding it difficult to form coherent sentences.

When she didn't answer, he nipped at her sensitive lips. Taking a couple of deep breaths, she dropped her eyes for a few seconds trying to work up the courage to tell him what she wanted, needed and desired. She gazed into his black eyes and pointed a rather shaky hand to the wooden cross on the wall.

"I want to be tied up and have the both of you pleasuring me at the same time," she whispered, blushing and dropping her head in shame. "But Jarryd..." She mumbled. "I want to be spanked, but..." she faltered.

Jarryd gently lifted her head so she was forced to look at him.

"You won't get hurt, I promise you, just enough to get you off," he said, caressing her face. "Blake has trusted me to do this, so you must too."

He waited for her to give her consent.

She thought for a moment, then gave the briefest of nods.

The man behind her didn't waste any time. He quickly picked her up and carried her to the cross, where he started to attach all the different straps and buckles. He gently placed her feet onto foot posts which held her above the floor by a few inches, and then her legs and arms were stretched open, buckled into place until she was standing in a star shape.

Her neck was gently placed into position, held in place by a wide padded neck restraint. Jarryd had watched her being shackled and now walked over, obviously aroused, and placed a blindfold over her eyes, shrouding her in darkness. She waited, trembling, for whatever was in store for her. He whispered in her ear.

"If at any time you want us to stop, just shout out Blake and we'll stop immediately. That is your safe word, baby doll." His fingers lightly caressed her face. She smiled, and nodded her head.

"Say it out loud baby doll, say it now," he ordered in a low, sexy voice.

"Blake." Her voice rang out, not betraying her by showing them both how nervous she suddenly felt. Her breast zips were undone and she closed her eyes behind the mask suddenly feeling a wet tongue flicking her nipple, making her moan. The neck restraint and collar were lifted and she felt a now familiar sting of a needle.

"No Jarryd! Why are you giving me that stuff?" she groaned as it started to work immediately.

"Blake told me to give it to you. He calls it your diminished responsibility, baby doll. You can't control yourself when you're given this drug, so it's not your fault what you do. Do you understand?" Jarryd said, again softly so no one else could hear what he was saying to her. He could see her expression and knew just how much this was killing her, to be acting so out of character. But it was killing Blake just as much if not more, as he had to watch the films. Watch everything Siobhan was doing, and having done to her. Jarryd didn't know if he'd be as strong as Blake was to hold off on trying to rescue her if she belonged to him. He'd spent the past month and a half at Blake's home working on a rescue plan with Nat, Alex and Ethan.

It'd taken a while to figure out where she was being kept, but Monique was vain and had left a few hints. Blake had eventually guessed and it'd been terrifying to watch his fury. He'd wanted to race over to France and free her.

Nat had to block his way and it'd been a terrible and brutal fight.

Both men had been so badly hurt in the struggle and had the scars to prove it – and to scar a vampire was no mean feat. But Blake had been made to see that they couldn't just walk in and rescue her, they had to round up all of their troops and go in undercover. If Blake or any of his known associates showed their faces here, it would be signing her death warrant.

So they'd finally agreed on a plan. And the first part was to find someone to guard her as much as was possible – that was Xandrella.

Her Order owed a huge debt to Blake and this was how he wanted them to re-pay it. Next in was a man who could pass Monique's sadistic tests and get to Siobhan – and that honour had fallen to himself.

When Jarryd asked Blake if he understood what he would have to do to her to be allowed frequent visits, Blake had looked him in the eye and nodded. His eyes had been dead of all emotion, but Jarryd could feel his cold, steely force simmering below the surface, barely contained. Jarryd knew, when the time came for rescue, every member of Monique's phoney Order would die a dreadful death.

He'd flown over a few days ago to negotiations with Monique, acting indifferently to all of Monique's plans for her prisoner. In reality, he was repulsed and disgusted – but he couldn't show any emotion and had encouraged her attempt to degrade Siobhan. It was Blake's idea to introduce the drugs. He knew it would kill Siobhan to be aware of everything that was happening to her and so he'd made Jarryd pass on the information about the drug. It made the female libido go out of control, so she wouldn't be able to take any responsibility for her actions.

Jarryd thought he knew all about love and respect, but he wouldn't have wanted a good and trusted friend and ally doing this to his beloved.

How will Blake act towards me after all this is over? He wondered? But Blake had reassured him, and said he'd rather it was someone he knew and trusted than a stranger who would hurt her.

And when an Elder asked you to do something, especially if that Elder happened to be Blake, you didn't have a choice...

"Jarryd...!" Siobhan called out, bringing him back to the present.

"Okay Si, remember it is Blake who is touching you," he whispered, hoping she would remember her safe word.

"Now you dirty little bitch, for your first lesson in pain, let me make you want to do all those naughty things you have been longing to do. You are one dirty little bitch!"

He snarled, completely changing his attitude towards her.

He was now dominant; the one in charge. With the drugs raging through her body she didn't care what he did to her.

She tried to struggle against her ties, but it was futile, she was held tight.

Suddenly, hands roughly unzipped all of her zips. Her breasts were already free and her main zip was undone, then his hands slid underneath, unzipping her from her ass to just above her pelvis. She gasped and spluttered as she was drenched in ice cold water. Her nipples hardened and her body thrummed in arousal. She needed to be fucked – and fucked good and hard – now!

"Jarryd..." she screamed, begging him.

Next she heard a whoosh and felt the white hot sting of her breasts being whipped, it hurt, it bloody hurt, but the pain turned into an ache that needed to be fulfilled.

She screamed wildly, her whole body bowing as the whip made contact again, right across her nipples. It felt like hot fire.

Just as she was about to scream out her safe word, she felt the lips and tongues of the two men gently licking where the whip had kissed her breasts. Her nipples had never been so hard and sensitive and she was gasping, breathing very heavily, just on the edge of an orgasm.

She stiffened as the whole cross moved away from the wall. What was going on?

It suddenly came to a stop. Siobhan quivered in anticipation, feeling hands stroking down her spine as well as her breasts being fondled, and she began to pant when a tongue lazily flicked across her super sensitive nipples.

She shrieked as she was spanked hard across the ass with a leather paddle. She liked this and groaned in pleasure begging whoever was doing it, to do it harder.

"Jarryd! Oh help me! Fuck..." She screamed as a large dildo was slipped into her, she was so dripping wet from excitement it fitted her beautifully. She tried tilting her hips as it was used to fuck her hard, but was so well bound to the cross it was impossible to move. Someone was sucking her bud at the same time as the dildo fucked her body. There were so many sensations going on that it sent her over the edge. Screaming out and bucking against the shackles, she came so hard it drained her. She'd never felt anything like it in her life.

But it was becoming overwhelming.

"BLAKE!" Siobhan hollered hoarsely and it all stopped immediately. She felt tears drip down her face with the sheer release of it all.

In her blissed out state, she felt the men releasing all the buckles and straps, and then gently laying her on the bed.

She sighed with pleasure as someone's lips caressed hers in a soft but very pleasurable kiss. The other man was gently removing her clothes.

But her blindfold was left on, as she went to remove it Jarryd whispered to her.

"Leave it on Si." She didn't argue and left it in place.

Once all of her clothes had been removed she felt the other man join them on the bed, so she was again sandwiched between them. She reached behind her to feel the man's cock, it had an incredible girth, making her gulp, and as she ran her hands up and down the length of him, she licked her lips in anticipation.

That's just not going to fit anywhere, she thought, a smile playing on her lips. But she knew she wanted to feel it pounding into her.

With the drugs still sizzling through her system she began to kiss Jarryd with a fever of someone possessed, the man behind her started to kiss and nibble her neck, slowly making his was down her spine to her backside which was still sore from the spanking a few minutes earlier.

His luscious hair ticked her on his travels down her body.

"Jarryd, I want to be fucked now!" Siobhan begged. She felt the other man's hands and tongue working at the entrance of her ass and wriggled, arching her back, silently demanding him to take her.

"You will be, baby doll, hold on."

Lifting up one of her legs, he placed it over his hips so she was in a scissor position. He slowly slid in his cock while the other man was gently probing her tight puckered hole with a finger. Jarryd tweaked one of her nipples, nearly making her go into orbit, as his other hand softly circled her sensitive bud.

She held onto Jarryd's shoulders while he slowly fucked her, there was no rushing now – just a slow grind in and a slow pull out. It continued until he felt her internal muscles clenching him and she was calling out.

"Jarryd, faster, now...!"

Grinning, he complied with her orders, ramming his cock into her so she was slammed into the man behind her. He in turn had got himself position so he could slide his cock into her from behind. It was so large she didn't think he would be able to fit, but he'd oiled himself and her, and he very slowly slid into her. She held on tight as both men fucked her, filling her in both holes at the same time.

It was incredible.

She shrieked with the pure enjoyment of it all; the delicious feelings of having two very large cocks in her soon had her whimpering, begging, crying out with need. It was her first ménage a trios with two men – and she was loving it.

"Oh my god, oh my god...!" she shouted. "Yes, oh fuck me yes...!"

She'd never, in her life, imagined that she'd be fucked by two men, but here she was, screaming with such sharp pleasure that she felt tears pricking her eyelids.

Suddenly she came, screaming Blake's name as her body rippled and bowed against them both. Slumping into Jarryd's hard chest she lay limp while the two men continued to fuck her until they came, their shouts of release filling the room.

Not giving her a chance to catch her breath, the men pulled their cocks from her and immediately she was roughly turned so the man behind her could kiss her. It wasn't a gentle kiss but it got the desired response from her.

Running her hands all over his body, she gasped. He really was huge, and he held her face in his huge palms so she was locked to his mouth while he was devoured her. She ran her fingers down his body until she could stroke his cock.

But just as she was getting excited about wanting his cock in her again, she was grabbed and pulled down to the end of the bed.

CHAPTER TWENTY SIX

She wondered what they were going to do next – until she felt a pair of hands tilting her head backwards. Jarryd, now on his knees, palmed his cock, pressing it against her mouth at the same time as the other man's cock entered her. She reached behind her, arching her back to accommodate them both, and caressed Jarryd's balls with one hand, while the other worked its way back to his asshole. Then she gently pushed a finger up inside of him.

He grunted.

"Oh baby doll, work me now..." he managed to groan. Reaching down, he pulled off her blindfold so he could stare into her eyes.

The other man leant forward, pinching her nipples with his huge hands and as he did she looked up and her eyes focused on the camera that was directly above her.

Now she understood why Jarryd had removed the blindfold, she would be staring directly into Blake's eyes while he watched this on film.

A single tear escaped and rolled down her cheek, but she kept staring at the camera. She was still sucking on Jarryd's cock as he pumped in her mouth and the other man was still fucking her. She was horrified at the situation that she was in.

But even more horrifying was the fact that she was bloody enjoying it...

Enjoying being used and abused, she couldn't understand how her body could feel pleasure when her mind was screaming against every touch.

Her hips kept rising to match the thrusting of the other man's cock and she felt him teasing another orgasm from her. Her fingers felt Jarryd tense his butt checks, so she knew he was very close to coming. She sucked his cock, her cheeks hollowing as she took him harder and deeper into her mouth and sucking slurping noises filled the room as they all took their pleasure from one another.

The other man put a hand underneath her ass cheeks, lifting her up slightly, his hips grinding into hers and her bud receiving more pressure until she was making little mewling noises around Jarryd's cock.

Jarryd came with a roar, quickly withdrawing from her mouth and releasing his pleasure all over her breasts. Once he'd stopped coming he lay down next to her, tilting her head, wanting to taste her and take her scream as she came. Her throat was hoarse with all the screaming they had drawn from her body already, but it was Blake's name she whispered against his lips.

Siobhan came slowly back down to earth, her heart racing as her body trembled. They were now alone in the room. She hadn't even felt the other man come and pull free from her.

Jarryd gently kissed her, and his hands offering a soothing touch. She waited for her heart to return to a more normal beat, then slowly opened her eyes and gazed directly into his.

"Tell me more about Blake," she whispered against his lips, trying to hide what she was talking about to him from the cameras.

"Let's go and wash off in the bath. The cameras can't pick up sounds so easily in there," he said. Getting off the bed, he lifted her up, cradled her against his body and carried her back to the bathroom.

Settling in the warm bubbling water, he sat on a ledge, placing her on his lap with her long legs wrapped around his waist, facing him, her head on his shoulder.

"My butt feels all bruised!" she grumbled.

"It sure has some bruising on it baby doll, but you did beg to be spanked harder and harder." He stroked his hand down her spine.

"The other man didn't say much, did he? In fact I don't think he said a word," she said, running her tongue along his neck and nipping his ear lobe.

"He can't speak, soon after he arrived here he did something to piss Monique off and we both know how easy that is to do. Anyway, she did something to his wind pipe or something, so now he can't talk," He explained softly, matching what she was doing on his neck, to hers, smiling to himself as goose bumps broke out all over her skin.

"I love Blake with all my heart, Jarryd, but I'm so scared when he comes and rescues me that I won't be able to face him. I can't understand everything that's being done to me, or even what I'm doing to other people. It was Blake who I wanted to show me all this stuff, not strangers – and not being forced to do it!" A tear rolled down her check. "And what happens if I can't have sex again without the aid of these drugs?"

Turning her face, looking at him, he kissed her nose and traced her tear track with a finger. Leaning forward he nipped her mouth.

"Firstly, I have known Blake for a very long, long time – and I have never in all those years known him to love anyone as he loves you now. It's like you're his piece of missing soul or something. The people here are using your body, but they can never touch your heart or your soul. They belong to you, and I think they also belong to Blake. Your souls are entwined; whatever happens here, they can't touch or hurt that. Secondly, the drugs you take are just herbal, you won't get addicted to them and you never know – Blake might want you to use them when you are together? If you can't trust anything here, then just trust in the fact that Blake loves you."

She raised her body upwards and let herself be lowered onto his swollen cock. They were hardly moving, content to sit there in the warm water, joined.

"He will come for you, but you must be patient. Don't do anything to put yourself in danger. I will be with you as much as I can without drawing any attention to us. And you have Xandrella to help keep you safe. Now baby doll, let me make you come again before I have to leave." He smiled as his hand disappeared below the water, finding her bud, stroking her as her eyes glazed over with desire.

God, she is beautiful, he thought, *this mission Blake has sent me on is going to be most enjoyable.* Siobhan peeped down at him through half closed, lust filled eyes and ground her hips down onto his cock and fingers. She pushed her breasts into him and he bent to suck on a nipple.

They were both breathing hard as their orgasms approached.

Arching her back and flinging back her head as she cried out, Siobhan collapsed against his chest as he gave one final push, then erupting in her as he cried out her name. He kissed her tenderly.

"I have to go now baby doll, but I will see you as much as I can."

Lifting her off him he placed her back in the hot water, and then got out of the bath, bowed to her and smiled before turning and walking out. Siobhan stayed in the bath for a few more minutes, then got out and used the shower.

As the hot water pounded her body she tried to come to terms with everything Jarryd had told her. Even though Monique was making her do all this, she didn't fancy being in her shoes when Blake came for her – and knowing that he would be coming for her made her heart soar. Siobhan felt exhausted, and ached in places she never thought possible, so she got straight into bed and fell asleep immediately. This time, she had blissful dreams of Blake coming to rescue her. How she loved him! In her dream she asked him to turn her into a vampire so she could be with him for eternity. But he wouldn't, he kept repeating that she wasn't ready and for some reason kept saying she had many, many more people to sleep with before he could.

She awoke some time later, her body still aching from all what had taken place with Jarryd. She couldn't be bothered to move, and continued to lie there. But she was filled with the happy knowledge that her friends were well and safe and that Blake still loved her and would be coming to get her. She just wished he would hurry up. The door was yanked open and Xandrella positively stalked to the bed, telling her in an abrupt tone.

"Get up and get dressed, we are going outside again." She knew Xandrella was on their side, but it certainly didn't feel like it at the moment. Siobhan got out of bed, moving slowly as her body wouldn't allow her to hurry, and walked over to her wardrobe to rummage through the clothes, trying to decide what to wear. The tiny school skirt and the blouse were the most "normal" clothes in there so that's what she decided to wear. Not that the skirt covered much or the blouse left much to the imagination, especially when it was teemed with the crotchless panties and pumps.

Xandrella didn't bat an eyelid at the outfit.

I bet she's seen a lot worse than this, Siobhan thought. *And besides, her own outfit is just covering the bits that need covering and only just.*

After attaching the metal lead to her collar, Xandrealla led the way out of the chateau and into the sunshine. She kept to the shade as it was a hot day and they walked was in complete silence.

Not one for small talk then, she thought. They arrived at a very private swimming pool, hidden by a dense wall of trees, giving Xandrella perfect shade, but Siobhan felt the sun by the water's edge.

The water looked so inviting, and as soon as Xandrella released the chain from her collar Siobhan undressed and dived into the cool refreshing water.

The swimming pool was huge and she began to swim up and down. She'd never skinny dipped before and it was wonderful to feel the water caress her skin. Reaching the pool edge, she rested her head on it and let her body float. The pool was covered in tiny mosaic tiles, in all different shades of blue.

"Siobhan come here!" ordered Xandrella. Quickly getting out of the water, Siobhan joined Xandrella in the shade.

"Turn around, I need to put some sun block on you. Blake wouldn't want you to get sunburnt," Xandrella leaned in and whispered. She had a small, knowing smile on her face, and Siobhan tentatively smiled back. She stood passively, letting the other woman massage the protection cream into her body, her hands rough and callused like a man's. Xandrella made sure the sun block was worked onto Siobhan's back before she told her to turn around and began the process again.

This time Siobhan closed her eyes, pretending it was Blake's hands that were roaming all over her body.

Xandrella took her time massaging the cream into her breasts and Siobhan remembered the man had said she liked the ladies. Once Xandrella was satisfied that her breasts were sufficiently covered, she slowly and methodically made her way downwards, onto her thighs – just grazing her hands over where Siobhan was beginning to want her to touch. She moved down the legs, ending at her feet, with firm strokes ensuring Siobhan was protected from the hot sun's rays.

"That's better, now hopefully you won't get burnt," Xandrella said, and once again retreated into the shadows. Siobhan dived again into the crisp, clear cool water.

She spent most of the day in and out of the pool, sometimes even managing to forget she had a minder. It was utter bliss to spend time in the sunshine and she felt her body beginning to change colour.

Every hour, Xandrella called her out of the water, putting on more sun protection cream.

Each time, Siobhan wished she would take it a bit further. She was feeling warm and rested and she would have liked it if Xandrella wanted to get friendlier.

Get me, she thought, a blush spreading up her neck to her face, *I'm acting like it's an everyday occurrence for another female to get a little friendlier with me,* she shook her head, but couldn't stop the little giggle that escaped.

As the afternoon began to disappear a gentle breeze shook the trees that surrounded the pool. She was lying next to the pool drifting in and out of sleep – fully relaxed, for once. Opening her eyes, she decided she wanted to know more about the woman that Blake had sent in to protect her.

So, biting her bottom lip and taking her life into her own hands, she got up and walked over to where Xandrella was sitting. She plonked herself down beside her, not at all worried that she naked. She felt comfortable being naked now, even around total strangers.

"Xandrella, tell me more about yourself. Like, how do you know Blake? What else do you do? And well, you know, other stuff."

She hoped she wouldn't take offence at being asked personal

questions and half expected the vampire to hit her or to tell her to piss off, but Xandrella looked Siobhan intently in the eyes before replying.

"My Order does not permit me to tell you a lot about myself. I told you yesterday as much as I'm permitted, but as to Blake, he has known me and my Order for as long as he has breathed really. We've guarded him and most of the Elders from time to time. But Nathaniel, Alexander and Ethan are his full time bodyguards now and they are good, the best – I should know as I trained Nat and Alex" Xandrella told her.

"You trained Nat and Alex?" Siobhan looked at her in surprise, impressed that she now had this talented vampire on her side.

"Yes Blake paid for their training and it took many years. They are, as we all are, still training every day of our lives. My Order stays in the shadows; we're not seen very often. But you saw the response I got from Raoul yesterday. We're much respected and feared." A now silent Siobhan watched her intently, enjoying the story.

"If you're not seen very often, how do other vampires recognise you?"

"Well, not very many vampires or humans go around dressed like this, do they? Also, I think, my staff." Pointing to the long bit of wood she carried around everywhere with her, *so that's what it's called,* Siobhan thought. "And my scars give me away. Plus as I said yesterday I've been in many battles over the years. I tend to get talked about."

She shrugged and lit up one of her funny coloured cigarettes.

Realising that was the end of the conversation, Siobhan got up and dived back into the water. She swam a few lengths but was restless now, so she got out, dried herself off and dressed.

"Xandrella, I need to see Blake so much, it hurts. Do you

know when he's going to come and get me?" she asked softly, walking over and sitting by her again.

"I have some idea, yes, but it won't be for some time yet. Talking of time, we have to get moving and get you back inside." Xandrella said, standing up, staff in one hand and her lead in the other. The lead was fastened to her collar once again and they walked back to the house in silence, once again.

After the sunshine, the chateau looked dark and forbidding. On their way to Siobhan's room they passed many people who looked at her with interest, but as soon as they spotted Xandrella they hastily looked away.

"Are you really this scary? Or is everyone overreacting?" She asked.

Xandrella just smiled, unlocking her door.

"Be careful Siobhan, I do not want anything to happen to you," she said, taking off the metal lead and gently pushing Siobhan into the room and locking the door behind her.

CHAPTER TWENTY SEVEN

"Jarryd!" She threw herself into his arms.

"I'm pleased to see you," she cried out, snuggling into him.

"Just as I am sure pleased to see you baby doll," he pecked her cheek. "Just look at your skin. Why, you are positively glowing." He ran a tanned but cool hand up and down her arm.

"And have you and Rella been naughty together?" He raised an eyebrow, grinning sexily. "Now baby doll, I would love to see that."

He's got on the same dreamy face that Blake had when he'd imagined me wearing the dominatrix gear, Siobhan thought, slapping him on the leg, hard.

"You men are all the same!" She rolled her eyes at him and tutted.

"Oh honey, I am just teasing you," he laughed. "Anyway, we have to get you ready, there is to be a small party and I am afraid you are to be the grand prize."

"What do you mean, I'm to be the grand prize?" Her happy mood slipped away.

"Monique has organised a treasure hunt – and whoever finds you will be able to claim you as their prize." He said, watching her shocked reaction. "The plan is, once they have found you, you will have to do anything they desire."

He pulled her closer as she wailed out her distress, trying to comfort her.

"But Jarryd, why don't you find me? It'd be okay then wouldn't it?" she said, taking a deep breath, trying hard to regain composure.

"I sure am going to try real hard to be the first to find you. But even I haven't been told where it is that you will be hidden. But I promise you I'll try. All I know is that you will be outside, bound and gagged." Jarryd held her as she started to cry. "Rella will be there with you, as it is outside, so you won't be alone."

"I didn't ask for this Jarryd, I didn't want to be dragged into any of this! Hell, I only ever wanted to be a vet! I never in a million years thought vampires existed, let alone that I would fall in love with one," she shuddered against his neck.

"Come on baby doll, pull yourself together; let's get you dressed so you are ready for when Rella comes for you." He gently dragged her over to the wardrobe and started pulling things out and holding them up to examine them. Finally, he decided on an outfit.

Before he let her put it on, he walked into the bathroom, returning with a large tub of body butter moisturiser which he started to massage into her skin.

Taking a sniff, Siobhan smiled. She loved the scent of coconuts, it always reminded her of holidays in the sun.

"That feels glorious," she moaned.

He massaged her breasts, using both hands and giving them his full attention. He chuckled, quickly moving down her body to do her legs. When he had reached the top of her thighs, she bit her lip – knowing where he would have to do go next. She licked her lips in anticipation and held her breath, waiting to see what he'd do – and he didn't disappoint. He made sure she was well oiled for this evening's game and paid particular attention to where her little gold hoop sat. Before long she was whimpering and moving her hips provocatively in time with his teasing fingers.

Her eyes were tightly shut, and she bit her lip as her head tilted back slightly.

He knelt in front of her watching her come apart on the end of his fingers. She was stunning like this, standing there taking what her body needed. He knew why Blake loved her as much as he did, she was very unusual, this female human. Stroking her bud, circling it, he made her hips buck as his fingers moved faster and she moaned for the last time and came. She watched almost sleepily as he leaned into her for a quick taste. His tongue flicked her bud alongside his finger, and he breathed in and enjoyed her very personal scent. He was going to find it extremely difficult to hand this woman back to Blake, but knew he'd die if he didn't.

Opening her eyes she smiled shyly at him and leant down to kiss him. Jarryd returned the kiss, then slowly stood up and led her back to the wardrobe to dress her.

He'd chosen a long dress made of black, very soft net, split down the front to her belly piercing which glittered against the black. When Imogen wore a low plunging dresses she used titty tape to keep her breasts in place, but Siobhan had no such luxury. There was nothing stopping her from popping out, but as everything was exposed anyway she felt it didn't make the slightest difference. Her aroused little nipples stuck out through the holes.

I may as well be naked, she thought.

The dress concealed absolutely nothing. It was like wearing a stretchy string vest with nothing underneath. He'd chosen extremely high stiletto ankle boots in blood red. She tottered around the room in them, was walking right up on her tiptoes. With her collar still in place she felt exposed in this thin mesh of a dress which had everything on show. At least she had a tan after a couple of days outside in the sunshine.

Finally happy with what she was wearing, he turned his head just as Xandrella walked into the room, without knocking.

"How's the party prize coming along?" she said.

"She's all yours," said Jarryd, giving Siobhan a gentle shove towards Xandrella.

Walking slowly on the highest shoes she'd ever worn, Siobhan waited as Xandrella attached the metal chain to her collar and then followed her out of the room.

But before they left, Siobhan turned to Jarryd and said:

"You had better find me!" He smiled back and winked, before Xandrella gave a gentle tug on the chain and Siobhan was forced to follow her.

"You must remember to be careful what you say and how you say it to Jarryd and myself. We're constantly being watched and filmed. If Monique, even for a second, thought we were on Blake's side we would all be dead," warned Xandrella as they made their way outside.

It took a while for Siobhan's eyes to adjust to the darkness and she stumbled a few times.

"You obviously have perfect night vision," she said to Xandrella, who gave her a curt nod. She had no idea where they were going and just followed Xandrella's lead. They halted at an opening in a very thick dense hedge, the start to a maze. Xandrella led the way, walking purposefully as though she knew exactly where she was going. They eventually reached the middle, where a chaise longue had been placed.

"That, obviously; is where you're to lie and wait for someone to claim you as their prize. When you are comfortable I will have to put on your restraints and your blindfold," she said. Shuddering with distaste, Siobhan arranged herself on the sofa. When she was ready, Xandrella cuffed her wrists together and then did the same to her legs. Then it was time for her blindfold. She felt like a prisoner, waiting here to be won in some sort of party game.

I've been reduced to a bloody party favour. She whimpered in anguish, but Xandrella placed a reassuring hand on her shoulder.

"I am standing right behind you, do not be afraid."

Easier said than done! she thought, blindfolded made the sounds of the night more intense. She heard voices, quite a distance away. But her heart pounded. *God, I hope Jarryd is the one who finds me!* she silently prayed, over and over.

"Just so you know, when they find their last clue and start the maze, they too will be blindfolded. So even if they are the first to arrive, they still might not find you." Xandrella said. "You might be shared between quite a few, or you might only have one person who claims you. We'll have to see."

The night was very balmy and muggy, and Siobhan wondered if a storm was brewing. In the distance she could hear the rumble of thunder and the gentle wind had picked up.

"Xandrella?" Siobhan softly called out. A hand was placed on her shoulder again, letting her know she was still there.

"Xandrella, I am scared, what if the person wants to, I don't know, like hurt me or something?" she whispered, in case anyone was near.

"The rules are that they have to stay here and that I'll be right here if they get too far out of hand. If I have to intervene, I'll have to make it look like an accident if I have to kill them," said Xandrella. She sounded so matter of factly about it; it was as though she killed every day.

Which she probably has, thought Siobhan.

Suddenly she heard voices, laughing as they made their way towards their goal, her. They sounded male and female. She held her breath, waiting for them to find her, trembling in anticipation of what would happen next. Then the heavens opened and it poured with rain. This was no summer shower and Siobhan laughed as she soaked wet in a matter of minutes. She raised her head so the rain could splash down her face.

Xandrella came over, crouched at her side and took hold of her arm. Siobhan felt the familiar sting of a needle being pushed into her skin and all too soon she felt her blood pounding in her veins as the drug took hold of her again.

But she couldn't even touch herself, to give herself relief as she was handcuffed. She gave a slow, low moan of frustration – she needed to be touched, now. She felt hands on her feet and braced herself.

The rain was still beating down, acting like a natural lubricant so the hands were slipping and sliding against her skin.

"We have a winner!" Came a sudden shout, making her jump.

In the distance, she could hear disgruntled players, unhappy that they'd been beaten.

"I have to leave you now Siobhan, but I won't be far away." Xandrella whispered in her ear. "You have been won by Jarryd, so I will leave you in safe hands."Siobhan heard her walking away, but still felt her presence nearby.

She felt male hands slowly crawl up her legs, and gentle licks and kisses followed. To be outside in the pouring rain with a man licking her and making his way far too slowly to where she needed him to lick was mind blowing.

Jarryd still hadn't said a word, but she was relaxed thanks to the drugs administered by Xandrella.

Suddenly, her dress was ripped from her and she was completely naked. She felt so alive, with the warm rain cascading down her body. Her body erupted in shivers of anticipation as she lay there, waiting for Jarryd's next move. She heard locks being open and her legs were now free of their cuffs. He laid her on her back, one leg casually bent over the back of the chaise longue, the other on the ground. In her previous life, she'd have died of shame at being this spread wide open before anyone, but now, here with Jarryd, she stretched seductively trying to entice him to touch her.

It's the drugs, it's the drugs! she shouted silently.

Her hands were still cuffed and he undid them quickly, then bent to gently kiss her wrists. The kisses continued up her arms and at last reached her neck, where he nibbled and used his fangs to scrape along her sensitive skin. His hands concentrating on her breasts pulling at her nipples, demanding that they stand up stiff and ready for his mouth to take possession.

But he was moving too slowly and still he hadn't said a word. His lips brought fire to her skin wherever they touched. Moving away from her neck he found her lips, hungrily kissing her, devouring her.

She ran her now freed hands up his wet back where his shirt was stuck to his skin, then onto the hard plains of his chest. Reaching his shirt buttons, she hurriedly began undoing them, wanting to feel his bare skin under her fingers. In the end, losing patience she tore the shirt open, and smiled as she heard the satisfying rip of material.

"Why you little minx. You only had to ask nicely and I would have removed it for you!" He laughed, his sexy southern drawl becoming more pronounced with the erotic pleasure he was feeling and it sent shivers of pleasure over her skin.

"I think I shall remove rest of my clothes before you rip the lot off. Not that I'd mind"

He moved away. With her blindfold still in place she didn't know where he was but she heard the zipper of his trousers and the sound of him kicking off his shoes, then his trousers being removed. She imagined his fabulous, rock hard body with his large cock standing proudly to attention and moaned.

She wanted to have it in her mouth, to taste him, to have him fucking her mouth. She held out her hands, trying to feel him, but all she felt was the rain on her skin.

CHAPTER TWENTY EIGHT

Jarryd returned quickly, not wanting to be away from her for long. The water from the rain made her beautiful body glisten and he heard her little whimpering sounds as she ran her hands over his firm chest, her hands travelling up to his neck and pulling him down to her, so she could kiss him fiercely. Their tongues danced, and his dominated hers as she held onto him loosing herself in the kiss, arching her back and brushing her breasts against his chest, not wanting to let him go.

"I love kissing you, Si, but I have a much more interesting place I want my lips and tongue to be right now," he murmured against her lips, smiling as she realised just where he wanted to go. "So once again baby doll, it is Blake's hands on you, Blake's tongue caressing you. Concentrate, and let him seduce you into having an intensely pleasurable evening." His mouth starting to travel down her rain-slicked body, to where she was throbbing with need. Her hips rolled upwards, seeking more of his touch, and she cried out as he took hold of her little gold hoop in his teeth, nibbling it. His eyes travelled up her body, watching her writhing on the sofa. He sucked her bud into his mouth, enjoying her begging for him to let her come.

Slipping his fingers through her already drenched core, he filled her, finger fucking her, while his clever tongue alternated between sucking her and flicking her bud at such a fast pace that she wrapped her leg around his shoulders, holding onto him, trying to ground herself while feelings of raw passion fizzled under her skin and her orgasm seemed just a fingertip away. She held his head firmly, her hands fisting his thick hair as she held him in place, and all the while the rain saturated their bodies, acting as another stimulant. He grazed her bud with his fangs, his eyes still wide open, watching her chest rising and falling, faster and faster.

"Now...!" she begged him. "I need to come now...!"She moaned loudly as her back arched off the sofa and stars erupted behind her eyelids. She ground her hips into his face, riding his tongue while he kept his mouth in place, sucking her bud, making her ride out all the waves of her release, making it last as long as possible.

After he'd wrung out every single moan from her, he allowed her to slump back onto the sofa.

But he only gave her a few minutes rest, before he lifted her up into his arms and carried her to the back of the chaise. Placing her hands on the top for support, he opened her legs and in one powerful thrust entered her from behind. She locked her legs so she didn't collapse, and groaned at the force with which he entered her. She rested her head on her hands, crying out as she felt every thrust. He slid his hands down her body, tweaking her nipples, making her cry out with pleasure and thrust her hips backwards into him harder. He found her swollen bud and stroked her in time with his pounding.

She jerked as another orgasm ripped her apart and her screams of pleasure filled the night.

"Jarryd! Oh yes Jarryd, like that! Don't ever stop!"

Her body was convulsing around his so much his arm went

around her waist to support her. He stood still and waited for her to calm down, enjoying the feel of her body pulsating as her inner muscles rippled around his cock, milking him with wave after wave of her release.

When she was sufficiently calm, he pulled his cock free, then turned her and picked her up. As she wound her legs around his waist, he pushed upwards slipping back into place.

With the rain erotically hitting their bodies, he took a nipple in his mouth and twirled his tongue around it. She clung onto him as her hips rose and fell, riding him as he reached up and removed her blindfold, needing to look into her eyes as she came again.

He loved how expressive her blue topaz eyes were and he watched the storm building in them. He wanted her to see him come, to know she was giving him pleasure.

Slowing the pace down, he withdrew his cock slowly, and then pushed back into her with slow, even strokes. They stared deeply into each other's eyes, breathing in unison. The hand which wasn't holding her up roamed all over her body, stroking, enflaming her wherever he could reach.

"Come again for me, Si."

And that was all it took for her to slip over the edge; it was exactly what Blake used to say to her, to make her come. She threw her head back and screamed, her throat exposed to him, as he watched her with a satisfied gleam in his eyes. Then he allowed his body to come with a roar, and held her close as the rain washed over them. Her heart was beating frantically as she rested her head against his shoulder. He walked with her still wrapped around him and sat down on the sofa. He was still buried deep inside of her and although he'd come he was still hard and she felt his cock twitch. Slowly and gently, she pushed herself up and rubbed her cheek against his.

Squeezing him with her internal muscles, she found a slow

sexy pace that soon had the pair of them gasping. He gripped her ass, lifting up his hips to meet her in the downward grind.

"Oh God Jarryd..." she whimpered, feeling one of his hands move between their joined bodies to stroke her. She felt her back ripple with pleasure as she strained to reach her goal again.

On the last push she locked her muscles, coming with a shudder, and with one last nip at her breast she felt his release beating into her. Letting her body crumple, she collapsed on his chest, his hands gently stroking her back as she came down to earth. Taking a deep breath, she looked at him and smiled.

"That was nice," she whispered, kissing him tenderly, although she knew the guilt would kick in at any moment.

"Well, I sure enjoyed it baby doll."They kissed for a while before he placed her back on the sofa, she curled up with her legs under her, resting her head on his legs, neither of them paying any notice to the rain, which was gradually abating.

"I've got to go soon baby doll, but Xandrella will take you back inside." Picking up her hand, he kissed it gently, sucking her little finger into his mouth and nipping at the soft pad.

"I'm glad it was you who found me." she whispered as Xandrella approached and stood patiently to one side.

"I hope to see you real soon baby doll," he said. Bidding her good night, he sauntered off the way he had come, his clothes flung carelessly over a shoulder. She watched his sexy saunter, admiring his ass.

He's got a damn fine body, she thought. She wondered if Xandrella had watched what'd taken place between Jarryd and herself. She shrugged, not really bothered. She couldn't believe how much she'd changed in just a short time, a few short weeks ago if she'd even suspected anyone was watching her have sex she'd have freaked out.

Xandrella, attaching her chain, led her silently back to her room.

"Tell me if I am being too nosy, but have you got a boyfriend? Or a girlfriend? Or whatever?" She asked her, kicking herself for her inquisitiveness. Xandrella's eyes glowed in the dark.

"In my Order men are banned, only used to breed with. I have a couple of playmates, as we like to be called, but in my line of work nothing usually lasts very long. We learn at an early age to enjoy sex for pure recreation and we experiment with many partners. Not tying ourselves to one specific partner, we as an Order are not meant to be monogamous," she said. Siobhan knew her eyes were like saucers, but she couldn't resist asking another question.

"Have you never been with a man at all then? Are you not in the least bit curious about how it would feel? Shouldn't you at least try it before you decide never to have sex with men?"

"To be truthful, I haven't given it much thought." Xandrella said as they reached her room. Undoing the chain lead, she gently pushed Siobhan inside.

"I never thought in a million years that I'd have same sex, sex, ever! But I've tried it and now I know I would try it again," Siobhan said.

She smiled at Xandrella shyly, blushing madly at what was left unsaid, and she was still completely naked but wasn't embarrassed and felt at ease. That was something she never thought she would be, naked in front of a strange woman and not worrying about it.

Seraphina would have been proud of her. She smiled a sad little smile as she thought of her friend, wishing for about the hundredth time that she was free and sitting in her lounge drinking with her friends.

Xandrella didn't follow her in like Siobhan was secretly hoping she would do, but gently closed the door, locking it.

There was food and wine waiting for her and she tucked in. *All this sex is making me hungry,* she thought. But at the same time she knew she was losing weight being here. After she'd eaten her fill she wearily got into bed and was soon sound asleep.

She was woken up by Xandrella prodding her with her staff.

"Wake up. It's time for your daily outside escape." Xandrella had on the same outfit as she wore every day. *Perhaps this is the only thing she's permitted to wear,* she thought. Siobhan pulled on a leather bikini she'd seen Jarryd admiring yesterday. It was black with a halter neck top which barely covered her breasts, and a thong bottom. Leaving her feet bare, she stood still while Xandrella attached her metal chain. It was sunny and clear, even after all the rain of last night. The grass was dry and felt wonderful under her feet.

"Are we going to the pool area again?" she asked Xandrella.

"If you'd like to," she replied, holding the chain lightly in her left hand, her staff held tightly in the right. Just like the previous day, every hour Xandrella would call to her to come and have the suntan lotion rubbed in all over her body.

Just why she stood passively and allowed another woman to rub it all over her, she couldn't think. But she didn't ask for the bottle so she could put it on herself.

She was beginning to enjoy the attention from this lady vampire.

Sometime after she'd eaten a light lunch, Xandrella jumped up, her staff at the ready. Siobhan had been snoozing, but she sat up to see what the matter was. Xandrella was stood to attention, ready to pounce or go into battle.

Holding her breath, Siobhan peered into the distance, watching to see who or what was coming their way...

"Stand down Rella!" A male voice shouted from behind the line of dense trees.

"Show yourself!" Xandrella shouted back, edging forward until she stood in front of Siobhan and put a hand on her shoulder.

"Stay sat and stay there!" she ordered.

Siobhan didn't even think of trying to move.

"Now, is that any way to treat an old friend?" The male voice asked as he breached the trees, turning and walking casually into the pool area.

"Trey!" Xandrella spat. "What hole did you crawl out of?"

"Oh, Rella, you know you want me really," Trey smirked.

She gave him a filthy look, which would have sent any normal man running for the hills. Trey could take the abuse Xandrella threw at him, but even he wouldn't dare to go into combat with her.

He didn't push his luck, instead, he turned to Siobhan.

"Siobhan, come here!" Trey ordered, his eyes glittered with arousal.

Siobhan closed her eyes briefly, then looking at her guard for help. But she knew Xandrella wouldn't protect her from Trey. He was far too important to Monique, not like Raoul, who'd come onto her the other day and earned himself a quick flying lesson thanks to Xandrella's staff.

No, she'd have to go to Trey and take whatever he wanted to do to her.

She wearily got to her feet and slowly walked over to him. He pulled her roughly to him, turning her until her back pressed against his hard chest. He bent her head to one side so her neck was exposed, unsheathed his fangs and bit her.

She screamed loudly, trying to fight her way free, but she was no match for a vampire. He drank her blood for a couple of minutes. The slurping noise was nauseating and she gagged.

Finishing, he threw her to the floor where she landed in a heap.

"You taste so fucking good! No one has drunk from you since I left have they?" he smirked, licking her bright red blood from his fangs and lips. "Rella, haven't you had a sample taste of our resident whore?" He asked nastily, pulling her up by her hair until she was standing once again. He moved her head so Xandrella could the two tiny puncture wounds made by his fangs. Siobhan whimpered and shook, wishing her ordeal was over.

"We all know what your preferences are, so tuck in. Don't mind me, I won't tell Monique that you had a little munch while on guard duty," he laughed.

Xandrella's eyes were now a dull black, and her face completely devoid of emotion. She coldly gazed at the blood still weeping from the holes.

CHAPTER TWENTY NINE

"I've already drunk my fill, thank you," she said, but Siobhan saw desire, or hunger, fleetingly flash across the female vampire's face. It was gone in an instant and Trey wasn't paying much attention to Xandrella.

"Oh well, your loss, as she's truly delectable." Trey laughed.

"Did you think we were friends after we fucked last time? Did you think you had me bewitched? Or that I was possibly cunt struck? I eat little girls like you for breakfast. We're going to have some fun tonight, baby. I'm hosting an orgy in my quarters and you will be the main event!" he shouted at her. Then she felt the slow slide of his tongue licking away the blood from her neck.

Tossing her aside, he stalked away from her.

"You will be brought to me at six o'clock tonight, make sure you have plenty of rest as you'll need it to satisfy my horny guests!" And with that, he disappeared.

She didn't move –she couldn't, she was numb with shock. She lay on the green grass where he'd had thrown her, like she was yesterday's rubbish. For the first time since being here she truly wanted to die. She began to sob as Xandrella knelt down and picked up Siobhan's head, resting it on her legs. Her hands stroked

Siobhan's hair, and she held onto her until she could cry no more.

"I can't do this anymore, would you please kill me and get it over with?" She pleaded. Xandrella ignored her, continuing to stroke her hair.

After some time, Siobhan whispered to be taken back inside. Attaching her metal chain, they made their way back inside the chateau. She was silent all the way and didn't say a word when Xandrella took off the lead.

"You will be alright Siobhan?" she asked.

"Yeah sure, I'll be fine..." Siobhan whispered, waving her away, wanting to be alone.

As soon as the lock had been turned she ran over to the wardrobe and threw all the contents onto the floor – not giving a damn where they landed. Next, she moved onto the wall of sex toys. They flew around the room, making loud thuds as she threw them against the opposite wall. Most smashed, broken beyond repair. *That's me,* she thought, *I'm now broken. No one will want me after this, I.Want.To.Die!* Her brain screamed at her.

Blake. Blake. Blake, his name all she could think of.

"I hate you!" She screamed at the top of her lungs. "I fucking hate you all!" She screamed until she was hoarse as she moved to the bed, crying uncontrollably at the injustice of her imprisonment.

Blake. Blake. Blake, again her mind shouted at her. She pulled off the shiny PVC sheets and hurled the pillows to the other side of the room. The table with the funny holes in was tipped over, and she threw, tipped over or broke anything she could move. The room was trashed and she collapsed to the floor, continuing to cry, scream, rant and rave.

Blake. Blake. Blake...

She didn't someone enter the room.

"Well, baby doll if you wanted to change the room around you only had to ask. I am sure Monique would have obliged you."

Jarryd drawled, his accent more pronounced. "You..." But he didn't get a chance to finish the sentence. She flew at him, hitting and kicking out.

"Kill me, please kill me! I can't take any more! KILL ME!" she screamed. Her nails raked his face and drew blood, and she punched him repeatedly.

In a sudden movement, he pinned her arms behind her back, lifted her, and calmly threw her on the bed. She landed in a heap but immediately crouched on her heels, ready to pounce again.

She was past caring about the repercussions of her temper tantrum. Her eyes flashed dangerously at him.

There was only one way Jarryd knew to shut her up. He shook his head quickly until he was a snarling vampire. Jumping onto the bed, he lifted her up by her shoulders and dangled her above him. She felt all the blood drain from her face, he was horrifying to look at, at his pointed teeth just waiting to pierce her skin and drink from her. His hooded feral eyes were now jet black and staring at her with animosity.

She felt sick and the madness drained from her.

"Now calm the fuck down!" he growled, slowly lowering her to the bed. She curled up into a ball, shaking with fear. He curled himself around her, holding her while she cried, until she gradually calmed down.

"Come on baby doll, you're okay, I am here for you. But you must surely know that Monique will punish you for wrecking this room? And there is nothing I will be able to do about it. At least she can't turn you, but I will tell you this, she has powerful, things, shall we say, working on the spell which protects you. You must behave or feel her wrath! She's a very old vampire, nowhere near as old as Blake and most definitely not an Elder – she bloody wishes!" he snorted.

"But in this chateau, her word is law – and if anyone breaks a law, you die. It's that simple. But when Blake arrives and the time is right, war will take place here. And if I know anything, Blake will win."

He talked to her softly, while holding her to him, battling to calm her; he knew the camera would have filmed her trashing her room, and dreaded what that bitch Monique would now do to her.

He felt her heart gradually return to normal, she was shaking less and the fevered heat that had flushed her skin began to fade. He turned her over to face him, but not before he'd returned to his human face.

She was limp and listless as a rag doll in his arms. Sighing, he pulled her to him, holding her head against his chest.

"Are you going to tell me what tipped you over the edge? What has frightened you so much that you risked Monique punishing you?" he said.

She sighed, tilting her head to look into his now friendly eyes.

"Trey paid me a visit today whilst I was at the pool. He told me that he is organising an orgy in his quarters tonight and I am to be the new toy, the main event. Oh Jarryd, I don't think I can handle any more. I wish Monique would get it over with and just kill me instead of drawing it out this way!" She shuddered, a sob breaking free as tears threatened to spill once again.

"Now listen to me, I am going to the orgy tonight. So of course I will take care of you as much as I am able to. And haven't we had fun the past few days? Tonight will be a doddle for you, now go and fill the tub while I arrange someone to clear up this room. Maybe we will be lucky and Monique won't have seen what you have done?" He patted her on the behind as she got off the bed and walked sullenly towards the bathroom.

He was worried about her. She was stooped, walking slowly with her face blank of any emotion, as if her mind had shattered and she was lost in a world away from here, away from the pain of being separated from her Blake. He wished Blake would come and rescue his damsel in distress before any permanent damage was done.

Sighing, he placed a call arranging for a cleanup crew to come ASAP to her room. He heard the water running, filling the deep tub and hoped a long soak would help to restore her to the woman he knew.

He didn't dare complete the next part of the sentence – of the woman he was falling in love with.

Thinking about what Jarryd had told her, Siobhan shuddered in the knowledge that Monique would now, no doubt, take revenge for the wrecked room. She shook her head sadly. The bath was soon filled and she removed the leather bikini, lowering herself into the warm water.

"Are you joining me Jarryd?" she called out. She heard him talking to other voices and guessed they belonged to the cleanup crew.

Jarryd walked into the bathroom and quietly watched her from the doorway. Her eyes were closed and her head was rested against the lip of the bath, she looked at peace and he didn't want to disturb her.

If only she didn't belong to Blake, he thought. *I would have made a move on her by now.* But he knew there was no way he could take Blake's place in her heart. He decided he'd just have to make the most of the time they had together.

He had enjoyed her the other night when their guest had presented himself – and he was looking forward to more fun and games tonight. There would be quite a few people both male and female there wanting a piece of her.

Quickly removing his clothes, he joined her in the tub. She slowly raised her head, smiling at him.

"You'll give me the drugs before tonight starts, won't you?"

she said, sure that she wouldn't be able to handle an orgy if she wasn't on them.

An orgy! She closed her eyes and took a couple of deep breaths as her insides quailed at the thought of what she was going to be forced to do tonight. Obscene images flashing before her shut eyes and she tried to clear them away. She wished it was only to be between the two of them again. She was getting to enjoy the attention he was paying her.

He was ridiculously handsome, with his short floppy hair which made him look like a young surfer dude, and the intense way his eyes followed her every move. It was as though he was reading her thoughts; he looked like he wanted to eat her up, whole. The muscles on his torso were an easy match for any body builder. As her eyes skimmed over him, she felt the first stirrings of lust flood her system. She longed to reach out and run a hand over his body. No not a hand, her tongue. Her body was acting on its own accord and she moved seductively through the water until she was directly in front of him.

She pondered what to do first.

Jarryd lazily relaxed, watching her approach, his eyes closing to slits, but he didn't move, wanting her to do whatever she had in her mind. She placed her lips against his, kissing him gently, and they stared deeply at one another. It felt incredibly sexy to be watched as she kissed him.

Breaking away, she kissed her way to his ear and nibbled on it, then licked and nibbled her way down his neck, trying to imitate his fangs, by scraping her blunt little teeth down his skin, making him smile.

Her hands were ahead of her lips, fluttering lightly across his chest and pinching his nipples. She felt him tense under her teasing hands, his chest muscles flexing as his breathing became laboured.

His nipples were now rock hard, as hard as hers were – even

though they hadn't been touched, yet... She bit on one and delighted when he let out a low hiss, his teeth clenching as he groaned.

Her hands continued their exploratory way down his body, intimately stroking, slowly and seductively working their way down to the place he was aching for her to touch. All the while he had to bite the inside of his mouth, very nearly drawing blood, to keep himself from touching her, from taking over and doing all the things he was longing to do.

She was inflaming him, this human, this woman, who he was supposed to be guarding and keeping safe for Blake. He closed his eyes, wanting to chase away any thoughts of what he was beginning to feel for her, knowing that Blake would kill him if he continued to feel this way for her.

Where her hands had touched, her lips followed, brushing against his cool skin.

Her tongue gently lapped its way down to his navel where she had to stop as the water barred her from his hard cock. She plunged her hands under the water at the same time her mouth found his, plundering his ever willing lips.

He held her mouth to his roughly, not wanting to ever let her go.

Using both hands, as he was so large one was never enough, she pumped up and down along his hard shaft, bringing him closer and closer to his release. He arched into her, his hips bucking, he was so very nearly there.

"Si," He moaned against her lips, not wanting to come, needing to give her pleasure before he took his own.

CHAPTER THIRTY

He shocked himself by feeling this way for a human. Before he'd met her, it was all about his pleasure and be damned about anyone else's. But with Siobhan it was about giving her pleasure and teaching her the many ways to heighten pleasure, whether it was receiving or giving.

Suddenly he couldn't hold back any more, coming with a low guttural moan, his eyes wide and holding onto her gaze while she watched them darken with desire.

Once spent, he grabbed her, lifting her up in a fireman's lift and throwing her over his shoulder, making her laugh and squeal loudly. She felt helpless dangling over his back, but couldn't stop giggling as he stepped out of the tub.

I keep forgetting just how bloody strong vampires are, she thought, looking at the view from upside down as she was carried through to her bedroom.

The room had been cleared, everything was back in its correct place. Anything broken had been mended or replaced, it was as though nothing had happened.

Placing her gently on the bed he quickly joined her and within seconds his hands and lips were making her body come alive. She was writhing in time to the silent beat he was strumming on her throbbing bud with his fingers. He kissed her, drawing her tongue into his mouth where he sucked it seductively.

Panting short breaths, she screwed her eyes tightly shut and he knew she was close to exploding. He flipped her over and lifting her ass so she was on all fours, winking at her as she turned her head. Her face was full of expectancy, waiting for him to enter her and put an end to her torment. With one powerful thrust he was in her, her back arching against him, willing him not to be gentle. He spanked her, knowing how much she enjoyed it and the slapping sounds echoed around the room as he watched her sun kissed skin turn a dark pink.

"You have such a pretty little ass, baby doll," he groaned. She shrieked as the spanks drove her closer to her release. His hand rose and fell at a steady pace, and she froze when she felt one of his long, slim fingers slip into her ass.

"Oh my God, Jarryd, now, fuck me harder now!" she shouted, her voice filled with desperation as her fingers clawed the PVC sheets.

Picking up the pace, he thrusted over and over into her – so hard she was being moved up the bed. It only took a few well aimed strokes and she was screaming out his name, collapsing as her legs gave way.

Pulling his cock out was torture and he almost growled at the way his body felt with her pulsing around him. He flipped her back over and reentered her while her orgasm still pulsated.

Slowing the pace right down, he tenderly kissed her while she wrapped her long legs around his waist. Lifting her hands she gently stroked his face, feeling all the contours. His eyes were filled with desire as he watched her watching him. They stared into each other's eyes, while he almost pulled his cock out of her, then teased her by slowly sliding back in, filling her right to the hilt. His long, lazy, slow strokes soon had her begging for him to fuck her harder.

Slipping a hand between their two bodies, she played with his balls, making him moan into her hair as she gently tugged them.

"Come for me Si, I need to feel your tight pussy contract around my cock," he whispered into her ear.

The trigger had her arching her back and crying out again as her world splintered, her body shuddered and trembled with her release.

Watching and feeling her come, he groaned, joining her, feeling his balls tighten just before they exploded into her. As her heart gradually slowed down, Siobhan watched as he pulled out of her inch by inch and fell onto the bed by her side, rolling onto his back. Then, gently gathering her body against his, he curled himself around her, holding her, not sure he wanted to ever let go. They relaxed, both completely sated and breathing hard. She looked into the camera lens that was pointed at the bed and thought of Blake watching her with this other vampire. She wondered what the repercussions would be for her or Jarryd once she was rescued.

Just how am I ever going to face the outside world, my normal world again after everything that's happened to me? Not only that, but how the bloody hell will I ever face Blake again after I know he's been forced to watch me being fucked by strangers and that I bloody enjoyed it? She wondered, *I'm in a no-win situation,* she shook her head sadly.

"Come on baby doll, don't get all melancholy on me. Blake will come and find you. And then all hell will be let loose. All those people who have drunk from you will be destroyed."

He whispered to her as he stroked her hair. He didn't want to let her go, but knew he had to so he looked at his watch.

"Let's get you ready for tonight's games."She joined him by the wardrobe, trying her best to look brave, but he saw every little hurt that flashed across her expressive eyes.

"Have you been to many of these parties before?" she said, watching him pull out and discard many items of clothing before finding what he was looking for.

It was a bra and panties set and she studied it curiously.

"Quite a few over the years and I find them intensely enjoyable, as will you," he said, winking cheekily. He held up what he'd chosen against her for inspection, nodded and flung it on the bed. Turning, he walked back to the bathroom – returning this time with a tub of shimmer body gel. He rubbed it all over her until every glorious, now tanned body part, glowed with tiny gold flecks. He paid particular attention to her nipples, and smiled as they swelled, deepening in shade to a glorious dusky pink. She watched him as he continued to rub the cream all over her body and glancing up he could see her desire building in her eyes.

"Jarryd..." she whimpered as he opened her thighs, making sure that every last bit of her was covered and the gel was worked into her skin. He stroked it down her legs, finishing by picking up each foot and rubbing the cream in, even between her toes. She giggled as he tickled her foot. Laughing with her, standing, he kissed her ready and willing mouth, then picked up the costume he'd chosen for tonight. She stared, not really sure what it was. It had the outline of a bra but was made of fine, gold coloured, chain mail.

As he put it on her she felt even more naked. The thin cold metal straps framing her breasts, which left them free and exposed. It felt like a thin, light harness. The panties were the tiniest g-string she'd ever seen. The small chain mail pieces were like a tiny metal belt around her hips, with a length going between her legs. It felt deliciously cold, rubbing her in all the right places. Jarryd knelt and put his hands between her legs, tugging the thin chain, making sure it wasn't too tight and arranging it so it fitted correctly. He took her gold hoop between his teeth and gave it a gentle tug.

Siobhan sighed as his tongue swept along her folds, but protested as he chuckled and stood up. He grabbed a towel and wrapped it around his lean hips.

"No point in me getting dressed, it'll save time by not bothering," he winked at her, grinning. "Sorry baby doll, but I have to attach the lead to your collar." He reattached the lead and she followed submissively.

As they walked through the chateau there were a lot of people milling around.

"Are we going to Trey's quarters, and where have all these people come from? Are they all vampires?" she said, watching a man dart past them wearing an undone white silk shirt and nothing else.

"Yes, its being held there and they are all vampires. But some humans will be attending, purely for feeding purposes." She shuddered at the thought of what was to come "The ones milling around are hoping to be invited to tonight's party. Trey's 'lifestyle' parties are legendary and he only holds a few of them each year." He leant in and whispered to her:

"Now before we enter, you must be very careful tonight. Remember, Trey is very important to Monique, one of her favorites. Do not piss him off; do whatever he wants you to do – no matter what it is he demands. I will try and protect you as much as I can, but you know I cannot afford to give my position away." He pulled her to him, and kissed her brutally, swallowing her moan as he injected her.

"I have given you a double dose tonight so it should last until morning." He could see the effects on her immediately. Her eyes half closed and her hand fluttered up to pinch a nipple.

"Touch me," she huskily begged.

"Baby doll I will soon, I promise. Hold on," he said, as they both entered Trey's quarters.

There were about fifty couples, fully dressed, and now staring in silence as he led her in like she was an animal on exhibition in a zoo.

"Greetings Jarryd!" Trey welcomed him, walking over.

Jarryd grinned, slapping him on the back as the two men hugged, laughing as though they were old, old, friends. Trey eyed her up, she was quivering with arousal as the drug overtook her normal sense of decorum. Her huge, scared eyes darted around the room – there was so much to take in.

This was much larger than the room she'd had been in before.

It was on the ground floor, and at the far end of the room, a huge triple set of French doors were opened wide as it was a gloriously warm night. But here eyes were drawn to the centrepiece – six super king size beds, covered in black satin sheets, and joined together to make one enormous bed. Her mind filled with images of what would undoubtedly happen to her on it.

The flooring was a black luxurious carpet, and as her feet were bare she curled her toes in it and thought it made a welcome change to the stone flooring that was everywhere else.

The walls were covered in very striking black and white silk, a plain white background covered with huge black velvet flowers. On a smaller room it would've been overpowering, but here it gave a very seductive feel. There were mirrors everywhere, all shapes, all sizes – and all strategically placed. Incense burners, lit by small tea lights burned a deep and highly erotic fragrance, she couldn't recognise what it was but it smelt like pure sex.

There were seats dotted around the room, from large soft black leather sofas to bed sized bean bags, little two seated love seats to bar stools. Just about every kind of seat that had been designed was here. Vampires were draped on all of them, watching her. Both Jarryd and Trey were eyeing her body, deciding what they wanted to do with it.

All heads turned as two young men dragged in a round wooden table, it only stood a foot off the ground and was on wheels. Two other men carried in an old fashioned wooden stock and stood it on the low table. Treys grabbed Siobhan roughly by the arm and she gasped, dread creeping up her spine.

"No!"He led her around the flat table, showing her off to the audience. One of the male vampires stood up, cheering as they walked past, so Trey turned her to face him and lifted her breasts up, flicked her nipples. He laughed loudly as she groaned in ecstasy, the drugs firing her blood and taking away all inhibitions. He ran his hands all her body, as though he was showing off a prize horse.

By now she was shaking with longing.

"Trey...!" she whispered, ashamed at herself that she was begging him to touch her, to humiliate her, in front of this large crowd.

Trey pushed her up onto the table. He removed her lead with one hand and pushed her down until her head and arms were in the stock, and then locked her in.

The stock was made out of a dark, highly polished wood, with black velvet covered cushions for her head and arms, so she would be in no pain, at least not from the stocks.

CHAPTER THIRTY ONE

She knew her butt with the thin metal chain was sticking out for everyone to see. She stood with her head and hands sticking through the holes and felt humiliated, but she knew a small part of her was enjoying everyone watching. Trey was standing behind her and she suddenly felt the sting of his opened palm as he spanked her. Her butt started to tingle and burn, but not enough to bring her the enjoyable outcome she craved. He checked the locks before he jumped down off the table and pushing it a little. She was on a giant Lazy Susan, and she could be turned around and moved by anyone. Trey clicked his fingers and a white spot light flicked on, bathing her in light.

"Now, you are my centrepiece. You can watch all the different scenes unfold in front of you but of course you cannot join in. You'll become more and more frustrated until you are begging for someone to release you, to allow you to come. Of course, anyone can come up here and have a play with you and do anything they so desire. You are our toy for the night. Have fun watching!" Before he walked away, he turned to her and whispered.

"I'm glad you're now on drugs that are so much stronger than the ones I gave you, They'll make you so much more sensitive to everything you are about to see."He laughed, then turned the table, making her face the huge bed.

"Ladies and gentleman, I'd like to thank you all for travelling here tonight. We're about to have a lot of fun. Let the debauchery...Begin!" Trey said, his voice low and deep and his eyes sparkling in anticipation of whatever evil he had dreamed up for Siobhan this night.

There was a gentle swell of excitement as males and females, dressed only in thongs, their bodies slick with oil, walked around the room carrying large decanters full of red wine.

No, not red wine, thought Siobhan, *it's blood.* The young waiters served their masters in any way they wanted to drink it.

Some wanted to a goblet, others smeared it over the bodies of the waiters and licked it off. In some cases the waiters filled their mouths with it and the vampires kissed them and swallowed the blood.

Music was playing in the background, the beat raw and as sexy as sin. It made the air sizzle with erotic promises. People were starting to group together, a kiss here, a touch there, fingers impatiently tugging off clothing. Siobhan watched, wide eyed, her head twisting as far as the stocks would allow her. Her eyes followed Jarryd as he found a chair, and sat directly in front of her.

Their eyes locked, while all around them, unimaginable things were beginning to unfold...

A young female vampire walked up to Jarryd, sat next to him and lightly stroked his thigh muscle, then her hand went underneath the towel. Siobhan couldn't bear to watch, but the images in her head were even worse. She opened her eyes again, only to find two females sitting either side of him, their hands up his towel. They were nibbling at his nipples and she saw their fangs scrape against the sensitive skin. But his eyes were still staring at her and they'd turned black. She could see his fangs, long, white and glistening, and his eyes closed to slits as pleasure rippled over him. Just watching them together was torture for Siobhan. Her body was almost humming with all the drugs in her system and now she being forced to watch people having sexual fulfillment.

And the party had only just started.

The female vampires began to undress, together, in front of Jarryd, slowly undulating in time with the music, both in perfect sync. They slowly teased him with little glimpses of skin, moving as if they'd trained all their lives, putting on an old fashioned burlesque striptease show for him. They were dressed identically, styling themselves as the fifties American film starlets. They had glossy, jet black, carefully curled hair, pale skin and bright blood red lips. Their outfits were old fashioned corsets with lots of frills and lace, making the two young vampires look even more glamorous. Their shoes were black and extremely high, and silky black stockings encased their long lean legs.

Others had stopped what they were doing and were watching as they shimmied and high kicked. Each time they removed a piece of clothing from each other the crowd cheered and clapped. They seemed to feed off the crowd's pleasure, stepping up the provocation of their routine. They came together and very slowly removed their corsets, fondling each other's breasts. Their nipples were covered in tasseled, sequin covered patches which they deftly twirled. They were now wearing just the patches, frilly knickers, stockings and shoes – but the crowd wanted more, so one of the girls knelt and pulled down her partner's panties. While she was down there she opened her lips and had a quick suck on her bud.

By now, the crowd was turning back to their own fun and games, but Siobhan couldn't take her eyes off the two girls, who were now on the floor in front of her. She was finding it hard to breathe and desperately wanted to be on the floor joining in on their own private party. She wanted to have one of the girls sucking on her bud, while the other one nipped at her breasts.

Groaning, she looked up and caught Jarryd watching her.

"Touch me...!" she mouthed at him, pleading with him to make her come. He rose as if to comply, but before he could reach her, Siobhan felt the base of the table moving slowly.

Now she was looking directly at another part of the room – and what she saw there made her gasp. This corner of the room was full of equipment like the stuff in her bedroom. There were cages of different sizes and inside them people were cuffed and blindfolded and in different stages of pleasure. Onlookers were touching them through the bars, caressing them, pulling at different parts of their imprisoned bodies or inserting different sized objects into any orifices they could reach. She could hear the moans and groans of their pleasure, which made it difficult for her to concentrate as she now desperately needed release.

One of the female party guests was receiving special attention from a caged male.

She teased him by placing her breasts through the cage, and he began to bite on them, nearly drawing blood. The woman threw her head back and was panting and Siobhan knew she was enjoying it. She didn't know what to look at next. A pretty black girl was tied in a swing, shrieking her head off as a hugely endowed black man pounded his oversized cock in and out of her. The swing was high in the air as the man was so tall; her legs were tied wide apart so everyone looking could see into every intimate part of her.

But her head was thrown back in exquisite ecstasy, not giving a fuck what other people were doing but only concentrating on what was happening to her. Siobhan knew what it felt like to be fucked in such a brutal way – and she desperately wanted to feel it now! She couldn't bear to watch and her eyes moved on. She tried to stifle a sob, but let it go as she found Jarryd. He was fondling a trussed up female. She was sitting, with her legs straight up in a V, her hands bound behind her back and her neck held high in an unnatural pose, supported by a black very thick leather collar. A range of white knots were holding her securely in place.

He pinched the girl's nipples hard enough to make her cry out, but Siobhan knew the girl was enjoying it. Her own nipples were erect and she was wishing someone, anyone, would come and play with her, punish her, anything... Jarryd stared at Siobhan, and never lowered his intense gaze as he slowly knelt behind the girl, stroking his hands around her body until he could fondle a nipple in each hand. Siobhan let out a long pent-up sigh as someone had took her own nipples and sucked, a warm tongue sliding around them.

Jarryd's fingers worked the girl's nipples and Siobhan was having hers sucked as they stared into each other's eyes. Whoever was enjoying Siobhan's breasts made noises of pleasure, but she knew she was enjoying it far more. They had ached with need ever since Jarryd had injected her earlier this evening.

Then as suddenly as they'd started, whoever was enjoying her nipples was gone and she was left feeling bereft. She moaned, and her eyes begged Jarryd to finish off what the stranger had started.

He walked purposefully away from the tied-up girl, leaving her in the throes of her orgasm, stepped up onto the low table and stood in front of Siobhan.

He slowly dipped a hand into her already soaking wet folds and it only took a few well placed strokes before she came with a scream that had her whole body shaking. If she hadn't have been in the stock she'd have fallen in a heap on the ground.

While Jarryd pleasured her, someone wheeled the table again and this time she was looking out through the open French doors. The night was pitch black, but was still incredibly warm and humid. On the huge decked area was a massive square Jacuzzi bubbling away. It had L.E.D lights under the water and its own entertainment system – the music that she'd heard earlier was playing through underwater speakers and hooked up to other speakers dotted around the room. A flat screen TV at one end of the room was turned onto a porn channel.

Who the hell needs to watch porn, when you can see it actually happening in front of you? she asked silently, watching twelve people cavorting and having fun. There was a mixture of same sex couples and man-woman couples, not paying much attention to what the others were getting up to, but occasionally having a feel of any body part close to them. A couple got out of the Jacuzzi, which was the cue for Jarryd to get in and join in the fun. He slipped into the warm jets just as a girl arrived, and without asking him, she sat on his lap. She leant forward to kiss him and Siobhan watched her tongue flicked, snakelike, in and out of his mouth. His hands roamed her body, and he dug his nails into her flesh leaving marks on her pale skin.

She arched and rippled under his talented caresses and Siobhan heard her moan. He picked her up and forced her back down onto his hard cock and her body took over, riding him in the water, making it splash against the couple sat next to them.

They stopped to watch and the man turned the girl's face to kiss her as she rode Jarryd. A frustrated spectator, Siobhan groaned and whimpered as her body cried out for exactly the attention that the other woman was receiving. It was torture to watch as she came on the end of his cock, knowing just how bloody satisfying it was.

It was what her body needed – now!

Finishing with his partner, Jarryd tipped her roughly into the water, and she joined in with the couple next to her.

Jarryd grabbed a passing waitress and poured a whole jug full of blood into his eager mouth. He couldn't swallow all of it fast enough and it spilled down his chest. Siobhan couldn't take her eyes off the blood as it dripped down his body. As it reached his cock, two female vampires got out of the water and slowly licked him clean.

Their clever pink tongues flicked over all over his body, and Siobhan watched helplessly as his cock swelled again. Both of them sucked it, their sharp nails raking up his body until they reached his hard nipples.

His eyes were once again black and he stared at her, baring his fangs for all to see, his lips pulled back in a fierce snarl.

Siobhan was panting, wishing she was one of the women sucking his cock; her heart beat erratically and she let out a sigh – someone had entered her from behind, fucking her ass. Whoever it was was massively endowed but well lubricated and she was so excited by what she'd witnessed that he slipped in without too much pain. His hands gripped her hips as he began a steady pace pounding into her.

She stared into Jarryd's eyes as her ass was fucked, and all around her others were being fucked in every hole imaginable; pumping and grinding and licking their way to oblivion.

She was panting as beads of sweat ran down her body. Her breasts were now being licked, and she looked down to see a girl flicking her nipples with her tongue, pulling them with her teeth to elongate them.

Whoever was fucking her ass was using his rough hands to spank her, hard.

The slapping noise could be heard over the slow sexy beat of the music. She was on the verge of coming when yet another man came along and shoved his cock into her open, willing mouth.

CHAPTER THIRTY TWO

She sucked him for all she was worth, all the while bucking into the man who was fucking her ass. She screamed while her mouth was fucked and the man came in long hot spurts down her throat. She swallowed greedily in one gulp.

He stayed in her mouth, ordering her to lick him clean and after she was finished he sauntered away without a backward glance.

The man fucking her ass finally came with a low grunt and he also pulled himself out of her and walked away, without a backward glance in her direction. She could feel his leavings running out of her and dripping down her thighs. Her ass checks were warm and tingly from where she'd been spanked.

The girl who'd been licking and biting her nipples moved to kneel behind her, gently licking her clean.

Jarryd had watched her come. Throwing off the two girls on his cock, he strode towards her. She stared at him in his full vampire face as he knelt down in front of her and fiercely kissed her, a rough, plundering kiss that seemed to go on forever. He sucked her tongue into his mouth and twirled it around his own. She looked into the never-ending depths of his black smouldering eyes.

"Jarryd...!" Siobhan moaned against his demanding lips. The girl had finished cleaning her with her tongue and moved to sit between them, on the floor at Jarryd's feet. In turn, she sucked at Jarryd's cock and licked Siobhan's swollen bud.

While Siobhan was lost in the kiss, the table was being moved again, not that she took any notice because she could feel she was about to come again. She pulled her lips free from his so she could focus on him, wanting him to watch her as the orgasm begin to take hold of her. He rolled her nipples between two fingers and kissed her once more, then heard her shriek and felt her little teeth bite down hard on his lip as she came again. As she slowly came back down to earth, her head lolled and rested on the stocks' cushioned headrest.

"Are you alright baby doll?" Jarryd breathed softly against her lips, watching as her eyes fluttered open.

"I don't know how much more I can take," she whispered back.

"Don't worry, I will be with you as much as I can, I promise," he said. Jumping off the table, he headed towards a bar in another corner of the room, which only served one thing, blood. There were tall fridges containing bags of blood and microwaves ready to heat it to the correct temperature. Siobhan watched as he was thrown a bag. Sinking his fangs into it he sucked it dry, then licked his lips, savouring the flavour. All around him, other vampires were doing the same.

Well, at least they're not biting me, not at the moment anyway, she thought, thankful they were drinking their blood. It gave her a short time to catch her breath and rest up.

Jarryd was drinking his third bag as his eyes flickered over her in lazy appreciation of her body. Suddenly, she was wheeled away.

A hush had come over the room and she felt goose bumps –

but she had no idea what was happening as she was facing the wrong way.

"Well, well, little one, you are having quite the adventure tonight aren't you?" Monique sneered, coming into view and standing in front of her. "Have you not noticed the camera crew following you around and capturing all your enjoyment for Blake to see?" She scratched a deep line on Siobhan's thigh and bent down to lick her blood.

"You do taste so sweet, it's no wonder Blake was keeping you all to himself." Monique purred, licking her lips to catch the last drops of Siobhan's blood. She glared at Monique, hoping her eyes would convey all the loathing she felt.

"I think you know why I am here? You have to be punished for your little disobedience in your room earlier today. And I want to be able to capture every little moan, every little gasp that will escape from your tender lips, so Blake will be able to watch your utter humiliation at my hands!"She slapped Siobhan's face hard on both sides.

Siobhan had ringing in her ears from the force of the slaps and knew she now had hand prints on her face. It stung so much she wanted to cry out, but she clenched her jaw tight and remained silent. Everyone was watching Monique as she snapped her fingers and three hooded men came and undid the shackles that were holding Siobhan's legs apart.

They then unfastened the stocks and dragged her off the table and over to the massive bed. The people on it scattered, allowing her to be placed in the centre. She was then tied with thick leather strips, they were pulled tight so she had no option but to stretch her legs and arms a star position.

Open wide, ready and waiting for anyone to use her.

Once she was in position the other people returned to the bed and were slowly starting to have sex all around her.

Her legs and arms ached and once her eyes found the camera man she looked directly into the lens. Trey joined her on the bed and her stomach flipped – Blake would see her yet again being fucked by someone he'd thought was on his side.

How she wished Blake was here, if he was with her then maybe she could relax and enjoy herself. She sobbed, turning her head away just as Trey reached her. He'd stopped along the way to join in with other people, have a quick suck or a lick, or to have someone do something pleasurable to him.

But he'd not taken his eyes off her as he got closer and closer.

She knew he was dragging it out so she would beg him to do anything he wanted to do to her. She desperately tried to locate Jarryd, who was also on the bed making his way to her.

They arrived at the same time, both naked, both hard and wanting satisfaction. Monique was watching as they both lay down beside her and took hold of a breast each. Trey bit into her, drawing blood and licking it off, relishing in her pain.

Jarryd meanwhile was sucking the other nipple as his hand travelled down to her little gold hoop. He gave it a gentle tug, the same time Trey was moving down her body, biting and sucking at her flesh. He moved to her bud, taking it into his mouth and she started to shake.

Grabbing her face, Jarryd turned her towards him, kissing her as he whispered.

"I am right here baby doll; I will stay with you forever," he kissed her on and on as Trey sucked her bud.

Two girls crawled over and joined in, each took a nipple into their mouths at the same time their hands pleasured the men. She watched their dainty hands as they used long, even strokes on their cocks, her breathing became laboured as her body spiraled up with the need to come.

Having this many pleasure senses being worked on was

overloading her brain. She tensed against the restraints and screamed as she came, her muscles stretched to the maximum. She felt her body lift off the bed as she came with a force in one of the fiercest of all the orgasms. Her bonds were cut and she was suddenly flipped over by her hips and Trey's cock was pushed into her with such a force she was moved up the bed. Jarryd bounced up with her, lifting her head so she was staring at him as he placed his cock into her open, willing mouth.

She was speared from both ends, her body pleasuring them both at the same time.

Her legs were lifted up into the air by Trey, his cock pounding into her. Only her hands were on the bed, her neck arching while she continued to suck Jarryd's cock. She felt movement under her body and instinctively she knew it was a girl, who was licking and sucking at Trey's balls and flicking Siobhan's throbbing bud with her tongue, while her fingers tweaked her nipples.

She couldn't concentrate any more – she was being abused and loving it, and in that instant she knew she would never be the same again.

Arching her back, her mouth still around him, her eyes pleaded to Jarryd that she needed to come. He nodded, smiling as she was ripped apart and came, her body convulsing around the two men. Trey came too, roaring out his release, letting go of her ankles as soon as his body stopped straining and the girl underneath her moved quickly as Siobhan crumpled to the bed, her body spent. Jarryd held her face in his lap as her body slowly calmed.

But they were not alone for long as new hands and new mouths quickly sought her out to use her body for their pleasure.

Jarryd stayed as close as he dared, always fucking either her or someone close by. He never took his eyes off her, feeling her pleasure rise each time and being there when she crumpled in a sweaty heap.

She lost consciousness at some point, but that didn't stop anyone fucking her or tasting her blood. Each time she came around, someone was filling her somewhere and she sought out Jarryd, knowing she was safe as long as he was nearby to keep a watch over her. Every time she came she was aware she was being filmed, and a little bit of her died, knowing Blake would probably be watching this tomorrow. Suddenly she felt her body being lifted off the bed, and looked around, beyond caring what was going to happen to her next.

She was lowered and bound to a padded table, her eyes covered with a blindfold. The table was similar to a hospital bed in which a woman gives birth, complete with stirrups to hold her legs up and apart.

Her hands were filled with two cocks which she held as they moved back and forth. She felt the padding compress as another man climbed up and felt his knees on either side of her shoulders as he placed his cock into her mouth for her to suck.

He ripped off the blindfold, forcing her to watch.

Between her legs, while her mouth was busy sucking him, she felt a woman's warm breath tickle her bud as she slid a huge dildo into her, fucking her very fast. Siobhan moved her hips in time with the dildo and the woman's clever tongue, which knew exactly how fast to lick to make her come.

Withdrawing his cock from her mouth with a grunt, the man moved down the bed, brushed the woman out of the way and threw the dildo across the room, pushing his cock into her with one hard thrust.

The woman returned to push a slightly smaller dildo up her ass and Siobhan cried out, straining against her restraints, panting as she was filled to the maximum. The cocks in her hands had reached their climax and were pulled out of her grip. The man fucking her didn't last long and with a grunt and a curse he came, quickly removing himself and pulling the dildo up her ass free and dropping it onto the floor before marching off.

She turned her head, panting hard and her gaze wandered to a row of showers in the corner. She looked enviously at people enjoying the water. They frolicked underneath, in different stages of undress. Her eyes sought out Jarryd, and guessing what she needed he walked over, unstrapped her and tenderly picked her up and they headed to the showers in silence. They stood under the warm water, still in silence as he soaped up his hands, before gently rubbing them all over her. She stood passively, resting her head on his shoulder with her eyes closed, enjoying the sensation as his hands gently washed her from head to toe.

"How are you baby doll?" he quietly asked her, bending his head down, kissing and nibbling the corner of her mouth.

"I'm a lot better now I feel clean. I don't feel as tired either," she said, kissing him back.

She felt aroused, even after everything she'd done tonight. He turned her so she was underneath the water and placed her hands against the wall, then gently bent her down from the middle. Kneeling directly behind her, he pressed his face into her ass. He used his hands to gently part her checks, his tongue already out as though he were dying to taste her, and he tongued her from behind. His fingers slipped into her, slowly sliding in and out, as she opened her legs a little more and leant further forward down the wall, giving him all the access he required to reach her throbbing bud from behind.

Her legs began to tremble and he knew she was close to coming. A woman in next shower was watching, and she smiled at him as she walked over and bent down to kiss Siobhan and fondle her nipples. Siobhan was enjoying the attention and she returned the kiss. Her breasts were certainly enjoying the other woman's gentle massaging, her rock hard nipples sending sparks of pleasure to where Jarryd's tongue was playing. She pushed her hard little tongue into Siobhan's mouth like a very small penis, and Siobhan sucked willingly.

Shuddering, she whimpered as her body stiffened and she came, his mouth sucking her and swallowing all she had to give him. He felt her internal muscles clenching his fingers and knew she wanted to feel his cock deep inside of her. The woman silently melted away to join in other fun and games, so he picked her up, tipping her upside down with one arm around her middle so they could perform soixante-neuf standing up.

CHAPTER THIRTY THREE

The water cascaded over their bodies as his tongue licked her bud while one arm held her securely up in the air. She wrapped her long legs around his neck while her mouth greedily sucked his cock. She was free to tease and enjoy his body and cheekily inserted a finger into his ass, feeling him moan into her. She changed to three fingers, slowly moving them in and out while sucking him using short fast sucks.

"God, baby doll, your mouth... it's heaven, smooth as velvet and hot as hell, take me there, finish me now!" His voice was low, almost a growl, letting her hear how much she was affecting him. His cock squirted into her mouth and she received the orgasm that swelled within him and flooded into her. She swallowed all of him, making sure she got the very last drop before letting go and coming herself. She pushed her hands against his thighs and arched her back to push herself further into his face, her mouth gapping open in a silent scream.

"Jarryd!" her scream made all those around them stop and stare as she fell limply against his stomach, trying to catch her breath. Turning her so she was the right way up, he carried her back through the heaving mass of bodies to the Jacuzzi. Making the most of the nearly empty tub, they sat side by side in a companionably silence, his arm slung lazily around her shoulders. Siobhan glanced at the porn that was playing on the TV and laughed at something the actress was doing.

"I don't think you should be watching animal porn, yet!" Jarryd laughed, changing the channel to a foursome taking place. As they watched, they realised it was being transmitted live. Siobhan turned to look at him in horror.

"Oh fuck, Jarryd! Is this going out live to the outside world or just inside here?" Anyone could be watching what she had been doing.

Blake. Blake. Blake. Her brain screamed silently. She imagined Blake sitting at home watching her, watching her perform and get enjoyment out of it.

"I have absolutely no idea," he replied, shock clearly showing on his face. She couldn't tear her eyes from the screen. There was Trey having his ass fucked by some huge black man, while he was licking a girl's bud, almost devouring her as his hand fucked her with a dildo. The girl in turn was licking and sucking another man's cock as it rammed in and out of her mouth.

Another woman started to bite the girl's nipples and Siobhan watched in silence as the girl's orgasm exploded on the screen, her whole body lifting off the bed straining with pleasure.

While she'd been watching the TV, she'd been unknowingly sliding her hand up and down Jarryd's thigh– and he'd been watching her hand on his legs. She turned to him now, even when she didn't realise what she was doing. Her hand finally made contact with his hard cock, making her gasp, but she didn't stop, just continued to slide her hand slowly up and down the hard length. Reaching her other hand under the water, she caressed his balls.

He reached over to tweak her nipples, which were floating on the water very near to his mouth as he sat on a lower seat than she. He sucked a nipple into his mouth and gently twirled it on his tongue, as she let out a sigh and arched back, looking for more of his attention.

His fingers began to lightly stroke her bud, side to side, fast little strokes, always making contact with the gold hoop.

She gently rocked her hips in time with his finger, and closed her eyes when her mouth made contact with his neck, kissing her way up until she reached his mouth. He pulled her to him, sitting her on his cock just as she came and he felt her body unravel, feeling all the delicious contractions milking him so he too could quickly reach his release.

"Jarryd, please!" They cried out each other's names as they came apart together, she slumped down onto his chest, panting while he stroked her hair, placing feather light kisses onto her forehead. Looking at the television, he realised that it was their turn to be the stars and he watched himself on screen as he kissed her, flicking his tongue over her swollen lips. He kept her turned to him so she couldn't see, but continued to stare into the lens, knowing Blake would be watching.

It sent a chill down his spine, knowing he was probably signing his own death warrant, but he was way past caring.

His hands travelled up and down her spine and dipped under the water, kneading her bottom. He continued to kiss her, to re-ignite the passion within her and she stretched her hands above her head. He took the opportunity to massage her breasts as she arched her back driving her breasts straight into his open hands.

"I can't believe how different I am from the person who arrived here. I thought adventurous sex was doing it doggie style! How little I knew..." she whispered against his lips.

He chuckled.

"Your knowledge has been gained by force, but nothing you

have done here is shameful. Remember that, anything and I mean anything that brings you pleasure is completely natural. So don't ever be embarrassed by your sexuality," he said seriously. She felt as though she was floating, she'd lost count of the number of times she'd come tonight and thought she couldn't possibly come again. But he was gently coaxing her body to produce another orgasm. He kissed her with such passion that she was soon seeing stars.

As she came she turned her head, gasping in shock when she realised that they were on the television.

"Well done little one!" Monique laughed, watching her shudder with her latest climax. She turned to face the camera.

"So, you see Blake, your precious little Miss Siobhan is more ours than she ever was yours!" She cackled like a demented witch. Jarryd held Siobhan tight to his chest as Monique turned on her silver spiked heels and stalked away to the main room.

"Do not retaliate, let her go!" he said. "Don't you see? She made a monumental mistake by openly admitting it is she who has you. Blake has every right to begin to put his plans into action!"

Siobhan's thoughts began to spin as she imagined Blake charging across the channel to France to save her. She knew she didn't have long to wait to be reunited with her only true love.

Jarryd looked sad as he realised he wouldn't have her in his arms for much longer.

"What will happen to you and me?" she asked softly and he dropped his gaze, not wanting to tell her. She gently lifted his face. "Tell me."

"Blake will come and rescue you and there will be hell on earth, a lot will die..." He said, leaving the sentence hanging.

"What aren't you telling me Jarryd?" she demanded.

"Truthfully? I don't know. You must know that I am falling in love with you? I know you love Blake and you are being made to do all these things with me. But after watching us together tonight,

Blake will know that I am in love with his woman!" he shook his head sadly.

"You're right, I am Blake's woman and me acting like this is so out of character that only the drugs could make me do it! But of course I have feelings for you; after what we've done to each other. You've taught me so much and I'll always be grateful it was you he sent in here to look after me. But I dread seeing him after he's watched me act this way with all these strangers, and enjoying it too! You've saved me; I would have wanted to die – and probably would have attempted it a few times by now. So Blake should be bloody grateful that it's you here with me, looking after me, and not be jealous of anything you think you're feeling towards me. I bet as soon as we're free, you will forget all about me!" She bent to kiss him again, thankful she had a friend in here that she trusted completely.

"The night's almost over. See, I told you it wouldn't be that bad," he changed the subject, stepping out of the Jacuzzi and holding out his hand for her to take.

As she stepped out, the water dripped off her body and onto the decked area He stood staring at her standing in the moonlight, then wrapped his arms around her. They stood for a while, enjoying the silence and the gentle breeze that caressed their bodies.

By the time he led the way back into the main room they were both dry.

"There you are, Siobhan. You're still here?" Trey called out as they approached the bed. Many of the partygoers were now sleeping or passed out cold, draped over the sofas or settees.

"I was just escorting Siobhan back to her room." Jarryd said.

Trey walked to them and threw an arm around Jarryd's shoulder, "did you enjoy yourself?"

"Yes, I always enjoy your parties, I wouldn't miss it for

anything. And this one is just an added bonus!" Jarryd laughed, slapping Siobhan hard on her ass, making her jump.

"So Siobhan, what did you think of your first lifestyle twist party?" Trey said, pulling her towards him and out of Jarryd's protective arms. "I saw you have a lot of fun with lots of different people tonight." He bent and pushed his fangs into her neck for a quick drink of her blood.

She didn't cry out, but Jarryd could see the pain in her eyes and watched a lone tear escape and slowly drip off her chin. Trey pulled away from her, licking his lips, and gestured for Jarryd to take a drink.

"Thank you, but no, I have already drank my full from your most generous hospitality." Jarryd said, with a respectful nod. "Anyway she is the wrong blood type, I am very particular about what I drink. My body is a temple and all that crap!" He attached her lead, bidding Trey goodbye as he led her from the room.

As they walked outside and through the chateau, she asked quietly.

"Am I really the wrong blood type for you? I didn't know there was a wrong type for vampires, I thought you weren't so discriminating. Is that why you and Xandrella haven't drunk from me?"

"No, that's not the reason why I or Xandrella have not drunk from you. Blake let it be known that anyone who tasted your blood will be hunted down and disposed of," he said as they arrived back at her room

Siobhan hurried over to the table, which was laden with food and wine. She was famished. Jarryd sat beside her, watching her eat. After all these years he still found it fascinating to watch humans eating. Once she had finished, he picked her up and carried her to her bed, tucking her in. She pulled him to her and they kissed softly while he ran a finger across her face.

"Now baby doll get some sleep, you must be completely worn out after your adventures tonight." He said, leaving her to her dreams. She was soon sound asleep, and dreamt she saw Blake with his men running through the chateau, opening every door they passed and killing anything in their way.

In the dream she was following them, calling out to them. But they couldn't see her or hear her; it was as though she were invisible. At one point she was stood directly in front of Blake shouting at him, but still he couldn't see her. They scoured the chateau but didn't find her; she could see Blake becoming frantic and watched as he sank to his knees shouting her name over and over again until his voice was hoarse and broken.

Waking up after only a few hours sleep, she felt disorientated and devastated at Blake's inability to find her.

She had no idea what the time was, but guessed it must be late afternoon or very early evening. The chateau was quiet and she thought everyone must still be resting. Closing her eyes again she relived what'd happened yesterday at the party, *no at the orgy*, she corrected herself, shivering slightly at the memories flooding her brain.

Her thighs felt bruised and her butt was sore with all the spanking and abuse it'd received, in fact she felt battered and bruised all over. She recalled walking into the room with Jarryd, and all the eyes that had watched her with longing. Being placed in the stocks, having to endure everything, because the drugs had made it ten times as enjoyable.

She shook her head, trying to forget what had taken place the night before.

CHAPTER THIRTY FOUR

I will take a long hot soak in the tub later on, she thought.

But for now, she wanted to stay in bed and relax. Snuggling under the covers, she spent most of the day lazing in bed, trying to ignore the camera, to just chill out after the hectic time she'd spent since being here.

It was good to spend some time by herself and not be worried about meeting someone else's needs. Staring at the wall full of different adult toys, she decided she wanted to take a closer look. She stood, hands on her hips surveying the assortment of vibrators, dildos and other things she had no idea what to do with.

She knew she liked the nipple clamps, and blushing slightly, she took them off the wall. Next, she helped herself to a large, smooth, black dildo, smiling as she remembered the man who'd joined her and Jarryd. She wanted something that buzzed, something she could hold against her bud. She admitted, if only to herself, that she needed to get to know her body, she was twenty-eight, for God's sake.

Gathering her choices together, she walked back to the bed and shyly got underneath the covers. She didn't want everyone watching the first time she pleasured herself.

Taking a deep breath, she closed her eyes, and suddenly it wasn't her hands touching her breasts, but Blake's. She imagined Blake's hands running down her body, touching her.

Her nipples stood up proudly as he gently and hesitantly sucked them into his cool wet mouth. She could hear him whisper how much he loved her and sighed, wishing that could be true. Her eyes closed tightly and she could almost feel his breath as he continued to tell her how much he loved her, how he adored her, that he wanted her and no other. His hands touched her body as they made their way to where she needed him to touch her most.

She'd never masturbated before but was beginning to relax and enjoy herself, finding it easier if she imagined her hands were Blake's hands and not her own. He'd now inserted the black dildo and the tiny bud tickler had been turned on and was held in place. The large dildo was slowly pulled in and out of her as she imagined Blake steering her towards her orgasm.

The metal nipple clamps she'd chosen were attached to her nipples and helped to edge her on her way, they made her nipples throb as the metal pincers held them in place. She arched her back as she felt the first tremors of pleasure creep up on her, past caring that the sheet had fallen away to reveal her breasts to the camera.

The bud tickler continued to buzz, giving her the most glorious feelings. But in her mind it was Blake's lips and fingers teasing her, gently nipping at her now swollen bud to make her come. Her whole body shuddering as she climaxed, her hips bucking against the dildo as her juices spilled free, soaking her thighs and the sheets, calling out Blake's name on a ragged breath.

She smiled a secret smile to herself as she withdrew and turned off all the gadgets, whimpering as the nipple clamps came off and blood surged back into them. Rubbing them gently as she placed the toys on the floor, and closed her eyes, wishing it really was Blake who'd just made her come.

Blake. Blake. Blake, where are you? She thought, curling up and slipping into a deep sleep.

Sometime later she was woken up by Jarryd, who was lying on the bed on his side, gently kissing the side of her neck. She smiled as he kissed his way up to her mouth, which was still a little tender from all the action it'd seen last night. He seemed to know this and the kisses were sweet, soft and tender. His hands were by his side not touching her – yet...

She loved to kiss; she could have stayed there quite happily kissing him and not bothered to move for some time.

"I watched you earlier on, touching yourself, it made me so hard. I just had to be with you. Was that your first time pleasuring yourself?" Jarryd whispered, all the while his lips were slowly devouring hers. Siobhan flushed a deep shade of red, not wanting to think of anyone watching her do something so personal, so private.

"Hey you, didn't I tell you that anything sexual you do is quite normal? Do not be embarrassed by it. It was highly erotic watching you touch yourself. Will you do it again, just for me to watch?" he said, pulling his mouth away from hers, wanting to look at her.

Her blue eyes were wide and her white teeth nibbled at her bottom lip. If she did this now when she wasn't under the influence of the drugs, would it mean anything? If she was honest with herself she knew she did have feelings for this vampire – but she loved Blake and she yearned for him right now. But Jarryd was here with her, and he was such a virile, sexy man she knew she couldn't say no. And anyway it seemed such a harmless, small thing to do for someone who was looking after her, putting his life in danger to keep her safe.

Closing her eyes, she slowly nodded. He picked up her toys and handed them to her as he kissed her with deep desire. Looking into his eyes she saw them darken, and she closed hers and tried to calm her nerves. This was the most personal thing she'd been asked to do.

I really was naive before here, she thought a little sadly.

She felt Jarryd shift his weight so his head was rested on his elbow, he was watching her every move with greedy, hooded, lust-filled eyes. She exhaled deeply, and turned on the buzzing device again, resting it on her sensitive bud, her breath caught and she let the erotic feelings wash over her.

Her other hand held the dildo and she pushed it deep inside her, feeling her internal muscles flex and ripple as it stretched her. He breathed in sharply as her hand moved it in and out, and she knew he was watching the dildo which now glistened with her juices. She was enjoying it more than she expected to do; with him watching. Her back arched as the sensations created by the metal and the plastic built up, demanding her body respond.

But Jarryd could take no more. He snatched her hands away from her body, replacing them with his own.

His mouth closed over one of her nipples and bit it hard. She yelped in pain but pushed it further into his mouth. He complied with her wishes. He had wanted to show more restraint, for her to show him how she secretly liked to be touched. He was sure she had never done anything like this for Blake and felt a little spark of triumph.

But he knew it was Blake she cried herself to sleep for, the one she no doubt dreamt about – and it was to Blake she would run to when he came to rescue her. Jarryd knew he was only on borrowed time when it came to the pleasure of her company. But would damn well make the most of the time they had left.

He loved the way she writhed under his expert touch, murmuring nonsense as she begged him to touch this, or to lick that. It excited him to hear her little moans and gasps of pleasure, to watch the way her eyes clouded when she was very near to coming. In all the years he had been a vampire, he had never felt the emotions he now felt for Siobhan.

He was maybe heading for his own self destruction but he couldn't stop himself. She ran her hands through his thick hair as he slowly and deliberately made his way down her body, taking his own sweet time to tease reactions out of her until she was gasping and begging him to complete his sweet torture. Shifting her a little so her legs were over his shoulders he made himself comfortable. And paused, his lips hovering over the part he wanted most in his mouth. He looked up and they stared into each other's eyes.

"Now, please," she whimpered, as she raised her hips and offered herself to him.

Siobhan watched through a lust filled gaze as he slowly opened her lower fleshy lips and continued to stare at her. She felt herself start to tremble under his scrutiny.

"Please...!" she whispered, willing to beg him again, until he dipped his head down and slowly licked her.

Siobhan moaned a long low moan and he knew that she was so very close.

"I hate to break up your tête-à-tête but Siobhan's presence is required elsewhere this evening," said Monique, who had entered the room unnoticed by Siobhan.

Of course Jarryd had heard her walking up the corridor to Siobhan's room, but he had felt disinclined to stop what he was doing. But now he knew he would have to, leaving Siobhan without her orgasm.

But he couldn't disobey Monique, and forced himself to pull away – listening as Siobhan moaned in discontent. He could feel her quivering with frustration, clasping her legs together to try and bring on her orgasm. She wailed as it wouldn't come about.

Monique laughed, obviously enjoying herself at her predicament.

"I have someone very special that I wish Siobhan to entertain for me tonight. I have brought in a few items that I wish for her to wear. Siobhan, please make sure that you are ready in half an hour. Someone you know will be here to collect you," said Monique, before marching out of the room. Siobhan dragged herself off the bed and silently walked over to the rail of clothes Monique had picked out for her.

There was a long white dress, off the shoulder with little wisps of puff sleeves. It was tight under the bust and fell away to the floor in a skirt which was made from metres of fabric. All of her womanly curves would be completely on show. Jarryd walked over to inspect it.

"It will look beautiful on you," he whispered, slipping it over her head.

The gossamer silk gently kissed her skin. It must have been made especially for her as it fitted like a second skin. It was tight across her breasts, and the stitching under them helping to lift them up, as though offering them as a gift; her still hard little nipples poked seductively through the thin material.

The sleeves sat seductively as though they'd slipped off her shoulders. Her naturally slender waist was hidden from view as the folds of material fell away to the floor, hiding her bare feet, while her silver blond hair made her look like an angel who had strayed into the very pits of hell.

Standing back so he could have a better view, Jarryd looked into Siobhan's eyes and saw the remains of the clouds of the storm that she had been feeling a few minutes earlier. He would have to send her on her way soon, but she needed a little something to keep her simmering on the verge of orgasm.

He lent forward and gently lapped at the skin of her breasts that were tantalizingly on show. He was rewarded with her breathing rapidly and her breasts rising and falling under his gentle licks. Her blue eyes fluttering shut to enjoy his attentions.

Just as she was lost to the pleasure of Jarryd's tongue, the door opened and Trey marched in. She watched him observe what Jarryd was doing to her. Jarryd slowly raised his head and winked at her before turning to the visitor.

"Trey." He grinned as he stood up, facing the other vampire.

"What an interesting picture you two make, the vestal virgin and the vampire." Trey mocked. "Considering what Siobhan's next little adventure into the arts of the erotic is going to be, she certainly looks the part. Our friend will be overcome with excitement when they see our toy."

CHAPTER THIRTY FIVE

"Do you know the story of the vestal virgins?" Jarryd said, turning back to face her.

"No."

So Jarryd told her the story in his low sexy, southern drawl.

"They were young pre-pubescent virgin girls in the Roman times, taken to serve the Goddess Vesta, goddess of the Hearth. Their job was to take care of the sacred fire of Vesta. All of Rome believed that if the fire was allowed to die, then great misfortune would find them and their health and prosperity would be lost. Now here's the interesting part, allegedly it was against the law to permit a single drop of the vestal virgin's blood to be spilt. If anyone hurt one or raped one it was punishable by death." He wondered if she would understand the significance of the story. Blake's word was law where he came from and he had also decreed that anyone who dared to taste even a single drop of Siobhan's blood would be punished by death.

Siobhan didn't understand what Jarryd was trying to tell her, but made a mental note to ask him later.

"Here, Siobhan let me attach your cape for you," he leant forward to attach a matching white silk cape, floor length with a wide hood. The clasp was a cluster of diamonds and the hood framed her face billowing out behind her. Her startling blue eyes betrayed her sexual awareness and with her blond hair hung around her shoulders the whole look was just as Trey had said: virginal.

Trey watched impassively until she was ready, then said:

"I have a present for you." He grabbed her arm roughly, and she felt the now welcoming sting of the needle. Her pulse raced, and she closed her eyes as some very erotic images started to dance before them.

"Come, we must make a move and deliver you," Trey ordered. Nodding goodbye to Jarryd, he attached the lead to her collar and led her from the room.

At the door Siobhan turned and smiled at Jarryd. Her eyes had glazed over and her desire was clear.

He blew her a kiss and grinned, but as they left Jarryd felt an uneasy knot form in his stomach. He hurried to find Xandrella, and see if she knew what they had planned for Siobhan tonight. Trey and Siobhan walked at a sedate pace, and every few hundred yards he touched her through her silk dress until her nipples stood proud and erect for all to see. She arched her body into his hard caress willingly, wanting a lot more than he could, or would, willingly give her.

"Trey..." she whimpered, feeling the familiar descent that would soon have her body demanding completion. He stroked his hands down the silk sheath that hardly covered her, then knelt in front of her and slid his hands back up under the dress, quickly slipping two fingers into her, feeling her throbbing around them. She clenched his fingers with her internal muscles and held him exactly where she needed him to touch. They were in a dirty, cold, old corridor and every so often someone would walk by, not paying the slightest bit of attention or surprise at finding a man pleasuring a woman with his hands.

As if it was an everyday occurrence.

And here in the chateau she was finding out that it was indeed an everyday occurrence.

She didn't care where she was, she was only interested in Trey continuing these utter bliss inducing feelings, as she was so very nearly at the point of no return. Realising she was just about to come, he snatched his hands away, making her cry out in sheer frustration. Her whole body was shaking with need as she watched him lick his fingers clean while staring at her.

It was incredibly erotic to watch as he made sure all of her pleasure was licked off each and every finger.

"Trey, please, touch me! Just one more touch, please!" She was disgusted with herself. What had become of her, if she was willing to beg him? But she was beyond caring, she had no self respect left as her body swayed seductively before him; trying to entice him to touch her.

But his eyes had a steely glint to them. He tugged at her lead and they continued to walk in silence.

Her eyes were on the floor as they walked towards a huge set of very old wooden doors that rumbled when they opened.

It was dark inside, only lit by about a dozen wall mounted torches. As Trey led her further into the room she realised she was in a church. She whispered.

"Trey, I thought vampires couldn't go into churches?"

He led her down the main aisle towards the altar, and to a man who was awaiting their arrival in silence, his back turned to them.

"Of course we can. Do not believe all the superstitions about us from the television or the movies." They stopped and waited for the man who was dressed like a priest to acknowledge their presence. Trey raised a finger to his lips, warning her to be quiet. Eventually the man turned, and looked briefly at Trey before his eyes rested on Siobhan.

She staggered backwards in shock. The man looking at her was Blake. She shook her head and stared at him.

"BLAKE?" she gasped.

Off in the distance somewhere she could hear Trey laughing, but she was solely focused on the man who looked like her Blake. No sooner was her lead undone than she turned and tried to bolt back down the aisle. She wanted to return to her room. Her insides were in knots and she felt sick to her stomach.

How could Blake be here?

"Stop," the man softly said, but her body immediately obeyed his command.

Trey bowed and turned, leaving her. She was shaking uncontrollably.

"Come and sit, my child," he said, sitting down at the nearest pew. The man who looked and sounded so much like her Blake and she found she couldn't stop staring at his face. Her hands drifting up to touch him, but remembering where she was and that he was dressed as a priest she pulled her hands away before she caused offence.

She silently took a seat next to him.

"My name is Father Anthony. Or it was when I was alive. You mistook me for my brother, the Elder Blake. I am not an Elder as he is; I am just a low ranking vampire. Not worthy enough to even lick his boots. Let me explain, after he turned and destroyed Monique all those years ago, she found me, and it was she who paid for me to get through priest collage. I had no idea who my rich benefactor was, at the end of my training it was she who turned me. I ran away from home at a young age. Not being able to live up to one's brother is soul destroying. All my life I had heard how wonderful he was, how important he was, what a life he was destined to live!" He took a deep breath, anger or insanity making his memories fall from his mouth in a hiss.

"When an Elder is born the whole family is brought into this world and looked after and protected till they die. Blake doesn't even know I exist! I haven't wanted anything to do with him for a good few hundred years. But now you are here and I have heard so much about you that I couldn't resist having you to myself for a few nights." He had the same intense green eyes as Blake and stared at her for a few silent minutes. But unlike Blake's green eyes, full of undying love, Father Anthony's were dead, devoid of any emotion.

"Anthony?" Siobhan asked. "Blake mentioned you, I know for a fact he'd love to know you're alive and well." She smiled at the priest but her smile faltering as his words sunk in.

"No he won't. You think you know my brother? You only know what he wants you to see, the image he has cultivated over the years. You think he loves you? He is incapable of true love, incapable of any true feelings. I was in love once; when I was still a human. She was a sweet young innocent girl, only fifteen years old, she wouldn't have hurt anyone. But my brother decided he fancied a bit of her for himself. He didn't turn her but she had to be put away in a mental institution after he had finished playing with her. You see he broke her; toying with her as a cat does with a mouse. Do you have any idea what it is like to watch someone you truly love slowly die before your eyes? Do you?" Anthony screamed at her as his green eyes turned menacingly dark.

She dropped her head, closing her eyes.

"And that wasn't the first time or the last he used and abused someone who fell in love with him," he growled, his hands balling into tight fists of anger.

Opening her eyes, Siobhan noticed a few females dressed like her, there were also a few young men wearing white loin cloths. They had begun to dress the altar with a white velvet cloth and huge blood red candles lighting it. It stood beneath a stunning stain glass window.

One of the girls held out her hand for Siobhan to take.

"Come, we have to prepare you for the hand of God to touch you," she said.

"The what?" Siobhan allowed her cloak to be gently removed.

She was led to the altar, then pushed down so she was laying lengthwise on it. The white velvet drape felt soft under her as her hands stroked it. Looking upwards she noticed a huge cross hanging from the ceiling – but this was no normal cross; instead, it was engraved with strange creatures doing obscene things to each other.

The beastly couplings were so well carved that the animals seemed to be moving, to be fucking each other, making her gasp. It was made of bronze and wood and the detail was extremely intricate and so detailed in fact that it made her start to enjoy the gentle, light touches from the girls.

Her arms and lower legs were now hanging over the edge of the altar. Her head was being held in place by a pair of masculine hands, so that all she could look at was the engraved cross above her. Father Anthony began to chant in a strange language.

It could be Latin, she thought idly

But that was her last coherent thought before hands started to move her dress upwards, ever so slowly. Her breasts were being caressed through the silk and her nipples were stood erect, proudly for all to see.

Leaning forward, a young man sucked one of her hard little nipples into his mouth, his saliva soaking the thin silk so it was very clearly seen through the white gossamer material. He gently blew on it, making her shiver, and then another man started the same process on the other side. All the while Father Anthony was still chanting but he'd moved and was now standing at the base of the altar looking at her.

His eyes were barely open while small female hands began to disrobe him. Siobhan watched in fascination as this man who looked so much like her Blake began to become aroused while looking at her. But she decided he did have an evil cold look about him. And that made her laugh a little bit hysterically.

Of course he has an evil look about him, you stupid girl; he's a fucking vampire and an insane one at that, she thought.

He was almost naked when he clapped his hands together, two young dark men rushed to stand in front of him and dropped to their knees. Her head was released and she watched, wide eyed, as they each took their turn to suck his large pale cock into their mouths. She could see as he grew in size and wanted to feel it herself. One of the red candles was extinguished and someone poured the red wax directly onto her distended nipples. She let out a shocked scream she felt the burning sensation of the wax through the thin silk.

At the sound of her scream Father Anthony seemed to grow even more excited, he sucked in a deep breath, pushing away the two men who were still pleasuring him. He climbed up onto the altar and stared at her dress, his eyes glowing as he looked at the two red patches left by the candles.

He crouched over her and held her head in his hands.

"Now my little temptress, confess to me what sins you have recently performed and I will seek your forgiveness from the good lord above!" he said as he took another candle with hot running wax and held it above her exposed pussy. She let out a hiss as she waited to see what he would do next.

Smiling evilly, his now black eyes glinted menacingly as he poured it directly onto her. Two men opened her legs to allow the hot wax to pour and wind its way along her sensitive bud. She bucked, screaming as the white hot flash of pain was immediately cooled – an ice cube following the same destructive path as the heat.

Gentle hands peeled the wax as it began to set.

No sooner had it all been cleared off then two soft tongues started lapping at her bud so gently that it very nearly made her come. But again she was left hanging as she heard Father Anthony laugh cruelly.

"Not so fast my little temptress. We have all night to find our mutual pleasures!" He was handed another candle and again poured it over her – and again she screamed.

The process of the hot wax being poured onto her bud, being cooled off and then licked clean was repeated over and over again until her body was bucking and she was begging them to let her come.

But Father Anthony, with infuriating inflexibility refused her wishes.

Each time she was brought to the brink of coming, her body bucking under the onslaught, she was cruelly stopped. He was a connoisseur of this infuriating form of torture and it was a sweet exquisite torture, the likes she'd never felt before. He clapped his hands again and the two men lifted and bent Siobhan's legs up until her heels were on the altar. Her sex was now open and on show for everyone to see, but she was past the point of caring. All she wanted was to be allowed to end this, and for her body to be allowed its release.

CHAPTER THIRTY SIX

Placing his hands on the neckline of her dress, in one fluid movement he ripped it from the neck right down to the hem. He knelt either side of her stomach, his impressively large, rock hard cock pointing directly at her. With her hands now free, she reached for it, groaning as she felt it bob in her hands while she fondled it. Feeling gentle hands on her breasts, she looked down, watching the girls play with them, one each, kneading them and rolling her sensitive nipples between their fingers.

She was now naked, lying on the tattered remains of her dress. Her skin was blushed and slightly shiny from a sheen of sweat from the torture of not being allowed to come. Her eyes caught a slight movement to the side, and she saw the camera crew who were of course there filming her every move.

She screwed her eyes closed, not wanting to stare into the lens of the camera, but they popped wide open when she felt something being pushed into her. It was a large gold ornate cross. Father Anthony was praying, his eyes shut as his hand worked the cross in and out of her. She couldn't believe what he was doing, but her body was betraying her, making her enjoy the almost ungodly union.

It's the drugs, it has to be the drugs, she thought, lost in the haze of carnal pleasure.

Leaning over, one of the men was flicking her bud, sucking it right into his mouth, while the cross was steadily fucking her. Just as she was about to come, Father Anthony dropped his head down, biting into her breast, drinking from her. This time he allowed her to come and with her hips bucking she screamed, feeling her world splinter with the sheer force of her orgasm.

It took a while for her body to come around from the powerful release, but when she looked down her body, she realised the cross was still stuck out of her and her breast was throbbing from the puncture wounds from his bite. She knew she should be fighting, screaming for her release – but the drugs held her body in such a high and constant state of arousal that her mind was not functioning correctly.

He licked his lips and razor sharp fangs clean, then without a single word he moved down her body, roughly pulling the cross out of her and throwing it across the church, where it landed with a dull thump that echoed around the vast room. In a blur of movement he turned back to her and before she could prepare herself, his cock was buried deep inside of her.

She screamed, bucking wildly as he filled her, demanding she stretch and allow him entry.

All around her, through the haze of erotic awareness she saw the men and women group together, having sex on the stone floor beneath them. She heard the animalistic sounds as they fucked harder and harder as though in a trance, and it made her body heat and beg for more.

Lifting her legs and letting her feet rest on his shoulders, he pumped his hips hard, making his cock reach places deep inside that soon had her writhing. Her hands grabbed hold of altar, worried they could tumble off and land on the hard stone floor. He was given a small handled flogger with lots of soft black leather strands and proceeded to whip her breasts and belly until she was screaming out with the onset of another orgasm fast approaching. Feeling the sting with each strike of the flogger, her body arched upwards, desperately meeting the onslaught – which only heightened her pleasure. Red welts were appearing all over her body but she closed her eyes, uncaring. She now understood the pleasure pain principle and it was the most phenomenal feeling she'd ever felt.

Her head thrashed on the white velvet and she shouted out incoherently, swearing at Father Anthony to let her come. He was chanting, praying for redemption, when suddenly his face contorted and he plunged into her for the last time, coming with a howl. Simultaneously, she lifted her hips up, locked her legs and came with a scream that rented the air apart. Siobhan collapsed on the altar, panting hard, just lying there while Father Anthony pulled his cock out of her and grabbed his robe. The women immediately stopped what they were doing to jump up and clothe him.

He stared at her, his black eyes taking in her disheveled, marked, sweat slicked body.

"Little temptress, that was almost divine. We will meet again, very soon."

He marched out of the church, all his helpers following him without a backward glance in her direction. The camera crew also departed, and she was left there alone, in the silence.

Taking her time, she slowly eased herself up, gingerly getting off the altar. Her body was painfully covered in welts and bite marks. She hobbled back down to the doors and had to push them hard to get them to open. Outside, a quick movement made her jump, and she found Xandrella standing there.

She took in Siobhan's battered body and grimaced.

Just as Siobhan was about to tell her what happened, she felt light headed and her world plunged into darkness. She came around slowly, feeling gentle hands rubbing some sort of cream onto her welts. She moaned as they gently massaged her bruises. Lifting herself up onto her elbows she saw Xandrella standing by the door, in deep conversation with Jarryd.

Whatever they were talking about, Xandrella didn't look happy. She looked positively furious, snarling and spitting, but stopped when she saw Siobhan was watching them.

Jarryd turned to face her, and he was also looking furious.

"Wh, what's up?" she stuttered, worrying what was wrong. Xandrella nodded to the girls and they quickly and silently left the room.

"Hey baby doll, how are you feeling?" Jarryd asked, sitting on the side of the bed and looking at her injuries.

"A little sore, but what are you both in such a temper about?" Neither seemed to want to answer her.

"Okay, here's the thing, Blake has always wanted to believe that his brother Anthony was turned and was still alive somewhere when he went missing. Blake found out he had become a priest, but what happened to him after that we just don't know. As no one heard anything from him or about him we all presumed he had perished. I had heard rumours of a priest that Monique kept here, but I didn't ever think it would be Blake's brother. I'd heard he is more than slightly mad and likes to inflict pain. And I now know this to be true just by looking at your body. I have to let Blake know – and I have no idea how he is going to react to this." As he whispered to her, Jarryd bent his head and pretended he was nuzzling her neck. They were all aware that they were being filmed.

"And the only way to see him is to leave you, which I am loath to do, now that I know about Father Anthony. It's going to be a rough few nights for you. He gets off on causing pain, but he also likes to have pain inflicted on him." Jarryd glanced at Xandrella.

Siobhan rested her head on the pillows. She understood now what Monique had meant a few nights ago when she'd told her she wasn't ready to inflict pain and wondered how she was going to get through the next few nights – especially as Jarryd was talking about leaving her.

"I'll be here and I will continue to watch over her." Xandrella said.

"Then I must leave today, I could be back in two days." Turning to Siobhan, he kissed her passionately.

"Tell Blake to hurry up and come and rescue me. Tell him that I love him and need to be with him and I miss him so very much," said Siobhan. She started to cry, heavy tears falling onto her cheeks.

"I will pass on your message baby doll." Nodding to her, he walked to the door, turned to wink at her and then was gone.

"You need to get some sleep Siobhan. I think your next few nights will be filled," Xandrella told her. "I'll stay in your room and watch over you."

"He's really going away?" Siobhan asked, her eyes round and filling with tears.

"Yes, we have to report this to Blake as soon as possible," said Xandrella. "Now sleep." She left the room. As she leant against the door, she hoped Jarryd wouldn't be too long delivering his news, Siobhan needed him here.

It's going to be a rough few nights, Xandrella thought, kicking at the stone floor in agitation. *We'll just have to see what happens now.* Siobhan slept most of the day away, only waking food and drink was delivered by a couple of silent men. She got up gingerly, her body aching still from Father Anthony's treatment, and made her way to the table, where she tucked in.

Xandrealla stood by the door, watching the two men leave. Siobhan ate naked; it now felt completely natural to be that way in front of Xandrella. The wine was heady and she felt a bit tipsy after downing the large goblet. She was surprised to discover that most of the welts and bruises had nearly disappeared.

How is that possible? She wondered.

"Xandrella, how did all this heal so quickly?" She mumbled, her mouth full of bread and cheese.

"The ointment put on you early this morning had very powerful healing qualities. You need to heal fast to be ready for Father Anthony again tonight." Xandrella walked over to take a closer look and nodded as she saw most of the previous night's damage had been repaired.

Siobhan froze as the door opened and in marched Trey.

"Oh, don't stop on my account," he said.

"You make a lovely image, stood there, the two of you. Would you like to continue your loving caresses on the bed perhaps?" He nodded towards the bed. "I promise I won't watch, much," But his face paled and smile vanished as Xandrella let out a shout and raised her staff to lift Trey off his feet by his throat.

His feet dangled off the ground.

"Rella, let me down! I apologize, come on now!" He grinned as she slowly complied. Xandrella couldn't do any real harm to Trey, but Siobhan knew when the time came Xandrella would enjoy every second of making him suffer. His feet back on solid ground, Trey turned to Siobhan.

"Be ready in half an hour, I'll come and take you to Father Anthony," he said and left, giving Xandrella a wide berth. Xandrella turned away and walked to the rail of clothes left by Trey's helper. The dress was again in long, white gossamer silk, but this time it was open in the front and held together with a simple tie. It left absolutely nothing to the imagination as Siobhan walked around the room in it. The sleeves were long and floaty and she felt very feminine.

She was barefoot, and apart from the barely there dress she wore nothing but her collar.

The half hour passed too quickly, and suddenly Trey was again leading Siobhan through the door. Just before he'd arrived Xandrella had called her over, produced a needle, and injected the contents into her thigh.

Now, walking along the dark corridors as Trey led her to Father Anthony, Siobhan felt her blood pounding in her veins as she gleefully thought about what was going to happen tonight.

She stumbled and fell against him, and her tie opened on the front of her dress, exposing her breasts. She watched his reaction to her body through lust filled eyes. His eyes blackening and he growled, steadying her. She attempted to fasten it back up, but he swiped her hands away and ducked down until his mouth sucked her nipple.

She groaned as his teeth nipped her sensitive peaks, her hands spearing into his hair, holding onto his head as to prison him, feeling his hand stroking down her body to play with her little gold hoop. Automatically her hips began to move in a seductive dance, in time with his fingers slipping along her slippery bud until he could fit three fingers up deep inside her, and slowly fucked her.

All the while he used his mouth to overwhelm her senses, sucking her nipple, swirling his tongue around it, teasing it. The drugs held her in a state of high arousal and she was just about to come when he pulled away, watching her body buck helplessly.

He tutted and tied her dress together, then yanked on her metal chain, forcing her to follow him. As they approached the entrance to the church, she began to tremble.

"Come on Siobhan, Father Anthony is waiting – and he's one man who does not like to be kept waiting. You'd be well advised to do everything just how he wants you to." said Trey.

The doors opened from within.

"Welcome my little temptress!" Siobhan heard Father Anthony's voice booming from somewhere deep inside the dark church.

Trey undid her lead and backed away and she was left to enter the church alone. It was still lit by fires and she smelt a deep musky smell of incense burning.

Her eyes soon adapted to the darkness and she saw Father Anthony in prayer, on his knees, his robes billowing out behind. He held a very large cross that was hung around his neck.

They really have got most of it wrong, the telly people, crosses really don't hurt vampires, she thought to herself, as she stood there not knowing what to do.

CHAPTER THIRTY SEVEN

"Come to me, my little temptress!" Father Anthony called.

Even his deep voice sounds like Blake's, she thought, walking slowly towards him.

The drugs were kicking in and her nipples had hardened to stiff peaks, clearly visible through the sheer fabric of the dress. A young man was lying flat on his stomach, stretched out in front of Father Anthony. His head was under the priest's robes, bobbing up and down vigorously, obviously performing for his master.

Father Anthony's pale face was locked in a grimace, trying to ignore what was being done to him, as he continued with his prayers. His eyes snapped open when she reached him and stood watching in fascination at what was happening.

"Stand over him and let me watch you pleasure yourself in the house of the lord." he hissed. Comprehension dawned and she blanched.

"Do not make me arise!" He barked. "Do as I say, or face the consequence!" He stared at her with the same green eyes as Blake, and she knew she could refuse him nothing, even if she hated him with a vengeance. She stood over the man on the floor, stared into Father Anthony's now hooded eyes and willed her hands to move.

Closing her eyes she fondled her breasts through the material, pulling at her nipples until they sent delicious spikes of pleasure all the way to her bud. Then she trailed her hands downwards until they found her little gold hoop and she gently squeezed it between her fingers.

Stroking her bud with one hand, she leant forward a little to slip a couple of fingers into herself. Her eyes snapped open when she felt a finger join hers. It gently brushed hers away and took over.

Looking down, she saw it was the man who had just been pleasuring Father Anthony.

He was now laid on his back, directly underneath her open legs and looking. She glanced at Father Anthony, who raised an eyebrow as if to say continue. She luxuriated in the sensations she was feeling. Her fingers were working faster and faster on her now swollen bud and the man increased his speed too, thrusting in a couple more fingers, making her rock her hips, riding the salacious feelings.

"Open your eyes my little temptress, I want to look into your eyes as you lose control," Father Anthony ordered, knowing she was so near to coming. She stared into his now black eyes, shuddering as she saw his fangs. He held his long thick cock in both hands, stroking it slowly up and down.

His eyes feasted on her, watching her every movement through hooded eyes. Just as she was about to come, she felt a white hot sting whip across her backside. She was being whipped. Two men held her arms as she tried to buck away from the source of the pain. She strained to see who was doing this to her.

It was one of the girls who'd helped her onto the altar the night before, her companion was stood behind her, watching the scene and awaiting her own orders. They were dressed identically in white PVC skin suits that covered their legs and arms, their pretty faces hidden by a tight-fitting hood with holes for the eyes and mouth.

Their eyes were black cruel slits, their lips painted bright red. The one holding the whip in her hand was waiting for the word to continue. Whimpering, Siobhan turned to Father Anthony. She was so close to orgasm, but she knew she'd have to consent to being whipped if she wanted to come.

He held her in a magnetic gaze, silently playing a waiting game.

Her brain screamed at her to shake her head and not to allow this to happen, but she felt herself nod. She bit her lip and readied herself for the kiss of the whip.

She heard it before she felt it and moaned loudly when it made contact. The man beneath knelt up so he could suck her sensitive bud into his mouth. His fingers were still buried deep inside of her, stroking her G-spot making her head roll back with pleasure.

The whip continued to flick across her ass, never the same place twice, it felt like fire kissing her skin. Siobhan felt her orgasm grip her body and as the last swish landed she let out a high pitched scream while her body convulsed, bucking and arching with the powerful release.

The two men on either side of her held onto her with a tight grip as her legs gave way. They removed her dress and as she was lowered face-down onto the floor. Father Anthony placed a booted foot onto her shoulder holding her spread-eagled body submissively beneath him. He continued a few more strokes on his cock, then shouted as he came in great white spurts which landed on Siobhan's newly whipped bottom.

"You're not worthy to even taste my milky offerings," he said nastily, walking away and leaving the girls to rub his seed into the hot welts on her ass.

Whimpering, she felt the sting from the recently whipped skin as it was caressed by the girls. They licked at her hot skin, with slow delicate little touches which she found soothing. Father Anthony was talking quietly to one of the dark men, giving him instructions. The other man nodded obediently before hurrying away. Siobhan closed her eyes as she lay on the cold stone floor awaiting her next orders. She heard ropes being pulled and a heavy sounding piece of equipment being lowered and looked up as the cross that she'd seen last night was being lowered to the floor. She walked over to have a better view, running her hands across the wood and the bronze; it felt warm to her touch. It was much thicker than she had thought, at least eight feet tall and about six foot wide and magnificent in an erotic way.

Once it was positioned where Father Anthony wanted, he manoeuvred her against the hard wood, placing her arms along the cross. A young man tied them in place. Her legs were opened and shackled to the small foot holders in the wood. She was trapped and started to tremble, feeling open and vulnerable with the carvings digging into her back. One particular piece of wood was rubbing against her in a most sensitive place.

The feeling was very pleasurable and she slowly moved her ass against it. One of the men, dressed only in a loin cloth, stepped forward, dipping his hand into a small pot that he was carrying. He stood behind her and slipped his fingers smoothly into her ass. The oil acted as a lubricant, so he could insert his long thin fingers all the way inside her. Siobhan moaned as he slowly withdrew his fingers but she was soon filled again, this time more fully, as the smooth piece of wood she had been rubbing herself up against was inserted where the man's fingers had just been.

It was chunky, filling her completely and she slowly started to pant as dark feelings began to erupt deep inside of her. She moved her hips back and forth in time with the movement of the wood. Whoever was behind her was fucking her ass and soon she was closing her eyes letting the feelings wash over her

The cross was being tilted, and she opened her eyes to find herself vertical, just a few inches off the floor. The wood was still plugged in her ass. Siobhan strained her neck to look for Father Anthony; he was sitting in a pew, looking at her as if she was putting on a play for his amusement. A man rolled underneath her and thrusted his penis into her open mouth for her to suck. He licked and sucked at her using his fingers to probe and slide into her, at the same time whoever was stood above her started to slowly slide the wood in and out of her ass. She was soon lost in a sea of feelings, staring into Father Anthony's eyes that they were so like Blake's. But where Blake's eyes were warm and loving, Father Anthony's were cold and calculating.

The priest sat in the front pew watching her in a detached way. He clicked his fingers and the two young girls knelt beside him, their hands disappearing under his heavy robes to fondle and stroke him. He looked bored, as if he couldn't be bothered. But as the girls stroked and teased, he slowly came to life and a cruel glint hovered at the back of his eyes. She quaked inside, not wanting to imagine what he could be thinking.

"Stop!" Father Anthony shouted. He jumped up, and throwing the girls off. Everyone stopped whatever they were doing, leaving Siobhan literally hanging. Her body was pulsing with desire, but the man had removed his tongue from her bud and his cock from her mouth. She felt feverish, her pupils were dilated and a glittering deep shade of blue. She was desperate to finish, to be allowed to come.

"Little temptress, I've an idea that I think you would enjoy. It's a bit hard core for you, but, well let's give it a go," said Father Anthony, he couldn't disguise the excited cruel glint in his black, hooded eyes.

"Tilt the cross so it's standing, I want my little temptress stood before me, all resplendent in her naked glory," Father Anthony told his willing servants. He was standing so close to her when the cross was finally in a place that she felt his cool breath caressing her cheek. He ran a pale finger across her breasts. "They truly are the work of the good lord, just perfect." He dipped a finger into her folds.

"You are wet my child, are you ready to come for me?" he said, taking hold of her little gold hoop and tugging it.

She let out a yelp as he leaned forward and bit hard into one of her breasts.

"Confess to me, my child, tell me all of your deep dark secret desires. I want to hear what you dream about when you are alone. Do you still believe my brother will come and rescue you? Or, perhaps you are enjoying yourself too much here to want him to find you? Are you ready to admit to the fact that you enjoy all that is happening to you here?" He asked as he continued to ravish her body, touching her in all the right places until she was writhing under his ever-watchful gaze.

As she started on the downward spiral to orgasm, he withdrew his hands and his lips and cruelly turned away. Siobhan wanted to beg him to continue, but instead watched him take a large whip from one of his minions. Her eyes widened as he walked back to where she was tied and bound. A girl stood before her, dropping to her knees as Father Anthony raised his arm. She gave her bud a long lingering lick and Siobhan closed her eyes waiting for the whip to make contact with her skin.

As the first shudders of her orgasm rippled over her body the whip struck her erect and very sensitive nipples. She screamed, her fists clenching. Her nipples were stinging but still so hard and Siobhan knew she was just about to come. It'd only take one more suck on her bud, one more swish of the whip and she would be there. He raised his arm up high again and the girl continued to grind in a couple of fingers into her while lazily flicking her bud with her tongue as Siobhan started to strain against her binds. She screamed as the whip kissed her skin for the last time and her world shattered as she came. She screamed her release. As soon as she was spent, the cross was lowered and she was cut free. She fell to the ground in a heap, trying to catch her breath.

Siobhan felt male hands lift her until she was standing. She felt weak and her legs were wobbly. Father Anthony stalked towards her, his robes were undone and he was fondling himself with his long thin white hands.

He was soon almost nose to nose with her.

"Well, little temptress here we are. Did you beg for redemption? Did you repent all your sins? Do you have anything to confess?" Father Anthony asked, still stroking his very hard cock.

His pale hairless thin body was all muscle, hard and unforgiving. His skin was so pale it seemed almost luminous in the fire light.

"I don't have anything to confess or to beg redemption for. All this is being forced onto me. God will understand and forgive me."

She hadn't intended to answer him back and she quickly lowered her eyes in terror.

CHAPTER THIRTY EIGHT

"I didn't know I was talking about your God?" He raised an eyebrow, and Siobhan knew she was in serious trouble. "In this building, this church, I am God, and it is my forgiveness you should be seeking."

In blurring speed he slapped her across the face, she screamed as her head snapped to the side.

He'd managed to split her lip, and he smiled a cruel smile as he licked it off.

"We could play this new game all night if you'd like? Let's see how fast you learn shall we?" He asked, watching her tears fall. "Now little temptress, do you have anything to confess? Do you want redemption?" She struggled to find an answer where she wouldn't get struck again.

Okay, okay, he wants me to repent, she thought, *so I'll just make up some bullshit for his benefit.*

She took a deep breath.

"Yes I'd like to confess. I'd like to confess that since being here I've learnt that I like to be whipped, that I like same sex partners; I also like sex with all different partners. I confess that I get turned on by being dominated and ordered around. And I confess that I want you to fuck me now," she said quietly, her eyes on the floor.

She hoped it was what he wanted to hear, and waited, biting her lip.

"Well little temptress, that wasn't so hard now was it? Everyone needs to confess at times – it helps to cleanse their soul." Thankfully, he seemed satisfied with her answer.

Her lips felt swollen and Siobhan wondered with dread what he was going to do to her next. As she raised her eyes, she saw Father Anthony seemed deep in prayer. All his helpers, slaves, disciples or whatever the fuck they were, had all dropped to their knees, also praying.

When he'd finished his prayers, he looked up and was instantly surrounded by his adoring slaves. He whispered to the two girls dressed in the white PVC outfits, making them giggle. With a nod of their heads, they walked over to her. Siobhan wearily wondered what they had in mind for her this time.

The two girls took her hands in theirs and gently led her to the front of the church, pushing her down onto all fours. One dropped in front of her and slipped beneath Siobhan, so she could take her nipples into her mouth and suck them. She used her fingers to slide and probe wherever she wanted to touch. Siobhan arched her back, the gentle sensations caused her to moan in ecstasy.

The second girl stood behind her. She had undone the zip of her suit and was gently massaging Siobhan's rounded behind. Siobhan felt the girl's breasts rubbing on her back, her hard nipples moving from side to side. The two girls seemed in no hurry to reach an end to their playing. Siobhan relaxed and enjoyed the gentle strokes and the soft caresses of the girls. She heard their giggles as they adored her body, and took pleasure from what they were doing. As soon as one had finished with a body part, it was quickly taken over by the other, so all of her major erogenous zones were being licked, stroked or tweaked. She was soon panting with desire, her back arching as she pushed against the tongue of one of the girls, wishing they would speed up and let her feel what her body was so very nearly feeling...

A knobbly dildo was slowly pushed deep inside her. It wasn't used to fuck her, rather, to fill her, stretching her internal muscles deliciously. At the same time she felt a man's oiled cock pushing past the tight ring of muscle and slipping into her ass while the second girl was still worshipping her bud. Looking around to see who was fucking her, she stared straight into Father Anthony's emotionless black eyes.

His lips were open and she watched, fascinated as he licked his fangs clean. They were dripping in deep red blood and reaching down between her thighs she felt a thick trickle coming from one of the veins at the top of her leg. She'd been so engrossed in what the girls had been doing to her that she hadn't even noticed she'd been bitten.

She watched through heavy eyes as he dipped a hand between her legs, brought up his fingers dripping in her blood and slowly licked it all off. He kept his eyes focused on hers, watching him drink from her. Everyone around them stopped and waited for him to give his permission to resume.

To Siobhan it felt like she was suspended from reality. She seemed to be watching from above. She was starting to feel woozy and she could feel her eyes closing. Shaking her head, she tried to keep awake but the next minute she'd passed out onto the hard wooden floor beneath her.

Siobhan came around slowly. She heard voices but was damned if she could open her eyes, everything seemed so far away, out of reach. She'd never felt so tired, so completely drained of all energy. She drifted off to sleep again, not noticing the drips pumping blood and other healing agents into her body. A few hours later she woke again, but still didn't have the energy to open her eyes. She sensed people peering into her face, prodding her or pulling her limbs.

But each time she came to she didn't realise she was rambling incoherently.

Finally she opened her eyes and slowly and painfully moved her head; she had a fierce headache.

"Jarryd." Her throat was gritty, hoarse and very sore and she coughed. She tried to raise herself up onto her elbows but fell back weakly.

At once Jarryd was stroking her face, he looked upset and worried.

"What...?" she croaked, but he shook his head and reached for a glass of water so she could take a sip.

"Slowly," he gently chided her as she tried to take a large gulp and choked and spluttered. He laid her head back on the pillows and she tiredly closed her eyes. When she next came to, the headache had lessened and her throat was not so sore. Jarryd was by her side in an instant.

"How are you feeling baby doll?" he said, worriedly. "Drink, it will help," he told her, again helping her with a glass of water.

"What the hell happened?" Siobhan asked, finding it hard to concentrate. As he took hold of her hand, she noticed the drips for the first time. "Jarryd, what has happened? Did I die or something? Did Father Anthony, you know, turn me...?" Her eyes were huge, begging him to tell her she was still human.

"No, baby doll, he didn't turn you. He got carried away and very nearly drained you of all your blood. You collapsed and were rushed back here and have been in and out of consciousness for of over a week. You contracted pneumonia on top of it all and for a while we thought we would lose you. It was seriously scary. I had just arrived back from England and found you being carried back from that animal in a horrendous state. You were so battered, bruised and broken I hardly recognised you."

He paced up and down the room.

"I had just flown back from England where I had to explain to Blake what was happening here. When he heard that his brother was still alive he was ecstatic. But when it was made clear to him what kind of vampire he had turned into and that you were his new toy... Well, I'm glad to be back here."

He sat down heavily in the nearest chair, head in hands, trembling. Just remembering how Blake had reacted scared him silly.

And I've seen some truly horrifying things in my time, but an angry Blake is an awesome destructive force... he thought.

THE END OF BOOK ONE.

If you have enjoyed reading this book, I would be most grateful if you would leave me a review.

TO BE CONTINUED IN THE NEXT INSTALLMENT
Book two in the, Journey of Innocence series.
Innocence Reclaimed.

AUTHOR BIO

Helen Johnston grew up in her home county of Hampshire, England. Her childhood dreams filled with the desire to become a dancer. An only child she was never alone, her years spent entertained with her vivid imagination. She met and married her husband not long after leaving school and soon after their son was born, their family is made complete with Helen's two cats that are spoiled rotten which results in them often thinking they rule the home.

Her life consisting of home life and a few jobs in the retail industry her vivid imagination refused to stay quiet and combined with her love of erotica and all things vampire she decided to try her hand at writing and has never looked back.

CONTACT

Facebook page:

https://www.facebook.com/pages/Innocence-Lost/178556542213717

Goodreads:

https://www.goodreads.com/author/show/6456359.Helen_Johnston

Twitter:

https://twitter.com/HelenJohnstonIL

26750375R00189

Made in the USA
Charleston, SC
18 February 2014